ORBS OF AZURE

NECROSEAM CHRONICLES BOOK II

NECROSEAM CHRONICLES

Available in eBook, Paperback, Hardcover, and Audiobook (for select titles)

Prequel 1: Princess of Shadow and Dream
Prequel 2: Princess of Grim

Book I: Willow of Ashes
Book II: Orbs of Azure
Book III: Pearl of Emerald
Book IV: Phoenix of Scarlet
Book V: Blossom of Gold

OTHER WORKS BY ELLIE RAINE
Adult
Nightingale: A Paranormal Noir

Children's Illustration
Ballad of the Ice Fairy

Orbs of Azure

NecroSeam Chronicles Book II

Ellie Raine

Orbs of Azure
NecroSeam Chronicles | Book Two

Copyright © 2018 by Ellie Raine

Cover Design by Ellie Raine
Interior Formatting by Tamara Cribley
Author Photograph by Melissa Giles Photography
Map © 2021 Chris Seckinger

All rights reserved. This book or any portion thereof may not be reproduced or used in any manner whatsoever without the express written permission of the publisher except for the use of brief quotations in a book review or article.

This is a work of fiction. Concepts, Names, characters, businesses, places, events, locales, and incidents are either the products of the author's imagination or used in a fictitious manner. Any resemblance to actual persons, living or dead, or actual events is purely coincidental.

Printed in the United States of America

ISBNs: 978-1-7320415-2-3 (Hardcover), 978-1-7320415-5-4 (Paperback), 978-1-7320415-8-5 (Ebook)

Library of Congress Control Number: 2018935665
First Printing, Edition I: 2018

Published by
ScyntheFy Press, LLC
www.ScyntheFy.com

For information about special discounts available for bulk purchases, sales promotions, fund-raising and educational needs, contact ScyntheFy Press at: www.ScyntheFy.com/contact

For special bonus features and up-to-date news, visit the official NecroSeam web site: www.NecroSeam.com

AUTHOR'S NOTE

Welcome back, Adventurer!

I'm delighted you decided to continue from your last save-point in the NecroSeam Chronicles. Watch your backs and take caution: the journey only grows darker from here. And if you get lost along the way, refer to the Nirussian Travel Guide in the back of this book for help.

Happy reading,
Ellie Raine

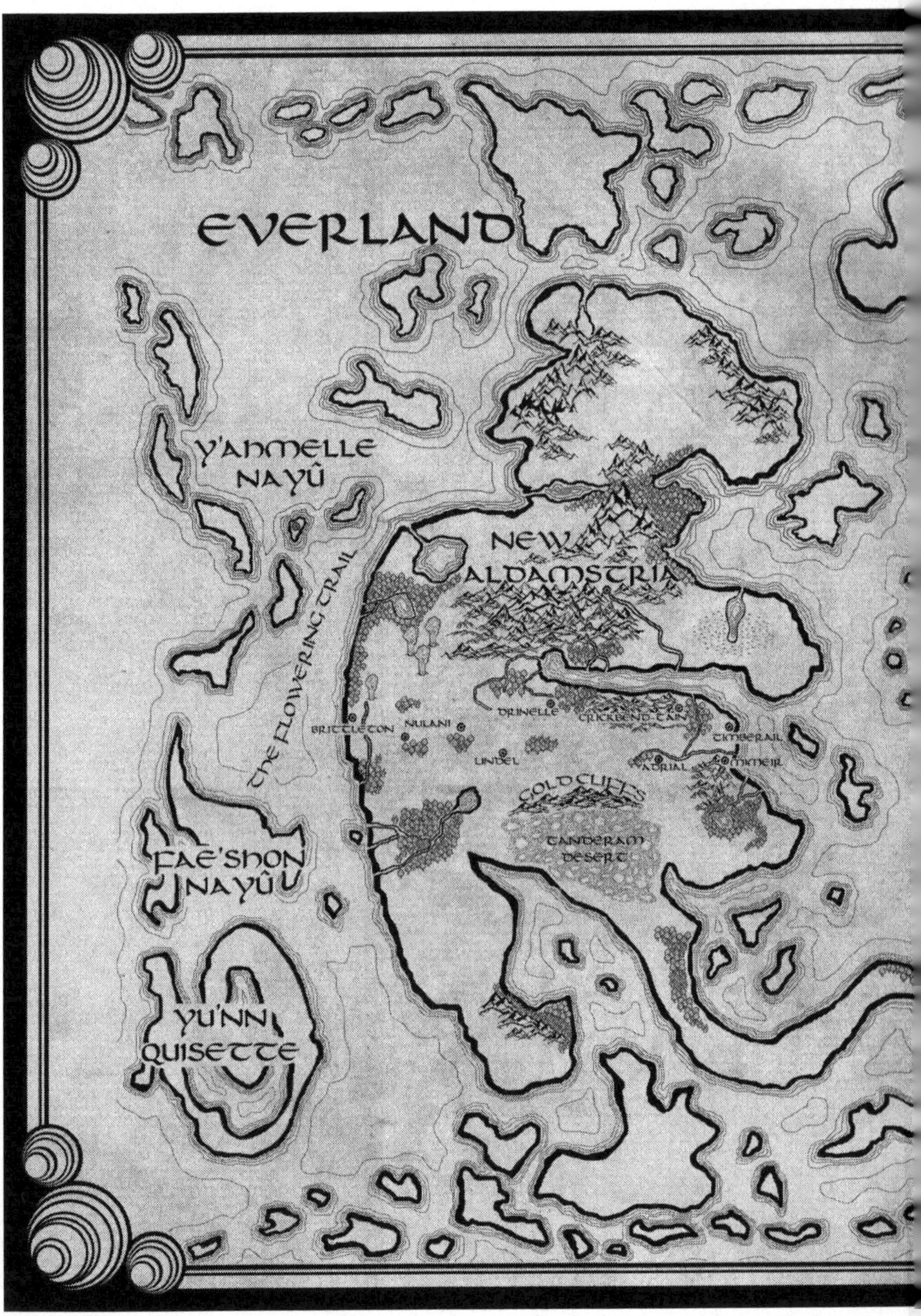

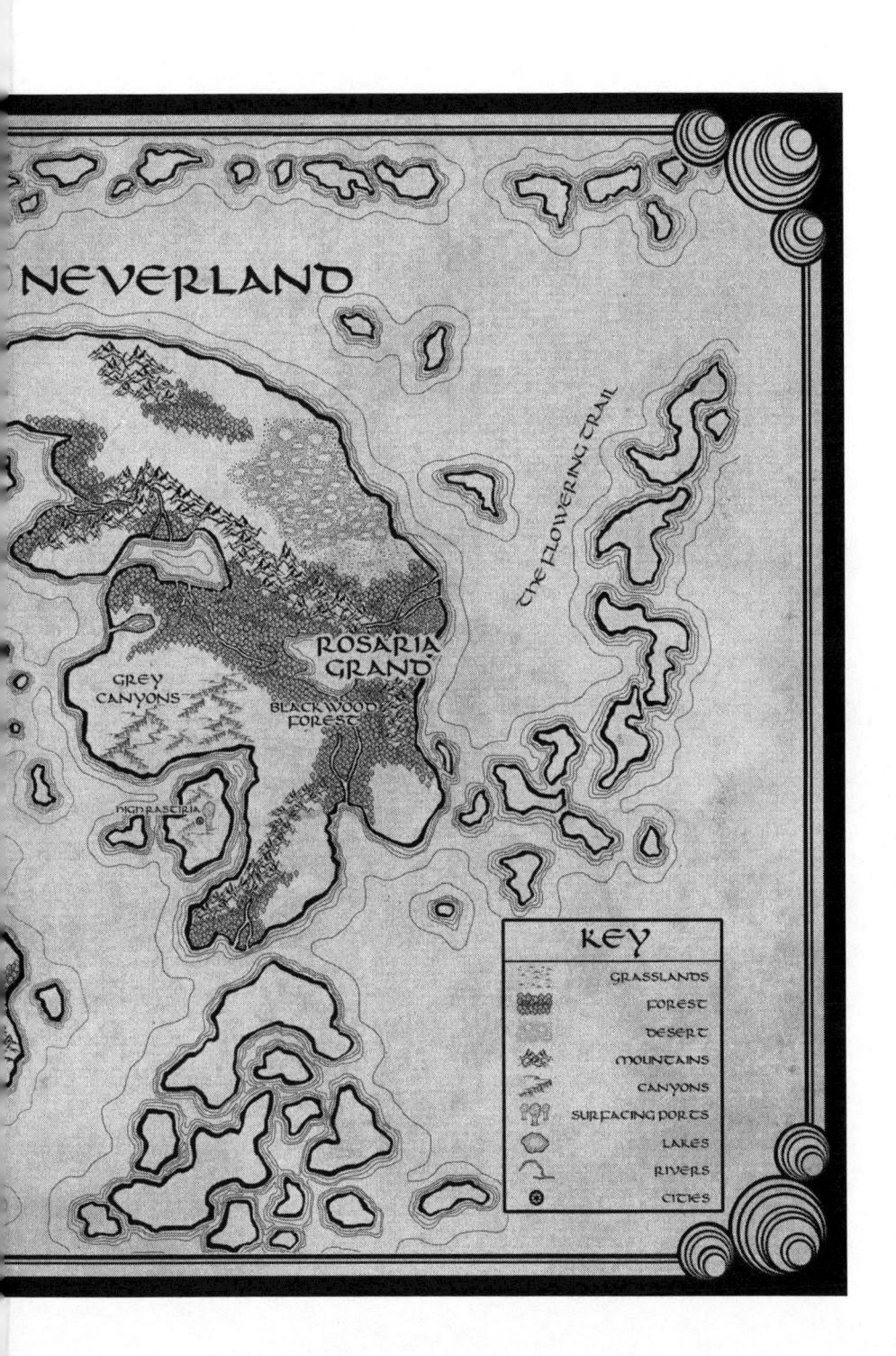

NEVERLAND

THE FLOWERING TRAIL

GREY CANYONS

ROSARIA GRAND

BLACKWOOD FOREST

HIGH RASCIRIA

KEY
- GRASSLANDS
- FOREST
- DESERT
- MOUNTAINS
- CANYONS
- SURFACING PORTS
- LAKES
- RIVERS
- CITIES

TABLE OF CONTENTS

Prologue: Soul Survivor 1
1. An Unwelcome Party. 6
2. Allies in High Places 15
3. A Royal Display. 22
4. Grim Findings. 31
5. Old Friends, New Companions 39
6. Raven Riot 44
7. A Displaced Dreamcatcher 46
8. Luring a Lion. 51
9. The Relicblood Gathering 55
10. If It Were a Snake 61
11. Unveiled. 64
12. Old Enemies 72
13. Devious 76
14. The Lost Father 81
15. Twin Princesses 84
16. Warcries. 87
17. Lost Comrades. 91
18. Contrived Council 96
19. The Siege 108
20. A Healer's Mission 114
21. Cat's in the Bag 121
22. Outlawed. 127
23. A Stolen Family. 137
24. Destination 139
25. Tanderam Prison 142
26. Foreboding. 150
27. Refuge 165
28. Stalemate 175
29. Royal Obligations 180
30. Desert Days 188
31. Preparations. 196
32. Blood and Water 204

33. Kin..212
34. Storming the Fortress................................218
35. A Haunted Past......................................225
36. Desperate Measures..................................229
37. The Undead Giant...................................233
38. While We're Young..................................239
39. Neverland's Heiress..................................243
40. Do Not Annoy the Alchemist.....................258
41. Family Reunion......................................267
42. The Truth...272
43. A Chance For Redemption........................284
44. Tactics and Torture..................................289
45. A Fresh Lead...295
46. Separate Ways.......................................300
47. Out of Hiding..305
48. Setting Sail..308
49. Rotten Regrets.......................................315
50. It's Never That Easy.................................320
51. Up In Flames..331
52. Found..341
53. Final Hesitation.....................................352
54. A Dance of Demons................................359
55. First Breath..361
56. Late Reunion..367
57. Caveats..374
58. The Archchancellor.................................377
59. Caught in the Fray..................................381
60. Familiar Faces.......................................386
61. A Daunting Task....................................390
62. A New Beginning...................................392
Epilogue I: Old Acquaintances........................397
Epilogue II: The Rightful Ruler.......................400
Dear Readers,..401
Book III Sneak Peek: Pearl of Emerald.............403
Nirussian Travel Guide.................................409
Character Reference List...............................411
Nirussian World Notes.................................415
Nirussian Minerals/Technology.......................419
About the Author..421

"Father, I've found him.

Though he is not what I expected. They are not what I expected. When will they be ready? When will they fix what I've done...?"

—The King of Dreams, 2081 A.B.

PROLOGUE
SOUL SURVIVOR

~~~~~~

JANSON

"*Die, Gods damn it!*" I ripped my scythe into the beast's sticky chest, *snapping* its rotted NecroSeam. Its corpse collapsed, blackened soul evaporating in a hiss—

Another Fera tore at my wing, feathers shredded, a yell scraping my throat. More leapt at me, one biting my arm, the others thrashing my side and legs. I tried to back away, but fell into a ditch and landed hard on my wings, screaming, the demons scuttling after—

"*Da'torr!*" my vassal, Rossette, screamed as she spread her green wings and flew between us. She thrust her hands at the Fera, vicious bolts of lightning shooting from her fingers and splashing over two beasts with a deafening *crash* of thunder, throwing the slithering things over the ditch.

The remaining beast shrieked and bolted for her.

"You eez watching self, Rossette!" My second, web-eared vassal called, sprinting to Rossette's side and swept a fogging hand at the demon. A pillar of ice crystalized from his fingers, encasing the creature in a solid, icy cage.

"Rossette…" I panted, groaning at my leaking side. "Nikolai… you should run. If you die again, I… might not… be here to resurrect you…"

"We cannot leave you to die, *Da'torr!*" Rossette stood her ground, she and Nikolai keeping back the demons that strayed into the ditch. "We swore to serve you to the best of our ability when we made the Bloodpact. If you stay, we stay."

The villagers' screams bleated over the ditch, curdled voices muffled overhead, their sobs dampened under the incessant whine in my ears. *Have I lost some of my hearing?*

I peered over the edge.

Those skeletal nightmares swarmed the burning valley, their skin slithering with black muck. Nira, the things were deboning villagers like feral fish in the dry glow of the fire.

My stomach churned, wanting to vomit, but I swallowed and ducked behind the rocky ditch. My palms were caked with blood, straining to keep hold of my scythe. I tried unfolding my wings, but winced as they stiffened back in place. My feathers were shredded… Flying away wasn't an option. Rossette couldn't lift me with her small muscles; her vessel was only a child, despite her soul's matured age… Even if she *could* have lifted me, I couldn't bring myself to leave Nikolai.

Fangs Lastings, I decided. *I have to call Fangs Lastings.*

I pulled out my communicator from my cloak pocket, fingers shaking as I dialed. The com's gears warbled to life, its cogs whirring as a screen of translucent light brightened, projecting from the vision-gem embedded in the center of the discus.

The screen's blue glow swirled in a slow, stirring motion, waiting for the other party to answer.

After a few panicked seconds, a wolf-eared man came into view in the framed light. Fangs Lastings drew back, alarmed at my grisly face.

"What in Land's name?" Fangs Lastings muttered. *"Who is this?"*

I raised a charred fist to my chest in salute. "Sir Janson Stane, requesting help, sir!"

"Help with… an attack? What is your squadron number?"

"13-A!" My voice fractured. "Trixer Sye's squad! Please, sir, I-I'm sorry for calling you directly, but I didn't know what else to do!" I ran a bloodied arm under my nose, blinking tears. "I-I… I need help, sir. Please…"

Lastings' brow furrowed as he shuffled through papers at his desk. *"13-A… you were sent to see to that distress call in the valley."* His finger traced down the documents, then he glanced at me. *"Two squads were already sent there from your sector. That much wasn't enough?"*

"They're all dead, sir!" I choked back a sob, shivering. "I-I'm all that's left…!"

His wolf ears dropped to his neck. *"Even Trixers Sye and Flerran?"*

"All of them!" My voice quaked, remembering the screams of my friends—of my Brothers. "It's just me, now, sir! We… we weren't prepared for this! It was an ambush! They were waiting for us…!"

Sir Lastings pushed his fists on his desk and hurriedly stood. *"Are you still in the valley?"*

"Y-yes, sir! And everything's burning! The Sentient girl is a Pyrovoker. She's not some lowly newborn either, sir, there's something not right about her!"

"*Get out of there, Dueler! If everyone's dead, then there's no one left for you to help.*"

A cloud of smoke clung to my throat, and I coughed blood onto my tattered white sleeve. "I-I can't move my wings, sir... And I can't walk out there—there's too many of them. I-it's like she's gathered an army."

"*How many?*"

I glanced at the turmoil over the ditch, my head light as cotton. How much blood had I lost?

"Too... t-too many," I reported. "Hundreds, maybe thousands. They're everywhere." My eyes stung from the smog, tears only flushing so much debris. "I... I'm going to die here, aren't I, sir...?"

"*Say that again, and I'll pull your Skull-pins from your cloak.*" He slammed an outraged hand on his desk, rattling the quill on his papers. "*Your squad leader's dead! That means you've been promoted to Trixer, soldier! And at your rank, you're not allowed to give up!*" His eyes flicked to my neck; to my white Death mark. "*What's your Hallows, Trixer?*"

I sniffed, hitting a fist to my chest. "It-it's death, sir!"

"*Do you have any vassals who could help?*"

I wiped the fallen ash from my eyes. "They're here now, but I... I don't know how much longer the two can hold them off. C... can you tell the others to cut my Seam when they get here, sir...?"

"*Damn it, Trixer, if you say that again, I'll demote you back to a Singer! I'm sending reinforcements your way, but you have to hold strong. Now get the Void out of—*"

Someone plucked the com out from my fingers.

An adolescent boy was suddenly standing over me. His skin was coated in bronze scales, brown hair grown to his chin with blond streaks.

"These devices grow stranger by the year," the young man hummed, firelight glinting off his half-moon eyeglasses. He tossed my com to the ground and absently scooted a severed head to the side with his boot.

He scrutinized me like a prize at an auction. "You're all that's left, are you?"

I shuffled back, fumbling for my scythe. "Stay back, Demon...!" *There are two Sentients? But... but where was the Pyrovoker?*

I stole a glance back at Rossette and Nikolai. They were focused on keeping the swarming beasts at bay, lightning and ice exploding in a chaotic frenzy. They hadn't noticed this newcomer.

The young man gave a disgusted sneer. "Do I look like those mongrels, you featherless twit?" His gaze lifted past me. "Did you hear that, Cilia? This ingrate thinks I'm one of your witless dogs."

A giggle bounced behind me. I spun so quickly, my eyes were late to focus.

The Pyrovoker!

The grey-haired girl crouched to meet my eyelevel and smiled. "Hello there, little bird. I seem to have missed you, haven't I?" Her green eyes flickered, white pupils bright and gleaming. She sighed dismally. "Oh, I'm terribly sorry. I hate to leave anyone out of a game."

She reached for me, and I cringed—

"Just a moment, Cilia." The young man knelt to me. "This one has a Death mark. And here I was beginning to think none from this lot were worth a damn... Tell me, Reaper: What is your Hallows?"

"Go Cleanse yourself in the Void, Demon," I spat.

He circled a finger over his temple. "This one lives to vex me... I doubt you're an Infeciovoker. Though I suppose another fire-thrower could be sufficient."

"Wrong," sang the girl, skipping playfully around me. "He's covered in burn scars. Fire cannot touch us Pyrovokers. I saw this one sewing his vassals to help, however." She nodded to Rossette and Nikolai. "He's a simple Necrovoker, to be sure."

The scaled man rose. "Interesting... Still, he'll be an imperative addition. Remember to keep his soul tied after you're finished, Cilia."

Her hand burst with fire. "Very well." She smiled. "It will be curious to have a corpse-raiser with us."

"St-stay away from me...!" I raised my scythe.

I was still losing blood, my head spinning like mad. *I can't fight like this. I-I have to get out of here.*

I scrambled up the ditch, forcing up my torn wings. I'd almost taken flight when the girl snagged my ankle and yanked me back to the dirt.

"I'm afraid you're too useful to let go, Reaper," she chided.

"I'll sooner be taken to the Void before I become one of you!" I turned my scythe round, pointing the tip at my own chest.

With a bracing inhale, I plunged the scythe into my ribs—screaming as the sharp metal slid through my breastplate and lodged into soft tissue.

Rossette and Nikolai screamed, dropping to their knees. They clutched at their chests, feeling my pain through our Pact.

"Da'torr...!" Rossette's voice was shrill as she spotted me.

Nikolai panted. "What eez... doing...?"

"I'm sorry...!" I gasped, the breath burning. I gripped my dripping scythe again. "I'm not... done yet...!"

I twisted the blade toward my Seam—

The Sentient ripped the blade out in a gush of blood.

Her enflamed hand raged with hot flames, and her fingers snatched my face, her claws sinking into my cheeks and scraping bone. I howled, the stink of melting skin simmering as her fire licked over my right eye and spread to my featherless head—

Something swooped down and slashed its talons across her face.

It was my messenger raven.

Nile!

The girl jerked away as the raven dove again, distracting her while I crouched over the dirt, bearing the pain of my melted skin.

I curled over the dirt, wheezing, my chest drenched in dark crimson, spots clouding my vision. I wanted to lie down and… and rest for a bit… just for a little while…

Your soul will rot, I remembered, sobering. *You'll be one of those damned demons!*

I found my scythe lying feet away. I heaved forward, crawling to it. *If I could just… cut my Seam…*

"Annoying little *rats!*" snarled the girl. She swatted Nile with a powerful *crack* and the bird hit the dirt in a puff of dust.

I screamed, my soul ripping in two.

"NILE!" Pain exploded, grief and panic slamming hard and sharp. I scrambled to my messenger and scooped up Nile, cupping the limp bird.

"N-Nile?" My voice cracked, tears flooding as the new pit in my soul shriveled. "Nile…! Please—No, no, no…!" I heaved gasps as I curled over the dead raven, the world shrinking away. "Nile…! Please… plea—*Hghck!*"

Something drove into my back.

Squrlch! Something wet squelched, an icy chill ripping from my ribs.

Everything went numb.

The girl sauntered around me, beaming like a proud child who couldn't wait for her promised reward. In her hands was a dark, drenched lump of muscle. It looked like a shifter's heart.

My gaze dropped, absently noting that the pulse in my ears was dimming.

Rossette and Nikolai's screams choked into silence. With my spotty vision, I saw their corpses were being scraped raw by the rotten beasts, their ghosts rising from their mangled bodies and huddling as the demons surrounded them.

"Keep his puppets from your beasts' teeth, would you?" the scaled man asked the girl, pushing up his eyeglasses. "I should think they'll make fair collateral."

"D…" Blood flooded up my throat, the taste of salty metal pouring over my tongue, vision blotting black. "Death save us…"

1
AN UNWELCOME PARTY

~~~~~

WILLOW

The cold gust rustled hundreds of leaves in a hushed storm, lifting my long, ashen hair and sweeping it aside. The Willow of Ashes loomed high within the misted cavern, glowing softly in its mournful brilliance.

Xavier stood alongside his brother before the ancient Relic, both watching me; waiting for me.

"Willow," Xavier's voice was thick with apprehension. The apparition's bearded face flickered, his strange eyes giving a warm stare as he took my hand. "Can you give the Call...?"

---※---

Thump, thump, thump—CRASH!

A thunderous clatter jolted me awake in the train's compartment seat. My tiny songcrow, Jewel, fluttered off my shoulder and whistled startled chirps as my gaze whipped to the carpeted floor.

Crushed beneath a pile of heavy luggage was a rabbit-eared girl. Her neck was snapped, brown skin covered in bruises from the fallen boxes, and her deadened eyes stared at my feet as drool dribbled on the carpet.

I relaxed and pulled my long, white hair over a shoulder, sighing. "Oh, Vendy, that's the fifth time this week."

The teenager's corpse offered no response. Nor did her ghost rise from her bones to reply.

"I see your strengthened NecroSeam is still keeping your soul attached when you die," I hummed. Jewel fluttered onto one of Vendy's rabbit ears and pecked at her skull curiously. "Odd, though, it's been nearly a month…" I tapped a ponderous finger to my lips. "Usually, soul-strengthening only lasts for two weeks. How strong had Xavier made it?" *I shouldn't be surprised*, I thought, *Xavier and Alexander have always surpassed us in Necrovoking training during our youth. Oh, how it would drive Matthiel to insanity—*

I stiffened, horrified. "Matthiel!" I hid my face in my hands. "Oh, Jewel, I Bloody forgot about my betrothal—!"

"What about our betrothal?"

I stifled a yelp. Xavier had appeared under the compartment's open doorframe.

His broad chin was cleanly shaven this morning, smelling of cologne, and he was dressed in white, silken garments. His wavy, grey hair was combed neatly over his brow, regal and suitable enough to be seen by the royal host we would meet today.

His heterochromic gaze regarded me quizzically. "Darling? Is something wrong?"

"No, no! Everything's… er, splendid." I craned to the crushed corpse under the pile of luggage. "Well, I suppose not *everything*."

Xavier glanced at his newly dead vassal and clicked his tongue. "Again? Blast it, Vendy, what have we told you about getting *help* to grab the luggage from the racks?"

Xavier's eyes suddenly switched places—the blue was now on the right, and the white on the left. Now, he was his brother, Alexander.

I rose from my seat as Alexander began Vendy's resurrection. With his hands glowing violet streams of light, Alex wove his fingers like a conductor before his orchestra, having the lights stretch and slither over Vendy's corpse. As the Hallows seeped into her skin, her bruises began to fade.

While Alexander continued the revival, Jewel fluttered back to my shoulder and fluffed her feathers until she was a small puffball of blackness. I rubbed her head with a finger, sighing.

Having traveled with the Devouhs for the better part of a month, I was slowly growing accustomed to the twins' shared-body predicament. It was astounding how commonplace it suddenly felt. *Seamstress, I should hope I don't grow TOO familiar with it.* I very well couldn't marry a man who shared a body with his twin.

Marry. The thought burned the memory to my skull in a cruel reminder. *Second betrothal. Matthiel.*

"Death!" I pounded a knuckle to my brow. "Xavier, there's something I need to discuss with—"

"Not Xavier," Alexander grunted, finishing Vendy's resurrection with a few final strings of violet light that sank into the rabbit girl's skin. "And... there we are."

Vendy breathed back to life, her neck newly healed, but she groaned to see the mess of luggage she now had to round up.

I deflated. "Ah, yes, right... Alex, I need to hold a... *private* discussion with Xavier. Could you perhaps go off and... and go wherever it is you both go when the other is in control?"

Alex snorted. "I'll still hear whatever you tell him. I can't simply block my ears in the psyche. I listen through the *physical* ears we share."

I grumbled. "Oh, fine... I'll save it for when you're both normal again." I glanced out the window, noticing the train was already stopped in the station.

We're already here? How long have I been asleep? The whistle sounded beyond the car's walls, echoes of gears and chattering crowds bouncing round the station outside.

I turned to Alexander. "Have we arrived—*oh!*" I jumped in a start, seeing Alexander's eyes had switched again. Now, I was staring at Xavier. I exhaled and lightly slapped his shoulder. "Death's Sorrowed Head, will you *warn* me when you change?"

Xavier chuckled. "Sorry. But yes, we've arrived." He checked his pocket-watch that was chained to one of his doublet's buttons. "Truth be told, we arrived half an hour ago. Master and Mistress have already left for Everland's palace. They thought it prudent that you rest more, considering your lack of sleep these past few nights."

I huffed and crossed my arms. "I recall seeing you pacing about the aisle just the same."

His grin was weak. "Well, I suppose it's been a rough month since... well, since what happened in Lindel."

I rubbed the crusts from my eyes. "*Rough* doesn't quite describe an entire city being leveled by a mountainous Stonedragon. Nor being overrun by Necrofera which provided the greatest death toll Everland has seen in centuries." I yielded to a shudder, holding a fist to my chest in prayer and whispered, "May Nira harbor their souls and deliver them to a safe rebirth."

Xavier hung his head as a silence grew. Then he cleared his throat and tugged at the long sleeves of his alabaster doublet. "Come, the porter is waiting outside with the others."

Jewel fluttered from my shoulder as I reached over the luggage racks and pulled down a wide-brimmed, decorative hat, donning it primly. It had been a gift from Mother Alice, so that I might find some shade from the surface's terrible sun. *Bloody thing.* From the compartment's window, I could see slits of those golden rays sprinkling into the station from wide windows, giving the promise of a clear sky outside these walls.

I checked to be sure my Storagesphere, which housed my shrunken luggage, was secured at my waist by a silver chain. It was wrapped around my new, golden gown that Mother Alice had purchased for me at the last stop. Now ready, I strode out the compartment.

"Wait," Xavier called.

—No, blast it, it's Alex again! How would I ever keep up with their constant switching?

Alexander's scowl was disapproving as he lifted a strand of my long, ashen hair. "Xavier failed to notice that you're forgetting something, Your Highness Death."

I stared at the strand. Then remembered.

"Oh!" I plunged a hand into my Storagesphere. The translucent, gel-like orb rippled as I sank my fingers inside and searched for the item I sought.

I plucked out a gilded earcuff. This held my newest illusion. The Devouh's family Dreamcatcher had purchased it for me in the first town this train had stopped in, and I'd used it to pose as Mother Alice's 'hopeful apprentice' during our travels.

When I slipped the cuff on my ear, I watched my long hair shorten to my shoulders and fade brown, the skin on my arms darkening like that of an Everlander's sun-tinted complexion. From my reflection in the window, I stared at the false face I'd grown accustomed to during my travels with the twins.

Alex nodded his approval of my disguise, then his eyes switched—*ugh*—yet again as he became Xavier once more, and turned to Vendy with a bright smile. "Thank you, Vendy, we'll have Dalen bring your uncle Henry to come and help you in a moment."

Vendy had stacked the luggage boxes into two towers and flattened against them in a hard pant, throwing up an approving thumb between gasps. "Th… thanks, *Da'torr*…"

He gestured toward the open door. "Shall we?"

I nodded and stepped off the hover-train alongside him. Smoke plumed from the many chimneys of other cars that were lined in this enormous, mountain-based station, perfuming the air with spiced scents. My eyes dried from the clouding exhaust.

Hydraulics hissed and squealed about the tall, tiled walls, and many trains whistled in their lines. Shifters bustled here and there, some leaving the mountain-city and others, like ourselves, now entering. There were vendors scattered throughout the station, fashioned like a bazaar, chatter and haggling bouncing off the enormous, domed ceiling—

"AAAH!" a woman shrieked from a nearby eatery, jumping out of her chair. "A rat! There's a *feral* in my sandwich!"

A furry head popped out between the slices of bread, the deli ham hanging from the weasel's teeth.

But it wasn't a rat. It was a feral ferret. One that I knew.

The ferret, Kurn, squeaked when the woman swatted her purse at him, and he ungracefully dodged and fell off the table, keeping hold of the ham as he scampered for me with his stubby legs. He stretched and grabbed my skirt desperately, snickering small pleas for help.

"Oh, get it!" cried the woman, hopping on one foot as she ripped off her slipper and lumbered toward me, flailing the shoe over her head like a maniac. "Get it, Roaress! Don't let it get away!"

I quickly plucked Kurn off the ground and spun on my heels, stuffing the long-bodied weasel into my hat and pulling down the brim to hide him.

"Roaress!" The woman shrieked at me, not seeing through my disguise. "Roaress, did it bite you?! Oh, the ghastly thing, it was so disgusting…!"

I shoved down my hat to keep the wriggly pet from escaping. "Oh, he *just* scurried into the drain! You ought to fetch the shifter in charge of this facility and file a complaint!"

Her face pulled into a dutiful look. "You're right! I should ask for my Mel back while I'm at it! They will not get away with this poorly-kept *farm*, having ferals skittering about the pipes…!"

She stormed off like a general striding to a promised glory on the battlefield.

Kurn popped his head out of my hat. I rubbed a finger between his round ears and chuckled. "That was a close one, wasn't it?"

"S-sorry!" A man shouted from the crowd then and shoved into view. "Crap, crap, crap, crap…!"

Ah. Right on cue, the ferret's owner came running over. Ringëd, our company's oracle and Footrunner, panted to a stop before me and wheezed over his knees. "S… sorry about him…!" He plucked the ferret by scruff and stuffed him in his messenger bag. "What did I Bloody tell you about running off, you fat little bandit? I swear to Bloods, if you get skewered by someone's umbrella, I'm just going to let it spill all that stolen food out of your stomach and…" Ringëd stormed out of the station.

"—'scuse me, miss," a winged man from our party, Dalen, said behind me.

I stepped aside for him and our company's Blacksmith, Henry, as they walked off the train with their arms full of luggage. It was the same luggage that had crushed Vendy earlier.

Behind them, I spotted three other freckled faces with Dalen's same hue of feathers. These were the Tesler siblings, part of our entourage. They were arms thieves, or I suppose ex-thieves now that they'd agreed to serve us along our journey in exchange for a full pardon from High Howllord Lucas.

The three in the back had given us a fair amount of trouble in Lindel, but their eldest brother, Dalen, seemed to have set their hearts straight again. Dalen himself was dead, but resurrected for a time by his new Necrovoking *Da'torr*: the twins.

Xavier stepped aside for the siblings as well, and chuckled. "You've forgotten what her guise looks like, haven't you, Dalen?"

Dalen peered round his bulky boxes of luggage and frowned at me. "Oh," said Dalen, his eyes popping open. "Right, sorry, Your High—"

I waved my falsely brown hands hurriedly. "No, don't call me by any of those honorifics, remember? If anyone overhears, this illusion will be for naught." I'd already been spotted in Lindel, but I was thankful Father Lucas fabricated a convincing story, explaining I'd escaped his watch and was still at large. He also assured me that my father needn't be informed… yet.

Seamstress prick me, I hope we end this trip before Father discovers I've left. I thanked Nira the local news hadn't caught wind of it. Only the Reapers knew of my presence here.

"Right, right," said Dalen, his brow scrunched as though he had a headache. "So, uh… what are we supposed to call ya again?"

"Ashleya," I reminded, adjusting my wide-brimmed hat as a gust nearly blew it from my head. "*Roaress* Ashleya."

Xavier rubbed his chin curiously. "You know, I've been meaning to ask. Why choose a name like Ashleya? It seems rather specific."

I shot him a piqued look. "It's my middle name, darling."

He winced. "A-ah. *Km-hmm*. Of course… I remember now."

"Somehow, I doubt that you do," I grumbled, lifting a finger as Jewel fluttered off my shoulder and instead alighted on my finger. She twittered at Xavier with offended chirps. "Why is it *I'm* the only thing from your past you don't remember?" I asked wearily.

Xavier scratched his neck. "It's not as if I've had anything to trigger the memories. At least, not until now. It took time to remember even Alexander, my parents, Jaq and Bianca…"

"Bianca?" I asked, clapping my hands excitedly. "That's right, your childhood Healing friend! You said she was here in Everland's capital, didn't you?"

Xavier smiled with delight. "Yes, she is! That's right, you've never met her… Well, perhaps we can correct that during our stay. You'll love her, I'm sure."

"From what you and Alexander have told me of her, I'm sure I will." I glanced at Jewel pleasantly. My little crow cocked her head in return, fluffing her feathers until she was a ball of black fluff over my finger.

I watched Dalen and his siblings haul the luggage outside into the trunk of a porter's hovering coach. It was a splendid, closed coach with gilded trimwork and vibrant lavender paint, bearing royal flags of Everland's crest: a series of golden diamonds made to look like a stylistic sword standing upright and wedged between two proud lions.

There was a second, identical coach beside it. *That must be ours*, I guessed.

From within its crystal-clear windows, I could see four familiar faces. There was Jaq, the twins' blond-haired viper friend; Lilli, my bat-winged Aide; Ringëd with his pet ferret wrapped around his neck; and Octavius, our party's poison-wielding Brother-in-Arms—

A pebble whistled past my ear and smacked Xavier on the cheek.

Xavier staggered in surprise, rubbing at the new red spot on his face.

"What're ye dirt crawlers doin', commin' to our town?" Piped a young, tiger-eared child. His fist was full of more pebbles, and he chucked another at Xavier, who hurried to dodge.

"Get out!" shouted the child. "We don't want none 'a your demons here!"

The child threw more, bypassing me and only aiming at Xavier—whose eyes quickly changed as Alexander took control and swatted a projectile away.

"Stop that!" growled Alex, swatting at another thrown pebble. The surrounding crowd noticed us, shocked gasps and angry murmurs filling the echoing station. Several shifters were grabbing nearby rocks and even some parasols, as if to use them as clubs. I spied a custodian brandishing his broom.

Alex swatted yet another pebble, not having noticed the swarming mob, and stamped a foot. "I said *stop that* you damned little bug!"

The boy threw another stone—

An armored man riding a feral stallion stepped between us and the enclosing crowd. Right behind him was a woman mounted on a red mare, her soft features contorted with focus, her grip tight on the reins.

Those two! They were the rebels that had boarded our train after what happened in Lindel. Kurrick and Anabelle.

Kurrick steadied his horse before it trampled the still-shouting boy, who yelped and scurried away from the warrior's brutish glare. "Move along, all of you," Kurrick barked at the tense crowd.

No one moved.

"I said," chewed Kurrick, grabbing the hilt of one of his swords. "*Move along.*"

Grudgingly, the mob scuttled away, but kept leery eyes on Alexander from over their shoulders.

Alex slid a hand through his shadowy, grey hair and exhaled.

Kurrick spit at the ground in a vile sneer, turning his horse away. He was a large man with an ugly, scarred face, his scowl as intimidating as the two swords across his back. Anabelle was his Healer companion, wearing a vermillion cloak with the hood drawn up to hide her curly, chestnut hair and crimson eyes.

I tucked a lock of hair behind my ear and glanced at Kurrick. "Where did you get those horses?"

"A man was selling them outside the station," grunted Kurrick.

Alex scoffed. "And where did you get the Mel for them?"

"Dream and his wife are funding us on this journey," Kurrick explained. "They believe it imperative that we accompany you to find your brother's corpse."

"*Body,*" corrected Alex—no, he was Xavier now. He'd switched out suddenly and had curled back one wolf ear, looking irked as he clipped, "We don't know if I'm dead or alive yet."

Kurrick snorted. "'Yet' indeed. This is a distracting trifle, I say. But then, it is not up to me, is it?" He flicked an annoyed glance at his woman companion, Anabelle, on her own mount beside him.

Anabelle wasn't paying him any mind. From atop her mount she was staring at me with discomfort. One of her lion ears flicked, causing her single, looped earing to quiver.

I smirked. "You still aren't accustomed to my guise, Miss Ana?"

Anabelle's mouth twisted, and she murmured, "I should think I'll never grow accustomed to it. Myra would always tease Kurrick and me with illusion disguises when we were young. I have yet decided if I find it humorous or irksome to see you following her example, Daughter of Myra."

My brow furrowed at the woman. "When you were young? How long have you known my mother?"

"Quite a while," Miss Ana said, sighing drearily. "Though, it has been some time since we've seen her. How I miss her so… At least I am able to spend time with her daughter instead."

Kurrick hummed dully, then nodded to me. "I'm glad to see your illusion is effective. The Everlanders are becoming more hostile toward you Grimlings." He threw his head at Xavier. "Best you head to the coach. Ana and I will keep guard from outside."

"Keep guard?" Xavier echoed. "I suppose you're our bodyguards suddenly?"

"I suppose so," Kurrick considered, scratching his greasy stubble. "If nothing else, claiming so will be an appropriate cover for us while in the company of the false king."

Xavier groaned and looped an arm around mine, leading us outside. "I hope you have the sense not call him that in his own Bloody palace. I'll have to warn Vendy and Henry to keep their lips shut as well..."

When we stepped into the sunlight I shielded my eyes with a hand. *Blast this sun!* My hat wasn't nearly enough cover. Both Xavier and I needed time for our sight to adjust to the sudden flood of blinding light, and he wiped at his watering lids just as well as I. We cave dwellers were not equipped for this ball of gas.

Although... Once the initial sting had settled and I could see again, the view out here was... well, it was absolutely breathtaking. The red and brown streaked mountains stretched the full span of the speckled city far below in the distance, like a mighty barrier from enemies. Wavering shadows spread across the slopes and rocky hills and the pointed peaks glittered with the golden light of the morning sun that rose from the east.

As horrible as this sun is, I thought, *I have to admit, it brings a beauty to these lands I never imagined.*

A warm breeze brushed past, nearly blowing off my hat—

—The breeze turned cold suddenly, the new gust rustling hundreds of leaves and lifting my long, ashen hair in its gentle currents.

The Willow of Ashes towered over me, magnificent and imposing as Xavier stood beside his brother before the ancient Relic. The twins watched; waited.

"Willow," Xavier hushed, his bearded face oscillating in and out of focus. *"Can you give the Call...?"*

"—All right, there?"

I blinked, the scene evaporating.

Xavier was looking me over, his hand clasped around mine in caution.

I massaged my eyes, that other face of his burned into my lids. When I looked at him again, I squinted at the harsh sunlight, focusing on his face. *This face. Yes, this was real.*

"I'm fine." I smiled and squeezed his fingers. But when I turned forward again, a heavy, sinking dread pulled down my lips.

That dream again. I stifled a shudder, despite the heat. *Why does it keep resurfacing...?*

2
ALLIES IN HIGH PLACES

~~~~~~

XAVIER

*B*rilliant.
    I sat slouched in the lurching hover-coach, my chin propped with a fist while I glared sidelong at Willow. She'd been dismissing it throughout the ride, but I knew something was wrong. She certainly wasn't discreet about it.

Willow's disguised, brown eyes would glaze, she would fiddle with her music watch, steal a glance at me across the buggy, look away when I caught her staring... even the little crow on her finger was acting anxious. And if a messenger was tense, it was a safe bet her Reaper felt the same.

Just Bloody brilliant.

I returned to glaring out the window, watching the mountain peaks bloom with golden halos as the sun rose behind them.

This proved it: The Gods hated me. First that lunatic pushed out my soul and tossed my body over a cliffside, I've been trapped in my twin for six damned years, and now my fiancée has found me before I've had a chance to fix it. All while that demon queen was still on the loose and no doubt stalking us somewhere behind those mountains.

This was not how I'd planned my reunion with Willow. It wasn't my Bloody fault she'd decided to jaunt over here during a demon invasion. It wasn't my fault I was stuck like this, and it damn well wasn't my fault she was sore about it.

But then, I couldn't expect her to look past it, could I? Were I in her place, I may have been more than a little... jaded.

I listened to the clopping hooves from the feral horses outside. Riding beside our coach on their own feral beasts were those two rebellion members, Kurrick and Miss Ana, serving as our personal guards.

Across from me, Willow's winged Aide, Lilli, brushed her black hair with pointed tenacity. The strange, yellow sunlight of these surface lands gave the strands a glossy sheen. Her bat wings were folded delicately at her sides over the leather seat, her messenger crow perched over her shoulder and preening its feathers. I noticed Lilli's hands were calloused and her neck still bore scrapes and scars from battle. It looked as though she'd tried to cover the damage with powder and creams, but the puckered blemishes couldn't quite be hidden yet.

On my side of the buggy, Jaq, Ringëd and Octavius muttered amongst themselves, regarding the latter two's new garbs that Mistress had given them.

Their movements were stiff in the silken doublets and pressed trousers. Octavius tugged at his high collar and long sleeves, his black cat ears grown in obvious discomfort. I grinned, promptly snuffing a chuckle before it escaped. Octavius and Ringëd would have to grow accustomed to such fine garments. We were to stay in Everland's palace as the king's guests for a time, at least until we found a new lead to Sirra-Lynn; to Octavius's mother.

My mood soured at the reminder. I glared at my gloved fists. If Octavius's mother truly knew where my vessel was, Nira, *please* let her help me get out of this borrowed skin.

"Jaq," I began, turning to the viper seated beside me. His sandy hair was combed back and lightly gelled this morning, patches of his grey scales shedding from his sharp, newly shaven chin.

"Remind me to contact Bianca first thing tomorrow," I said. "Now that we're in the capital, we may as well go to the primary source for our mission."

Jaq slipped off his rectangular eyeglasses to rub the scratched lenses with his sleeve. The crow on his lap fluffed her feathers before tucking her head into her wings and returning to sleep.

"May as well," Jaq agreed, slipping his eyeglasses back over his nose. He ran an endearing thumb over his crow's skull. "Been a few years since we've seen her anyway."

Octavius's head perked, as had his white-cheeked raven from his lap. "Bianca?" he asked. "Was that the friend you mentioned? The one who told you about my mom?"

I nodded. "Her Master Healer claimed he'd seen your mother on an island to the west… which, I suppose, matches *your* observation regarding your visions of me, Ringëd."

The officer grinned and threw up his thumb approvingly, the feral ferret on his shoulder nibbling on a dried apricot. "Told you," he said smugly. "I know my homeland's language anywhere."

"Did the doctor follow my mom?" Octavius asked.

"He tried." I shrugged. "The island was very crowded. She was lost in the masses, we hear."

Octavius looked dismayed. Glancing down at his raven, he stroked its feathers for comfort. His tensions leaked from his shoulder at the touch.

The coach had fallen silent, save for the messenger's quiet croaks as they received attention from their Reapers. Despite what had happened in Lindel, everyone seemed at ease due to the birds' presences. From what I'm told, this was the effect messengers had with their Reapers. The Bond was said to be incredibly sacred, since they shared emotions with their companions.

I scowled up at my brother's raven, Mal. He had elected to perch on the curtain rail and was biting at an itch, briefly cocking his head at me before returning to his more important priority.

Lucky bastards, the lot of them.

I should be brimming with good cheer. Willow was here, I was regaining more memories, and after so many years of rigorous training, I was finally inducted into the Brotherhood of Reapers.

But now that I was here, official badge pinned to my breast pocket and recognized as, dauntingly, a war hero…

I didn't deserve it. I was an imposter. How could I dare call myself a Reaper if I had no messenger?

Where is your brother, Mal? My stare turned stale at the raven, a sickness balling in my stomach. *Where is my Chai—?*

The horses screamed at the front, and the coach lurched to a bumpy halt. My wolf ears sprouted and lifted, hearing shouts erupt outside.

I jerked my gaze out the window and found that our two rebel bodyguards had dismounted and drawn their swords, disappearing around the front of the coach. The sounds of scraping steel punctured the air, the clamor of battle roaring.

"Bloods!" I hurried to pluck a scythe-sphere from the chains around my neck, pressing the sealing rune etched on the ball. The ball gleamed with a golden light and melted in my hand, stretching with glowing ripples until it curved and sharpened into my short-handled blade, solidifying to keep its crooked shape. "Tell me it isn't the Necrofera again?" I pleaded.

"It ain't." Jaq spat venom off to the side, unwinding the long chain that was wrapped around his wrist and had his crooked scythe materialize at the last link. "The messengers have been as quiet as feral gophers."

"He's right," Lilli agreed. "I haven't felt any strain from Dusk."

"Nor I from Jewel," Willow rumbled, her fox ears curled.

"Shade's fine, too," added Octavius nervously.

I heard Alexander call from my thoughts, *"As is Mal."*

"Yes, yes, I get the point," I muttered. *Spoiled Reapers and their damned companions.* I ripped open the door and leapt out.

Blocking the mountain path was a wall of men, their faces veiled by lion-shaped masks, swords and Shotri drawn as they came at our bodyguards with full force.

Our coachman stumbled off his bench in fright, the man's hound ears fully grown and folded fast to his neck.

I grabbed his shoulder. "Who are they? What's happening?"

"B-b-bandits!" The coachman squeaked. "I-I've heard rebels have been raiding porters with royal flags—oh, Gardener sow me, it's actually happening!" He stumbled off in the direction we'd come, away from the bandits.

I glared at the lion-masked men. *Rebels?* Like our bodyguards? If those two had anything to do with this…

No, our 'guards' looked set on killing those men, if needed. The warrior's two large broadswords clanged noisily against the blades of his adversaries, and the woman guarding his back had lifted a portion of the road with her golden-glowing hands to fashion herself an impressively thick blade out of the bits of rock, the pieces melding together under the shimmering light she controlled.

That's right, the woman is a Terravoker as well as a Healer. I'd nearly forgotten that detail. Dual-Evocators were a rarity. Those fortunate enough to be born with any Hallows were typically restricted to one element. Unless you were a Relicblood, like Willow.

The others tumbled out of the coach behind me and sprinted toward the battling mass. But before we stepped more than five feet, two rabbit-eared figures leapt out of the second coach behind us, hollering at the band of rebels. It was Vendy, my teenaged vassal, and her uncle Henry.

"Hey!" Vendy shouted, waving her hands like a maniac at the masked men. "Wait up, wait up! It's just us—*GLCKK!*"

An arrow *cracked* through Vendy's skull, the force so strong it threw her backward several feet, and she collapsed to the dirt.

Henry rolled his eyes at her new corpse and trotted toward the men responsible. He rolled up his sleeve and held up his thick arm, displaying a tattoo in the shape of a lion reared back in a proud roar, a crown elegantly curled around the image in a circular frame of flower petals.

"I Bloody told the Lord Servant we were coming," Henry snapped at the men. He pointed at Vendy's corpse. "And you're damned lucky my niece is already dead, else I would have strangled whoever shot that arrow!"

The masked men staggered. Then the one in front lowered his sword. "Is that… Henry?"

"You're Bloody right it's me," Henry snorted. "That sounds like Lotten. Did the Servant make you a captain since last I saw you?"

The front man, Lotten, laughed and stabbed his sword in the dirt, leaning on the hilt. "That he did! Good to see you, Henry. And, er, sorry for your niece."

Henry swatted a dismissive hand toward me. "The Howllord will bring her back in a minute."

I sighed and put away my scythes, striding to Vendy's corpse. "Will you tell your friends to take more care in knowing with whom they cross blades?" I muttered.

Lotten stared at me from under his mask. He pointed and asked Henry, "Is that he? The High Howllord…?"

Henry gave a bearded grin. "It sure is. Like I said on my last call to the Servant, my niece is their vassal."

The men removed their masks in awe, murmuring amongst themselves and sharing excited whispers.

I groaned and rubbed my eyes. "Bloody rebels and their damned delusions…" I supposed they believed Alex and I would find their 'rightful king', just like Henry and Vendy—*and* Miss Ana and her burly companion. *Lunatics.*

I crouched over Vendy, examining her latest corpse. Luckily, it seemed my strengthened NecroSeam still held, even after a month. I thought it was odd since my parents' vassals never lasted more than a fortnight, but I supposed my halved-magic must be amplifying the Evocation.

Two feet shuffled by her head, and my second vassal, Dalen, whistled above me. "Twice in one day?" He scratched his cheek as his wings gave a curious flap. "Does she just like dyin'?"

I hummed, plucking the arrow from Vendy's skull in a spurt of blood. "You're one to talk, Dalen. It seems like you and she have made a sport of finding the most curious ways to die, this last month."

Dalen crossed his arms in a grumble. "Hey, *I've* been a ghost longer than her, *without* my body. I'm still getting' used to bein' alive. Well, sorta-alive."

"All the same." I flicked my eyes upward and called for my brother. "Alex? Some assistance?"

A groan sounded in my thoughts. *"And here I thought we could finally have a day of relaxation without worrying over these two. Cheery Bloody birthday to us."*

I felt a tug at my soul, and was *yanked* backward. The sensations of touch and smell vanished along with the physical world until I found myself floating in the empty abyss of my brother's psyche, with naught but a single window to show me the outside world through Alexander's eyes.

I watched through the window as Alex peeled off his gloves and evoked his Hallows. His fingers gleamed with violet lights, his birthmark of three black diamonds shifting white and changing into a Death mark under his knuckles.

The lights stretched and engulfed Vendy's corpse, mending the hole at her skull, and when Alex pressed his hands over her chest, he poured the Hallows into her heart—which *thumped* back to life.

Vendy's eyes flew open, her rabbit ears perking straight up in a gasp. "Bloods!"

"Perhaps next time," Alex muttered to her, "you shouldn't charge into the cross-fires of a skirmish?"

Vendy rubbed her neck and laughed nervously. "Heh, right…"

Alex's work done, he threw himself back into the psyche, which pulled me back out to the physical world. I pushed to my feet and helped Vendy up, turning to see Henry was still speaking amiably with the band of rebels. The captain, Lotten, was on a com call, holding the device to his ear and keeping the screen-option off.

When he ended the call, Lotten trotted to me and bowed.

"Forgive us, Howllord," he said. Without his mask, I saw two stubbed antlers were sprouting from his forehead, his brown bangs draping along their sides as a forest of stubble dressed his chin. "We didn't realize you were among the passengers. I've just contacted my Lord Servant, he has vouched for your company. He welcomes you to the mountains."

My stare turned askew at the man. "*Who* welcomes us?"

"Land's Servant." The man rose proudly. "If you're to stay with the king, be on guard, Sir. The imposter family is not to be trusted."

"What do you mean?"

"It's simply a precaution." He tipped his head and gave hand signals to his men, all of whom withdrew down the mountain path. "Welcome to New Aldamstria! Good day to you, Howllord. Glory to the Heir!"

They said farewell to Henry, apologizing to Vendy again, and dispersed into the winding roads down the hill.

Henry laughed and came beside me, slapping my back cheerfully. "Lotten, a captain! Never thought I'd see the day."

"Never thought I'd have a rebel welcoming party, yet here I am," I muttered, cocking an eyebrow at Henry. "Did those men know of our… er, predicament?"

Henry shook his head. "Nah. They only know you've got some role in getting back our true king."

I sighed. "Wonderful."

Our 'bodyguards' strode to my side, Miss Ana clinging to her warrior's back as the scarred man glared after where the rebels had left. "I should hope we will not have any more visitations during our stay."

"In that, sir, we agree," I said.

The burly guard put away his blade and retrieved his stallion, taking the beast by the reins as he adjusted the saddle's girth.

Miss Ana mounted her red-coated horse and patted its neck. She whispered something to the warrior.

He grunted a response. "Perhaps."

"What did she say?" I inquired. Did that woman ever speak louder than a whisper?

"Land's Servant seems to consider you a person of honor." He swung himself onto the saddle, sniffing. "Though, the question of why is concerning."

"Ah—yes, this Servant person everyone is on about." I folded my arms. "Who is he?"

"He is the rebellion's leader in Everland," said Kurrick, sounding unimpressed.

"Ah. And is he the one spreading rumors of our affiliation with your supposed 'lost heir'?"

He only shrugged, then took a separate breath and said, "Where is our porter?"

I threw a thumb over my shoulder. "I imagine he's soiling himself up the path."

"Blast it all, I don't know the way from here… Come, Ana."

"Yes, Kurrick," I heard the woman whisper dutifully, and I shielded my eyes with a hand while watching the two trot after the driver. Their silhouettes were outlined in gold from the rising sunlight that spilled from the mountain peaks.

3

A ROYAL DISPLAY

XAVIER

"Bloody Land!" Octavius gaped out the coach's window when we arrived at the palace gates, marveling at the towering architecture of Everland's grandiose castle. "This place is huge!"

I tugged on my gloves and hummed. "I suppose it's quaint."

"Quaint?!" Octavius gawked at me. "It's practically the size of five houses!"

"As I said." I shrugged. "Quaint."

Willow eyed the building beside me. "Oh, it's adorable! Is this really a palace? Mine is perhaps thrice that size in Grim."

"Even our manor is twice as large," I murmured. "Odd, I expected more from 'the mighty King of Everland'."

Octavius hunched back in his seat and snorted. "Spoiled rich people…"

Though, as unimpressive a stature as it was, the palace did seem incredibly sturdy. Built like a fortress, the stained-glass windows were the only delicate features it had. From the east and west wings hugged the mountainside, like a mother cradling her child, and the palace's teeth-like parapets circled the four towers that cast long shadows over the fortress's thick walls.

The hover-coach stopped after looping round the circling courtyard, and we each filed out—

Brr, brr, brr, BRR, BRRRRrrrrRRrr!

A loud blast of melodic notes burst to life, and we cringed at the out-of-tune croaks, squeezing our ears shut.

"My… my lord Alexander!" a man in a servant's uniform panted, tucking a bugle—the cause of the hideous noise—into his vest. He then threw a fist-full of wilted rose petals in the air, the things fluttering down in an ugly display as he cleared his throat. "His Majesty, the… the king welcomes you…" He paused to wheeze and dab at his sweaty brow with a kerchief. "… and your company… to his palace…! And he wishes you a… a cheery birthday!"

The servant plucked out his bugle again and trumpeted three pathetic notes. "Please f…! follow me…!" His voice dwindled miserably at 'me', then he shuffled off, huffing and puffing as if ripe to faint.

Jaq and Vendy erupted with snorting laughter, and Lilli and Willow politely turned away to stifle their giggles. Officer Ringëd clasped a hand over his mouth and shuddered with a snicker while Henry and the Tesler siblings chortled and mimicked the man's silly presentation.

Octavius glanced at me, bewildered. "Uh… is *that* normal for rich people?"

"Not even slightly," I muttered, scratching my chin as we followed the exhausted servant down the pathway. "At least, not in Grim…"

"And it's your birthday?" Vendy asked from the back. "Why didn't you say anything, *Da'torr*!"

I sighed. "Why does it matter? We aren't exactly in a position to celebrate."

"Oh, nonsense," Willow chided, her disguised, short hair flicking when she shook her head. "We're visiting foreign royalty. What better time to celebrate one's *Rae'u Shelic*?"

Behind us, Dalen's brow furrowed at me, his wings fluttering. "*Ray-you-what now?*"

Jaq tossed a scaled hand his way. "*Day of Life*, it's a Grimish term. And I'm with 'Roaress Ashleya' over there—it's a freakin' *castle*. Enjoy it."

I grumbled, "I was hoping to have my own body before I turned twenty."

Jaq slapped my back. "Get over it! We ain't bein' chased by demons no more, we ain't gonna have people throwin' stones at us—I say take the break while ya got it."

My head tilted. "Fair point…"

I twisted, noticing that Miss Ana and Kurrick had fallen behind. They were giving their horses to a different servant, perhaps to be stabled. They strode down a separate path, as did Henry and the Tesler siblings with our luggage, still laughing at the boisterous welcoming.

When we reached the towering, oak doors, the servant heaved them open and led the way inside.

I heard gasps of wonder from the others, the light from the stained-glass windows flitting in colorful patches of red, green, and yellow, giving life to the maroon carpet under my boots. The servant shuffled down the halls, still panting, and led us to a new set of doors which he swung open and guided us into an expansive, carpeted dining hall lined with rows of more stained-glass windows.

The many faces seated at the long table turned to us, and the servant bowed, still winded as he announced, "The Hi…! High Howllord Alexander and…! and company have…! arrived…!" He produced his bugle and blew a weak fanfare, gasping for breath he threw a handful of wilted rose petals into the air like before, then sagged out of the hall with his horn dragging over the floor.

My mother and father rubbed their ears from their end of the long table, shooting the theatrical servant piqued glares, then gestured for us to sit in the available seats beside them.

On the other end of the table was, I could only assume, King Galden and his wife. Their end of the table was lined with an insane number of children of varying ages, all with glossy yellow hair and sun-bronzed skin.

The king, having been caught biting into a large leg of what smelled like lamb, quickly chewed and gulped it down, wiping juices from his scraggly beard.

"There you are, lordling!" His Majesty bellowed. "We were waiting so long, we broke fast without you."

Alexander muttered from my thoughts, *"Lordling?"*

I resisted the urge to grumble my own complaint, but bit my tongue and bowed. "Forgive us, Your Majesty." I turned to my parents and bowed even deeper. "My Lord and Lady. We ran into complications on the ride over."

"What complications?" Father rasped. He was dressed in a pure white suit, which I noted held a single brown stain on the sleeve. He was now trying to clean it with a wetted napkin, his moustache tugged in a displeased frown.

"We were ambushed, actually," I explained, lowering into the seat beside him. The others claimed their own spots, chair legs grinding softly against the carpet and the cushions' springs squealing.

"Ambushed?" Mother questioned. "By whom?"

"By a band of rebels." I plucked the gilded spoon set in front of me and stared at my stretched reflection—and Alexander's fainter reflection—in the bulbous curvature. "They supposedly thought we were someone else, and withdrew once they saw we were not, in fact, their quarry."

Mother snorted, her grey wolf ears curling. "Thoughtless fools. If we find them, they will be swiftly punished."

I grunted dully and examined the expansive hall. I counted a total of six princesses prattling away while they ate, their goblets clinking and engraved, gold utensils squalling over their plates. They were stealing glances at me over their shoulders.

The cutlet lamb in front of me was drizzled with green syrup which, I discovered after taking a bite, gave it an odd, candied flavor. There were very few vegetables accompanying the cutlet. I could only spy a few slices of onions and crumbs of dried parsley.

"They're just so *pale*," I overheard one of the blonde princesses hush to another. "Their skin's just as grey as their hair. And here I thought the forest folk were the lightest I'd ever…"

She caught my eyes and looked away in a blush, she and her sister sharing an impish giggle.

Sighing, I cast Willow a sidelong glance from the chair beside me, glowering at her disguise. The dark woman next to me was beautiful to be sure, but she didn't look like my fiancée. It was more than a little disconcerting.

A lighthearted laugh made me turn back to the royal family. Sitting nearest to King Galden was a lean but muscular man in his mid-twenties. With that sharp, stubbled jaw and yellow hair, he was practically the spitting image of the king, only leaner. I could only assume this was his son. On the train ride here, I remembered Mother informing us the crowned prince was named Cayden.

The prince was dressed in thin silks embroidered in shimmering gold and brown patterns. His waist was wrapped with a maroon sash matching his loose, wide-hemmed sirwal and gold slippers. He was accompanied by a Roaress this morning, his enthused laughter and shameless fondling of her bare shoulders suggesting he was courting her. And they seemed drunk. *Was that wine in their cups at this hour?*

I lifted my gaze to the head of the long table, observing His Majesty Galden as he ate his "breakfast" want of grace.

"Ambushed!" His Majesty called to me from across the table, his voice raised so he could be heard over his daughters. He drained his goblet of purple wine before pouring himself another from the carafe. "My own guests, ambushed, right here at home! Shel, but I'm glad you made it to us safely. My deepest apologies. But I wouldn't give those rebels more fuss than they're worth. This 'Land's Servant' they follow is only a pesky vigilante. The resistance's total members can barely fit inside a latrine, let alone threaten thousands of trained soldiers."

The Roaress under Prince Cayden's caressing fingers scooted to the edge of her chair with interest. "Oh, but Your Majesty," she said, "several soldiers were killed by rebels, weren't they? My brother is a Runner down in the city, and he insists…"

The king's amiable smile vanished suddenly, replaced with a wicked glare aimed solely at Cayden's guest. His lion ears were curled back and his teeth were now sharp.

A tensed moment passed before he relieved the Roaress of his stare and instead addressed Cayden. "How unbecoming. Cayden, would you kindly remind your guest not to speak out of turn?"

The Roaress shrank in her seat, murmuring an apology. Prince Cayden gave her a patronizing pat on the hand. "Perhaps what your brother thought were rebels were only disgruntled civilians?" he considered.

"Hah!"

I winced. That laugh had been Willow beside me.

Now, all heads were turned to her.

Prince Cayden lifted an eyebrow. "You find something amusing, Roaress?"

Willow took an indignant sip from her cup. "They were no disgruntled civilians. She is correct. The resistance is larger than you think and they're killing your men."

The Prince's neutral expression darkened slightly, but he kept an even timbre. "You sound intimately familiar with this, Roaress." He let slip a chuckle, his tone quizzacious. "I don't suppose you're a rebel yourself, eh?"

"I can't rebel against a nation I've no citizenship in, just as you can't be prince of another's palace."

"Roaress, I've met many shifters who say the most outrageous things simply to turn a few heads. None of them ever provide evidence to support their—"

"I've seen it myself." Willow interrupted. Her falsely darkened eyes barely capped her annoyance. "I watched your knights die at the hands of a single man from their ranks. He was a horrid man who claimed loyalty to the lost Relicblood."

This made the blonde princesses giddy, the dangling coins sewn to their garments jingling throughout the table.

"Tell her to shut it," Alex snapped from my thoughts. *"Before she all but gives our bodyguards away!"*

"Pardon, *Roaress*," I hissed to Willow under my breath, "you can't tell the blasted king we have rebels with us."

She murmured back, "I don't mean Ana and Kurrick."

Vendy's rabbit ears draped to her neck. "Uh, what about *us*—?"

The king slammed his hands on the table, quieting his chatty daughters.

"Young Roaress!" he shouted down the table at Willow, "I have had enough of this blatant disrespect. If you cannot act properly—"

"Father." Prince Cayden raised an appeasing hand, his voice calm. "I prompted a bold discussion. It's only reasonable that she provides a bold argument." Cayden's voice began to sour, "However, Roaress, this isn't evidence. How do we know you haven't tailored this little story yourself?"

"Because I can describe the man for you." Willow's fox ears had already sprouted, though they were brown because of her illusion disguise, and they curled against her skull. "He was a goat shifter with prophetic Hallows. He called himself Linus."

The prince's chair legs scuffed the carpet with a soft *scriiiff* when he rose. "L…" He sounded winded suddenly. "Linus…?"

Willow looked pleased by his reaction. "So, you've heard of him, have you?"

Cayden looked ill.

The king stroked his beard ponderously. "Linus, eh…?"

I was beyond puzzled now, rubbing my temples. "I don't understand, Your Grace," I said. "Who is Linus?"

Prince Cayden abruptly left the table, his lady friend following after him in distress. Once Cayden was gone, the king slumped in his chair.

"Linolius," said Galden, "was the son of my former Hand. Roarlord Renneguard, his father, was… tried for slaughtering a Raider's family. His wife, his *children*…" He poured himself another cup of wine. "There was no reason for it. Renneguard was a madman. His mind was twisted with hate, fueled by the rebellion's propaganda. I had him executed. I… had no choice."

He glugged his wine, staring hauntingly at his reflection in the goblet. "Linolius was there beside him when he killed that family. Delusional lad… Linolius took the man's wife for himself before they killed her. Made her children watch as the boy disgraced her. I would have sentenced his death as well, but he fled after his father's beheading. He had been a very close friend of Cayden's before then. But after what he and his father had done, Cayden hasn't uttered his name since. Wants nothing to do with the scum."

There came a resounding silence when the king finished. *Bloods.* I squirmed and loosened my collar string. *What a pleasant topic to open with.*

"My lady," a breathy voice greeted from behind me.

I turned in my seat to see that the beautiful Yulia, our family's private Dreamcatcher, now stood between Willow and me. A few of the male servants in the hall had slowed to ogle her, and even the handmaidens lingered under doorframes.

If Yulia noticed her audience, she paid them no mind and brushed back her short, white hair. She bent to Willow and held out a rectangular, velvet box. "I had these polished, as requested. I apologize for taking so long, but I could only carry out the errand this morning when we arrived."

Willow's eyes brightened, and she took the box with eager fingers. "Ah, yes! Thank you, Howless."

Willow opened the box, revealing a pair of sparkling engagement-vines. Tiny diamond facets glittered from silver chains, and butterflies embedded with azure gemstones were carved along them. Willow wasted no time in clipping the chains to her hair, leaving the third piece, the diamond droplet, in the box.

I stared at the silver strings now dangling from either side of her disguised hair. I stared long and hard. Then I pointed. "Aren't those..."

"The engagement-vines you bought for me those years ago." She kept her voice low to keep any royal ears from eavesdropping. Luckily, those chatty princesses drowned us out. "I brought them hoping they would spark some of your lost memories."

I vaguely remembered purchasing those. I'd found them on display in a jeweler's shop I'd wandered into after being told I needed to find a suitable set for our official engagement announcement, for her thirteenth birthday.

"Death's Head, how long it's been." I delicately lifted one of the nostalgic vines. Would we have wedded by now if I wasn't trapped in my brother?

"Of course you would find this an appropriate time for sentiments," drawled Alex from my thoughts. *"She's supposed to be in disguise. Those will give her away."*

"And what will it give away, exactly?" I muttered. "That the Roaress Ashleya is engaged to an unnamed man whom she has no obligation to reveal?"

He grunted, but offered no further protest.

She turned to the Dreamcatcher, who I only now realized was still lingering behind our chairs. "Thank you for having these polished, Howless," Willow told Yulia, "I do appreciate it."

"You're very welcome, my lady." Yulia bowed and took an empty seat beside Willow. I supposed the place had been reserved specifically for her, as Mistress had likely seen to. Yulia was more than a simple Dreamcatcher, truthfully. She'd been with our family for the entirety of Alexander and my upbringing. One could say she was more of an older sister.

A ghostly head suddenly popped up from the table, rising out of my plate. It was our winged vassal, Dalen.

"Dalen?" My brow knitted. "Bloods, have you died again? And did I forget to strengthen your NecroSeam?"

"Yeah, uh, funny story." Dalen sounded more than a little embarrassed as he scratched at his translucent nose. "See, I kinda forgot I was resurrected and jumped a few dozen floors too far in the stairwell. That tower's so cramped, I couldn't open my wings to fly, so..."

I sighed. "Spent too much time without adhering to physical boundaries and physics, have we?"

The ghost shrugged. "Ya get used to it."

"Yes, well, I suggest you reacquaint yourself with the concept of mortality." I snapped my gaze at the snickering Vendy, who choked into silence and pretended to be distracted with her glass of juice. I sighed and rose from my seat, folding the napkin that had been on my lap and placed it on the table. "I suppose there's nothing for it—"

"Talking to ghosts, Alexander?" His Majesty called from the end of the table.

I stared at him in shock. I may not have been Alexander, but he was bold enough to call my brother with no honorific?

"It must be interesting," the king mused with fascination. *Or was that distaste?* "Able to see things one shouldn't, enslave the dead to do your bidding."

Silence smothered the table. I could feel it squeezing my limbs. Even the blonde princesses were stock-still, their attention directed at me.

Vendy scowled and pounded her silverware on the table, her rabbit ears curled back. "Hey, *I* asked him to make a Pact with me. And it damn well took a whole lot of convincing to get him to even accept—"

"Oh, you poor dear," the king lamented, though his eye twitched in disgust as he scrutinized Vendy, as if learning she was a walking corpse made her little more than a dirty beetle. "Has he ordered you to say this—?"

"A Bloodpact is not enslavement," interrupted Father sternly. His glower was cause enough to make one soil their trousers. "It is a consensual agreement made between the vagrant soul and Necrovoker. The soul is given protection from others with our Hallows in exchange for service."

The king offered a wry smile. "Consensual, yes… and what of the previous Necrovoker in your position?" He lifted a finger and wagged it in a playful tempo as he sang a familiar nursery rhyme.

Watch your head, watch your insides, else they ride with the Death King's Eyes.

The hall echoed with the song, all other voices absent.

Death and cinder, steps like tinder, here comes Endsler the Bloody Ender.

His Majesty dropped his finger, his face falling into a sneer. "Did the Bloody Ender's vassals agree to an oath with him, hm? After he had them executed to enslave their ghosts?"

At the mention, I watched a haunted Yulia quietly take her leave.

My father nodded to the Dreamcatcher on her way out, then took in a smooth breath. "Howllord Endsler was a tyrant, Your Majesty," he said. "He held no respect for the dead. And I would keep in mind that I've brought a soul or two who had once been enslaved by Endsler here with me. I would ask you to kindly mind your words, else you upset them without your notice."

"Hurry 'n wake this idiot up!" the youngest brother, Rolen, demanded with a sharp flap of his wings. "It's too cramped for us to fly with this dope draggin' us down!"

"Sorry," Dalen offered with a shrug, though the ghost was unheard except by me. Usually the three siblings were wearing masks that allowed them to see and hear their brother, but their faces were bare today. It was likely they hadn't seen a need to wear them since their brother had been, until recently, resurrected.

Vendy whistled as she looked over Dalen's crooked limbs and snapped wings. "Well, dangit, I guess you win today," she pouted enviously.

I tapped an impressed knuckle to my chin. "Yes, you've done quite a number on yourself, haven't you? Alex, could you assist?"

My brother grunted from my thoughts, then I felt a tug at my soul as I was dragged back into the psyche. All sensation vanished as the darkness swallowed me, and I was surrounded in pitch black, nothing in sight save for this loathsome window that was my brother's vision. Gods, but the day I'd be rid of this place wouldn't come soon enough.

Alexander was quick to resurrect Dalen's corpse, his hands glowing with violet light that stretched around Dalen's lifeless limbs like slithering tendrils. Thankfully, I didn't have to spend too long in isolation. I returned to the physical world and wove Dalen a temporary, violet-glowing NecroSeam, making sure to give it more strength so that his ghost would remain tied when next he died. The ghostly thread quivered and waved like twisted, vine-like strings as I sewed the soul to his newly risen vessel.

Now that he was resurrected, Dalen stretched tall, spread his wings, and brushed his servant's vest with a look of distaste. "Aw, damn. There's blood everywhere."

"You may as well change," I suggested, starting back up the steps. "And I mean all of you. I have a feeling the palace staff isn't well acquainted with Necrovokers and their frequently dying vassals. I'm sure the blood will cause alarm."

The siblings all mumbled their agreements, punching Dalen ruefully.

"My lord!" a winded man's voice called from the top of the stairwell. Footfalls echoed, the steps hurried. "My lord Alexander…!"

I stopped when that bugle-trumpeting servant from earlier came trotting down to me, panting in shaken breaths. He handed me a folded piece of parchment. "Your f…! Your father sent me to fetch you! He and the High Howless have departed for the city!"

"They've what?" My brow furrowed as I unfolded the parchment, reading its contents.

Alexander, the note read, *gather your company and come to the Reaper headquarters immediately. The Second Fangs has made a grave discovery.*

Bring your vassals and the Blacksmith.

My father's signature was scripted underneath.

I peered over my shoulder at Dalen and Vendy. "It, er, seems we've been summoned into town. You'd best hurry and change, Dalen. And Vendy, please fetch your uncle."

Vendy saluted and hopped up the steps to comply, and Dalen muttered about his ruined clothes as he stepped past the servant alongside me.

After a long coach ride, our company—sans Jaq, who had been dragged to his grandfather's manor within the palace gates—arrived at the Reaper District in town.

In contrast to Everland's culturally flat-roofed, sandstone buildings, the Reaper District resembled a tiny portion of Grim. Spired rooftops, enormous cathedrals, meticulously-maintained cemeteries, grey-haired Grimlings bustling in the markets filled with Grimish imports and food, all wedged into a miniature segment of New Aldamstria's mountain city. It was easy to see why the locals called it *Little Grim*.

We reached the Reaper Headquarters and strode inside. There, a receptionist at the front desk directed us to the conference chamber where she claimed our parents were meeting with the Second Fangs of this continent. I led the way and soon stood outside the polished conference doors, barely hearing the muffled voices within.

When I rapped my knuckles on the glossy wood, the voices quieted, and a wolf-eared man cracked open the door.

"Sir Alexander," Second Fangs Lastings greeted with a bow. "Thank you for coming."

The man's tousled hair was bark brown, his skin barely a shade lighter than the thin beard lining his jaw. It was safe to assume he wasn't a Necrovoker—and therefore had no soul-sight. Brown hair meant Landish descent, which also meant he wouldn't be able to see the difference in Alexander and my eyes. The Landish shifters didn't have our Hallows from Grim, unless their blood was mixed. And I doubted this was the case for Fangs Lastings.

Lastings scrutinized the company behind us, looking oddly disappointed. "Where is Sir Jaqelle?" he asked, craning his head to peer further down the hallway. "Fangs Alice was just telling me of her star student."

"He is in conference with the High Roarlord," I informed. "Their… discussion is taking longer than expected. We'll brief him of our findings afterward."

Lastings glanced at the rest of our party. Vendy waved to him, Henry lazily saluted, Octavius ducked his head sheepishly, Willow—in disguise—coughed behind a fist, and Dalen shifted his weight to one side. Dalen's siblings had elected to wander the markets, armed with their newfound wealth that came with their services and eager to spend it. Ringëd had left to find himself a meal, since Kurn had cut his first attempt short at the palace, and Ana and Kurrick were posted outside the building to be sure no 'rabble-rousers' disturbed us.

Fangs Lastings puckered his brow when he found Lilli and regarded her with a second bow. "High Howless, good morning."

Lilli nodded primly, her leathery wings giving an appreciative flutter. "Good morning, Honored Fangs. Pleasure to make your acquaintance."

"Believe you me, the pleasure is most certainly mine, Sil Lilliana." He smiled, but his lids dripped into a frown when he spied the rest of our group. "And, er, I see you've brought others."

I gestured to Dalen and Vendy beside us, "We've brought our vassals, as requested." I nodded to Henry next. "And our Blacksmith."

Lastings nodded to them with respect, and stepped aside to permit us entry.

Mother stood by the corner of the table, thumbing through reports that lay scattered on the conference table. She didn't wear the same gown from this morning's meal. She'd donned thicker, less lustrous trousers and an alabaster coat with padded shoulders and military patches that adorned the arms, chest, and high collar. This was her general's uniform. Her shadow-grey hair was braided and fell over one shoulder, her wolf ears perked intently as she read through the classified documents.

Father sat in one of the leather chairs, the fabric creaking and rubbing quietly when he turned to us. He wore his spectacles to read over the reports Mother hadn't claimed for herself, and he settled the frames to the tip of his nose to peer at us.

I straightened and locked my arms behind my back, announcing, "We've arrived as requested, honored lord and lady."

"At ease." Mother wafted a hand at me, her attention dedicated to the files. "And latch the door. These are not details I want leaked to passing ears."

Willow was the last to enter, and she bolted the latch behind her.

Fangs Lastings frowned at Willow, who was still disguised, then he pointed and turned to my mother. "Is this a… a new apprentice, High Howless?"

Mother barely tossed her head, her equivalent of an impassive shrug. "A hopeful ward. I'm preparing her entrance exams while she carries out minor tasks."

Lastings nodded, seeming stuck on a thought as his gaze drifted to Octavius. "And this is the one you mentioned?"

Mother hummed to confirm, her eyes darting left and right while scanning those files fervently. "Octavius Treble, yes. The student I didn't meet until he graduated."

Lastings belted a laugh and thumped Octavius on the shoulder. "The man himself! I'll be. You ought to be right proud of yourself, Sir Octavius, not just any soldier impresses Fangs Alice that swiftly."

Octavius flushed scarlet.

Lastings's laughter ebbed to a pleasant chuckle, then he glanced at me. "From what I saw on the Screens, you all earned those badges rightly. Bloods, it's a miracle your team survived Lindel without more Brothers."

I grunted. "I doubt it would have made much difference, Honored Fangs. Though, it would have been more encouraging. We're only thankful to be alive."

"I bet you are." He scratched at his nose with a sniff. "And I expect you're being compensated properly? Active duty pays decently, but taking on so many hordes of Necrofera *and* two Sentients makes you eligible for certain allowances. Not to mention *killing* one of the damned beasts, for Land's sake."

"Oh, we've received quite a bit of our earnings, Honored Fangs." I smiled, pride bubbling as I straightened taller. "Of course, it's barely been a month. Much of those allowances are still being processed. But I'm more concerned about our missing demon queen at the moment." My gaze flicked to Octavius, who cast me a wary glance.

It seemed Octavius was still coming to terms with his lineage. Cilia, the aforementioned demon queen, was likely his ancestor. I wasn't sure how *I* would have processed learning that I was related to a five-hundred-year-old demon. Octavius wasn't certain how to handle it either.

"Yes, regarding this queen." Lastings's tone dulled. "We've not had another sighting of her. Though her soldiers have still been terrorizing several more cities, the queen herself has been absent. Licking her wounds, I wager."

"Her absence could be a good omen," Father rumbled, tapping a finger over the table. I noticed his messenger raven, Barrach, was perched on one of the chairs, its greying chest feathers puffed and dipping with each breath beside Mother's smaller, canary-sized black bird.

"Then again," Father sighed and removed his spectacles. "It could be an ill omen. But I'll ask more on that later. My son is here for a different matter, Roden."

Lastings nodded, singling out a particular folder from the table and handed it to me. I examined the reports and glanced at the accompanying photographs.

"This is the file from Entrial Valley, Howllord," Lastings explained, "where this queen was first seen."

"No survivors…" I murmured as I read. "Save for two children?"

"They were hidden in the cellar of a Rockraider's station," said Mother, glancing up from her reports at last. "Two brothers, one eleven and the other six. The older boy said their father was a Raider, and took them to a hidden room underground when the Fera first attacked."

"The father did not survive, obviously," Father added. "But his body was missing, along with half the village populace. His corpse was eventually found and identified… among one of the Necrofera bodies that *your* team killed in Nulani."

Sobering news. I asked, "Where are his sons now?"

"They've been admitted to an orphanage here in New Aldamstria," said Lastings. "Since this is one of the few cities that hasn't been hit by the Fera, we thought it the safest choice."

"But the next concern," Mother said and flapped her folder closed, "is about the cellar they were found in."

"The cellar?" Lilli asked doubtfully. "Why is that a concern?"

I flipped the page in my folder. Then my gaze widened at one of the attached photographs. "Because they found *this*," I said.

Pictured was the cellar in question, looking like a hidden armory. Stacked upon wall mounts were a number of radiant swords, gleaming with a brilliant blue light. It was akin to our own weapons.

"These," I began, "are made with Spiritcrystal. Aren't they?"

"Do you know of any other rock that emits such a light?" questioned Mother. "Based on the brightness of the swords, I imagine those are not alloyed. That is pure Spiritcrystal, to be sure."

I murmured, "Then the reason you asked Dalen and Henry to come…"

Henry took the file from me with a low frown, and Dalen loomed over his shoulder to look himself. "Ya think a Raider took the scythes from Lindel?" asked Dalen. "And framed *us* for it?"

Father's fingertips pushed against themselves from his seat at the table. "That is precisely what we think, Mr. Tesler. We don't know how many other Raider stations have these hidden armories, if any. And we don't know how many have stolen Spiritcrystal, like this one. You claimed someone who wore our cloaks made off in the night with our weapons?"

"Yeah," Dalen muttered, folding his arms. "That was the bastard who cut my Seam early."

"Well." Father exhaled. "Whether he was an actual Reaper or not is yet to be seen. But it seems logical that the weapons are being shipped to the Raider stations. It's all too much of a coincidence... thus, why we've asked you to come and review these files as well, Mr. Cauldwell." Father nodded at Henry. "As a smith who can forge our crystal weapons, I wondered if you'd been approached by someone of Everland's military requesting these weapons."

Henry flipped through the file, his brow furrowed angrily. "Not directly, myself... I'd only made *one* crystal sword, and that was for my niece. But hers is legal, since she's the vassal of a Reaper. Though, I've heard rumors from the other smiths about people asking for it. But I thought those were outliers, you know, one-time jokesters... Gardener sow me, if you found this in a Raider's station... Bloods, I need to tell Land's Servant about this, see if he knows any..."

Henry kept mumbling to himself and slapped the file on the table and stormed out, pulling out his com and vanishing into the halls.

I peeled open the file again, staring at the photograph of the crystal swords. "Does this mean the king is involved?" I asked.

Fangs Lastings' head wavered. "It's possible some of his knights are acting on their own. But I personally find that unlikely."

"Death..." I closed the file, handing it to Willow when she reached for it. I looked at Mother uncertainly. "What does this mean for our nations? To even possess our weapons is a breach of the Death Laws."

Willow read the files, her tone augury. "It means we may be at the brink of war with Everland."

"War?" I echoed.

Alex scoffed from my thoughts. *"Impossible."*

"But Grim hasn't gone to war with another country in nearly a millennium," I protested. "Surely this isn't reason enough for something as drastic as war?"

Willow handed the file to Lilli. "It would depend on the king's stance," she explained. "How far does his involvement go? Is he gathering our weapons to prepare for something? Does he expect his country to be without Reapers in the near future?"

Mother growled, "All points that we intend to broach with Galden this evening."

I stared at Mother, baffled. "You plan to waltz up to the blasted king the very day you arrive at his palace and..."

—*crcrr*-CK, CRACK! SMASHHHH!

A disturbing *crunch* tumbled from outside, shouts bursting after.

Everyone hurried out to the hall and I trotted after them, following the bustling knights out to the streets. Close by, a wagon had overturned off the side of a tall cliffside and crashed to the stones. I followed the knights who were on their way to oversee the incident.

A passing nurse with rabbit ears rushed by me—

My attention locked onto her.

She hadn't noticed me as she hurried to the blood-spattered scene, trailing behind the other Healers, her orange hair swishing to and fro in a frazzled tail.

She was an ordinary thing, plainly dressed, her brown face naked without powder or creams. Pale-orange rabbit ears twitched from her head, her face dusted in tiny specks of freckles. The woman wore a simple yellow nurse's uniform with a patch on the shoulder that read 'Healer Apprentice'.

She lugged a bag of medical tools behind her elderly mentor, who saw to the crushed patient on the stretcher with quick efficiency. Whenever he would ask the young nurse for a medical instrument, she would fish inside the bag and hand it to him.

Well, well, well. I watched the nurse like a feral hawk while she tended to her work. *How very convenient.*

Once the victim was stabilized as best he could be, he was brought into the hospital. The rabbit woman gave an exhausted breath, dragging behind the rest of the group. Her urgency seemed depleted now that the victim was safe and being treated. Judging from the bags under her eyes, it looked as though she hadn't slept in days.

I slid in front of her.

"Where do you think you're off to?" I clipped, chin to the air.

The woman gasped and dropped her bag of tools with an overjoyed squeal, then hooked me by the neck.

"Guys!" She laughed brightly. "Oh my Gods! You're already here?"

"Arrived just this morning," I said as our old friend, Bianca, released me. I smiled. "Jaq will be envious he wasn't here to see you."

"Where is he?" She puffed out a tired breath, stretching her arms while searching about the street, probably on the lookout for the viper.

I grimaced. "With his grandfather."

Her face creased with a disgusted look. "Ew. Guess he was ambushed when he got here?"

"Swiftly." I watched her elderly mentor rush inside the hospital with the crushed patient. "Well, er… I suppose your master is now preoccupied with an emergency surgery?"

She shrugged. "Looks like it. Why?"

"We've lost our latest lead on Sirra-Lynn. We were hoping Dr. Hendril could help us find the trail again."

Her nose wiggled in thought. "I can tell him you want to talk when he's done?"

"Please." I clapped my hands appreciatively, then laughed. "On a separate note: wonderful to see you again."

She hit my shoulder. "Seriously! How long's it been? Three years?"

"Just about," I wagered.

"Too Bloody long." She slipped on a pair of red-rimmed eyeglasses that had been clipped to her breast pocket. Her nose scrunched as she examined my eyes.

"So, Xavier's out," she concluded. The eyeglasses had a soul-seeing Evocation sealed into them, like Jaq's glasses, so she was able to see my eyes. I was the one who'd sealed the Hallows in those glasses years ago. The etched rune was still visible on the rose frames. I was surprised she still used them.

"Where's Alex?" asked Bianca, knocking on my skull. "Still in there?"

I lamented, "If he wasn't, you'd see two of us."

"Good point." She rubbed her arm. "Will he be coming out this time?"

I glanced up, questioning him, "Well?"

Alexander was silent for a moment. Then he sucked in a preparing inhale before I felt him tug at my soul. I let myself slip into the psyche, watching from the discus window as he fidgeted in front of our friend.

He seemed to be searching for something to say, but surrendered and simply waved.

Bianca slipped off her glasses, grinning. "Hey, Alex. Been a long time, huh?"

Alex squirmed, scratching his neck vigorously. "Ye… Yes…" The bottom of my window bowed upward. Alex must have been smiling. "I… I'm not sure what to say. Perhaps it's been too long."

"Well, it wouldn't kill you to call me on com for once, like your brother does."

He idly folded his arms behind him and swirled the dirt under his boot. "I… w-well, see, I was hoping to be normal the next time we met, and…" He coughed into a fist. "How are your studies?"

She rolled her eyes, but replied, "Brutal. Master Hendril has my schedule packed full-time, since I'm his only ward."

"Ah. Good. I suppose…"

"—Who is this?" Willow suddenly asked from behind, making Alex jolt.

The others had come to surround us, all peering curiously at the new rabbit woman.

Alex cleared his throat behind a fist and tugged at his lapel, then gestured to Bianca. "An old friend. Everyone, this is the Lady Bianca Florenne, apprentice of Dr. Roarlord Hendril."

Octavius frowned. "*You're* Bianca?"

"That's me." The rabbit gave a not-so-dramatic flourish.

Octavius gawked at her, confused. "But they said you were from Grim?"

"I am." She placed hands at her hips and lifted one of her long ears. "I know, Landish skin and hair. My foster family found me alone up here when I was young and took me in. Long story."

Beside us, Willow asked, "Do you remember your real parents?"

"I don't even remember being up here in the first place." Her lids squinted at Willow's disguised face. "Hang on." She threw a thumb at Octavius. "I've seen *him* on the Screens." She pointed at Willow. "But I don't think I've seen you on there anywhere."

"Ah, that'd be my cue," I proudly called to Alex from the psyche.

Alex hesitated, stealing a glance at Bianca. "Now? But I only just…"

"You know damn well how long I've waited to introduce these two," I muttered, "You can catch up all you like afterward. It's your own Bloody fault you never hear from her in the first place."

He clicked his tongue, taking another moment to think it through. Then he sighed.

I took control again, blinking my stinging eyes when the harsh sunlight hit my retinas, but took Willow's hand with a grin.

"She's under an illusion now," I told Bianca. "So you'll have to trust me when I say she doesn't normally look like this. *Khmm-kmm!* Bianca." I waved a ceremonious hand at Willow. "At long Bloody last, meet my betrothed."

Bianca stared at Willow for a moment. Then her dark skin flushed. "Oh, Death!" She hurried to bow. "I-I mean, you *are* Death, so that doesn't really…! Um, I'm so sorry, Your High—!"

"No, no!" Willow waved for her to rise. "No need for that, miss. You must understand, I'm not meant to be up here."

"Then, um…" Bianca blushed. "If it's all right to ask… what *are* you doing up here?"

"Finding my fiancé." Willow glanced at me. "Well, half of him. But I suppose the other half will come with time, once we meet with your master Healer."

Bianca swallowed. "So you… uh… know about them?"

I glowered and circled a hand in the air, muttering, "It's a rather tedious story."

"I'll not say a thing to my father," Willow assured. "I expect to find Xavier's vessel before my father is even aware I've left."

Bianca's face sagged incredulously. "The king doesn't know you're gone?"

"I should think not. In truth, it was my grandfather who sent me up here to find Xavier. He wanted me to reunite him with Alexander for some cryptic reason he never explained."

"As he'd done with our bodyguards over there," I said and threw a thumb toward the two lion rebels, who lingered by a fountain in the distance, watching us. "Two of our newest recruits, as you can see. The frightening fellow over there is dubbed Kurrick, and his smaller companion is Miss Anabelle...They think we're going to lead them to the lost Relicblood of Land, or some such nonsense. Bloody daft, it is. As if we have the heir tucked away in our other coat pocket—"

A loud *crack* sounded, followed by a tumble and loud screeches.

A young apprentice Reaper had dropped a crate of trapped messengers. It'd split open and the boy yelped in a panic as he hurried to retrieve the birds that'd scattered.

Then I heard a scratched, injured wail, more piercing than the other screeching fowls.

"Mi*ne*!" the low croak blurted. "Mi*ne*, mi*ne*...!"

There was something odd about that pitiful wheeze. The sound of it stirred my blood, and it... it felt so...

I drifted over, leaving the others behind. The cries came from the broken crate. The bird trapped under it was trying to pry its thick beak underneath, but didn't seem to have the strength to lift it. It gave another helpless wail as I knelt to pick up the box.

"It's all right," I hushed, freeing the patchy raven of its cage and set the box aside. "There—"

Craaaaww!

The raven scrambled, flapping its clipped wings but couldn't take flight, feathers fluttering everywhere and drifting to the stones. The raven hopped onto my chest and clung to my doublet, its talons pricking my skin underneath.

"Ow-*ow*!" I fell to my rear, the bird flapping hysterically as it clung to my chest. I tried to pry its talons from the fabric gently. "Stop that, will... you..."

It nestled against the crook of my arm. Now, it was perfectly calm.

"Mi*ne*," croaked the raven, its beak nuzzling against my neck.

—Shock slammed through. It was an icy surge, my lungs cinched and strangled, shriveling as if *air* were a virus. The raven laid there on my chest, cradled in my arm and looking more relieved than it'd ever felt in its life.

Is... My breath went ragged. *Is this...?*

"Chai?" I ran a shivering thumb over the vertical scar that adorned the raven's right eye. I heaved a ragged breath, almost a laugh, and cradled the raven warming my chest. I felt it. I felt *everything*, his pain, his anger, his last burst of sheer joy to be here...

His fear, to know he was dying.

"My Chai..." I held the feeble raven tighter, tears stinging. "Gods have mercy, what have they done to you?"

6

RAVEN RIOT

XAVIER

So much *pain*.

Chai's weakening heartbeat synced to my throbbing pulse, and I held him fast, my lungs splintering with blistered gasps. I-I couldn't breathe... He couldn't breathe.

"Xavier?" Willow called above me. She reached a hand toward Chai. "Is this—?"

I jerked Chai away from her, shaking. "What have they done?" My voice fractured, and I cradled Chai closer, as if the air itself threatened to smother him.

Pain, so much *pain*...!

"What's happened?" I heard my father boom from behind. "Has he been injured?"

Willow murmured, "I think... I think Xavier's found his messenger."

Everyone shuffled around me, whispering.

Father's gruff tone faltered. "He's come...?" I felt his hand press down my shoulder, his face blooming in my peripherals as he beheld the raven in my trembling hold. "He's come at last? He is yours?"

"He's mine." I said, throat raw. I couldn't face Father. I didn't dare look away from my Chai. Twenty years of waiting—twenty Gods damned years of hoping, of doubting, of giving up—he was here. He was real.

And he is dying.

I rubbed his bare patches of missing feathers with trembling fingers. "Help." I could barely whisper, my vision flooded as the raven's trauma rooted deeper, sinking like fangs. "H-he's in pain. He's dying. Please, *help*...!" My throat closed.

Father tightened his grip on my shoulder. "He will be helped. Praise Nira, he'll be helped immediately. Come, I'll..."

"My lord!" a Reaper called to Father, rushing to him with a fist to his chest. "My lord, Fangs Lastings is asking for you. He says it's urgent, you're needed right away."

Father hesitated. Then after a moment of silence, his grasp vanished, and he barked to the others. "Take them to messenger care immediately! There isn't time!"

"I'll take them," said Bianca, and she grabbed my arm, yanking me to my feet and dragging me along. "I can pull strings over there if we need to."

I fumbled to keep up with her as we left the others behind, keeping the wheezing raven pinned to my chest. *Chai, please.* I secured my hold gently, seeing he'd fallen unconscious. *Just hold on a little longer.*

We turned four blocks and crossed the bustling road, then Bianca shoved open the doors to the Messenger Care Clinic, a wall of sound hitting my grown wolf ears with noisy chatter and frantic veterinarians who rushed in and out of the lobby, ravens and crows screeching in a fury.

Bianca stormed through with me in tow, shoving open the door that led into the back rooms. Nurses and vets were in even more of a frenzy back here, all the rooms filled with several black birds and surrounding staff.

Bianca peeked into each room, then found who she was looking for and pulled me inside with her.

"Roaress Tonya!" she called to the woman inside. "My friend needs your help! *Now!*"

The elderly vet turned to us, her brown wings fluttering in a start to see Bianca scowling so drastically—and then seeing me beside her, my face caked in stale tears. My arms which held Chai were trembling.

"*Shel*, Bianca!" The woman abandoned the room and scooped our backs with ushering hands, guiding us through the halls. "Is this the High Howllord's son?"

"Yeah," Bianca panted. "Xav… A-Alex said this raven is in critical condition."

"H-h-he's dying," I sputtered, then flinchingly shielded Chai from the passing nurses and vets. "Please, I… I only just found him, I…"

The vet twisted back to look at me, her expression cracking with heartbreak. We halted outside a surgery room, and—

She ripped Chai from my grip.

"*No!*" I roared, lunging for him, but Bianca grappled my waist and heaved me back.

"Calm down!" the rabbit ordered, and I watched in agony as the elderly vet disappeared behind the door with my Chai. Bianca shoved me back. "Chai will be all right! The Roaress is Master Hendril's wife, she's the head veterinarian of the clinic. If anyone can help Chai, it's her."

"Nira, please, *please*…!" I slid to the floor, clasping my hands… and prayed. "Please let him live…"

7

A DISPLACED DREAMCATCHER

RINGËD

"<Cruel!>" Kurn cried in his breathy language, rolling to his back on the wooden table and flailing his stubby paws. "<Heartless! Villain! Sadistic, tyrannical butler…!>"

I swallowed the last of my grilled trout and shot the ferret a curdled glare. "Quit your whining. After that stunt you pulled in the palace—*and* the station—you'll be lucky if I let you out of that bag for a week."

"<But I didn't…! But it wasn't…!>" He breathed wounded *dooks* and rolled to his belly with a heavy head. "<Oh, I couldn't *help* it, Ringëd! I admit, the station was poor judgement, but the palace cuisine was just so succulent…! And where better for an exiled emperor to feast than a royal hall?>"

I *thunked* my elbows on the table and rubbed my eyes in a groan.

Kurn was my delusional little pet. He thought he was the exiled emperor of a planet called *Hcah-Ah-Ah-Hcah*, sent to this world after the rebellion took siege of his palace, yadda, yadda, yadda… something like that. Long story short, he thinks I'm his butler. But I just bought him from a random peddler in my home island, Y'ahmelle Nayû. That nose of his has been pretty useful for investigative work, but *Oscha*, did it get him in loads of trouble sometimes.

"Well, Kurn," I sighed and picked up my trash, walking it over to the wastebin. Kurn scuttled to my shoe and climbed up my leg until he reached my shoulders, then curled around my neck. After tossing my trash in the bin, I got out a smoke and lit it up, blowing out a smooth stream of grey. "We'll have to make sure those princesses don't see you again. There's no telling how long we'll be staying up there, but if they see you, they'll catch on and probably kick us out—"

"*Kha-hooph*—!"

An antlered man slammed to the ground at my feet.

"The High Howllord ain't giving handouts," a Reaper spat over the guy, tromping away. "Sod off."

The elk pushed up, his breath cracked when he shouted, "I don't want handouts! I just want to find…!" He threw a hoofed fist at the stones, cursing. He was covered in dirt and soot, the wrinkles on his hooded vest looking weeks old.

I tossed my trash in the bin and crouched to the guy, reaching a hand to him. "You all right, pal?"

The guy flicked his tired eyes at me and took my hand, letting me pull him up.

—*Screams drilled his ears, ash and smoke plaguing the city, a skeletal fiend tearing open a woman's insides as he stumbled and shoved his way onto the fleeing train's rear compartment, clinging to the railing*—

The vision vanished, and I stared hard at the antlered man, flicking the ashes off my smoke. "You're from Lindel, uh?"

He wiped an arm over his soot-ridden face. "Uh, yeah… barely made it out."

"I saw that."

His brow furrowed. I took a hit from my smoke, then waved it at him. "What business you got with the High Howllord?"

He rolled back a shoulder. "I'm looking for his son."

"Uh-huh," I grunted, cocking an eyebrow. "What's your reason?"

He hesitated, looking worried at me, like I might pull out a knife.

"There's a… a girl with him that can help me out," he explained, "Obviously, I lost my flat, the whole damn city was leveled, which means I'm out of a job. I need to file for a relocation, but my ki… my boss doesn't know where the Void I am."

"And what's the girl going to do for you?"

"She's my boss's granddaughter."

"Uh-huh." I took another hit from my smoke, thinking. *Granddaughter?* Obviously, he was talking about Her Highness Willow. Who was her grandfather? *Wait, she's the first hybrid Relicblood. The Princess of Death and…*

"Ah!" I snapped my fingers. "Your boss is King Dream. So, that must make you a Dreamcatch—*mmmmf!*"

The elk slapped a hand over my mouth in a panic, my smoke dropping to the ground. "Shut up!" he hissed and flicked his eyes over his shoulder. "Bloods, I already lost my city, I don't need to be driven out of this one!"

I lifted my hands in appeasement. He squinted a cautious eye at me, then finally freed my mouth. I laughed. "Hey, it's all right, pal. My uncle's one of your Brothers down in Brittleton."

He grunted, unimpressed. "Yeah, well, *he* doesn't have to find our missing king and file for relocation."

I frowned. "Your king's... *missing?*"

"Yeah." He didn't sound too happy about it, crossing his arms. "No one's seen him in months. *OR* the queen. All of the cities in Aspirre have bulletins filled to the brim with inquiries for him, but he hasn't answered a single one *anywhere*. Not even in the other realms' subconsciouses, from what I hear. And trust me when I say he and the queen *always* answer inquiries."

I tapped my heel broodingly. My Uncle Lawson once mentioned how the Dream realm had cities before, but I never thought about how Dreamcatchers were able to contact their always-traveling king in there. The bulletin thing made enough sense... but if he hasn't been around...

"So, what's he doing that's so important?" I asked.

He snorted. "Only the Shepherd Bloody knows. But I need to *eat*. I need my paycheck. I need a new station, anything! I met his granddaughter in Lindel a while back—she was pretending to be someone else, but I knew better—so I figured she's the best shot I got at contacting His Majesty Dream."

"Sounds like it..." I stole a glance at Kurn from my shoulder, who cocked a round ear. I sighed and set hands at my sides. "Well, you sound sincere enough... you said you met Her Highness before? In Lindel?"

"Yeah," he exhaled miserably. "But I don't even know if she's still with the High Howllord. It's the only lead I got, so I at least need to try."

"Right. Give me a sec." I pulled out the new com I bought at the last town and dialed Her Highness's number, the device's gears and springs warbling to life as a screen of light projected up from the embedded gem at the center of the discus machine.

Her Highness, still wearing her illusion disguise, fuzzed onto the screen. *"Ringëd?"* She began, confused. *"Is something wrong?"*

"Not really sure, to be honest." I rubbed my neck, then threw a thumb at the elk behind me. "But this guy's one of your Grandad's Catchers. He's from Lindel, says he met you there at some point. He's name's, uh..." I twisted to him, raising an eyebrow.

The guy looked shocked as Void at me and stuttered, "U-uh, tell her it's Jimmy! The one who helped with the stone-throwing mob!"

"Says his name's Jimmy," I said in case she didn't hear him. "Something about helping with a mob?"

"Oh!" Her Highness clapped her hands. *"Yes, I remember Jimmy. He's here in New Aldamstria?"*

"Yeah. He needs to talk to your grandad about a relocation, but apparently Dream's missing. Have you heard from him lately?"

She took a minute to think on that. *"The last I heard from him was when he gave me this mission to find Xavier... but that was over a month ago. Perhaps Miss Ana and Kurrick could be of better assistance? I have a feeling they've heard from him more recently than I."*

"Got it. know where they are right now?"

"Yes, they're standing guard outside where we are. The Messenger Care Clinic, between Crossings Street and Trepid Landing."

"Alrighty. Thanks, Highness."

She sighed. *"You're quite welcome, but again: it's 'Roaress' for now. Honestly, does everyone forget?"*

She ended the call, and I grinned at Jimmy. "We got a lead."

Jimmy laughed and followed me down the road. "Bloods, you didn't mention you were *with* her! I owe you, seriously!"

"Don't mention it." I tossed a hand back. "You can buy me a drink later and…"

"… is just brilliant," a woman's husky voice sounded up ahead. *Oh, hey, it's Yulia.* The Devouh's private Dreamcatcher. She was outside a hovering coach that was leaning drastically at one corner, the horses flicking their tails idly as she inspected the lowered end of the box. "Are you sure there's nothing you can do?"

"Sorry, mum." The coachman pulled off his gloves and tucked them under an arm. "This side's lost its Levi-stone. She ain't going to lift any time soon."

"How long will it be?" Yulia asked.

"Depends on how fast the delivery lad can run a new stone over. I'd say nine hours, minimum. We're running low on staff these days, and the nearest supply is further up the mountains."

She groaned, combing grey fingers through her short, silky white hair. "Far too long… Very well. I shall go on foot. Thank you for taking me this far, at least." She rummaged through her Storagesphere, which was chained to her curvy waist, and gave the man three gold Mel beads. "I hope your vehicle is repaired posthaste, sir."

He smiled and tipped his hat. "Thank you kindly, mum."

I ran up to her in a laugh. "Hey! Howless Yulia!"

She stopped and turned, blinking at me. "Oh. Officer Ringëd. And his little exiled emperor, good day."

Kurn snickered appreciatively from around my neck. I patted Jimmy's shoulder. "Got one of your Brother Catchers here. He's from Lindel."

Yulia's breath caught. "Oh, you poor dear! I suppose you wish to find His Majesty, then, like the others?"

"Uh…" Jimmy's jaw dropped at her, blanking out like a feral guppy.

Oh, right, I thought, *should've seen that coming*. People usually had that reaction when they saw Yulia. Couldn't blame them, either. She was built like a delicate Goddess, with skin as smooth as polished marble and long, black lashes that fluttered over sharp, Grimish eyes. I guess I was just used to her crazy perfect looks by now. Besides, I was an engaged man. Soon to be a *married* man, if I kept my end of the bargain by the time I got back to Mika.

Actually. I rubbed my stubbled chin in a grinning afterthought. *I have a new com. Maybe I should give Mika a call and check on her? It's been a long while anyway.*

Giddy now, I pulled out my com and started dialing—

A feral horse almost slammed into me, and I jumped back and dropped my com.

SMASH!

The damned creature crushed the com under its hoof, the thing shattering into a million pieces.

Crunch, scrunch!

Other horses harnessed to a passing hover-coach trotted over it next, and by the time the coach left, the tiny vision-gem that made the thing work was crushed into shards, some of the pieces skittering into a storm drain.

"Aw, come *on*!" I groaned and scooped up the pieces mournfully. "Not again…!"

8
LURING A LION

LUCAS

"They're doing what?" King Galden held a disgusted hand to his throat. He looked as though he'd be sick, his lion ears curling back as his livid voice filled the private conference room of his palace. "How detestable! My knights are meant to work *with* the Reapers, not harm their companions like savages!"

From my seat across from him, I rubbed the beard at my jaw, gauging his reaction. "You claim ignorance?"

"Howllord, I swear on my life, this is the first I'm hearing this. I... probably shouldn't admit this, but—and I tell you this in confidence—I'm not as informed about my men as I should be... My workload has been more than a burden lately. I can't be expected to keep up with every soldier in every blasted station. I've left that responsibility with my generals. But now..."

He rose and began pacing, eyes darting around in frantic thought. "It seems I need to issue a thorough investigation on the Rockraiders. Every station must be inspected. I suppose campaigns against these crimes will have to be reinforced as well, possibly tripled... regular monitoring must be administered as a precaution... Bloods, this will cost us so much..."

If this was an act, it was a commendable one. Galden held all the signs of a nervous ruler on the verge of a breakdown. The confident, discriminating king that had just this morning given snide remarks was now unraveling.

Galden paced the conference room, muttering ideas to himself on how to fix his current dilemma. He was clearly worried, there was no denying that.

But is he worried over the debt? I folded my arms behind my back. Or worried he's been caught?

I flicked a sideways glance at my wife, who sat beside me. Alice said nothing, though I could tell from her scowl that she didn't trust him. She clearly had a few words waiting on her tongue. Given her glare, they likely weren't the most *tactful* words. Alice was an exemplary military woman, but she was no politician. Gentle words were not her specialty.

We'd left our messengers with our accompanying vassals, Nathaniel and Aiden, hesitant of bringing them in here with us. This man may very well be responsible for the torture of thousands of black birds—including that of my son's.

My hands balled, a rage brewing in me. I should have stayed with him. I should have insisted that I was needed there, not here in this Gods forsaken place. Just remembering my son's pained face…

Nira have mercy on this man, should he be responsible. My wolf ears threatened to sprout, the fury reminding me why I could serve my son better here. *For I shall not offer it myself.*

"I understand your concerns." I attempted to quell my growing ire, but found it too intoxicating. "However, there have been other matters brought to our attention."

Galden's eyes flashed with dread, fiddling with his wedding ring. "What matters?"

I glanced at Alice, who nodded, and I slid the envelope of report papers over the table for Galden to see. The king raised a blond eyebrow before searching through the envelope's contents.

"These were found in the cellar of one of your Raider's stations, in Entrial Valley," I said while the king flipped through the reports. "Do you recognize what is shown?"

"It seems to be… swords," the king replied. "What of them?"

"Their blades produce a very distinctive glow. A pale, blue tone, very subtle, yet beautiful."

"Yes, beautiful. Brilliantly forged, I suppose. But why does it matter?"

"Only one mineral is known to give off such a light. A crystal from *our* caverns in Grim." My gaze darkened. "Those swords are forged with Spiritcrystal. And from the brightness of their glow, I imagine they are of *pure* crystal. Only Death Knights, apprentices, and their vassals are permitted to wield weapons with that mineral. So tell me, Your Majesty. Why do your knights have swords forged with our crystals? And *how* did they come into the Raiders' possession?"

Fury creased Galden's face for a moment, but was quickly replaced with a calm, amiable laugh. "Surely you jest, High Howllord? These photographs—how do we know they're legitimate? Any Decepiovoker could have easily manipulated the image—"

"Second Fangs Lastings confirmed their authenticity," Alice clipped. Her wolf ears curled back, grey tail waving round her skirt. "And other weapons of this sort have been found in other stations in Everland. Their numbers are equal to those of our scythes that have been stolen from the armories here for years. How can you explain this coincidence?"

The king's tone was guarded, ignoring Alice, and he looked at me. "High Howllord, I swear, I had no knowledge of this. Thank you for bringing it to my attention. If it's true, then I must call for an inspection of my knights."

He set down the file and turned to leave.

"There is the other matter," I called gruffly, making him turn. I saw his fingers ball for only a second, then I hummed, "of your fatality rate over the last few decades. It has been rather odd. The number of Necrofera reported have declined significantly."

Galden's hands clenched again. Unclenched, then balled a third time. He breathed out sharply. "Why, yes. That's been my goal since I became king."

"But how have there been so few attacks…" I lifted my hands, weighing the issues. "And yet, there are so *many* demons populating your lands now? Those numbers have increased two-fold. But the deaths caused by the Necrofera have *decreased*. Is it possible all these attacks haven't been reported?"

"I suppose. You can't expect to account for every—"

"And with fewer reports." Alice failed to suppress her biting growl. "That means the Reapers are not receiving the accurate number of statistics needed every year. Could it be that your Rockraiders have taken our weapons, shaped them into swords, and taken on *our* duties for themselves in secret?"

Damn it, Alice. I grimaced. My wife was never one for passive aggression. She always wanted to get to the point of things.

Galden's face paled. Then his cheeks reddened. "Are you accusing me of defying your laws, High Howless?"

She stood her ground. "Perhaps. Do you deny it?"

"Howllord, I suggest you tame your wife," he sneered. "I provide you my home, my food, my graces—I've shown you nothing but hospitality! And you repay me with suspicion?"

"I heed you take this matter seriously, Your Majesty," I said calmly, though the rage threatened to sprout again. "Such actions are grounds for war."

"You dare speak of war?" He slammed his hands on the table. "It's *your* Reapers who've brought the demons upon my people! Your very son, even! If you threaten war, then you'd best remember who started it!"

Alice and I drew back in surprise. He's already turning the accusation on us? Death's Head, we have him.

"We've started nothing." I kept my wolf ears from growing. Showing hostility would only worsen the situation. Alice didn't have a choice in showing her ears, though, they were her primary shift. Her teeth and claws, however, were still sharp. I wished she would keep them retracted, but that woman often did as she pleased. Her anger was known to get the best of her.

I exhaled. "You'd best think carefully. Beginning a war with the Death realm will cost your kingdom countless lives, not to mention raise the debt you're so concerned about. The demons will overrun the nation, every soul will go un-reaped without us—"

"Everland doesn't need the Death Knights," he snorted, his lion tail whipping behind him. "We've been faring on our own for decades. With the proper weapons, we can be independent of Grim."

Alice rose, her claws digging into the table. "Then, you admit to stealing our weapons?"

"I admit to improving my nation. You even said yourself that the death rate from the Necrofera has declined."

"Because the attacks were not reported!" I bellowed, unable to keep my wolf-ears suppressed. "Do you live in a delusion, man? The deaths are still happening! According to your own statistics, your population is dropping. It appears your people are disappearing without a trace! Your methods are not helping your people, and it is a crime for anyone but our knights to possess our scythes. Not to mention the capture and torture of those messengers!"

"Either cease your crimes and step down as Everland's ruler," Alice's patience had waned, her voice seething. "Or the Council of the Relicbloods will take the crown from you. The Death King will spare your soul from destruction if you agree to relinquish claim to the throne. You will still be tried and executed if found guilty, but your son will be crowned in your stead, though he will be monitored until proven trustworthy. If you defy us, we cannot guarantee your afterlife will be a long one. Concede, and you have a chance to plea before the Death King for your soul. It is your choice."

Sweat beaded the king's brow, his lion ears folding in fright.

9

THE RELICBLOOD GATHERING

DEATH KING SERDIN

Rain applauded outside the window.
    Beyond the drawn, maroon curtains I watched the storm fester, strings of light bursting from the brewing maelstrom.

"<Did your daughter say where she was going, Rojired?>" I inquired of the Sky King, speaking his native language of Culatian. Thunder rumbled gently outside, and lightning brightened the night.

Culatia was known for its incessant storms. I rarely remembered a time when the rain was absent while I was visiting the islands.

Rojired wore his usual, sleek robes, his molting wings sprouting from the buttoned flaps on the back of the rubber-like fabric. The trim of his clothing was smooth with minimal adorning, contrasting my own, embroidered hems.

His hood was drawn down to his shoulders so we could see his brown face, which was creased with age and bubbling from disease.

All four Relic Bloodlines were present tonight, circling the rounded table in Rojired's palace conference room.

My messenger songcrow, Locke, had perched himself on a curtain rail above me, the bird giving a low whistle.

My wife, Myra, stood poised and stoic beside me, made up with dark powder that dusted her lids, which were lined with sapphire lashes. Normally, she would have worn ebony silks like myself, but for this particular occasion, she was here to represent the Dream Bloodline in place of her father. Wherever that bastard was.

She wore her old, pale-orange cloak which jingled faintly with small bells that hung from her long sleeves, and her dark gown draped to the floor and covered her feet. Her greying, azure hair tumbled over her bare collarbone and curled round her enticingly swollen bust.

Myra and I stood together at the foot of the table. The Ocean King waited at the right, and the Sky King was placed at the head.

There was one empty chair at the table, as always. That seat would normally have been for Land's Relicblood, had there been one left. It was a dismal reminder to all of us. Four of the five Bloodlines were left. And one, it seemed, may well disappear soon as well. *If that day comes, these meetings will be hauntingly empty, with only three of us.*

"<My daughter…>" Rojired wheezed from his seat, his breath strained and weak as he spoke the Culatian tongue. It seemed every breath brought him pain. "<Said nothing… of where… or *what* she was doing… not so much as… a warning…>"

Rojired was a sorry sight. His usually bright, scarlet wings were faded and tattered, patches of feathers missing, even from his head. His dark skin had strange, purple splotches and looked to be deteriorating. His scarlet eyes had lost their luster, nearly blind. The downfeathers framing his chin were ragged and scruffy, and every time he scratched there, some would fall onto his grass green robe.

I'd been sure to keep my distance from the man, else I be bombarded with his struggle. Infeciovoking could be a curse at times. When around the terminally sick you could do nothing but feel them waste away from the inside. We felt their pain, their weakness, their body rushing to heal, but they were doomed to die in the end… It was truly a wretched experience.

Still, I did my best to ignore the static of disease and asked him, "<Do you think she left to find your son? How long has it been since *he* disappeared?>"

"<The prince…?>" Rojired gave a series of hacks. "<It has been… three years… but…>" A flash of guilt crossed his pockmarked face. "<There is something… I have kept from you all… about Prince Roji…>"

He hacked again, his coughs loud and obnoxious before he went on. "<He did not run away. I… banished him from the kingdom…>"

There was silence.

The Ocean King, Ninumel, seemed unsure of what was happening. He looked at me, no doubt trying to gauge my expression hoping to assess what Rojired had said. Ninumel couldn't understand Culatian. But whatever scowl contorted my face now seemed to stiffen Ninumel's posture.

"<*Banished?*>" I asked Rojired, baffled. "<Why in the five realms would you banish your heir?>"

"<Years ago…>" Rojired began distantly. "<Roji came to me with a request I could not… agree to…>"

"<What request?>"

The swallow shot a rueful glare at the Ocean King. "<He wished... to form a union... with *that thing's*... sister!>"

The Ocean King's green brow furrowed, not having understood.

Ninumel was a fairly young Seadragon, barely into his thirties. His emerald hair was thin and textured like fins, same as the long moustache hanging from his lip. His skin was coated in smooth scales, and they shimmered under the lamplight. He wore muted burgundy garbs to contrast his green hair and eyes.

The Seadragon's webbed ears gave a questioning twitch when he glanced at me, seeming to take my distress as a sign that he shouldn't be pleased.

I let out a hard breath, wishing Ninumel would just agree to learn Culatian. Though, it would also help if Rojired spoke Landish for everyone to understand, but the damned swallow wouldn't let it go. I had the irking feeling he enjoyed leaving Ninumel confused in these meetings.

I stifled a peeved groan, once again playing translator as I explained Rojired's words in Ninumel's language. "*Ma'tessît Ninumel,*" I began, choosing less-offensive terminology. "*Quanmëd Rojired... foyey.*"

Ninumel's emerald eyes splintered as his face flooded with rage. "*Foyey?!*" The Seadragon bellowed. "*Ma'tessît?! Quanmëd pschal frettre renn?!*"

I winced. On second thought, I decided it was a blessing Rojired didn't understand. Ninumel had just called him a feather-headed idiot.

The Seadragon exploded with new insults now, his drooping moustache wavering as his words tumbled out so chaotically, I could hardly keep up. I managed to catch the words 'kidnapped!' and 'That irresponsible bird will drown!'.

Rojired began arguing back with equally prejudiced insults, both kings only guessing what the other was saying, but not letting that quell their anger. Rojired's Sky mark brightened scarlet on his chest, electricity sparking between his fingers; Ninumel's Ocean mark shone emerald on his neck, palms spreading with fogging ice—

"Enough!" I slammed a fist on the table and evoked my fire Hallows, an inferno spreading from my fist and bursting outward between them, leaving a burnt streak on the lacquered table, bubbles forming at the surface.

The kings jolted back, their heads snapping to me. Now that I had their attention, I called the fire back, having it snuff out in a puff.

"That's enough!" I shouted in Landish, my wolf ears grown to emphasize my impatience. I tugged on my lapel and addressed Ninumel in Marincian. "<Your sister wasn't kidnapped, Ninumel. As I said before, she seems to have eloped with Prince Roji of her own volition.>"

"<Dalminia would never leave with a reckless storm-brewer!>" Protested the scaled man. "<Never!>"

"<Well, it seems that she has.>" My wolf ears curled back, warning him not to push me further. "<And Rojired banished his son over it. Which means wherever the Sky Prince is, your sister will likely be there as well.>"

I turned back to the Sky King, switching languages so he could understand. "<And if Zylveia left to find her brother, it's a safe bet *she* will be with both of them. Perhaps it is time we all began a worldwide search for the Sky Prince again?>"

The Sky King grumbled and folded his arms over the lacquered table, wheezing. "<I should think... *you* be in charge of it, Serdin. You and Myra are... responsible for my son's poor decision in the first place.>"

I paused, not having expected that. "<Excuse me?>"

"<My son... tried to persuade me to accept his union with... that slimy fish girl.>" Rojired's gaze smoldered. "<He... wished to form a stronger alliance between the two kingdoms... as you had done with the Dream and Death realms. But he did not understand... your case did not hold the consequences other Bloodlines would have faced.>"

I bristled. "<Meaning?>"

"<Aspirre has always had... the same ruler,>" explained Rojired. "<The original... Relic Child. Dream has ruled the sub... subconscious plane for... two thousand years. And he still does today... Aspirre is in no need of an heir. Your daughter... is only obligated to rule in Grim.>" He coughed again, shifting his weight. "<If a union ever happened between two kingdoms... who *both* needed an heir... Well... one Relicblood cannot rule two kingdoms.>"

"<You realize Ninumel has a son?>" I pointed out. "<His sister wouldn't take over Marincia next.>"

"<Ninumel's son is but a child, nearing seven years. If something were to happen to Ninumel, like it will surely happen to *me* soon... A child... cannot rule a kingdom. And so Princess Dalminia would... have to take the throne until the boy came of age... And to form an alliance with those *fish*... would have both kingdoms in an outrage!>"

I rubbed my eyes. "<Rojired, we must find your heirs. We cannot risk another Bloodline dying out, just look what it's done to the Land realm. The continents are practically at war again! Their 'peace time' is crumbling right before our eyes, do you want this to happen to Culatia?>"

Rojired's faded eyes soured, gazing at the empty chair by the table. He said nothing, but I knew his answer.

Then Rojired blinked, looking at my wife. "<Dream Princess?>" he hummed to Myra, puzzled. "<You have been… rather quiet…>"

Myra had been studying the conference table with particular scrutiny, her manicured nail scratching at a bubble my fire had created in the lacquer. She didn't respond to Rojired's questioning, still scratching away at the table idly, lost in thought.

Damn it all, I knew that look.

I changed to the Landish tongue. "Myra, if you've had a vision, out with it."

Of course she would have a vision now. When addressing an issue like this, how could she not? I grit my teeth, having a dreaded feeling that whatever my wife had seen with her prophetic Hallows couldn't have been in Rojired's favor. Not with that blank stare on her face, which, I noted, held just the slightest hint of gravity.

Myra didn't look up when she finally spoke, but it wasn't in Landish. She spoke in Grimish. "<Serdin. There is something I haven't told you.>" She glanced up with a dead expression, save for the slightest hint of remorse in her arched, azure brow. "<I think the time has come.>"

I staggered. If she was speaking Grimish, she clearly didn't want either man to understand us. That did not bode well. "<Time for what?>" I asked, bracing.

This is it. She was going to say the Sky realm would soon fall, just as the Land realm had. Rojired would die, his heirs wouldn't be found, the birds of Culatia would be in complete turmoil and all Void would break loose between the Sky and Ocean realms…

"*Myel a'ynash,*" Myra finally sighed, snapping me out of my panic. I frowned. She had said *you're wrong.*

"*O a'ynash yechet?*" I asked, confused.

"<About the Relicblood of Land,>" she said. "<The line did not die.>"

I paused. "*Oha?*"

"<The child that would have taken the throne those years ago still lives.>"

"*Myra.*" What was I supposed to say to that? "<It's been five hundred years. How could anyone…>"

She gave me a pointed look. "<Serdin, tell me. How old am I?>"

I loosened my collar. What was that number again? How many centuries…?

"Er," I began. "<Five… hundred…?>"

"<Five hundred and eleven,>" she corrected, though there was no outrage in her tone. She remained rather calm, her voice gentle. "<And how old do I look?>"

I was sure to remember the golden rule when asked to guess a woman's age: *round down.*

"<I suppose… early forties?>" Was that too high? I amended. "<Perhaps even thirties?>"

She gave no hint of offense *or* flattery, merely continuing, "<How, would you say, is such a thing possible?>"

"<You and your family have lived in Aspirre for centuries. Time doesn't exist in…>" I grasped her arm, pulling her aside. "<Are you… are you saying the lost heir's been in *there* this whole time?>"

Myra gave a soft nod. "<My father has housed the heir after the last Land King was killed. The child was too young to rule, so we've kept the heir hidden until the time came for the Shadowblood to take on his duties.>"

"<Whose duties?> I demanded. "<Myra, you're not making sense! Why would your father keep something like this hidden? Does he have any idea what a disaster he's caused for everyone?>"

"<There are changes being set in motion as we speak, Serdin,>" she said. "<And we are not prepared. My father has done everything in his power to set all the pieces into play, but there is only so much he can do. The current heirs have done their part and fled at my father's request—>"

"*OHA?*" I shouted, jabbing a terse hand at Rojired and Ninumel. "<You mean to tell me all of *THIS* is your father's doing?!>"

Impressively, she didn't flinch. "<Serdin, you must understand. This is greater than all of us. My father did what was necessary.>"

I slammed a smoking hand against the wall, my fire aching to leak. "<He told the Sky and Ocean heirs to run away, *and* kept Land's heir hidden for five centuries?!>" I massaged my temples, growling, "*Hu'choft Necros…!* <I'm only glad Willow is still at the palace, otherwise I would have thought the world was in shambles!>"

I paused when Myra bit her lip, her hands fidgeting. "<Actually, Serdin.>" She cleared her throat gently. "<Please don't be angry, but…>"

I paled. "*A! A, Myra…! Myel a'thoul kes…*"

"<Willow has her role to play as well,>" she argued. "<Perhaps the most important, being Death's incarnation. I've Seen visions of her progress, Serdin, and she's doing splendidly. She's even found—>"

"*OENN UL LIZ'U YEYTSCHE, MYRA?*" I bellowed, wolf ears curled and teeth deadly sharp. "*WHERE IS WILLOW?*"

10
IF IT WERE A SNAKE

~~~~~~

JAQ

"And is she eating enough?" Grandad asked and set his rook on the ebony square that held my pawn, taking my ivory piece. "The peasant is at least able to feed her?"

I pushed up my glasses while examining the new board and threw a lazy leg over the cushioned chair in Grandad's private library.

"His name is Yoric, Grandfather," I muttered, moving my knight to take his rook. "And if Mother starved to death, you'd have heard it from my Da by now."

Grandad scoffed and moved his queen forward two spaces. *Idiot move.* "He doesn't have the money to afford a com," he grumbled.

"He has a job, Grandfather, he isn't destitute." I moved my second knight to take his queen, the piece hitting the board with a felt-muted *tpt*. "Check."

Grandad squinted at the board, and hurriedly moved his king one space left to keep away from my knight's *L* path. Then he mumbled, "Yes, the noble job of a simple cobbler. How very profitable in these times."

I slid my last bishop down and took his final rook, clearing a path for my queen to take his king. "Check mate."

Grandad's scaled brow raised in surprise. He bent over the board and scrutinized it carefully, curling a finger over his lips and pushed up his reading glasses.

He clucked. "By Gods, it is! Very impressive, Jaqelle. Not even the king's treasurer has beaten me yet."

The old snake heaved out of his chair. "Well, I suppose it's time to get to business, then."

"Business," I muttered. "And here I thought you only wanted to catch up on the family for once."

"You know well this is in the family's interest."

"Your family. Not mine."

"You and I are of the same blood, despite your peasant father. I'm only thinking of your future." He went to his desk by the corner of the library and picked up a long piece of parchment. "I've updated my Will as of last week. Some changes have been made that will hopefully... well, sway you to take your place as my heir."

I snorted. "The last time you added changes, I was suddenly engaged to some prissy snake girl up here."

"Yes, well, I've canceled the arrangement with Roaress Caullur. And I do hope you appreciate that. It was a damned nightmare between her sobs and her mother's threats to my lower regions."

I snickered, stretching my back over the chair and reached a hand for my crow's nuzzling beak. Bridge perched on a desk lamp and tended to her tattered feathers. I could feel from our connection that she just wanted this to be over. *I feel ya girl.*

"So," I sighed, letting Bridge climb onto my outstretched arm and nestle over my chest. "Is that the only change?"

"No," he said. "I'm also allowing you to... to keep your peasant name."

I jolted upright, Bridge fumbling to my lap. "What?"

"You can keep the Mallory name as you wish." He looked and sounded angry to say it. "And the question of whom you marry will be decided by your own volition."

I gawked at him. Those were the two items he *never* wanted to give up. What the Void was going on?

My lids narrowed at him. "Grandfather... are you dying?"

He rubbed his scaled knuckles vigorously. "In a manner of speaking, we're all dying, Jaqelle. It's just that I... I-I might have less time than the rest of you."

I pushed off my chair, Bridge alighting on my shoulder. "Are you ill?"

"No, no," he assured, wafting a hand as he went to the open window and shut it, drawing the curtains. "Nothing like that. I'm afraid that with tensions rising in Everland, my line of business could be *extremely* dangerous for me."

"You're worried the people will revolt against the king?"

He laughed. Hard. "Quite the opposite." He lowered his voice to a quiet hiss, gripping my shoulders sternly. "Listen well, Jaqelle. The last man in my position was a goat named High Roarlord Renneguard."

I frowned. "You mean that guy who slaughtered a whole family with his son?"

"That story was a cover up that Galden fabricated." His jaw was set like an iron block. "The Renneguards were nowhere near that family that night. They were both with the rest of us."

"The rest of who?" I squirmed under his vice grip. I didn't like where this was going. Or… well, okay, I *really* liked where this was going.

"Jaqelle, there is something you must understand." He slid his hands off my shoulders, tugging his lapel. "As my heir, I think it only right that you know my true line of business."

"Oh, man." I felt a weird mix of excitement and fear twisting my gut right now. "Grandad, if you're with the rebellion…"

His moustache lifted when he smirked. "With? Jaqelle, you humble me. I am its *general*."

I clapped my hands in a laugh. "That's why you knew I was here this morning! *You* knew we were coming. *You* must have been told by Land's Servant when Henry called! Or—oh, Holy Bloods, Grandad, are *you* Land's Servant—?"

"No, no!" he contradicted, sounding more relaxed, "no, I'm not Land's Servant, good gracious. As I said, I am his general."

Oh. Well, it was still cool as Void. "So," I began, "So you know who he is? What does the rebel leader look like?"

"Even I don't know," he admitted. "He's never taken off his mask, not even for me, the secretive bastard." He chuckled. "But you were right, it was my Lord Servant who told me you were coming. Though, the real reason I've brought you here…"

He sucked in a breath, looking over his shoulder even though we were alone. "Jaqelle, I've come to warn you. To warn all of you. For the last month, Galden has been gathering his generals behind closed doors. He has been sneaking weapons to his men and gathering them for intensive training. I've managed to overhear him talk of war on the eve of next month."

I swallowed. "War with the rebellion?"

"No." Grandad looked me dead in the eye, and snarled. "War with the Reapers."

11

UNVEILED

~~~~~

XAVIER

Craaaaw!

I jolted awake—crashing to the floor when I fell off my chair, startling the Messenger Care Clinic's staff and the disguised Willow beside me.

A ripple of chuckles washed through the waiting room as I sat up on the carpet, groggily smearing a hand over my face. "Hrmm... what..." I yawned in a stretch. "How long have I been asleep...?"

Willow helped me to my feet. "Five hours. Even Alexander nodded off when he took over for you."

I *cricked* my neck. "I suppose he's still asleep, then. I don't hear him in there—"

Craaw!

My head snapped to the backroom door.

Dr. Tonya was there, holding a tattered raven in her arms, a cast fastened to his broken leg.

"Chai!" I fumbled over, gingerly taking my wounded raven, who croaked at me cheerily. "Oh, thank Bloods..."

Dr. Tonya chuckled. "He gave us a scare, but he pulled through in the end. I'm prescribing him these supplements, to ensure feather growth and proper mending." She handed me a bottle of square, chewable capsules, as well as a bag of corn. She lifted the latter with a smile. "And *these* are treats."

"Co-*rn*!" Chai flapped eagerly from my arms, his beak nudging toward the bag. "Co-*rn*!"

I laughed and brought the bag to him, letting him feast as he wished. "Thank you, Doctor," I said wearily. "I'm glad Bianca got to you so quick and..."

I paused, searching the waiting room and finding most of our company present. Octavius was here beside Lilli, but Bianca had left the seat she'd once occupied. In her place was a different rabbit girl—Vendy, who waved with a crooked-toothed grin.

I turned back to Dr. Tonya. "Where *is* Bianca?"

The Doctor wafted a dismissive hand. "Oh, my husband called her back to her duties for tonight. She invited you all to our manor tomorrow night, to discuss the questions you had of Sirra-Lynn."

"That sounds wonderful—*ahh!*" Chai shoved his beak in the bag of corn more fiercely, and it fell out of my grip and spilled over the carpet. I winced at the mess, holding Chai tighter and cleared my throat. "Er, apologies…"

She gave a wrinkled grin. "We'll clean it up. That one needs as much strength and energy as he can find—"

Craaaw?!

A piercing screech blurted from a different raven near the back, one still stuffed in a crate with several others and held by a young apprentice Reaper, who fumbled with the now wobbling crate.

CRAAW!

The crate bounced out of the apprentice's hand and *cracked* open in a mess of splinters on the floor, freeing the many black birds. They scrambled through the waiting room, flailing and hopping, their clipped wings fluttering uselessly as they dove for the pile of corn in a hungry frenzy.

I rubbed my neck, shrugging weakly to the doctor. "Er, sorry…"

Dr. Tonya snorted. "Well, I suppose Chai isn't the only one needing energy, eh?"

Lilli and Willow's messengers fluttered off their Reapers' shoulders to join the feast at my feet, Jewel having trouble finding an open path amongst her larger brethren. Mal flew down from a chair's back and shoved his way in, pushing Jewel farther back. Chai wriggled in my arms, our Bond straining slightly, and I gently lowered him to the newly formed murder. I watched him carefully as he hobbled over with his casted talon, ready to pull him up again if the others pushed him aside as they'd done Jewel. But, to my surprise, Chai cocked his head at Jewel and used his beak to push the others aside, providing an opening for Jewel to steal a single piece of corn—which was all she could fit in her tiny beak—and flutter back to Willow's shoulder to enjoy her meal.

Willow chuckled. "He's yours, all right."

His task finished, Chai hobbled back to my feet, fluttering his clipped wings and pulling on our Bond again. I picked him up and hummed cheerily. "Aren't you the little gentleman, Chai?"

From Octavius's head, Shade flew down to join the others, pecking at the bounty fervently—

Shade knocked heads with a new raven, one with a white diamond pattern between its eyes, and the two paused, staring. Their feathers ruffled, and they stood taller.

Crrrrrra!

They belted startled cries, fluttering as they circled one another, knocking beaks like old friends. Octavius rose from his seat, befuddled, and crouched to the ravens. "You know this guy, Shade?"

His white-cheeked raven bobbed its head excitedly. "Kn-*ow*!" croaked Shade. "Kn-*ow*! Bro-*ther*!"

Octavius blinked. "Woah. Really?"

I crouched beside him, watching the ravens. "Fascinating… Mal wasn't the only one to find a sibling among the stolen lot, then."

"Apparently not," a voice grunted groggily from my thoughts.

I perked, flicking my gaze to the ceiling. "Ah, awake, are we?"

"How could I sleep with all this noise?" Alex grumbled.

Octavius laughed and rubbed Shade's head eagerly. "Hah, that's cool, Shade! Hey there little guy—*ow*!"

Shade's brother bit Octavius's finger. Then the new raven paused, cocking his head to the side to scrutinize Octavius with one eye. It bleated a triumphant croak and hopped onto Octavius's shirt, climbing up with its sharp talons, Octavius wincing with each step, until the bird nestled into Octavius's hair. It didn't seem to want to move.

Octavius grumbled and reached for the intruder. "All right, uh, *guy*, time to get down—*ow, ow, OW!*"

The raven clung to his hair, then bit his fingers again.

Octavius shook his hand. "What the Void!"

Dr. Tonya curled a thoughtful finger to her lips. "Hmm. He seems attached, doesn't he?"

"Why?" Octavius glared ruefully at the raven, and Shade flew to his shoulder to screech at his sibling. "*I'm* not his Reaper. I already have my messenger."

"It's possible," the doctor began, "that he thinks he'll find his Reaper if he goes with you. Either that, or he feels safe around his brother… Oh, why not take him? The poor dear must have been through a lot. Here, let me fetch you another bottle of that feather-growth prescription!" She rushed through the backdoors and disappeared.

Octavius grimaced, his head weighed down by the new raven, and the one screeching on his shoulder. "Great…"

Night had bloomed when we left the Messenger Clinic. Chai ruffled his tattered feathers in my arms, and I fed him his prescribed supplements. The raven ate the chewable capsules grudgingly, but cheered some after I offered his reward: a new bag of corn. Chai pushed his head against my jaw, cooing contentedly.

"Is this what I've been missing?" I scratched under Chai's beak. A calming wave flooded my chest, surging from the Bond I shared with my new messenger. It was a wonderful feeling... One that I strangely couldn't describe with fair accuracy.

"It's different, isn't it?" Alex hummed from my thoughts. *"It's an otherworldly experience. When I first Bonded with Mal, my perspective of everything changed."*

"I suppose I see what you'd meant now." I gave Chai more corn, his beak digging eagerly into my palm. "I only wish he hadn't suffered. If he'd come sooner..."

Willow, walking beside me, patted Chai on the head. "He looks happy to be here now, at the least. I'm sure he was just as anxious to get to you as you'd been to wait for him."

"In all honesty." I fell quiet. "I was beginning to doubt he even existed. It'd been so long, I thought, perhaps... Nira hadn't chosen me. Not as a Knight and not as a shifter. I thought She hadn't chosen me to live at all."

Lilli stroked her own messenger from her forearm to my left, sniffing while dabbing at her tearful eyes. "Oh, this is all so touching...! Congratulations, Xavier. Truly."

I heard Shade croak twice from Octavius's shoulder behind me, and Octavius laughed. "Seriously. Welcome to the Brotherhood. Weird as it sounds coming from me."

I gave a toothy grin. "I find it fitting, actually." My gaze flicked to the *second* raven screeching from Octavius's head. "And should we welcome you a second time? Two ravens, two inductions?"

"Shut up..." Octavius grimaced, the new raven squawking on and on, Shade croaking back.

Vendy lifted to her toes and poked at the new bird, scrunching her nose. "What a weirdo—*yowch!*" The raven bit her finger, and she sucked it tenderly. "Bwoohy Bwirhhd—!"

Tmpt!

Something dropped from the roofs suddenly, startling us. There was silence for a time. Whatever or whomever had leapt down was watching us quietly. I could barely make out a humanoid figure outside the lamplight.

"Howllord," the man in the shadows finally rasped. "Good evening…"

I shuffled back, straining to see in the darkness, but it was nearly pitch black outside the light.

The figure rose, his voice a gritty rumble. "I believe you and I have business…"

I held tight to Chai, the bird's tattered feathers brushing my arms. "What business? Who are you?"

"A friend," growled the figure. He made no motion to approach, but he lingered there, watching me. "I hear the king may well have broken the Death Laws…?"

Once my eyes adjusted, I saw the dim outline of his plumed hat and clothed mask. Glinting in the light was a green bead that hung from a strand of deep, auburn hair.

I hesitated. "Our affairs with the king are of no concern to you."

"All affairs with the false king are my concern." His voice rattled as if needles pricked his throat. He stepped into the light. "I hear rumors that Galden is a suspect of more than a few crimes in your realm. Not surprising… he is a fool. It's only fitting that he paves the quickest route to his own death. It certainly makes my job easier…"

"Who are you?" Willow questioned, her tone guarded. "Are you part of the rebellion?"

His laughter was dim and sordid. "I *am* the rebellion, dear Roaress." He bowed. "They call me Land's Servant…"

Vendy let out a squeal and dropped to one knee in awe. "My Lord Servant!" She squeaked excitedly. "My-my parents fought for your cause, sir! I'm following in their footsteps and-and I've formed a Bloodpact with the High Howllord here—the one our Seers have had visions of, and—!"

An irritated snort came from the back of our group, and Kurrick shoved in front of Vendy, Miss Ana trailing behind him meekly. "Cease your groveling, girl," grunted Kurrick, his lion ears curled as he turned to the rebellion's leader. "What business do you have here *Servant*? Speak or be gone."

The "Servant" bowed again with his arms spread, his tone appeasing. "As I've said, I am a friend. I merely wished to greet the Howllord and his company."

"Greetings have been had," said Kurrick. "Your goal was met. Now off with you, Lord *Servant*."

The Servant's head cocked, the long, striped feather in his hat wavering along with the green bead in his hair. "Not the reaction I usually see," he rasped. "My name is either met with reverence or the draw of a blade. You do neither."

"You think your quarrel with the monarchy is of a single dichotomy?" Kurrick folded his arms. "There are those who seek the Old Kingdom's return outside of your ranks."

He gave a guttural hum, turning his gaze to Miss Ana. "And I suppose you're of like mind as your associate, Miss?"

I saw Ana shrink, and the mousey woman sidled behind Willow, who glanced at me with a raised eyebrow. I shook my head, turning back to the Servant.

"You didn't simply want to greet us, did you?" I called, stepping from around Kurrick. "You mentioned the king is suspected of breaking the Death realm's laws. You want us to give you information?"

"You misunderstand, Howllord," he said. "I wish to *trade* information. If you need further evidence to convict Galden, I have an informant in the palace who can provide it."

"And what would you have in exchange?" I asked.

"A promise." I could imagine the smirk that went with his tone. "As it seems your dear vassal has informed you, many of my oracles tell me that you, Howllord, hold a great importance to our cause."

My stare narrowed at the Servant. "If you expect us to lead you to Land's lost Relicblood," I said, "you're wasting your time. As we keep telling Vendy, *and* these two, we don't give a damn about any lost heir. We aren't concerned with your politics."

"Then, I'm saddened to say, Howllord." He gave a coughing laugh. "Our politics will soon *become* yours. When the time comes for Grim to war with Everland, know that my men will be at your service. You have the rebellion's support, wanted or not."

My teeth barred. "You can't just…"

Kris la vheh, weh shae'beahl hu'leigh…

I stopped, my wolf ears perking. What was that voice in the distance? Someone was… yes, someone was singing. A small voice lilted in the night, singing in Grimish, echoing through the streets. *Don't I know that prayer?*

Willow's fox ears grew as the voice carried on. I saw her fingers trace the music watch around her neck. "The Requiem…?" she hushed, forgetting all about the rebellion leader.

She drifted down the street.

"Will—R-Roaress!" I snapped, barely missing a swipe for her wrist before she broke into an impulsive dash around the corner.

Land's Servant blinked at her sudden retreat. "W-wait now, Roaress! I wished to ask something of you…!" But she was already gone, disappeared into the night.

"Blasted girl!" Lilli growled, taking flight after her, leaving the rest of us on the walkway.

The Servant's tongue clicked, the grittiness gone from his suddenly undisguised voice. "Damn it all…! She's the only one who's heard from Linus!"

My head snapped to him. *Wait a Bloody minute.* I knew that voice. "Prince…" I began, incredulous, "Cayden?"

I was met with silence. The Servant, it seemed, had grown terribly still.

"I…er…" The Servant floundered for a reply. Then he growled, "Oh, dash it all. I suppose if it's you, Howllord…"

So, so painfully slowly, the Servant pulled off his mask.

The man's previously olive eyes bled crimson and his brown hair shifted blond, as if that mask had been enchanted with an illusion. Bloody Death, it was indeed Prince Cayden. Galden's heir.

"I must say, Howllord." The prince's lips made a frustrated puckering sound, and he scratched behind one of his lion ears that had been hidden under his wide-brimmed hat. "You're an astute one. Annoyingly so. Now, I should hope you don't take my reveal lightly. If my Seers hadn't thought you pertinent to our victory, I'd normally open your throat right here without a thought."

I groaned and smeared a hand over my mouth. "What in Death is this about?"

"But," Octavius stammered next to me. "In the palace, you said… I thought…"

"Bloody Death, you've been conspiring against your own father?" I threw up my hands. "*Why?*"

Prince Cayden snorted. "The list for "why" is far longer than the contrary, Howllord. A sack of feral bison dung could rule Everland better than that fool."

"Yes, but see, you talked about *killing* him," I emphasized.

The madman simply shrugged. "My father needs to die. It seems to be the only way to correct the corruption in our kingdom. Besides, my family was only meant to be a temporary replacement until the lost heir returned. My father believes the change was permanent, and so he will not step down from the throne should the heir arrive to take it from him. Of course the most logical solution is to kill him."

"Then why not do it earlier?" Octavius looked to be suffering a headache. "I mean, I don't think you should, but you live with him. If you wanted to kill him, why'd you wait so long?"

He cocked an eyebrow. "Sir, I might be the rebellion's leader, but as of today, you and I are the only bunch who know it. If I were to kill my father and take his place, no one would believe that I was Land's Servant. I would have countless assassins after me once I took the crown, and likely be accused of killing the *Servant* and taking his identity as some ploy to gain the affections of the people."

"Well then, that doesn't seem the least bit farfetched," I muttered, adjusting my hold of Chai as he squirmed in my arms. My Bond with him was pulsing with warm signals of doubt, the raven glaring suspiciously at the prince.

"With all due respect, Howllord," said the prince, "I've been around these people for some time. I know their string of logic regarding politics, however paranoid and exaggerated it may be."

Vendy shrugged. "Yeah, he's got a point."

Kurrick grunted his agreement as well, but didn't seem set on admitting it verbally—

Something caught the warrior's eye over the horizon. I watched the color flee from his skin as Kurrick's grip tightened on his sword. "What in the five realms…?"

I followed his gaze, as did Octavius. *Strange…* Over the lamp-speckled mountain paths, there was an enormous shadow cloaking the roads. It was hazy at first, and seemed to change shape over the cluster of orange dots that lined the winding pathways.

"Um," began Octavius, "What is that?"

"Land's Blade…!" Prince Cayden cursed, watching as the flood of blackness split apart and poured into the city.

Mother of Death!

It was the Necrofera.

12
OLD ENEMIES

~~~~~

WILLOW

O myel heist timbriw lahla'beahl?
Murrderes craw hellacha lola'beahl…?

I hurtled over flour sacks that a vendor had set aside in the bazar. The Grimish merchant shouted after me, but I paid him no mind, weaving between booths.

The singing voice reverberated off the buildings. My fox ears were grown and flicking toward the echoes, the Requiem unmistakable. But who was singing? It sounded like a child. How could a child know of this prayer?

Heist craw'u lole fret myel ena…

I rounded into the back alleys, puffing, and crept along the maze of enclosed walls. Around the next corner was the child, singing the Requiem. He was a dark-skinned boy with feathered, chestnut hair that fell to his shoulders. His back was turned to me, wings draping at his bare heels. He was shirtless, wearing nothing save for ratty, tan shorts and a red-and-black striped scarf round his neck. He was so small… I doubted he was older than five.

I know him. Wasn't this the child from Lindel? The one who'd stolen apples from the vendor?

A crow was perched on a pile of wooden boxes beside him, its flat tail fanning out when I approached, showing a white, clover shaped mark on its tail feather.

Jewel fluttered off my shoulder to greet the singing child.

Yechet wuw kemn droh la wuw kemn thal...

The boy stopped when Jewel fluttered in front of him. He turned to me, and I was met with a pair of wide, yellow eyes. "Took ya long enough!" He huffed and folded his boney arms, looking about the alley as though searching for others. "Aw, Land," he muttered, snagging my fingers and trying to pull me along. "Wrong future. com'on, we gotta get everyone else!"

"P-pardon?" I dug my heels into the paved stone, anchoring us. "Where did you hear that prayer?"

"From you," the boy said. He tried to shove me forward, his tone straining as he pushed my stubborn weight. "It's what ya sing…! At the tree…!"

"Tree?" I scowled. *The Willow of Ashes.* "What do you know of that place? It's forbidden."

"Well, I only See it in the later parts." He mumbled. "Ya take the wolves there. Now come *on…*"

"What wolves? Do you mean the twins?" I questioned. "I've never taken them…" *No,* I realized, *I have taken them there. In my dreams.* "What do you know of that?" I demanded.

"He knows quite a lot, actually," a new voice answered above. My skin crawled to hear it was familiarly pleasant. "He knows more than any of us, in fact."

My gaze lifted in a grimace. Sitting on an iron patio and swinging his legs over the ledge was a goat-horned man.

My teeth sharpened. "Linus…!"

"Forgive my rudeness," he called down, "but your new look doesn't suit you, Your Highness Death." Linus blithely slid down the iron ladder, leaping at the last rung to touch down.

I drew out my scythe, snarling. "No further!"

He kept his distance from my blade. "There's no need for that," he said, bowing theatrically. "You're not my enemy, your grace."

The Raiders he'd slaughtered in Lindel's prison came to mind, and my fox ears curled tight. "But you are mine."

The winged child tugged my arm suddenly. "It's all right," said the child, his tone urgent. "We need Linus. I can't talk 'bout it right now, though, we gotta leave. They're coming."

"Who is coming—?"

"Willow!" A new voice cried from the sky. Lilli had soared down to perch on the patio, folding her leathery wings and scowling at me. "You can't run off like that and expect us to leave it be!"

The child's yellow eyes brightened at Lilli. He took a shocked breath, then cried, "Mama!"

Lilli frowned at him, looking to me. "What's all this?" She noticed my scythe was drawn, and her hand cautiously reached for the glowing spheres at her neck. "Who are they—?"

"Friends," Linus answered before I could speak. He nodded to me. "I'm glad to see you brought reinforcements, Your Highness. You'll need them."

The child tugged my arm again, his crow fluttering to his head. "Come on, Auntie Low! We gotta get outta here. And-and you too, Mama!" He glanced up at Lilli now. "Come on!"

Auntie Low? I squinted an eye at the boy. *Mama?* Why use such names?

The boy unfolded his wings and soared ahead, beckoning for Lilli and me to follow. I glanced back at Linus with narrow eyes. The goat didn't bother to meet my gaze, chasing after the boy on foot with a suspicious urgency. Something was certainly wrong.

Lips pursed, I darted after the child. Lilli followed while Jewel and Dusk fluttered ahead—

I faltered.

A dark shadow engulfed the mountains in the distance, a blur of blackness spreading down the rocky hills toward the town.

Bloody Nira! I sped faster, keeping my scythe poised behind me. *Demons!* Just when I'd thought we were through with these damned invasions, here they were, thousands of them, heading our way. *Again!* Cilia's army had grown two-fold, by the looks of it. And they were about to swarm the capital all at once, using the surrounding mountains as a funnel.

Bloods, I'd been a fool. Of course we weren't rid of Cilia. The day she was Cleansed from our lives would be the day I sent her to the Void myself—

A figure dropped down from the roofs and blocked my path.

It was Miss Ana, that rebel woman of ours. *Where had she…*

Ana clasped her arms round my waist, and I stiffened. "M… Miss Ana?" I asked skeptically.

Her bare feet slid into a prepared stance. They glittered with golden Hallows, her grip strong around me. "Keep hold," she whispered.

A sinking feeling twisted my nerves. "What are you…"

I screamed when we launched off the ground, shooting through the air, and I was suddenly reminded that this woman wasn't just a Healer—she was a Terravoker as well. She was evoking her rock Hallows through her feet and using our weight against the ground to push upward, the stones cracking in our wake as we flew in a rush of wind, passing the now startled Lilli who flapped beside us.

We dipped and rose as Ana skipped from rooftop to rooftop, using the bricks as anchors. I yelped in fright, the road shrinking and growing nauseously beneath us.

"Blast it, can't we run on the ground?!" I screamed.

Ana's crimson gaze was hard, as was her voice. "There is no time! I must see you safe, for Myra!"

"Oh, why are you always on about my moth—*aaah*!"

We dipped again with more hustle, and I screamed as we sped from roof to roof over the city.

13

DEVIOUS

~~~~

XAVIER

Our messengers screeched and fluttered wildly, the Necrofera reaching the city's perimeter.

Chai shrieked from my arms while Mal fluttered from my shoulder. Shade—and the other raven following Octavius—croaked in a scream as the cloud of blackness stretched down the mountains, blanketing the edge of the capital. Sirens blared as cloaked Reapers hustled out of their stations to take arms, heading for the horde that was coming from the horizon.

"Hey!" Someone hollered within the crowd. "*Da'torr!*"

I found our vassal, Dalen, flying over the sea of heads toward us, his three siblings trailing behind. They landed in heavy puffs, and Henry shoved through the crowd to join. The Blacksmith was covered in sweat, and he quickly unloaded a Storagebox full of weapons and armor, passing them around to our group as needed.

"Plate-up!" Henry called and tossed me a suit, giving another set to Octavius. He turned to Dalen and tossed the bird a pair of glowing, Spiritcrystal daggers. "These are yours, thief," Henry said to Dalen. "The vassal of a Reaper needs the right weapons."

Dalen grinned wildly and tested a few swings with the new blades. "Nice! These're seriously mine?"

"You bet," Henry said smugly. "Took me a while to get the crystal, but here they are. Now, I say we—" Henry tensed suddenly, spotting Prince Cayden standing with us. His teeth sharpened threateningly. "What in the five realms are *you* doing here, Princeling?"

Vendy hopped between them and shook Henry's shoulder. "It's *him*, Uncle! He's Land's Servant!"

Henry's brow knitted. "The crowned *prince*?"

I tossed a dismissive hand. "Absurd, we know, but apparently true. Your Highness, I presume you're trained in the sword?"

"Aye," Prince Cayden grunted, his lion-ears curling as his hands glittered with golden light. The road beneath him *ripped* apart and formed into a sword in his hand, and he held it at the ready. "You have my blade and my Hallows, Howllord."

"Good to hear," I said, my gaze sweeping the chaotic crowd. "First priority is finding Willow—"

"Alex!" Willow called suddenly from… above us? "Xavier—*oh*!"

Two figures dropped to the street—and accidentally landed on Vendy, knocking her on her stomach. The culprit, Miss Ana, blushed and apologized as the disguised Willow climbed out of her arms, looking ill. Lilli landed beside her, folding her leathery wings.

"Thank the Gods you're… all right," Willow panted, her nausea seeming to ebb. "There are…"

"Demons. We know." I gripped her arm. "Come, we must leave."

"To where?" Lilli demanded. "The Fera have already infiltrated most of the city. There's hardly a path clear enough to get through without conflict—"

"Alexander!" yet another voice called from the crowd. Bloods, we were popular today. And why was everyone presuming *he* was out, anyway?

A white-haired woman pushed her way to us through the frenzied shifters. It was the beautiful Lady Yulia.

"Yulia?" I questioned. This was the last place I expected to see her—especially at a time like this. "What in Bloods are you doing here?"

"Your father sent for me to… to check on you," she wheezed, dabbing at her sweaty, slender neck. At her heels were Ringëd, with his pet ferret clinging to his shoulder, and a newcomer: an elk shifter with spiked, bowing antlers. *Wait a moment, I know him.*

"Jimmy?" I pointed dumbly. He'd been the Dreamcatcher from Lindel, the one who'd helped us quiet the rioting townspeople. "What are *you* doing here?"

Willow smacked her brow and gasped. "Oh, I'd forgotten! Ringëd called while we were in the Messenger Care Clinic, Jimmy is looking for—"

"Tell me later!" I shook my head and turned to Yulia. "Find shelter indoors with Jimmy," I said, giving Chai to her, the raven croaking in protest. "And please watch after him for me?"

The Catcher fumbled with the raven, but secured her grip as best she could, thankfully with great care.

I glanced at Ringëd. "I suggest you accompany them, Officer. Neither are armed."

Ringëd's stare flattened at me. "All I've got is a Shotri. That won't exactly kill any Fera."

"It can still fend them off if you need to escape. But—actually," I paused and turned to Vendy, who'd recovered from being flattened and had drawn her Crystal sword beside Prince Cayden. "Vendy, lend them your blade."

She glanced from her sword to Ringëd, rumbling a reluctant grumble, and tossed her weapon at Ringëd's feet in a clatter.

I clapped a hand over my eyes. "It's a figure of *speech*, Vendy... just go with them."

"Oh." She quickly grabbed her sword again and grinned. "Right."

I sighed, plucking the scythe-spheres from the chain around my neck, having my scythes materialize. Willow drew out her long-handled scythe, and Lilli followed suit, readying her dual-blades as Octavius hurried to grab a handful of throwing-scythes from the holsters at his legs.

"All right," I called to the group. "If there are no more interruptions, everyone, move...! Er, out..."

I belatedly noticed two figures lingering behind Yulia. One was a child; a winged boy donning a red-and-black scarf. He looked vaguely familiar. *Hadn't we seen him in Lindel, before the leveling?* Alongside him was a goat-horned man, his grin disconcertingly wide as he caught my gaze.

I turned to Yulia, pointing at them with a scythe. "They shouldn't be here," I said. "Get them somewhere safe."

The child tugged my arm. "Wait...! Ya have to get outta town!" The boy had a small crow resting on his head, the bird dipped up and down urgently. *Ah, that's right, he'd had that messenger back in Lindel.*

The child looked skeletal and starved, his boney grip quivering over my sleeve. "Come on," he pleaded, looking ripe to bawl. "Ya gotta come with us, Uncle Xavier. It's the only good way."

"Listen to him, Howllord," grunted the goat-horned man who stood next to the child. He stepped in front. "He knows much of—"

"By Shel's grace!" Prince Cayden blurted and shoved me aside. By Gods, the man was almost in tears. "Linus?"

The goat, Linus, gripped hands with the prince, the two sharing a heartfelt embrace like long lost friends. "Cayden," Linus chuckled, though it was half-hearted. He seemed more concerned about the hysteria encircling us. Still, he murmured absently, "Or, I suppose, my Lord Servant. It's been a while."

"You Bloody fool!" Cayden wiped at his eyes with a thumb. "It's been nine Bloody years! Of all the times for you to come back, you choose now?"

"I haven't time to explain, my friend." The goat trotted ahead and waved all of us on. "Come, we mustn't dally. War is upon us."

I groaned, and jabbed a scythe toward the encroaching wave of demons. "Yes, we're *aware*, thank you."

"I don't speak of the Fera," Linus contradicted. "No Reapers shall fall this day, by the claws of the Necrofera."

I frowned. "Excuse me?"

"If you wish for answers, you need only ask the owl." Linus gestured to the winged child. "He's Seen your fate, should you stay here."

I didn't move my attention from the man. Then I asked, "Who exactly are you?"

"He is High Roarlord Linolius Renneguard," Cayden answered for him, his toothy smile stretched wide. "He's one of the Seers who told me of you when we were young, Howllord."

"One of three Seers, at the present," murmured Linus curiously. "I've Seen your present; little Oliver, your future. As for your past... well, I believe that's him there." He glanced at Ringëd, who exchanged a skeptical glance with the ferret on his shoulder.

The child, Oliver, suddenly flexed his wings and flapped past me. He landed in front of Lilli, making her gasp when he grabbed her hand. "Come on, Mama!" Oliver urged. "We gotta go!"

Lilli wrenched her hand free, befuddled. "What did you call me?"

"Mama, come on!" Oliver whined, tugging at her skirt. "*Please* come on?"

"Use your eyes, you mangy little grub," Lilli scowled. "I'm no one's moth..." Oliver started crying. His piercing wails made her cringe and clasp her ears. "A-All right, fine! By the Gods, how can someone so small make such a sound—!"

A black, fanged creature slammed into a tin wastebasket from the mouth of an alley, its slithering skin spraying from the impact and squirming back to the beast like disgusting slugs.

"They're here!" I roared.

The Fera locked its sights on the wailing child, shrieked in wild excitement, and scrambled for Oliver.

Lilli snatched the boy with an arm, sidestepped around the charging demon and *ripped* one of her blades into creature's chest, its NecroSeam giving an audible *snap*. The corpse thudded at her feet and Oliver clung to her neck, sobbing still, black blood evaporating off his cheeks.

"*Bloody Death!*" Alex cursed from my thoughts. "*Xavier, look! The hospital, from your peripherals!*"

My head whipped to the building. Winged Fera swarmed the hospital's outer balconies, shattering windows as screams curdled from inside. One scream in particular was familiar.

"Bianca!" Alex and I breathed, my brother swiftly taking control. He bolted for the hospital. "Bianca…!"

His arm was seized by Linus and he twisted back, glaring at the goat.

The man didn't loosen his grip, his Dream mark gleaming from his arm as his eyes grew stale. "The Lady Bianca is safe," he said. "She's being taken to a secured bunker. There are many Reapers guarding her and the other doctors."

Alex glowered at Linus. "You Saw this in a vision?"

Linus nodded. "She will be safe. Though, I can't say the same for Lord Jaq."

Alex cursed, shoving a hand over the Seer's chest. "Where is he?"

"Alex," Willow gasped behind us suddenly.

Alex whirled, a growl burning his throat as he scowled at the disguised Death Princess. "*What?*"

His anger dampened. Willow's back was turned, gazing at the city's skyline, a hand cupped to her lips.

He followed her eyes to a clock tower's roof.

There, a girl stood poised and watchful, keeping hold of an iron spire as she danced over the shingles. The Necrofera swarmed round her as she waved her free hand, mock orchestrating an intricate musical piece for an opera.

It wasn't Cilia.

Long, white hair thrashed about in the wind, a black dress clinging to a pale body as a long scythe glinted in the moonlight. There on the roof, orchestrating civilian deaths…

Was Willow.

Everyone came to surround us, seeing Willow perched on the tower, commanding the Fera beneath her.

"Uh." Octavius looked at our own, disguised Willow. "Why are there two of you?"

"It's an illusion," growled Willow, her voice curdled. "Cilia wants everyone to think *I'm* ordering the Necrofera."

"Mother of Death." Alex cursed. "We've walked into another ploy of theirs. What do we…"

Willow darted back the way we came, heading for the clock tower.

"Damn it all!" Alex muttered, and bounded after her, Lilli following from the skies.

14

THE LOST FATHER

~~~~~~

OCTAVIUS

Great!

I chucked one of my throwing-scythes at a demon, hitting it square in the chest and killing it with my poison Hallows.

Just Bloody great!

I was dead in the middle of the warzone, huddled with the only people who weren't equipped to kill demons worth a damn—well, except for Vendy, but the others just ditched us—and I was running low on ammo.

I was also holding this stupid, extra raven, and Shade was losing it on my head. The new bird's wings were clipped, like Chai's, so I guessed he couldn't fly away, but thankfully Shade hurried to perch on Yulia's shoulder to keep out of my way. The *annoying* bird didn't want to leave. I had to pry him from my arm to get him off—and winced when his sharp talons seared my skin open. A tingling sensation radiated from the bleeding cuts, static festering as the prickling senses from my Infeciovoking detected germs.

Damn this stupid bird!

I ignored the pain and shoved the new bird to the antlered Catcher, Jimmy. He wasn't doing anything anyway. "Keep this guy away from me for a sec!" I hollered.

Jimmy fumbled with the raven, but did his best to keep it pinned.

I flung four throwing-scythes at two Fera coming for me, coating them with infection Hallows. When they hit the Fera, they crumpled in pained howls and dropped. When they were dead, I plucked the scythes from their chests to keep what little ammo I had left.

Vendy and I kept the things back as we all bolted inside the nearest building, two of the Tesler siblings—Herrin and Rolen—barricading the doors with furniture and boxes.

I fumbled to the window, watching the frenzy between Reapers and demons. Out in the distance, the Death Princess—I mean Cilia?—was still perched on that tower's spire, a black blur of boney figures circling her like a dense squall.

My eyes narrowed at the disguised demon; at my ancestor. Then I bolted up the stairs, heading for the roof.

"Tavius!" Ringëd called after me from below. "Where're you going?!"

"I'll be right back!" I called down. "There's something I've got to do…! Keep everyone safe with Vendy while I'm gone!"

I ran up the rest of the stairs and threw open the roof door, sprinting to the ledge and leaping onto the next, close-by roof. I thanked Land most of these buildings were crammed together, it would make it easier to travel up here than down in the streets. *I just hope Yulia will keep a close eye on Shade.* I didn't want him coming after me in this mess. Though, part of me was screaming to go back and get him—the part that was shaking—but damn it, I'd rather he stayed *away* from these things.

What did I expect to say when I got to Cilia? I thought as I hopped another roof, this one conical with thick shingles. *Does she even know who I am? Does she know we're related?* I knew this was probably a stupid plan, going to see my murdering ancestor, but I wanted some answers, damn it! She could have killed me in Lindel, but she didn't. *Why?*

When I hopped the next roof…

I stopped, almost slipping off the ledge. There was a man on the next building. A man I *knew*. His bronze skin practically glowed in the setting sunlight, his black hair greasy, chin hidden under thick stubble. His yellow eyes glinted when he saw me.

Piss whatever I was doing.

"Dad?" I absently headed to the edge of my roof. "*Dad…?*"

"Who is that?" he ordered sharply. I hadn't heard that voice in six years, but Bloods could I recognize it anywhere. It was him. It was actually *him*…!

"If this is another trick, Macar," he spat, "you can piss off."

"Dad, I… i-it's me!" I toed the ledge, trying to yank out something—anything—I could possibly say. Of all the times he could have shown up…! "It's Octavius!"

I had a list of questions prepped for years, waiting so long for this… but Gardener sow me, why couldn't I remember any of it?

"Tavius…?" Dad's tone was hollow. He took a step, but stopped himself. He glared at me for a long minute, then jerked his head the other way. "No. Go to Void, Macar."

"Dad, really, i-it's me!" I stupidly pushed a hand to my chest, like I hoped it would somehow make me more believable. "I mean, I know it's been a while, but…!"

Craaaw!

Shade suddenly came out of nowhere and fumbled onto my head. His landing came in too fast, he ended up snagging my hair to keep himself grounded, screeching hysterically.

"O-*ow*!" I pried him off, my scalp stinging bolts. "Damn it, Shade, I told you not to come!"

"It can touch you?"

I snapped back to Dad. His eyes were red now, and I swore it looked like they were welling.

I looked at Shade, keeping the wriggling bird pinned to my stomach. "Uh, what?"

"It can touch you." Dad cupped his mouth, his voice softening. "You're real…?" He stared at Shade. Then he cursed.

"Where're the others?" he asked, panicked. "Are they with you?"

"I… what? Ringëd's here, but everyone else is at home—"

"Go back and get them out of there." He hopped onto the far ledge of his roof, grinning so wide I thought his face would rip open. "If you're out, Macar must be slipping. Get them out while you can, keep them safe. I'll come and find you."

He leapt off, catching himself on an awning before jumping onto the street and breaking into a run.

"Dad!" I hurried down an iron ladder nearby and sprinted after him—

A flock of Fera scrambled for me.

In a reflex, I plucked two throwing scythes from my holsters and shot them at the nearest demon, both sinking into its chests, where my infection Hallows spidered.

Its friends came after me, but Shade soared down, shrieking at the dripping creatures. They stopped cold, looking at my white-cheeked raven with bright, white eyes. Then, for some reason, they left. They just Bloody *left*!

"Dad…" I looked after where he'd vanished, my brow furrowing. "What's going on?"

15

TWIN PRINCESSES

~~~~

WILLOW

My doppelganger waited above me on the looming tower, clinging to the long spire and swinging herself in playful circles round the conical roof. Her white hair—*my* hair—streamed in the gentle gusts, the scene oddly serene considering the ruin that lay beneath her.

She obsessively searched the streets for something, her hands languidly tossing flames at the homes below as if the city was nothing more than a pile of wooden blocks a child had built, and she the destructive older sister.

"Cilia!" I roared up, scythe poised at my side. My lungs were coated in the thickening plume, but I mustered as much breath as I could. "This ends now!"

Cilia glanced down, her head cocking at me. With a frown, she skipped off the roof and dropped, the ground cracking on impact, a nearby fixture of charred wood splintering apart and coughing up a dust of bright embers.

She crouched there at the center of the fractured road, staring at me. With *my* azure eyes.

"You know my name?" Cilia asked. Her—*my*—pale face was crossed with suspicion. "I don't believe we've met… did I kill someone you knew?"

Death, I thought, a chill shivering my nerves, *it's like looking in a mirror*.

"Remove that illusion at once!" I commanded and flung off my earcuff. My ashen hair bled into its true color, the bell tinkling from its ribbon. "I'll not have Fera scum defile my name!"

"Ah, Her Highness Death!" I watched myself—Cilia—chuckle. "Now, isn't this interesting? We match."

"Not for long, we won't. I am ending this now."

"So sorry dear, but you're rather late. Admirable work ethic, though, truly. Gold star for you."

"Go Cleanse yourself, you dead bitch—"

Someone flew from the sky and *cracked* to the ground beside me. It was... Kurrick?

Ana was in his arms, she must have used her Terravoking to bring them here, as she'd done with me. When Ana was set on her feet, she stood dutifully beside Kurrick, who withdrew the swords from his back, the blades shining gold and stretching longer, and scrutinized me.

"Death had been wearing gold before this," he said, looking at my silken, golden garbs. He grunted. "It was foolhardy to run off alone, Daughter of Myra. Your mother would have our heads if you met your end under our care."

"As if I'm in need of another's care," I muttered.

"Willow!" Lilli suddenly called from above. My Aide touched down and eyed me warily. "Injuries?"

"None," I reported, amending ruefully, "save for my reputation."

Alexander, or maybe Xavier, came running to my other side. I studied his mismatched eyes, taking note that Alexander was in control.

"Is it she?" Alex questioned, panting. "Is it Cilia?"

I nodded, and yet another scuffle sounded behind. Octavius came panting over, sweat coating his face and staining his clothes. His cat ears were grown and all but latched to his dripping neck.

Cilia's eyes lit up when he arrived.

She ripped off a necklace that had been sparkling from her throat and tossed it aside. Her false features dissolved, the usual grey haired, tanned girl revealed, her white pupils gleaming within green irises. That necklace must have been what held the illusion, I guessed.

Cilia swerved around the rest of us and came to a dead halt before Octavius.

"Descendant!" She bubbled, snatching Octavius's hand. "You had me so worried, I'd looked everywhere...! Oh, come, come! You may stay with me. You'll be safe from those bumbling ink stains and..."

Octavius jerked his hand free, looking disgusted. "Get away from me."

Death, Octavius! Could he be asking for his death any plainer?

I prepped my scythe, expecting her to rage, but she remained where she was, her shoulders slacking. By the Gods, she looked heartbroken.

"Descendant..." Her voice faltered. "Please. You've nothing to fear. You carry my blood."

"So what?" he spat, drawing out his slender sickle. The blade radiated a soft blue light over his fingers. "Your blood's rotten anyway...!"

I saw his hands yield to the slightest tremor, but commendably, he kept it stifled.

Cilia's throat tightened—and my grip did likewise on my scythe. If she snapped, I'd have to reach her before she reached Octavius.

"If…" she began, her voice a hollow quiver. "If that is your decision, then I…" She fell silent. Then her next glare was nothing short of feral, resolve rekindled. "No…! If my absence risks your death, I'll not allow it! I'm keeping my family safe—"

"Get *back*!" Octavius's hand burst with black veins, the sticky threads crawling over his sickle and blotting out its light.

He slashed for her and she ducked to the side, but he managed to slice her arm.

She screamed, clutching the wound, staring in horror at the black veins that were slow to fade.

"That Hallows…" She was trembling. "We have such an element in our blood…?"

An opportunity! I bolted past Octavius, driving my crooked blade into her back. She shrieked and ripped out my weapon, snarling at me.

"Stay away from him!" I sneered, displaying my sharpened teeth.

Her joints unhinged and cracked as she crouched from a safer distance, stealing a final glance at Octavius. Her cat ears curled. "Fine." she rumbled. "I see I've overstayed my welcome…" She rose and brushed her hair aside, releasing an airy sigh. "While I do enjoy playing with you all, I'm afraid I must retire. I did aught for my part, regardless. But I'll find you again, Descendant." She flashed Octavius an intent gaze. "I'll see you safe with me yet…"

She sauntered into the mass of her retreating horde.

"No you don't!" I roared, diving into the horde and cutting down the flock that blocked my way. But I soon found myself swinging at empty air. The Fera were making a wide perimeter around me, retreating with their queen, but avoiding my bubble at all costs.

I whipped my gaze round the mass, straining to find that damned queen, but she was nowhere to be seen. The Fera dissipated from the roads, scampering out of the alleys, surfacing from the sewers… Within mere moments, they were gone. All that was left were the shriveled corpses and mangled skeletons of the fallen.

I threw down my scythe, the weapon clattering over the ash-flooded cobblestones. "Nira hang it all!"

16
WARCRIES

LUCAS

My com chirped in alarm from my doublet's pocket. Befuddled, I pulled it out, its gears turning and the screen projecting to life. A name was scrawled across the screen of light: *Thateus*. My vassal and private butler from our manor in Grim.

Da'torr, I heard Thateus's voice sound from my thoughts. My vassal was channeling our mental connection instead of waiting for me to answer the call. *His Majesty Death is on hold for you. I've redirected his call here. He stressed urgency.*

My bones iced. Serdin was calling?

"Excuse me," I said to Alice and the shivering King Galden, moving to the back corner of the room while my wife kept an eye on him.

Clearing my throat, I answered the call. The com's gears clicked and warbled as the face of a pale man appeared on screen. His hair was ashen and his eyes were emptily white, grey rings surrounding the irises. A silver skull-crown sat atop his head, and his cleanly shaven jaw was set hard.

"Lucas," the Death King rumbled. *"Good, you're available. Are you alone?"*

"No, my lord."

"Be so."

I glanced at Galden, curtly motioning for him to leave. "My king wishes to speak in private. If you leave this hall, Galden, so help me, I will have my vassal roast you alive."

The pitiful man nodded rigidly, glancing at Alice before he took his leave.

Turning back to the screen, I shivered at Serdin's tight expression. *He knows something*, I realized. Gods help me, had he learned his daughter was missing?

I cleared my throat again, the cords incredibly dry now. "It is solely Alice and I now, my lord, if this suits you?"

"It does," he said. *"Myra tells me you have my daughter. I wish to verify her good health."*

Blast it all! Right to the point... I'd forgotten the Death Queen's visions were strong.

"She... escaped during the chaos in Lindel, my lord," I said, using the same excuse I'd used to lead the other knights astray. "Forgive me, Sire, we're trying everything to find her again."

Serdin frowned. *"Escaped? Myra tells me she's with your son. Is he not with you either?"*

"Of course he is, my lord, but Alexander tells me her highness had—"

"I don't mean Alexander," he interrupted. *"I hear Willow is with Xavier. Myra claimed he was with you, in New Aldamstria."*

"I... Xavier, my lord...?" I feigned shock. "Xavier is dead, Sire. Perhaps the queen has mistaken—"

"She is sure there's no mistake, I've asked countless times, believe you me. You may not have been aware. Your son is alive... And Willow has apparently found him."

"I... I'm not sure what to say..." A distraction—I needed a distraction. "This is perhaps the worst opportunity to tell us. Sire, you may be on the brink of war with Everland."

He took the bait, stiffening. *"What?"*

Alice pushed to her feet, explaining for me. "Sire, we've discovered King Galden has been ordering his Rockraiders to steal our scythes, and they've used them to do our duties. He has neglected to file reports of Fera attacks, and has been responsible for the capture and torture of countless messengers here on the surface."

Serdin's horrified face sported deep creases. *"What in the Bloody—"*

The door burst open, and King Galden stormed in, shouting, "What is the meaning of this?!" The man blustered over and flicked on a large vision-screen that was embedded in the wall.

On the screen, the Death Princess was standing tall over a spiked tower. *Cackling.* She looked to be ordering a flurry of Necrofera upon the town. The camera angle was upright, as if it were lying on the ground and zoomed on Willow. The lens had been cracked and spattered with blood.

"You dare come to my kingdom...!" Galden shook with rage, causing the looped bracelets around his wrists to rattle. "Accuse me of seeking war, and send your own princess to slaughter my people?!"

Serdin gaped from my com screen, looking at the reports himself. *"Illusions!"* He slammed a fist on the desk he sat before. *"That is not my daughter...! Willow is highly acrophobic—!"*

"I will not allow my kingdom to suffer your kind a moment longer!" spat Galden—and in a flurry, gold-armored guards clattered inside, their swords drawn at the ready.

Hang me, he must have gathered them the moment we let him out! A foolish oversight on our part.

Cursing, Alice and I plucked the spheres from our neck-chains, drawing out our weapons. I thrust my long-handled scythe in front of me as Alice held the chain connecting her dual blades taut, adjusting her footing.

When the king fled down the hall, his knights charged.

"Nathaniel!" I shouted, driving my scythe's crooked blade into one man's breast plate.

Alice plunged both her blades into a second and third man's neck. "Aiden! Return!"

A new Raider charged forward—but an arrow shot into his skull.

Thank Nira! Under the doorway were our vassals: Nathaniel and Aiden. Thank Nira we thought to resurrect them before this. We knew a contingency plan was needed if this conference didn't go well. It seemed our preparation paid off.

My vassal, Nathaniel, cracked his burly knuckles, his hands bursting with flames as his Death mark gleamed white from his thick neck. "Got a bit o' trouble there, don't ye, *Da'torr?*"

Beside him, Aiden kept his crossbow aimed at the remaining four guards with one hand while the other wielded a Shotri. "The next man to lift so much as a nail to my Mistress," began Aiden, his brown-and-red wings giving a threatening flap, "becomes my personal pincushion!"

"Aye," grunted Nathaniel—

A knight's curved blade slid through Nathaniel's chest from behind, and the bear's eyes grew dim. He dropped to his knees before thunking to the floor, blood pooling around his corpse.

"Sloppy, Nathaniel," I chided in a low rumble, evoking my death Hallows over his slowly aging skin and bones.

The surrounding men let out disgusted gasps as my Hallows seeped into the dead bear's muscles, his skin regenerating. Within seconds, Nathaniel was on his feet again, and he twisted round to pluck the still-stuck sword out of his back.

He turned to the man who'd felled him, cocked an eyebrow—then sank a leaded fist into the man's nasal cavity, a *crack* sounding as the fellow crumpled to the floor.

Nathaniel hefted his new, bloodied blade over a shoulder, his free hand igniting into flames. "We're already dead, lads." His laughter seemed to rattle their legs. "Kill us, and we're commin' right back. Now unless ye lot got a trick like that up yer sleeve…"

The guards hesitated, one smelling like he'd soiled himself. Slowly, they each lowered their arms, sidling against the wall toward the exit until they reached the halls, whereupon they broke into a terrified run and shouted for reinforcements.

Nathaniel came to look me over, his bear ears folding. "Ye in one piece, *Da'torr?*"

"At the moment," I said, snatching the com I'd dropped during the fight. Serdin's face still gazed helplessly from the screen of light.

"Sire," I addressed while leading the way through the corridors. "I do hate to cut our call short, but—"

"Find my daughter!" he ordered, white wolf ears curled. *"And Gods help us, gather the troops!"*

17

LOST COMRADES

~~~~~

XAVIER

I sprinted through the ruins of the Reaper district, hurrying back to where we'd left the others.

Many rattled citizens were now shuffling out of their homes, peeking through their shutters to see if all was clear at last. Reapers rushed here and there, tending to the wounded and the dead, searching for any wandering souls that may be lurking and in need of help.

The crowds quieted when we passed, their gazes latched on Willow, who strode at my side *without* her disguise.

"She doesn't look as she did on the Screens," I heard a merchant woman murmur to her neighbor. Her smock was in tatters, ash and grime layered thick on her cheeks. "Why is it different?"

"A trick, to be sure," grumbled the neighbor, looking troubled while wiping his dirtied brow with a cloth. He hacked into it next, muttering. "I says the Fera have a Decepiovoker in their midst. One of the Wakened dead, from the tales."

"You think?"

"Aye. If that be Death, no chance she'd be all the way up there on that tower. They says Death never fancied no heights, not one incarnation."

I saw Willow's fox ears sag, a growl rupturing. "Brilliant. My damned phobia is my single voucher."

I muttered. "Better than nothing."

She sent me a blazing glare, and I kept my tongue sharply bitten. I turned to Octavius, who was glancing over his shoulder, seeming intent on a search. Was he looking for Jaq?

—Jaq. Blast it all, Jaq!

"Dalen," I called, tapping into both our vassals' connection lines. "Vendy, report. Any casualties?"

None from our group, came Vendy's reply.

"Location?"

Dalen answered that one. *Right in front of you.*

My head snapped up. Dalen was there waving at us, the others huddled behind him.

"What the Void happened?" Dalen asked when I caught up. "Did they just leave?"

"It was a ploy," I said. "They were merely here to kill anyone moving, except us, I think."

Willow spat next to me. "Cilia wanted to make sure the Everlanders blamed the Reapers for this."

"Any sign of Jaq?" I asked Dalen hurriedly. "We didn't see him in the streets."

Dalen shook his head. "If he came by here, we didn't see him."

The goat man from before, Linus I believed, came to clasp my shoulder. His eyes glazed at the touch, his Dream mark gleaming from his arm, and before long, he said, "Jaq is safe for now. He's on his way here."

Had he just had a vision of it?

That winged child fluttered out of Yulia's arms and went straight to Lilli, tugging her skirt. "Come on, Mama, we gotta get him and go! We're gonna lose him!"

Lilli raised a brow at the boy. "Lose him to what? The demons are gone, little urchin—"

Sirens blared again, but this time they were accompanied by a fizzling voice.

"Noble citizens of Everland," it boomed, *"This is First Fangs Basin, chief general of the valiant Land King Galden. The Death King and his Reapers have soiled their agreement to keep peace with our fair country. This act of terrorism has been dubbed a declaration of war. All Grim peoples and those who show them sympathy will be imprisoned or killed if caught within our borders. I repeat: we are at war. Prepare, and hold strong. Repeat: we are at war. Prepare, and hold strong..."*

JAQ

"Repeat: we are at war. Prepare, and hold strong..."

"Well, crap!" I muttered, holding Bridge tighter. We bounded through town to find the others, the war announcement stuck on a loop and echoing at every corner building.

Rockraiders stormed the district now, trying to advance through the last-minute blockade of Reapers who desperately tried to keep them out of the district's residential block. Grimlings and Grimlette's alike were scurrying out of town while they could. I saw whole families hauling luggage out of their homes and high tailing it out of there.

Most were heading for the Surfacing Port at the mountain's geysers, thinking they could hop back down to Grim before they were caught. I doubted that was going to work. If Grandad was right, Galden probably made plans to shut the port down before this.

I ducked into an alleyway, keeping Bridge secured against my chest. I felt the crow's little heart beating furiously, her wings squirming against my grip.

"Sorry, girl," I hushed, stopping to catch my breath behind a dumpster. "No flying right now. Got to keep you safe and out of the skies."

On the way here, I nearly had a heart attack when I saw the bastards snatching up messengers—even killing some, if the birds were too violent. There was no way in Death I'd let that happen to my Bridge.

But now what? I sucked in a breath, vigorously rubbing my face, trying to think faster. Master and Mistress were in conference with the king during all this, weren't they? If Everland just declared war, then what happened to them at the palace? My guess was, they were either locked up, dead or getting the Void out of here. Hopefully it was the last one, and if so, the rest of us needed to follow their example.

But where are the twins? Yep. Priority One set.

Seeing that the coast still wasn't clear on the open streets, I ducked into the back alleys and sprinted on.

XAVIER

Shockspheres zipped and sparked from every direction, citizens scrambling out of homes and shops to escape the Raiders who now stormed into the district.

I bustled beside Willow, all of us following Linus and the disguised Prince Cayden through the frenzy. Above us, Lilli flew with Dalen and his siblings. They were shooting spheres at the winged Raiders.

Little Oliver flew at Lilli's skirts, seeming panicked when he fell even an inch behind her—

A winged Raider was sliced in the throat by a combating Reaper, and the man's corpse slammed into Oliver, the boy's wings crushed as he and the corpse spiraled toward the streets.

Horrified, Lilli put away her scythes and dove for the child, catching him—but a grounded Raider shot a sphere the moment Lilli touched the ground. Both she and Oliver collapsed, spasming on the stones. The Raider looked pleased with himself, reaching to collect them.

Before I could do it myself, someone cracked a fist at the Raider's face. The Raider clutched his now bloody nose, bewildered, and the scaled newcomer scooped up the unconscious child and helped Lilli to her feet.

"Jaq!" I panted. "Where have you been?"

"Busy!" the viper shouted, lugging Oliver at his side as he and Lilli hurried to lead us in a different direction. "Story time later! Run now—"

Kshat!

Jaq was hit with a Shocksphere in the side, both he and Oliver flung to the ground with lightning shocking their limbs.

"Jaq!" I bolted for him, but jerked back to avoid a new stream of Shockspheres. The moment my foot stepped back, it caught someone's corpse and I stumbled into the wrecked bed of a wooden cart, biting down a yell when one of the splintered planks drove into my right tricep. I plucked it out, the splinters soaked red, and felt around the wound to yank out a small piece that was still stuck—

Crunch!

Something glass-like broke under my boot. I lifted my foot and found a pair of eyeglasses lying there, one of the lenses cracked. My brow furrowed as I snatched them up to examine the ripple-like runes that were etched in the frames. They were runes that *I* had etched, years ago.

These are Jaq's. They must have been thrown off his face when he was hit with the spheres.

A scream sounded, wrenching my grown wolf ears straight up. That had sounded like Lilli.

I pocketed the eyeglasses and fumbled around the broken cart, ducking away from a pair of Raiders that nearly slammed into me—and I found Lilli laying on the other side of the street.

She was lying beside Jaq and the young Oliver, all littered with electric static that snapped about their limbs, their muscles spasming violently.

A cluster of Raiders surrounded them. The three were knocked out with sharp cracks to their skulls, then tossed in a barred wagon that was already brimming with prisoners.

Crack!

The steersman at the wagon's bench whipped the feral horses into action, their hooves bursting over the stones as they hauled the hovering wagon down the hill and out of sight.

I shoved after them, but a squad of Raiders blocked my path. I was forced back when one swung an axe at me, then another took aim at my head with a Shotri. I lurched and side-stepped as the Shockspheres whistled past, and a second squad of Footrunners came bounding after me.

Then, someone snagged my arm and yanked me into an alley. I spun and raised my scythes, but saw it was only Linus.

"This way," he directed, motioning for me to follow with an urgent hand while he started into the backstreets.

I stood where I was, puffing. "They have Jaq and Lilli!"

"We will retrieve them." He doubled back to seize my wrist. "The path to them is thick with Raiders."

"Then we'll find another!"

"They all lead to *death*." He halted, turning on me, the beads in his dreaded hair clattering when he shook his head. "Jaq and Lilli won't be recognized by these Raiders. What awaits them is imprisonment. But you, Howllord, *will* be known. What awaits you is death, should they catch you. You'll be of no use to your friends if you're dead."

My hands balled, wolf ears folding. "I…"

"Your head is now the most profitable bounty in Everland," he emphasized. "The son of Lucas Devouh will be Galden's greatest asset. Give him what he wants, and we've lost this war."

Damn it… Damn it, damn it, damn it, damn it, damn it…!

Biting down a string of curses, I followed Linus through the backstreets.

18

CONTRIVED COUNCIL

~~~~~

SERDIN

WEEKS AFTER

"Any sign of her?" I asked Lucas through my portable com's projected screen, stepping through my palace's orchards alongside my wife. We'd arrived home this morning and were roaming the grounds to decompress. Such was our personal welcoming gift, one could say. The Seamstress knew I needed it. "Even a whisper?"

"None, my lord," Lucas reported. His sapphire eyes grew dim as he slid the helm from his skull. He and Alice were hours away from our first siege attempt on the surface. Our target was High Drinelle, the city directly above Lucas's home in the caverns. Lucas was certainly dressed for battle, but his hesitant expression and heavy tone suggested otherwise as he shook his head. *"Alice and I haven't even heard anything of our son since the first attack at the capital..."*

I gave a dismal sigh, my head weighing heavy. "I see... please, Lucas, if you hear anything, let me know immediately."

He nodded, and I ended the call, pocketing my com.

"No sign of Willow?" Myra asked beside me, worry absent from her humming tone.

"None," I said, feeling the urge to rip the hairs out of my scalp. "Bloods, I don't know what to be more concerned over: My missing daughter, our new war with Everland, or Rojired's blatant insults *and* accusations regarding his own missing heirs." I drew out a long breath. Obviously, my first priority was to my daughter. But there was little I could do down here, so far away from her. The fact that no news had cropped up was certainly a good sign. Galden's soldiers hadn't caught her yet, but that did nothing for my nerves. To top it all off, Sky King Rojired had to use her as the subject for his finger-pointing.

"One of these days, Myra, I fear I'll kill Rojired myself," I muttered, stalking ahead in the palace orchards. Rojired was truthfully farther down the list of priorities, but somehow, the subject seemed more relaxing by comparison. I swatted away a low hanging branch, keeping it peeled back to let Myra pass as well. "I'll Bloody kill him. I don't care if he's going to die before I have to Reap his Gods damned soul. When he dies, I'll resurrect him so I can kill the bastard again myself."

Myra strode ahead, plucking a pale, green apple from a branch and inspected it for blemishes. "Honestly, Serdin," Myra murmured, turning her apple in hand. "Would killing the man make you feel any better?"

"Yes," I said, folding my arms over a branch. "In fact, it would."

She tucked a strand of greying, azure hair behind her ear. "Then at least be sure the man is clothed when you resurrect him, hm? A king on his second deathbed ought to keep his dignity."

She bit into the apple, then gave an impish chuckle and pressed the fruit over my own lips. Sighing, I took a bite, taking it in hand while chewing on the tart piece. A refreshing breeze ruffled the trees, the cool air washing over my heated skin. Small wisps of steam slithered from my bare arms, my sleeves rolled up, my Pyrovoker's internal heat ever boiling.

Myra wore a casual, ebony gown, though wrapped around her shoulders was a warm, fur coat. Her breath was thick with fog, her hollowed cheeks painted in a most becoming red as she yielded to a tremor.

I ducked under the branch and reeled her in, warming her. "Nearly twenty years, yet still, you find my caves so cold?"

She gave a wan smile. "I was raised in a void without temperature. There was no heat, nor was there cold. I'm afraid I shall never acclimate here without a fire-brewer."

"Then best you stay close to one, hadn't you darling?"

She placed a thin hand over mine, her delicate knuckles dwarfed by comparison. I never understood how bones could differ so incredibly. And strange how the older we grew, the more prominent our skeletons gleaned under our skin.

Stranger yet, I could never quite fathom how age only made this creature more beautiful. Myra was a serene, reflective pool. When undisturbed, her smooth surface was as radiant and clear as the finest crystal. But with the slightest touch of a Fallen Light on its waters, the gentle ripples left you entranced.

I cupped her chin, losing myself in the depths of those azure pools of hers. "Why is it," I said, my mood growing dismal, "after how hard we've worked to make the world look past our lineages, we still have challenges to hurdle? Haven't we finished with these trifles?"

"It would seem we haven't," she sighed, her arms circling my waist. "Do you ever wonder if we've made a mistake…?"

I snorted. "Never."

"But Rojired raised questions I hadn't considered. Willow's Hallows are weakened due to her sheer number of elements. And since she's the first hybrid among the Lines, we have no way of knowing how this will affect her children, and their children, and…"

"Myra," I hushed, taking her hand. "You've been listening to my brother again. Our blood does not define us. It's merely a tool to keep our hearts beating and our bodies warm. Nira has no use for it. It is our souls which the Seamstress stitches to these empty vessels that matter."

I released her and sank my claws into the bitten apple, prying it apart near the center. The seeds within did not make their star pattern, but had split two to three on either half. I placed one piece in Myra's open palm, and the second in my own. "They say destined lovers are those of the same soul, split and cast apart into different vessels." I brought my half of the apple over hers, our fingertips meeting along with the pieces. "I found the rest of my soul when you popped into existence at my doorstep, Myra. And damn me, Rojired—and one day my brother—will respect us and our cherished daughter."

For the first time in a long while, the woman blushed. A rare sight these days.

We sat on the soft grass, sharing the apple and watching the servants bustle about the orchard and back vineyard. The palace had been hectic since we arrived this morning. Our welcoming home may as well have been an afterthought to the personnel.

Unsurprising, I thought. In the time Myra and I had been in Culatia, Willow had disappeared and we'd gone to war with Everland. Obviously, the servants and guards were still frantically making preparations. They were so deep in their work that many didn't even notice we'd returned.

Except, of course, for Morice and Conrad; my master servant and head vassal.

I saw the two men were approaching us from the stone pathways now, looking rather frantic.

"S-S-Sire!" Morice squeaked, his double chin quivering as the thick man failed to tame his trembling limbs. He seemed to have lost a bit of his hairline since I'd left. He clutched a notepad and quill tight to his chest, the nub quivering over the paper. "The reporters have been slinking through the gates left and right to get a statement on the war!"

"And on the princess!" added Conrad's antlered ghost feverishly. "We declared she was traveling overseas as you asked, but the public is in a riot over why!"

Myra sighed and tucked another strand of blue hair behind an ear, keeping a whimsical smile that I suspected was merely for their benefit. "Tell them we'll hold a press conference," she instructed, "first thing tomorrow morning."

Morice scribbled it down furiously, then crossed two 't's and turned about to take off. But then he seemed to recall something and spun on his heels. "Also, er, Your Majesty…" he said, his throat sounding dry. "There's been an immediate summons for you in the Court. They requested your presence the moment you returned, and demand that you place your vote on a new bill."

I scratched the coarse scruff on my neck, rumbling. "What new bill?"

"They wouldn't say until you arrived. But they stressed urgency. They're all gathered and waiting for you at court in town."

I rubbed my stinging eyes. Thank Death I was back in the caves and away from that blistering 'sun'… "I'll be in tomorrow," I said. "It's been… a long trip, Morice. I wish to rest."

He swallowed and fished into his coat pocket, pulling out a crinkled, sweat-ridden scroll that was tied with a black ribbon. It held the Court of Lords' insignia: a simple script of a C and L.

"I'm afraid they've demanded your attendance *today*, sire," said Morice.

Scowling, I took the scroll, untying the ribbon and rolled it open.

Chanerr yechet wu droh, read the opening salutation,

It is with grave importance that the Court requests His Majesty, Serdin Lyriel Ember V, Lord of Grim and Blessed King of Death, to appear for an immediate review and vote of the proposed bill now under discussion. The Court has placed their votes in turn, though His Majesty's is yet pending.

We await his presence and answer. Urgency is emphasized, as it relates to the fate of the heiress.

Thala wu sheft,

The Court of Lords

My eyes fixed on the last line, reading it again. *As it relates to the fate of the heiress…*

"Morice," I growled, my wolf ears sprouting. "Fetch my court robes and call for the coachman. Send for my Hand."

"Howllord Tessinger is already there, sire." Morice bowed. "He received his own summons an hour ago."

I cursed, shoving to my feet. "Then tell the coachman he is an hour late."

The courtroom rang with voices, the echoing whispers and hushed mutterings bouncing about the domed ceiling.

The rafters and buttresses arched like sharp ribs throughout the marble-dressed building, fogged lamps radiating with Fallen Lights, their brightness so brilliant I was sure they were newly fallen.

I paused under the wide entrance of the room, assessing what I was to face during this session. All representatives seemed to be in attendance, the many Howllords and Howlesses stirring in the benches. The loudest voices filling the room were, as usual, the Lord Scholars, particularly the departments of Evocational and Physical Sciences. The robed lord and lady representing those sects were in another heated argument, both trying to convince the other why no conclusions could be drawn regarding a soul's physicality and why it had any influence on the tangible plane at all.

I smoothed my embroidered, silken robe over my chest and stole a glance at my faint reflection in the glass of a Lord's portrait. My silver crown gleamed in the lamplight from my brow, fitted snugly over my ashen hair. Death, but my eyes were bloodshot. *How much sleep had I lost this past month?* My white irises may as well have been glowing against the redness.

A low whistle sounded, and I turned to the large songcrow that was perched on a lamp. Locke thickened his chest feathers, his sharp head revolving toward the courtroom. He was nervous.

"As am I, Locke," I said, extending an arm to the crow.

Locke climbed onto my arm and gently wrapped his talons over the ebony sleeve. He let out a soft, alto song. Feeling a new sense of calm now that Locke was settled, I crossed the carpeted floor.

The Head of Council, a tall, slender woman with a hawkish face and beaked nose, was shuffling through papers at her podium. She noticed my entry, her glower piercing, then promptly returned to her paperwork.

The lords and ladies hushed and stood, bowing as I made my way toward my risen bench.

My royal Hand, Daniel Tessinger, was seated beside me. "You took your damned time, you ruddy bastard," he grunted quietly.

I sat, letting Locke climb onto the wooden desk before me, he and my Hand's messenger exchanging flutters.

"Had your fill of the councilwoman's harassment, Daniel?" I muttered.

His reply was a sour stare.

I noticed a packet of documents had been placed on my desk. Sighing, I produced my reading spectacles from my robe's pocket and examined the documents. "What is this nonsense about a new bill, then?"

"You won't like it, Serdin." Daniel's leathery wings fidgeted behind him, flexing and retracting repetitively. He dabbed a kerchief over his sweating brow. "You won't like it one Bloody bit. I would have warned you, but the Head of Council came to me herself and offered to 'escort' me here."

"With a proverbial scythe to your throat, no doubt." I flipped the page of the packet.

So far, all that was written was a list of attending lords, their titles and positions, the traditional salutation of what a pleasure and honor it was to have them with us today, a reminder of the court's rules and regulations, a schedule listing the various proceedings.... Bloods, why were these introductions so arduous?

I murmured to Daniel, "Which page on this Gods' forsaken textbook is the actual—?"

CLACK!

The head councilwoman struck her gavel, the loud bang echoing in the dead silence. "Now in session!" announced the councilwoman at her podium.

She set down the blackwood gavel and patted her pinned up, raven-black hair, primly clearing her throat. Her primary wolf ears swiveled forward as she nodded to me, her tone venomous. "Thank you, Your Majesty, for joining us so soon after your arrival. Your punctuality is most appreciated."

I kept own ears tame, despite them itching to grow hostile as I returned her nod, though tersely. "Your ladyship. What is this about my daughter's fate, exactly?"

A grin cracked her painted lips. "Straight to the matter, then... I am most pleased that my lord performs his duties with such alacrity." When I gave no reply, she went on. "We've recently received news that Her Highness abandoned the palace to surface to High Everland. Is this correct?"

"She did not abandon anything," I said. "Quite the opposite, in fact. My daughter heard news of the Necrofera plague and was driven to assist. She informed me before leaving, and I approved the decision. I've kept in contact with her all the while, and I apologize for the delayed announcement. At the time, I was in council with the other Relicbloods in Culatia, so I felt it was not as crucial."

I glanced at Daniel, who gave me an encouraging nod. Good, I at least sounded sincere. The truth was, I hadn't heard a damned thing from Willow since I left. I only heard of what happened by Myra, then by Daniel, then on the Bloody news when Everland declared war with us. *That blasted girl will have much to answer for when she returns, she can be sure of that.*

The councilwoman placed a pair of spectacles over her nose, scrutinizing the papers on her desk. "And what was the nature of this meeting, may I ask?"

Death, where to start? "In light of his heir's disappearance years ago," I said, "Sky King Rojired recently gave the title of next-in-line to his daughter."

"So I've heard." She tapped a manicured nail over her lacquered podium. "And why was my lord called to council for it?"

"Because his daughter is gone," I explained. "She has… disappeared from the Sky country, just as her brother did."

Chatter erupted in the courtroom, and the councilwoman struck her gavel to demand silence. When the murmurs lowered to hushed whispers, she continued. "Why has she left?"

"We haven't confirmed any answers at the moment," I said, "but King Rojired believes Zylveia went to seek out her brother. Rojired has asked *me* to personally oversee the search effort for his daughter. I predict she'll be found within the mid-realms, perhaps on a Marincian province."

"Pardon my confusion, my lord…" She circled a delicate finger over her temple. "But why do you think that, specifically?"

"This is assuming she *is* looking for her brother," I clarified, "while taking into account that her brother eloped with the Ocean Princess—"

I was drowned by the sudden roar of flabbergasted shouts. The councilwoman pounded away with her gavel, barking for silence so she could address me at a reasonable volume.

"The Sky Prince…" She pushed up her spectacles, gawking at me in disgust. "*Eloped* with a different Relicblood?"

I muttered. "It would seem so."

"Were offspring involved?"

"Not to our knowledge."

She bit her curled finger. "I see why my lord was appointed for this task… This elopement looks most certainly like the indirect result of *your* crossed union with the Dream Princess. If we have another abomination born from this…"

My wolf ears grew despite myself. "Was there a reason for this summons, your ladyship?"

Her eyes fluttered back into focus, and she leafed through the papers before her. "Ah, yes, of course… You see, in the time of your absence, Sire, there's been a proposition. Many of us here wish to lower the age minimum at which an individual will be considered a legal adult in Grim. As a result, this will involve lowering the age minimum of, say… a participant in Death's Duel."

My shoulders jolted stiff. "Excuse me?"

"I said—"

"I heard what you Bloody said. You can't change the age minimum of the Duel. It's been set at age twenty for nearly a century."

"Which is why," she said and kept her voice at a low scratch, her chin raised indignantly. "We believe it's a bit… *outdated*. Most of the lords and ladies here agree, and have cast their votes. To speak true, we already have 4/7th *for* the bill, so it will pass regardless of what my lord votes."

Agreeing murmurs came from the court, some of them passing me apologetic shrugs and others glancing away in shame. I shot a glare at Daniel beside me, and was relieved to see his bitter stare sending me a solid denial.

The councilwoman peered through her lenses over her beaked nose. "Your vote, my lord, is still unanswered."

"As it will remain," I spat.

Her brow cocked, and I saw the hint of a sly grin cross her lips. "Interesting… you thought your daughter mature enough to surface on her own and enter a war, but not to accept duels here at home?"

My retort died.

"Very interesting…" She picked up a quill and dipped it in a bottle of ink. "I suppose even the king thinks her odds in the ring are slim… I'll mark your vote as—"

"Yae!" I barked before her quill nib could drip one blot on the ballot. My wolf ears curled. "I vote yae. My daughter has been prepared to face any challengers since her seventeenth year. I pray swift departures for the fools who wish to cross her."

Her lids turned into slits. I matched her glare twofold.

Soon she huffed and marked my vote, sliding off her spectacles. "Then the law is passed. As for the 'fools' who cross your daughter…" The gaze she cast me blazed with resentment. "Let us hope my dear niece is prepared for what her cousin has in store for her."

She slammed the gavel one last time, dismissing the court. Howllords and ladies rose from the benches and began their lively chatter again, many coming to bow to me and give their sentiments. A good number of those present, it seemed, voted either 'nay', or 'yae', in the belief that Willow was ready. *Death, do I hope so.*

Daniel and I waited for the room to empty. Once I was sure it was clear, I stalked up to the councilwoman, who was now stepping down from her podium. It seemed my ashen-haired brother, Yvan, had come to meet her from the back entrance. Just as well. This was no doubt *both* of their ploy anyway.

"Rovinne, Yvan." My throat clicked. "Whatever grudge you hold against me, you've no right to take it out on my daughter."

Rovinne placed a boney hand on her hip. "That vermin has no right to the throne to begin with. It was only a matter of time before she came of age, regardless."

Yvan's chuckle was a twisted purr. "The only difference now is how much shorter that time is. Thank you, Serdin, for seeing the need for this law."

"Need for it my Bloody ass. How much of the court did you bribe? Wouldn't be the first time, and I doubt it'll be the last, if you wish to see your son on the throne after me."

"That," he smiled. "May be more than a wish, soon enough."

Rovinne let slip a giggle, and I shot her a dangerous glare. "You find the thought of my daughter's death amusing, Rovinne?" I growled.

"Not so much amusing, Serdin," she said, "but more… *satisfying*."

"She was close to being your own daughter once. You wouldn't have found it so satisfying then."

"My own daughter?" Her composure fractured, a scowl creasing her thin face as her voice drained into a disgusted hiss. "You saw that she *wasn't* my daughter, bedding that blue-haired freak…! And during *our* betrothal no less!" She bit back her tone and recomposed herself, examining her manicured nails. "Or perhaps you've forgotten?"

I shuddered, resisting the urge to clutch my groin. "Forgotten?" My laugh was more of a grimace. "Hardly a man in existence is soon to forget having his unmentionables smashed by a candlestick…"

"Perhaps I should have used a fire poker." She muttered. "At least that would have stopped you from making that atrocity you've plagued the Bloodline with. Tell Her Highness she best be prepared when she returns to Grim. I have a feeling the moment she sets a single claw on this soil again…" She and Yvan strode toward the exit. "Grim will have a new heir."

They left, leaving Daniel and I alone in the courtroom.

I slammed a fist against the empty podium. "Damn them! Damn them…!"

Daniel clasped my shoulder. "Serdin, calm yourself. Willow's not home yet."

"She can't come home. It's too soon. She isn't ready…" I whipped my gaze at Daniel. "Daniel—send word to Lucas. If he finds Willow, tell him to keep her away from Grim."

He nodded gravely, leaving to carry out the request. When he was gone, I slammed another fist on the podium. It gave an echoing *thunk*! "Damn it…! I will not lose my daughter like this…!" Another strike at the podium, reddening my knuckles.

"Now that doesn't seem very fair."

I jolted at the boyish voice, which hummed behind me again, scolding, "That poor box did nothing to you, yet you threaten to burden it with holes. For shame, Serdin."

Bloody Void. I groaned and thunked my brow against the wood, rolling my head back to glare at the intruder.

The teenaged boy was reclined over one of the long desks, his propped-up legs crossed and one barefoot bouncing idly as he read through the packet of documents that had been left behind, keeping the papers lifted over his straight nose.

He wore a commoner's baggy sweater, the sunset-orange fabric lacking any sort of luster or ornamentation, as was the case with his loose, brown trousers. His hood was drawn up, a tuft of curly, azure hair spilling over his brow where a crowned Dream mark was displayed. A white-gold crown with foxes etched round the rim had been set aside on the desk by the boy's head, and a less-than-splendid shepherd's crook was leaned against the side. The staff looked like nothing more than a splintered tree branch, a bell tied at the knob with a black ribbon lined in butterflies.

"Dream." I pushed off the podium, walking to the young man. "Where in Death have you been?"

"If I'd been in Death," murmured the boy, still reclined on the desk as he flipped a page in the packet. "I imagine your wife wouldn't exist, and I'd be without my favorite son-in-law."

My stare flattened at him, but if he noticed, he made no comment.

He continued his reading, finally sitting up and dangled one leg over the edge of the desk. He scratched his head under his hood, then brushed a thumb over his lips and flipped another page.

"I suppose the bill was passed, then?" he asked.

I grunted, sinking onto the desks beside him. "It was. I suppose you already Saw it coming, then?"

"Why do you think I told Willow to leave so abruptly?" The skinny boy rubbed a finger under his nose. "Even if I warned you before you left, the result would have been the same. But then there wouldn't have been any delay in the Duel. So, since I had a favor to ask of her anyway, I thought it best she left posthaste."

"I… Thank you." I clasped the young man's shoulder, giving a short, appreciative squeeze. "You may well have saved my daughter's life."

"Well, I can't have my granddaughter dying before me, can I?" The lad's neutral tone dipped slightly, his icy eyes moving to me as he set down the documents. "But now, you must realize she cannot stay up there forever? She'll have to come back sooner or later. It may be months, even years before then, but she will return."

"I know." My tone was little more than a whisper. "But it may be enough. If she trains…"

"Oh, I'm not worried about the Duel." He pulled down his hood, letting his azure hair tumble into view, and plucked his crown from the desk to sloppily place it on his skull. "Willow holds the soul of my dear sister. Death has never lost her throne to a challenger, regardless of the incarnation. What concerns me is *after* the Duel."

He slid off the desk and took up his shepherd's crook, the bell jingling as he propped it over a shoulder and bounced it absently. "What comes after that trial," he said, "no training will help. At least, not for her. But she will be integral to her betrothed's training, along with his brother."

That last bit had one of my wolf ears perking, and I leaned forward, lacing my fingers. "Her betrothed… you mean Xavier?"

"Naturally." He balanced the staff over his shoulder and hopped onto the desk, walking past me as if performing a tightrope act. "Since Xavier is alive after all, I imagine Willow intends to cancel her arrangement with Lord Inion."

I ran a hand through my hair under my silver crown. "I… suppose you knew for some time that Xavier was alive?"

"Yes and no," he admitted, his shrug jingling the bell tied to his crook. "I knew his soul was still here. Whether or not he was a Necrofera was a different matter. But luck was on Willow's side, it seems."

"But where has he been? What's become of him?" The thought of surviving the fall was one thing, but I could only imagine what he must have gone through all these years on the surface, alone, away from his family… And Lucas didn't even know, for Nira's sake.

Dream had a placid smile on his face. I was familiar with the forced expression. The boy often struggled with showing genuine emotions.

"I'll let Willow give you those details some other time," he said and leapt onto the floor. "For now, I'm glad you agree that it's best she stay away from the palace. I'll inform my Catchers to make sure she remains on the surface, if they meet her."

He dipped a hand into his sweater's pocket and pulled out one glittering, azure orb. It glimmered in the lamplight, a mist seeming to swirl within the glassy globe like wondrous galaxies. The orb began to gleam as Dream stared into its depths. I knew what that meant, and stopped him with a breath. "Wait."

The Orb still gleamed bright, but Dream glanced at me curiously. "Hmm?"

"Is it true about the Relicblood of Land?" I asked. "Myra mentioned… You've been keeping him in Aspirre? He's alive?"

That same emotionless smile broke his lips. "Be strong, Serdin. We both have a war to win. With Everland, and afterward."

The Orb flashed a blinding blue light, forcing me to hold a hand to my eyes. By the time it dimmed… he'd vanished.

19

THE SIEGE

LUCAS

"Bring down the gates!" Shouted a fully plated Alice. "Secure the frontline!" Our troops charged for the enormous, stone wall surrounding the city of High Drinelle. I watched through the slits of my visor as the Reapers erupted with war-cries, our Brothers and Sisters clambering toward the iron gates. The Landish Rockraiders were perched on their towers, and from my vantage, I was pleased to see they seemed frantic and on the defensive.

I hoped to both the Father God and Mother Goddess this would be a clean, simple siege. We at least held some advantage, attacking both outside *and* inside the city. The Surfacing Port in the nearby geysers had already been overtaken by our ranks under and above ground.

Our enemy had brought out cannons and armored tanks, weapons of which we hadn't the luxury in enemy territory. They were firing enormous Shockglobes—and many Flameglobes—at our blocks, littering the barren land with craters and blowing our men off their feet.

I was sure to keep my visor lowered, the swelling scent of cooked flesh permeating even from inside my helm. I hustled beside Alice, my staved scythe held ready as I quickly surveyed our progress.

One squad of Reapers lugged a battering-ram within the safety of our formations, and once they reached the wall, they *slammed* the ram onto the wooden gate. They struck twice, then thrice, and finally splintered the wood.

Our frontline scrambled inside. Alice and I hustled after them, rushing inside with our weapons in hand…

Yet most of the guards, it seemed, had already been taken care of on the inside. Bodies lay strewn on the cobblestone. Citizens barricaded themselves in their homes and civil buildings. Chimneys spewed smoke and some structures were crumbling at the mortar.

It smelled of warm death. Not at all like the scent of decay. It reeked of fresh blood, the smell ungodly... Why, for Nira's sake, was I growing accustomed to it? *Sorrowed Death*, I thought, *what horrors did you endure in the Great Wars?*

This concept of warring with other nations was new to all of us, in this era. Such hadn't been seen since... since... *Oh, what year was Death's last conquering? 0026 A.B.?* In that respect, Everland held the advantage. Their conflicts with the sister lands had made them recently practiced in the field.

A mere trifle, I decided. These are but men. We've spent two-thousand years exterminating far more dangerous creatures. Now was the time to push forward.

"Nathaniel!" I barked.

My vassal was several yards ahead, across the roadway. The bear-eared man sank a fiery fist into an enemy's face before he turned to glance at me.

Aye, Da'torr? Nathaniel called through our mental connection. He was too far for me to hear directly, and so his voice sounded in my thoughts.

I motioned to the rooftops. "Search for scouts and guards up above. Either bring them in, or do away with them, but secure the higher ground."

The bear grunted his confirmation, taking off to do as ordered. I glanced over to see Alice requesting the same of her vassal, Aiden. A good idea. Aiden could reach the roofs easier with his wings.

A shout from a nearby soldier caught my ears. My gaze snapped up in time to see the volley of Shockspheres and Hallows-infused arrows raining down. Alice screamed for the shield-toting Reapers to take formation and they slammed down the padded slabs of iron in a tight perimeter around us, blotting out the sunlight and drowning us in darkness. The rattling of splintering shafts snapped. Glass pellets shattered, and the metal walls echoed like funeral bells. Luckily, our shields' insulations were made of rubbery material to dampen any electric shocks. But those left outside our enclosure could be heard screaming, most of their cries cut short with liquidy gasps.

When the shields were lowered, we pushed forward...

Then drew to a halt.

We weren't the only ones fighting the Raiders. Several of the citizens had taken action against them as well, street brawls scourging the alleyways and parks.

And shouting orders at the rebellious civilians was someone I never, in all my life, would have expected.

"Keep your formations!" Roarlord Apsonald Coult, Hand of King Galden and Grandfather of my wife's favored student, drove his sword into an attacking

Footrunner. He then flung hand signals at his men. "You're not some disorganized bunch of imbeciles! Order! Unity! Honor…! Remember the words of Land's Servant! The enemy of our enemy is our ally! Hold fast and claim victory!"

He caught sight of me and saluted with two fingers to his brow, trotting over. "High Howllord! Good to find you in one piece."

"High Roarlord…" I staggered, not sure how to react. "You're with the rebellion?"

"I'm the Servant's appointed general," he explained, eyes darting around, still not at ease. "There'll be time for explanation later. We must find the guard's captain. No one may leave here after seeing me. I can't have the king knowing."

"Clearly. I'll call for my vassal to search for this captain—"

"There!" yelled Alice. My wife jabbed one of her scythes at a Raider in the distance.

His armor gleamed brighter than the others, dangling ornaments of rank on his shoulder guard. He was also surrounded by other knights protecting him.

Apsonald motioned more hand signals to the rebels, and everyone sprang for the captain. His guards were swiftly cut down, leaving the captain alone and quivering where he stood. He was quick to drop his sword and Shotri with a clatter, the dangling ornaments on his armor shaking with the rest of him.

"P… please," he stammered, swallowing the knot in his throat and lifting his hands. "I… I relent! Relent!"

Alice kept her scythes raised, but I lowered my staved blade, exhaling. "A wise decision."

"Indeed," muttered Alice, her wolf ears curled back and sharpened teeth gritting threateningly at the cowering man. He sank to his knees, letting loose an undignified sob and threw his hands over his head.

Alice snorted, allowing herself to relax. "It isn't wisdom that drives this one."

Apsonald removed the captain's helm. The viper frowned at the man's tuft of orange hair and draping hound ears.

"This," he began. "Isn't captain Yorke."

The scrape of metal sounded behind me, and Alice roared, "Lucas!"

I barely spun round when a helmed Reaper, wielding a sword he'd filched from the ground, brought the blade down at my neck.

Screeee—clang!

With the swiftness of a man half his age, Apsonald slid in front of me, raised his sword that glinted oil in the sunlight, and blocked the opposing blade in an earsplitting ring of metal on metal.

The foe was pushed away, making to run, but Alice flung one of her chained dual-blades and caught him by the arm. The knight screamed at the pain when Alice jerked her weapon and tugged him toward her. When he stumbled over her feet, she took him by the neck and shoved him against a wall.

"Crafty," she commended sourly, removing the man's helm to reveal a scarred, Landish man underneath. His glare was sharp as glass as Alice peered down at him with one eye narrowed. "Captain Yorke, I presume?"

He spat a glob of saliva on her cheek. She didn't flinch, instead continuing. "Surrender this territory, or surrender your life."

"I'll not relent to a dirt crawling bitch," he snarled.

"That dirt crawling bitch," I clipped and towered over him, my shadow blocking the sun from his gaze, "is not a woman you wish to cross. Unless you fancy being castrated, then by all means, continue."

His tanned skin paled white as my ancestor's ghost, and I turned to stride off. "We claim High Drinelle as Reaper territory," I said to our new prisoner, then turned to a nearby Reaper captain. "No one is to enter or leave without our approval."

Alice called after me, "and what shall I do with the trash?" She threw her head toward the captain, who was still caught by the neck.

I waved brusquely at her, sliding off my gauntlets. "Do with him what you will, dear. He's your claim."

She eyed him with a scrutinizing leer. "Not the most pleasing to look at, but I suppose I've had uglier men… You may yet be in luck, captain: perhaps I'll have use of your lower extremities after all."

His jaw locked, face turning green. Alice broke character and chortled, shoving him to the ground and gave an emphasized kick to the ribs with her pointed, steel boots. After dusting her hands of him, she came to follow at my side.

"Enjoying ourselves, are we?" I asked, sliding off my helm and tucking it under an arm.

My wife was still grinning with amusement. "He looked as if I'd broken his fragile little mind."

"You may as well have, given the patriarchic culture he was raised in," I mused, stopping our pace once reaching Roarlord Apsonald. I shook hands with the man. "I can't tell you how thankful we are for your support, High Roarlord. And I believe I owe you my life, on top of it all."

"Ah, well, call it an investment." Apsonald slid his sword in its scabbard, giving a hearty laugh. "My grandson speaks more highly of you than he does me. If I ever want him to take on his role as my heir, I thought letting a lowly guard cut you down would ruin it all."

"Then I bless my wife for recruiting him." I scanned the terrain to see the fruits of our victory.

Rebels were putting out fires, Reapers were hauling our captured Raiders to the prisons, others were going from home to home and assuring the civilians they were safe, should they submit and agree to keep within the city gates.

"This siege went rather smoothly with the rebellion's help," I commented, peering questioningly at Apsonald. "But how did you get here before us? I could have sworn we left you at the capital."

"I was able to take the train system directly. My other daughter, Helda, is married to the duke here. I told Galden I wished to bring her to the capital safely, guessing you'd attack Drinelle first anyway."

"And you knew this how?"

He shrugged, his plate clattering. "Low Everland's capital is directly under here, isn't it? You could say this is your home, or at least above it. And since it also comes with a Surfacing Port in the geysers down the ways…" He shrugged again. "The odds told me you'd start here."

I chuckled. "Clever. Well, again, thank you. We could have lost more men than we did."

"As could we. But now… to be honest, I'd hoped…" He glanced past me, searching the Reapers who scuttled among the streets. "Is Jaqelle here?"

I gave a quiet, sickly sigh. "He and my… son have been missing since the capital went on lock-down."

"Do you have an idea where they are?"

I caught Alice dabbing at her eyes. She tried to pretend it was an itch, but I knew better. I knew *her* better. She hadn't taken our sons' disappearance lightly. And neither had I. The battle had distracted us, but still, even a simple reminder like this brought back the rude reality that we may never see our sons again. Either of them, in one body or not. The business of war was hectic and unpredictable, especially when in enemy borders. To have been separated at the very start may well be an omen for what's to come.

"There's been no word," I said. "No sign. But there's still a reward out for my sons' head, so we can only hope that means they managed to escape and are lying low."

Apsonald's lips pursed, concern creasing his brow, but he nodded nonetheless. "It's the wisest strategy, right now. I'll… have to trust that you taught them well."

So will I.

Reapers came to stand around us, so many exhausted faces among them. They seemed to be waiting for me to give further orders. I stepped forward, drawing a breath deep from my lungs to declare, "High Drinelle has fallen to both Reaper and Rebel forces! We claim this territory as our own, and hence bind allegiance with the resistance!"

Cheers roared from the crowd, causing a ripple throughout the city.

At least we have one obstacle out of the way, I considered. *But there are so, so many more to come. I only hoped finding my sons was next on the list.*

20

A HEALER'S MISSION

BIANCA

"Come on, come on…!" One of my rabbit ears folded down, my toe hammering the tiled floor of the hospital as the com screen whirled. "Pick up, you stupid venom-spitter…!"

The call dropped, and I groaned. Jaq still wasn't answering. I'd already tried calling Alex and Xavier, but that was a waste. Didn't anyone bring their Coms before ditching me?

"Bianca?" Master Hendril called from the doorway behind me. "Is everything all right?"

Master was an old goat, his curling horns cracked and dull at the tips. His face had countless wrinkles and his hair was an aged grey, making him look more like a Grimling than an Everlander, if not for his dark skin. He had a scraggly beard hanging to his portly belly, and tiny glasses rested on his nose as he stared at me, questioning.

Sighing, I pocketed my com. "My friends aren't answering, Master Hendril. What if they were nabbed? Or…"

"I'm sure they're fine," he patted my shoulder. "They probably just lost their Communicators in the raid. I'll keep an eye out for the 'captured' list. Now come and help me with the patient transfer. We don't have much time to move, according to our eviction notice."

I grumbled, but nodded all the same.

It'd been over two weeks since the raid. Everland's declaration of war with Grim was stressful on us, here in the Reaper District. Luckily, we were given leniency since we weren't actually Reapers. The Healers were given a choice: Stay loyal to the 'righteous' king here, or help the Reapers and be hung for treason. *So* hard to choose…

I followed Master Hendril to one of the patient rooms. There were two winged girls here, one in the patient bed and the other sitting beside her, waiting. The non-patient girl had the same shade of brown skin as me, and she had scarlet wings sprouting from her back. Her face was hidden under a sand-yellow hood, which she yanked over her eyes the minute we walked in.

There were two archery bows set against the wall, and a pair of quivers filled with arrows beside them. One was a crossbow, looking pretty high-grade, probably the latest model. The other was a more traditional bow with curved edges, and it wasn't strung.

I also spotted several pouches of empty Metaspheres tied to the quivers. Those little things, when wet, could be stretched to incredible extremes, and just about anything could be housed in them. Lightning was usually harvested in these things, the inside somehow impervious to any elements, though the outside was as vulnerable as any typical glass. The spheres could be pushed back down to size and allowed to harden, too, and that's how Shockspheres and Flamespheres and a whole lot of other elemental ammo for Shotri was made.

I'd done a lot of research on Metaglass. It was just so mysterious… and it had an alluring potential to further scientific advancements, if I could just find a way to utilize it in a way no one's thought of yet.

But anyway. I shook out of my daydream, focusing on what was happening now. If they had that many Metaspheres along with copper-coated arrows, they must be Stormchasers.

The Sky Knights were the ones who harvested the lightning for the world. Culatia's technological advancements and engineers provided us with new electronics every year. There was a science to it, just like with medicine, but different.

Then again, I heard they've started using electro-shock therapy in the medical world now, so maybe the line separating the two isn't so solid after all? What would happen if I used electricity to heat mixtures instead of our usual fire—

Focus.

I blinked back to real life again, looking at the Stormchasers. *Did they come from the Chaser District here in the capital?* My eyes narrowed at their colorful, bright wings. No, the Landish birds didn't have scarlet and blue feathers… What were Culatian Chasers doing in Everland? Maybe they were transfers.

I smiled and approached the girls, who were talking to Dr. Hendril already. I had to remind myself not to stare at the patient on the bed. She was… well, just plain weird. Her skin wasn't exactly dark, but I wouldn't call it light either. It was more of a pale beige color, and on her back were blue, feathery wings that were white underneath. Her hair—mammalian hair—was snowy white, and she had cat ears that flicked up every time Master Hendril's voice made a cheerful inflection.

Hybrids were rare. This girl looked like a mix of Culatian and Grimish. The red Sky mark on her bare foot and white Death mark on her forehead made that clear.

A hybrid AND Dual-Evocator? I noticed the hybrid had a broken wing, her feathers torn by what could have been jagged claws and teeth. Necrofera wounds. She was lucky to be alive, after that massacre.

Master Hendril cupped his hands and gave the hybrid girl a wrinkly smile. "And have the nurses treated you well, miss El?"

The hybrid looked like she didn't understand, her cat ears folding in question.

The visitor—the red-winged friend—babbled something in Culatian to translate. The hybrid's face brightened, and she gave the red girl an answer.

"She say," the visiting friend began in awkward Landish. "She ees the happy one with Healing helpers. But she ees the sad one, too, to be changing places."

Hendril's smile fell slightly. "I'm terribly sorry for the trouble. I'm afraid it's not in our power to defy the order. Do send her my apologies."

Red Wings translated for Blue Wings, and Blue grumbled a quiet mutter.

"She say, we have bad timing in visiting," grimaced Red.

"Yes, well," Hendril rotated a hand. "I wish the situation were different. Now, miss El, would you please come with me? We have to go through some examinations before the move. Bianca, could you please help this other Sousül with their things?"

Sousül? A Culatian noble was traveling here at *this* time? Death, that was harsh luck, having their holiday ruined by this disaster. I hurried to pick up their bows and quivers, smiling helpfully at the red-winged Sousül.

"Come with me, Sousül," I said as Hendril led the hybrid out of the room. "There's coffee and tea in the waiting room—"

A scream came from outside, followed by frightened babbling in Culatian. Master Hendril was shouting also.

The Sousül and I rushed out.

Oh, Death. Blue Wings was being dragged over the floor by a troupe of Rockraiders in the lobby. She wiggled and kicked when they grabbed her feathers, pulling her wrists in painful angles. She was shouting in Culatian. The Death mark printed on her forehead shone with a white light, and her hands burst into flames, making the Raiders lunge back.

One shot a Shocksphere at her, and she collapsed, spasming as they fastened dampening gloves on her hands and feet.

Red shoved past me and ran after them in a full sprint down the hall. "El!" Her hands suddenly exploded with snapping, electric strings.

An Astravoker! No way! Have I ever seen one of those up close?

She shot a bolt of paralyzing lightning at a knight who was carrying her friend away. He went down, and the others drew out their swords. One still had his Shotri out, and he shot at her in a panic. She dodged one, was hit by another—it didn't affect her much, but the Raider dropped into a paralyzed spasm, since he was stupid enough to fire the thing at close-range.

The Sousül ran for her friend—

A different Raider came behind and knocked the Sousül out with the hilt of his sword, and she went down.

"Sousül…!" I hurried to crouch over the unconscious Sousül to shield her from the looming Raider. He scowled down at me, his sword still raised and glinting in the lamplight. My rabbit ears went limp. *Idiot!* I never think these things through.

"Stop!" Master Hendril pushed his way through the Raiders, waving for them to lower their swords. "That is my ward! Put those blasted things away!"

He whipped his head left and right, finding the shackled hybrid and the unconscious Sousül I was protecting. Master roared, "What is the meaning of this?!"

"We got orders," the knight hovering over me said. He sheathed his sword with a sliding click. "All dirt crawlers be deemed traitors from here on. Same with Dreamcatchers. Anyone what with white and black hair—a Death mark—a Dream mark—a pet bird—we bring the blokes in. This one has a Death mark, *and* white hair." He folded his arms with a proud grin. "Grimlette."

I went cold. Did that mean *I'd* be arrested, too? I may have been Everlandish by blood, but I was raised in Grim by my foster family. My eyes inched up at the Raider, but he didn't seem to notice me. I guessed they were only going by looks. I relaxed, but only slightly.

"But she's Culatian." Hendril's goat ears grew as the Raiders hauled the hybrid away. "She doesn't even speak Landish!"

"A Death mark's a Death mark," said the Raider. "I didn't make the law. And I'd mind me tone if I was you. We lock up sympathizers. Now mind, I'd like not bring in a good doctor, so if you'd be so kind as to piss off, mate?" He made a shooing motion.

Master glared behind his tiny glasses. He picked up the unconscious Sousül from the floor.

"Come, Bianca." His wrinkled face deepened with a scowl. "We have a new patient to check in."

The wall clock ticked away in the clinic room. I sighed, my posture slacking in the seat beside the patient bed. Master had stepped out, so I was in charge of watching over the Sousül while she rested. She was moving only a little in her sleep, her breaths sounding upset.

"Roji...?" She murmured, shaking her head from under her covering hood. "Roji... *Yeme ză kegtcha...? Oltorofv...*"

Her head shook more vigorously, exhaling groggily when she woke up.

"Roji...?" The Sousül sat up, seeming confused as she clutched her head. "Re... E-El?" She twisted to look around the room. "El? *Yeme ză, El?*"

She frantically pulled down her hood, and I saw her narrow face for the first time. Her scarlet hair was feathered and cut like a swallow's tail, and her eyes were an electric shade of rose-red.

"They took your friend," I said, rubbing my knuckles. My rabbit ears draped down. "I'm sorry. There was nothing we could do..."

The girl looked scared at first, but then she clenched her fists. "I have to be getting back El. Where they take?"

"I'm not sure. Maybe you can ask the prison guards uptown, or..."

She flung out of bed, grabbed her bow and quiver—and shoved her friend's crossbow in my hands.

"You take, *Külleschkov.*" she ordered. "Keep safe for El. We go find now."

I fumbled with the crossbow, not having a clue how I was supposed to hold it. "W-we?" I stammered. "But I can't..."

"Go with her," Master suddenly said from the doorway.

He had a thick textbook tucked under his arm now, and his wife was suddenly here, too. Roaress Hendril's wings ruffled, and she gave an approving nod to Master.

"Wh... what?" I asked the elderly man. "But Master, I have to be here. My apprenticeship—"

"Is over." His sagging face was the coldest I'd ever seen. "Consider this your final task as an apprentice, Bianca. It isn't right, what this king is doing. We'll not be a part of it any longer."

"We can't stand another minute in this prison camp," his wife spat, her talons grown long. "Those monsters have been killing the black birds in my clinic! We've lost so many because of their damned raids—they're slaughtering them for Bloody sport now! I've had enough. We both have. We're joining the resistance and leaving tonight."

"And I can't ask you to make such a dangerous decision yourself, Bianca," Master went on. "It's not my place to tell you what side to choose—"

"Of course I'm choosing your side!" I blurted. "Everland's at war with Grim, and I'm sure as Bloods not Landish! I'll come with you. I'm not just going to leave you, Master."

He paused, a smile breaking his wrinkled face. "Thank you, Bianca... But as of today, I'm not your master. You're fully graduated. I've already filed the papers."

I felt like I'd swallowed a giant block of dry ice. Me, *graduated*? So early...? I still had another five years left—holy Death...!

"But I..." I squeaked, trying to contain my glee. Or was it confusion? Was I really qualified to graduate now? "I can still come with you, can't I? I mean, I really need to find... um..." My face got hot.

I apparently didn't need to finish, because Roaress Hendril grinned. "You need to find Alexander?"

I blushed harder, but nodded. "I haven't heard from him. Or any of them." My eyes started stinging. "I-I don't even know if they're still alive and..."

"I'm sure they're fine, dear," she sighed and came to hug me, stroking my hair. "We would have heard about it otherwise. The Devouhs are still marked as missing, if one was found and killed, it would have been reported by now."

"In fact..." Master tapped a finger to his peppery beard. "I wouldn't doubt if they were with the rebellion this very moment. In a war against King Galden, it seems fitting for the Reapers to ally with Land's Servant and his resistance."

His wife cocked an eyebrow. "They already have. It wasn't just the Reapers who captured Drinelle a few days ago. The rebellion shares it with them now."

Drinelle? How far was that? "I'll pack my stuff at the manor!" I said, hurried. "I'll be quick, and...!"

Hendril glanced at the red-feathered Sousül beside me, his eyes sliding into a thoughtful glaze. "Just a moment, Bianca. There's still this Sousül's friend to think of... Here, I have an idea. Keep your com with you, and we'll keep ours. Tanya and I will head for Drinelle and ask for shelter. They should let us in, since we'll be delivering the injured messengers. But you should go with the Sousül and find her friend, then meet us in Drinelle. We'll be there. But take this with you while you're gone."

He held out the thick textbook he'd brought. It was labeled *Lady Jilume Herdazicol's Advanced Tonic Brewing: Formulas for the Practicing Alchemist*. It was dated as a 19th century text, but it was marked as *Edition V*, a more modern reprint.

"You were an excellent student," he said. "Better than any I could have hoped to train. It was a miracle I found you in Grim, of all places."

I fumbled with the bow and quiver and took the textbook, my nose scrunching. "*Formulas for the Practicing Alchemist?*" I asked. "What is an Alchemist?"

He winked. "I'll leave you to read for yourself. But I have a feeling this will help you in dangerous times such as these. It had no use during peace, but now, I believe the times call for it again."

"But what *is* it?" I asked skeptically, clutching it tight so he couldn't wrench it away. Whatever was in here, I was at least sure I *definitely* wanted it.

He smiled. "It is something, I suspect, you will be most proficient in."

"Master... I—"

The red-eyed girl shoved me forward. "Very good, come now! *Prev'lae* ees needing me!"

Master Hendril chuckled and waved me off encouragingly, the Sousül dragging me down the hall. I started crying, shouting a final farewell to him and his wife, who hurried on in the other direction as we left the hospital.

21
CAT'S IN THE BAG

MIKANI

The night was finally coming to an end at the café, and Brittleton Beach was closing to the public.

I had Neal close everything up, and Connie went to help him clean dishes. Now that Octavius wasn't around, chores had to be split between the three of us. That stupid kid and his stupid bird. *Why did he have to leave?* If it wasn't for that Devouh kid, my brother and Ringëd would still be at home where they belonged.

Grumbling, I went upstairs and shut my door, heading to the private washroom.

I turned on the shower and waited for the water to heat up. In the meantime, I went to the sink to brush my teeth. When I reached for the paste, my hand found a long, black box made of soft velvet. It'd been buried under combs and cans of sunscreen. I pulled it out and opened the box.

It was my engagement-vines. The ones Ringëd gave me years ago.

Been a while since I've seen these. Checking to make sure the door was locked, I took out the gold vines and clipped them to my hair, staring at them in the mirror. Bloods, they were still beautiful. They shined in the light, the strings glimmering even though the coating was tarnished.

Why haven't I been wearing these again? I leaned over the sink counter and sighed, swatting at the vines with a finger.

Man, I remembered when he first gave me these things: he'd taken me for a night walk on the beach, ended at the pier, then got on both knees, bowed and presented the vines while singing a weird song… He'd said it was the traditional proposal in Marincia. He looked like a damn idiot the whole time, and it didn't help that he was tone-deaf…

I snorted a laugh at the memory. I'd laughed then, too, and he thought that was a *no*. But I shoved the vines on my head mid-laugh, so that made it clear in the end. Then he brought me to his flat, we made crazy love and…

And morning came.

Mom was dead.

I ripped off the vines and stuffed them back in the box, snapping it shut. *Oh, right.* I grimaced. *That's why I never wear them.* But that was forever ago, right? Wouldn't Mom want me to finally get married and start a family already?

Start a family? I cringed.

I couldn't even keep *this* one together anymore. At this rate, we might lose our house and have to move in with Ringëd if things go bad—

Bang! Bang! Bang! Bang!

Pounding came from the café's door downstairs. My annoyance flicked with each knock, my cat ears growing. I pocketed the box, turned off the shower and stomped downstairs to see who the Void was knocking at this hour.

I ripped open the door. "What do you want?" I barked at the Rockraiders waiting outside.

There were two Footrunners with them, both I recognized. They were from the Seeker Department, from Ringëd's branch. Yule and Jared, I think. New guys.

My scowl softened to see the familiar faces. "Oh. Sorry guys, we're closed. Come back tomorrow."

I started to shut the door, but one of the Raiders kept it open with a thick hand. "We're not here for a meal, ma'am. We're looking for…" He looked at the folder in his other hand. "Claude Treble?"

My eye twitched at the sound of Dad's name. "He's… out."

"Sirra-Lynn Treble?"

"Dead."

"Then, are you Mikani Treble?"

My lids narrowed at the Raider. "Yeah. Why?"

He cleared his throat and turned to the other knights. "All right, careful with this one. Her file says she has a Death mark. Watch for fire. Take her in and find the others."

CRACK!

They kicked the door open, throwing me back. They drew out their swords and Shotri and I was caught by a flurry of Shockspheres, spasming in pain. Two of the Raiders came behind and strapped dampening gloves and shoes on me, blocking my fire from exploding at them.

"What are-are you do-ing?!" I shouted in a stutter. The shocking bolts started to wear off, and I tried to wriggle out of the Raider's hold—but he forced me to my feet.

The Raider who'd first knocked on the door smiled and unrolled a long scroll. On the back of the scroll was the royal crest: a thrashing lion above a flowery collection of diamonds, looking like a sword standing upright, a crown resting on the lion's head.

"All Grim blooded shifters are to be imprisoned, as declared by King Galden in consequence of the war with the Death King," the man read aloud.

I gawked at him. "Are you stupid? We're Everlandish!"

"Black hair, Death mark…" He sized me up. "Looks like a dirt crawler to me—"

A carving knife shot right past my face and ripped through the scroll, throwing it out of the Raider's fingers and *thunked*! against the wall beside us. The paper hung there as the knife quivered in place.

"Get your damn hands off my sister."

Neal came from the kitchen with his cat ears curled, a cigarette burning between his lips. His belt was stuffed with every cutlery knife we owned. Neal noticed the Seekers standing under the doorway, and his brow furrowed at Ringëd's coworkers. "Yule, Jared, hurry up and get those things off her."

The Seekers hesitated, their eyes darting away.

I stared at them. "Guys…?"

One of them, Yule, pursed his lips. "S-sorry, Mika… we didn't have a choice."

"Everyone who didn't tell them where you were…" The other Seeker, Jared, looked shaken. "They're dead. Everyone's dead, Mika. Everyone but us. They said they wouldn't hurt you guys if you didn't fight, s-so…"

Are you Bloody…? I started crying. Damn it, I *hated* crying. Damned, Bloody bastards…

The Seekers didn't have anything else to say to me, looking at their feet as the Raider started dragging me out the door—

Neal threw another knife, hitting the Raider's hand with a quick *splicsh* of blood and pinned it to the wall next to the paper scroll. The knight screamed in pain, trying to pry his hand free, but Neal's blade was so deep and precise, it'd cracked the wood and was determined to stay stuck there.

"I said let her go, asshole." Neal flicked his smoke to the floor and snuffed it with a shoe. He pulled out a large cleaver from his belt. "Or are you not very *attached* to your hands?"

One Raider pulled out a Shotri and let loose a stream of spheres.

Neal leapt and rolled behind a support-beam, ducked around the other side, and flung the cleaver at lightning speed. The Raider twisted out of the way and the blade cracked against the wall.

The café was a warzone as they alternated shots, Neal's blades leaving a trail of splintered wood. One finally hit the Raider, but he'd lunged left and was only grazed on the arm.

Neal was out of ammo.

The Raider was out, too, but his buddy finally yanked the carving knife out of his pinned hand and tossed *his* Shotri to the other knight. "You deal with him!" he seethed at his bleeding hand, grabbing my arm with his non-injured one. "I'll put this one up, *away* from that maniac—"

A high-pitched scream came from the kitchen door, and both Neal and I found Connaline lingering at the doorway.

"Connie!" I barked at the young, cat-eared girl. "Get outta here!"

She didn't move. Neal jumped for her. "Move it, Con—!"

Neal was shot with a sphere, and he crumpled to the floor. The Raider was quick to cuff him, kicking his gut for good measure before jerking Neal to his feet.

Connie finally ran for it, and the Raider brought the thrashing Neal over to follow his buddy—who was dragging me out of the café.

"Should we grab the imp?" One Raider asked. "And there should have been another kid, with a Death mark. This one doesn't have any."

"The, um, other kid left town weeks ago," Yule squeaked while hustling after us. "Do-do you have to worry about the younger girl? I-I mean, it's too much of a hassle and all, right?"

"Eh... yeah, true." The Raider shrugged. "She doesn't even have Grim hair, like these ones, so what's one loss?"

"The captain said to be thorough," the other knight snapped, cursing while babying his stabbed hand. "She still has Crawler blood, and—"

"Fine, fine, then torch the place. See how long she survives on the streets. They have stoves in there, right? Call it an accident if the locals start asking."

Neal and I were thrown into a caged wagon, and I pounded on the bars when the knights locked us up.

"Stop!" I screamed, watching as our home—our memories, our childhood, *everything* we ever owned—went up in flames. "Please...!"

The horses at the front of the wagon were whipped into motion, and we lurched forward, the café falling out of sight.

CONNALINE

I wheezed for air, scuttling through the streets, wishing I was in better shape.

I swore I was starting to see spots. I couldn't even go a few streets without passing out?

Looking over my shoulder, I saw the café was a pillar of fire now. I flattened myself against an alley wall, peeking around the corner. It looked like the coast was clear, so I snuck across the road, heart thundering.

Where was I supposed to go? Octavius was gone, Mika and Neal were arrested, Ringëd left weeks ago… and apparently, the other Seekers had ratted us out.

Yule, Jared… My eyes welled. I overheard them. They gave us over to the Raiders for some stupid new law! And because of them, I was alone now.

I wiped my eyes, sniffing. *Okay, Connie, calm down. Think. Where do I go from here?*

Maybe my school friends could help. *Can I trust them?* I shook my head, deciding that was a bad idea. If they hid me and the Raiders found out, they might kill my friends, too.

A glint caught my eye by the corner walkway. There was an opened case lying on the ground, with two gold engagement-vines and a detached droplet.

Those are Mika's!

I swiped the box and clutched it to my chest. Their prisoner wagon must have come by here. Did she drop them?

Footfalls scuffled down the street, and I sprang for the nearest alley for cover. I hid behind a wooden dumpster, trying to stifle my ragged breath. I rubbed away more tears, smearing a hand under my running nose.

Three patrolling Footrunners passed the alley, spears held lazily over their shoulders as they chatted about how they couldn't believe what the dirt crawlers had done in the capital. They said the Death Princess was even seen there, commanding the demons along with the Reapers.

That couldn't have been right. If Octavius was supposed to be a Reaper, then the Reapers were good. Weren't they?

The Runners passed, and I hurried to the next block. There was only one person here I knew I could trust. If he wasn't here, then… I swallowed, deciding I'd figure it out later as I made my way to his upstairs loft and hammered the door with a fist.

At first, there was no answer, but Shel had mercy on me when a cream haired man swung the door open.

The flat-nosed guy started at me, then grabbed my arm. "Bloods be good, girl, get in here!" He dragged me in and shut the door, turning the lock.

"M-m-mr. Fleetfûrt," I sobbed to Ringëd's uncle. I couldn't help it. I felt like a little girl again, scared and one-hundred-percent useless. "They took my brother and sister. And-and my house is gone. I—*hic!*—I don't know what to do…!"

He squeezed me in a hug. I could see the azure Dream mark printed on the back of his neck from this angle.

"It's all right, Connie," he hushed. "Calm down… I had a feeling they might pull something like this. Here—you can come with me. I'm leaving tonight."

I blinked away tears when he went to a couch, where a bag of luggage waited. "Where are you going?" I asked.

"To Drinelle, in the Reaper territory." He picked up the bag. "The Raiders are looking up hospital files for anyone born with a Death or Dream mark. Catchers like me are considered traitors. It's not safe for any of us."

He slung the duffle bag over his shoulder and opened the door, guiding me out. I sniffled up at him. "What's going to happen now?"

He looked troubled, his round ferret ears sprouting. "I don't know. Let's just focus on getting out of here. Where's Ringëd?"

"He-he went to find Octavius, I think. And *he* was at the capital, last we heard. Did they get Octavius, too?"

"I'm sure he's fine." He led me down the stairs to sneak through the streets. "Come on. We'll stowaway on a train and get out of here. I'll try and find some of my Brother Catchers, see if they've found a good place to hide. We'll be fine, sweetheart. Don't worry."

He ruffled my head and I nodded, swallowing the knot in my throat. I felt like a dumb baby, crying instead of being useful. But what was *I* going to do? I only had remedy Hallows, and wasn't very good at it. I could patch up a little scrape, but if anything serious happened, I'd be helpless.

I decided to just go along with Mr. Fleetfûrt, since he actually had a plan. *Maybe I could find Octavius along the way? And he could help get Mika and Neal back?*

My cat ears folded, sniffing to keep determined. That was my plan, now: Find Octavius. Everything would be better after that.

Wouldn't it?

22

OUTLAWED

XAVIER

Alex smashed his fist against a tree—yelling in pain.
He clutched his fist, now bloodied and splintered, cursing obscenities. It'd been over two weeks since the raid at the capital; two weeks since Jaq and Lilli were taken.

We didn't know where the Raiders carted them off to, but we were Bloody sure going to get them back. We'd hiked from town to town, avoided the main cities, and were now camped in a nearby forest of dried up, nearly dead trees. It seemed like the only safe place for us.

A fire crackled at the center of our refuge. Willow kept the flames up with her Pyrovoking, her Death mark gleaming white from her chest.

Ringëd was keeping watch a few yards off with Dalen's ghost, accompanied by Vendy and her Crystal sword, in case any stray demons decided to visit. We had Dalen's vessel contained and shrunk in his Storagecoffin, which was clipped and dangling from our belt. His siblings, Rolen and Carrie, were on patrol beside him, both looking thoughtful. Or was that boredom?

Herrin was sitting against a tree and reading from a book, his wings curled tight behind his back while he squinted at the pages in the dim light of the fire. *Where did he get that thing?* I don't remember stopping off at any libraries recently.

Linus sat watching Willow's flames absently, either trapped in a vision or brooding over a thought. Henry sat beside him scraping one of his swords over a whetstone and inspecting the blade's sharpness every so often. Jimmy and Yulia sat together beside the princess, trying to keep conversation to help calm her. My tattered messenger, Chai, was on Yulia's lap, receiving endearing scratches from her and Willow. Dark circles were puffing from under Willow's lids, and her face was coated in dirt.

It'd been days since any of us could sleep soundly. We always had to be alert, in case the Raiders came hunting.

I found Miss Ana sitting against a tree farther away from the fire, staring into the woods in silence. Kurrick had gone to hunt for food with Prince Cayden earlier, and the lioness seemed distressed without her scar-faced warrior. She hadn't attempted to make conversation with any of us while he was gone. She only stared after where he'd left, like a lost puppy waiting for its master.

I watched from the psyche as Alex cast down his gaze and slammed his back against a tree, clutching his bleeding hand.

We'd just gotten back from Batterdale, searched their prisons for Jaq or Lilli, and come up short. Again. We wondered if they were moving them from prison to prison. *But where was the end?*

Alexander seethed from his raw knuckles. Our antlered Dreamcatcher, Jimmy, rose to his feet to head for us. "Calm down," said the elk. "We'll get them back."

"You're damn right we will," Alex gripped the glasses Jaq had left behind. "We'll find them. Even if we have to search this whole Gods damned kingdom, we'll find them."

Jimmy thumped my brother's shoulder. "You bet we will. The next time'll be the last, guaranteed. So, save your strength. You'll need it to help them out."

"Hey, Jimmy!" Ringëd called from the woods, throwing a thumb over his shoulder. "Trade shifts?"

"Sure!" he called back, the antlered Catcher trotting to take his place as lookout. The Catcher waved his hands, his Dream mark glowing from his right palm, and the elk's form multiplied into five copies, all fizzling into existence before walking silently into the woods to scout.

As Ringëd made his way back, he slid a cigarette between his lips and lit the end, exhaling a cloud of smoke.

I watched Ringëd from the psyche's window. Then Alex glanced down at Jaq's glasses, which were still clutched in his hands—and an idea struck me. *"Alex!"*

My brother's eyes snapped up. "What?"

"Seers! We have Seers with us!" My tone was hurried. *"They can find Jaq and Lilli with a vision!"*

Alex blinked. "Mother of… Ringëd!" Alex thrust the glasses into the Footrunner's hand. "These are Jaq's. Can you use these as a medium? To find him?"

Ringëd scratched the scruff at his neck, studying the glasses. "I guess I can try?"

He closed his eyes, clutching Jaq's glasses. His Dream mark gleamed blue from his shoulder, eyes opening, yet unseeing. His pupils had dilated and gone stale.

Soon enough, his mouth twisted and he clicked his tongue. "No good. All I'm getting is the academy yard with you two, in Grim. When you guys met."

"Try again!"

He sighed, but complied, his eyes dimming a second time. Then, "A cell block. The first one we checked, weeks ago. Too old, we already know he's moved since then."

"Again!"

"Look, I deal with past events. Whatever glimpse I'm gonna get is going to have already happened. No telling how long ago it'll be. But we do have another Seer…" He twisted back, calling. "Hey, Linus!"

The goat lifted off the log, wiping his hands of dirt and grinning, already knowing what we wanted. "Give those lenses here."

Linus stepped next to the Officer and was handed the glasses. The goat went silent for a long while, his Dream mark gleaming bright from his arm. Much like Ringëd's, his eyes went stale. Then his head cocked, wiry dreads tumbling over his dark shoulder, and after a few minutes of still breath, his brow furrowed.

"What terrible vision," he murmured. "No wonder your friend needs these… Well, there is good news and bad. I've found him. He's in a wagon, I think. It's blurry, but I can just make out others there, and it's lunging something violent. I think I see a pair of wings on someone beside him. I would guess that is the High Howless Lilliana."

Alex breathed in relief. "Then they're alive?"

Linus nodded, pursing his lips. "The bad news is where they're headed… I can hear the guards talking. They mentioned the name Tanderam."

Alex prodded. "And? Where is that?"

Ringëd answered for him, his tone dreaded. "It's a high-grade prison up on the Golden Canyons. It borders the Tanderam Desert."

"Then let's hurry there!" blurted Alex. "We've wasted enough time!"

Ringëd shook his head fiercely. "Not that easy. Tanderam Prison is the most secure, isolated, and *largest* prison in Everland. It's on fractured canyons that drop a mile down to the desert below—which, if you survive the fall, will swallow you in its sandpits or drown you in its currents."

"How can a desert have currents?" Alex questioned. "From what we've read, deserts are just piles of sand."

"Not Tanderam." Ringëd grimaced. "I hear the sandstorms are so violent there, it actually *moves* the sand in current-like waves. That's why they call it the Dancing Desert. The other Runners say only the most dangerous criminals get locked up there. We might get ourselves killed trying to break out, let alone *in*."

"We have to chance it." Alex took back Jaq's glasses and pocketed them. "It's either that, or we let our friends rot in there."

My tattered raven, Chai, started croaking from Yulia's arms near the fire.

I asked Alex to switch, and he complied, slipping into the psyche so I could come out and take Chai. The raven grumbled and rubbed its head against my splintered hand, comforting me. I hushed Chai with a soft stroke, Mal squawking as well at my feet as I sat down.

"It's all right, Chai," I sighed—then two other messengers fluttered to my lap beside him: Bridge and Dusk.

These were Jaq and Lilli's crows. They were left behind when their Reapers were captured. Had Jaq and Lilli told them to follow us? The Raiders were killing messengers on sight now. If these two had stayed with their masters, they would have met the same fate.

I flicked my eyes up when another, younger crow perched on my head. This one had a white, clover-shaped patch on its tail feather. *Oliver's messenger.* He also came with Bridge and Dusk, for safety. *I think Linus said this one's name was Clover?*

"We'll find them for you," I assured the birds. "We aren't going to leave them behind."

They screeched solemnly and flew off, except for Chai, who stayed on my lap while Mal stayed by my feet. The murder went to the pinestraw near the fire, and that pet ferret of Ringëd's scuttled over to play with the crows. The weasel snickered and hopped about them, rolling in the straw with naught a care in the world.

Ringëd and Linus exchanged uncertain glances beside me. Then Linus scratched between his curling horns. "I suppose you're quite set on this..." he said.

"Yeah." Ringëd crossed his arms. "And I guess you guys are practically like nephews to us, in a weird way. I don't like the idea of going into a deathtrap, but I guess if we can find a way to..." He paused, looking past me suddenly. "Tavius? What's with you?"

I twisted back and found Octavius was leaned against a tree trunk, looking distraught. Shade was in his arms, and that other raven with the white diamond between its eyes—we'd started calling him Shade Two, for lack of knowing his real name or the Reaper he belonged to—was on his head.

Octavius didn't seem to hear Ringëd. His green eyes were blank and distant.

Ringëd tried again. "Tavius!"

That caught his attention, making Octavius jump. "—Huh, w-what?"

"You've been wound up tighter than a feral flounder on a hook," Ringëd observed. "Go on, spill it. What's wrong?"

Octavius swallowed. "Um… I was just… you know, just thinking."

"About?"

He shrugged. "I don't know, I… I'm just tired. Need sleep, I guess."

"Uh huh." Ringëd headed for him, his hand outstretched. "Did something happen? Something we should know about?"

Octavius shot to his feet and backed away from Ringëd's reach. "I-I said it's nothing!"

"Doesn't look like nothing." Ringëd drew closer still. "What's got you so riled up—?"

The crunch of pine needles made everyone stiffen.

But we relaxed when Prince Cayden and Kurrick made their way to us. The men hauled something large and bulky over their backs.

They carried a slumped man with black wings, his flight feathers dragging over the ground and collecting dried leaves. He was wearing a ripped-up Reaper's cloak, stained with old blood.

I heard Willow gasp, and I looked over in time to watch her abandon the fire and leap to her feet. "Sir Janson…!"

Every messenger started shrieking at the newcomer, fluttering wildly.

We all gave a few whistles in command to hush them, else anyone heard. Chai wriggled in my arms when I rose to hustle over to the new Reaper, and he hopped out to shy away.

I gave the raven a questioning glance. "Chai?"

His throat let slip a threatening grumble, creeping back with his head ducked and neck feathers flared. I frowned. I'd heard once that messengers acted strangely around crow or raven shifters, but something felt… wrong. Chai was clearly tense, our Bond strained and festering with warning.

But why? Other than the horrific scars crawling over the man's face and the dried, red blood soaked into the fibers of his cloak, I couldn't see anything out of place with him.

Still, Chai hobbled to my foot and grabbed my torn trousers' hem with his beak, trying to drag me away.

"We found him on our way back." Prince Cayden was out of breath when everyone crowded them.

Kurrick ordered Ana to see to the Reaper's wounds, and the woman obediently began checking the source of the bleeding. Willow dropped to her knees to help, asking Ana if there was anything she could do.

I crouched beside the Death Princess, gently shooing Chai off my leg. He remained close by, but bobbed up and down restlessly when I turned to Willow. "Do you know him?"

Willow brushed her greasy, white hair behind an ear. "He was watching over me when I first surfaced here." Jewel fluttered by her head, tugging a lock of her long hair. The little songcrow looked just as rattled as Chai. "He helped me kill the Fera following me."

"A lot of help..." The Reaper coughed sorely, trying to laugh, but it looked too painful. "I was... Now everyone thinks you're responsible..."

"That wasn't your fault," she hushed, tenderly removing his hood. She examined his face in horror, the skin scarred and blistered like an old burn wound. His bald head was scraped and one eyelid sealed closed; his opened eye was black and bloodshot.

"Gods..." I whispered, cupping a hand over my mouth. It was painful to gaze upon the poor man. *What terrors had he endured...?*

"—um," Octavius blurted suddenly from behind me.

I twisted back, seeing Octavius had grown rigid.

"Your Highness?" He said to Cayden, pointing warily. "I think you're being haunted."

Cayden looked over both his shoulders, puzzled. "What? Where?"

It was true. Cayden was indeed being followed by two ghosts that hung at either of his sides. Though, without soul-sight, the prince was left looking about his flanks with blind nervousness.

One soul was a woman with feathered wings. The other was a fin-eared man with scales that coated his translucent skin. The ghosts stared at us in silence, possibly wondering if the rest of us could see them.

"Where did you two come from?" I asked the specters, rising away from the injured newcomer.

Both ghosts glanced at the winged Reaper. The woman answered. "We serve *Da'torr* Janson."

Vassals, then. So, the man was a Necrovoker. I rubbed my chin where coarse whiskers had grown thick and itchy.

I glanced at the now unconscious Reaper. Janson, Willow called him? He had two skull-pins on his cloak's collar, marking him as a second ranked knight: a Dueler. Lieutenant of a squad leader. On all the fingers of his right hand were silver and black rings with Nirian symbols etched on them. *A Nirian Purist?*

The Purists were a branch of the Nirian religion who, unlike us Harmonists, believed the Mother Goddess was the only deity that existed. Alex and I had met a few of them in the past, and all had worn those rings as well. I couldn't quite remember what they stood for.

Cayden and Ana heaved the Reaper near the fire together, binding his wounds as Ana began her Healing.

ANABELLE

I ripped the cloak from the Reaper's shoulders, freeing him of the black, uniformed shirt underneath.

Now that his marble chest was bare, I could view his many cuts with ease. But there was still so much blood... if I sealed the cuts now, they may well grow infected.

"What do we do?" Prince Cayden asked me, running a bloodied hand through his blond hair. His arms were stained from the Reaper's blood, just as mine were.

My face warmed, not sure if I should answer the prince. *The Servant*. Kurrick had advised me to stay silent around him... yet was there further need for silence? The Day of Revival was nigh upon us. Just at our fingertips! Now that the twins were nearly reunited, it was only a matter of trivial years, perhaps months—

"Miss Ana?" Cayden questioned, looking concerned that I still hadn't answered him. "Will he be all right?"

I held his eyes for as long as I could manage, but quickly shifted my gaze to my warrior, who knelt beside me.

Seeing I was requesting his ears, Kurrick asked. "What do we need, Ana?"

"The water," I whispered. "What you collected from the river."

Kurrick rose to fetch the pail we'd stolen from a stable in the last town we had passed. Kurrick had filled it with river water earlier this morning, and it sloshed from the rim as he brought it to me.

I ripped off a clean piece of the Reaper's cloak and dunked it in the water, wringing it out before wiping off the man's blood.

There was so much... and a lot had dried and caked, making it difficult to scrub off. When most of it had been cleaned, I gazed at Kurrick.

"Please, bring Octavius," I whispered next. "The Infeciovoker."

Kurrick stabbed a finger at Octavius, who flinched. "Cat!" Kurrick barked. "You've been summoned."

Octavius gulped visibly, his legs taking a rigid step forward. Then another. Then he found the rest of his confidence and crossed the camp, kneeling beside me. "W-what?"

I bit back my inherent bashfulness. "Could you please…" I began, voice tightening to a loud whisper. "Could you… scan his injuries? For infection?"

His cat ears perked, concentrating on my quiet words. When he was sure I'd finished the request, he let out a breath. "Oh. Yeah, sure…"

He waved his hands over the Reaper, hovering just above the skin. Then his brow furrowed. "What the…"

Prince Cayden's lion tail swished anxiously. "What's wrong?"

"I don't know." Octavius tried waving his hands over the man again. "He's all fuzzy… like, *everywhere*. There's no place on him that isn't prickling."

Cayden frowned. "'Prickling'?"

"It's complicated…"

"So?" Kurrick demanded. "Are his wounds infected?"

"I-I don't know." Octavius seemed distressed now. "Like I said, all of him is fuzzy. It's masking the cuts. Maybe all that blood messed it up?"

The Shadowblood was standing above us, and he raised a skeptical brow. "'Messed it up'?" the Shadow echoed. Though incredulous, the voice was gentle, and his brow was arched in concern rather than impatience. *This must be Xavier*, I decided. "Has that ever happened with you?" asked Xavier.

"No. Maybe? I…" Octavius exhaled, biting his lip in panic.

The Shadow rested a hand on his shoulder, but looked just as tense. Shaken, even. "Try again. You've always been accurate before. Maybe you just… just need some rest after this? Your Hallows may not be as effective when you're tired—"

"That's not how it works," snapped Octavius. "Guys, something's seriously wrong. I don't know what the Void's going on. Shade's going crazy and it's freaking me out, and now my Hallows is all wacked out? It's too weird. I think I've felt something like this before, but…"

Myra's long-haired daughter came beside them to see what was wrong. "Where else did you feel it?" she asked.

Octavius shook his head. "I don't remember. But I have a really bad feeling…"

"What feeling?" The Daughter of Myra's voice turned shrill. "Is he going to live? Have you felt this with another dying man?"

"I-I don't know. Maybe? It's hard to—"

"Just tell us if he's going to die or not," the Shadowblood ordered, his face contorting into a scowl. *Ah, Alexander now.* "We don't have time to figure out your little problem. Our Brother is dying."

"I can see that!" shouted Octavius. "And I don't know what's going on! It's like he's *covered* in an infection!"

"But does he have a chance to survive? For Death's sake, we don't need to know what it is, just if he's going to live—"

"That's not how it works!" Octavius shot to his feet and shoved past the Shadowblood, his cat ears curled. "I don't know what's wrong! All right?! It's just…! Just…! Argh, never mind. If you can't feel it, then you won't get it. Shade! Come here!"

The white-cheeked raven screeched from the huddle of black birds farther away, keeping their distance.

"Shade?" Octavius paused. "What's wrong?"

He pushed past the Shadowblood to retrieve his timid raven—cursing when that bigger, diamond-marked raven fumbled to his head as well.

"Damned bird…" he grumbled, clutching Shade to his chest. He stormed into the woods.

"I'll get him," Ringëd muttered and chased after him; the feral ferret climbing to his shoulder.

They disappeared as Myra's daughter began arguing with the Shadow, demanding that he apologize to Octavius. He didn't see the need for it. Their argument was becoming heated.

Why are the Reapers frantic? I wondered if it had something to do with their messengers' behavior. The Bond was said to be an empathetic connection… *Perhaps the apprehension is becoming a subconscious emotion?*

I shook my head, focusing on the task at hand. This Reaper needed his wounds sealed right away, cleaned or not. There was so much blood lost already, any more would surely kill him. I decided it was best if I closed the wounds and kept a close eye on him—

My breath caught.

When I looked back at the Reaper, his wounds were already sealed. Closed. Cleaned. But I hadn't used my Hallows yet. *How did they heal?*

Before I could gasp in surprise, Kurrick patted my shoulder. "Good, Ana. That was quick work."

He and Cayden went to lay the now unconscious Reaper on a pile of soft straw, Jimmy and Yulia dragging a log over to elevate his legs.

Myra's daughter engulfed me in her arms, making me flinch when she kissed my cheek.

"Thank you," the ashen haired princess sighed in relief. "He'd helped me when I first surfaced here. If we'd lost him, I wouldn't be able to repay him."

She thanked me again and left with the Shadowblood. Xavier must have been in control now, I caught him squeezing her fingers gently before the two went to speak with… well, they seemed to be talking with no one. *Perhaps they're conversing with the ghosts they mentioned earlier?*

Everyone carried on as usual, unaware that I *hadn't* been the one to heal the winged man. *Hadn't they seen? Were they not paying attention?*

"Ana," Kurrick called. "Your job is done. You may return."

I rubbed my knuckles. Then sighed, scuttling to Kurrick's side. *I must have healed him while I was distracted with the Reapers' bickering*, I decided. *It wouldn't be the first time my Hallows came about subconsciously.*

Still. Perhaps Octavius was right. Something was certainly… off.

23

A STOLEN FAMILY

~~~

RINGËD

I hurried after Octavius, passing by the Carter Siblings—uh, *Tesler* siblings—who were still posted as lookouts.

"What happened over there, Runner?" Carrie Tesler demanded, her wings fluffing as she put a hand on her hip.

"Did someone get in?" Rolen peered over the edge of a tree to see the newcomer. Herrin had been reading again, and looked up to listen for an answer too.

I shook my head and kept heading for Octavius, accidently phasing through a copy of Jimmy in the process.

"It's another Reaper," I said, Kurn clinging to my sleeve as I sped after Octavius. "Just keep at your posts, it's taken care of!"

Octavius went ahead for another five minutes. When he finally stopped, he slumped against a tree, trying to slow his breathing.

"<What in *Drrrok-koh* is the matter with that one?>" Kurn asked in his snickering language, stretching up to my face and rested his paws on my cheek. "<He looks sickly! Has something happened?>"

"Don't know," I whispered, scratching his round ear. "He's…just got something on his mind."

"<Like what?>"

That's what I want to know. I crossed my arms and leaned on a nearby tree to let Tavius cool off. It was dark, but the moonlight flitted through the forest canopy enough to show Octavius's miserable figure.

"Are you going to tell me what's wrong?" I sighed. "Or are you just going to sulk there all night?"

He still didn't look at me, but after a minute, he answered. "This is because of him, isn't it? He helped start the war, he's responsible for what happened to that Reaper…"

I waited for him to explain what the Void he was talking about, but he shut his trap after that. I decided to push more. "Who's responsible?"

His arm stretched out, offering for me to grab it and See for myself. I complied, clasping my fingers around his arm, my Third Eye opening.

"Where're the others?" a familiar voice demanded, the face bleeding into view as I looked through Tavius's eyes. "Are they with you?"

My face drained. No. Bloody. Way.

"Go back and get them out of there," Claude Treble told his son. "Keep them safe. I'll come and find you…"

Octavius jerked his arm free. "It was *him*, Ringëd," he said. "It was my dad. He was acting like he knew what was going on."

"Holy…" It'd been six years since anyone saw Claude. But that was *recent*.

Octavius saw my expression and bristled. "Why was he there, Ringëd? He didn't even bat an eye during the invasion! Is he working with the demons? Is that why he hasn't come back?"

I sucked in a tight breath. "I hate to say it, but… it does look like…"

Octavius ran a hand through his black hair. "Great! First I have a demon queen for an ancestor, and now my *dad's* part of them, too?" He gave me an intent glare. "Don't tell the others. I need to figure this out first, before they find out my dad might be responsible for all this."

I licked my lips as Kurn crawled to my other shoulder, demanding to know what we were talking about. I ignored the ferret. "What was he saying about your siblings, though?" I asked. "About keeping them safe?"

"Land if I know," he spat, an uncharacteristic sneer darkening his face. "That whole thing didn't make any damn sense."

A sinking feeling came, and my eyes narrowed. "Do me a favor real quick: think of your sister. And give me your arm again."

His brow furrowed, but he complied and let me grab his arm.

"…Mikani Treble?" a gold-armored Rockraider asked at the doorstep of the Café. The point of view was coming from someone who was standing beside the knight.

"Yeah," Mika began, looking irritated. "Why?"

—The door was kicked down, she and Neal were shot with spheres and clapped in irons. There was struggling, Mika shouted, she was crying—

The vision vanished, taking my breath with it as I sank to my knees. "Mika…?"

Octavius's tone was worried now. "What? What happened?"

"They…" I could barely whisper, my voice tight. Gods, I couldn't… I couldn't breathe… "They took *my Mika*."

24
DESTINATION

~~~~~~

XAVIER

"What are your names?" I asked the two ghosts who'd come with the new Reaper.

Willow stood beside me, listening. She would occasionally glance over at the unconscious Reaper who rested by the fire, probably to make sure his condition hadn't changed.

The first ghost to answer me was the winged woman, looking hesitant. "I am… Rosette."

"Nikolai," the fin-eared fish followed.

Neither said anything else, an awkward silence growing as the other members of our camp continued with their tasks of gathering firewood, fetching more water or changing shifts for scouting.

I tried for another attempt at conversing. "What happened to your master?"

Nikolai answered in a thick Marincian accent. "Our *Da'torr* was capzured by ze Raiders. He escape, but did no have scythe, and fell into nest of demons."

"We escaped," Rosette finished in plainer Landish. "But not easily. *Da'torr* fled to these woods afterward."

Willow's gaze turned tense. "How far was this nest?"

"Not far enough," the woman said. "They were following us, but I don't think they were many in number. They may have fled after sensing everyone in your party."

I rubbed my chin, glancing at the black birds near the fire. Chai caught my eyes, ducking his head and shot me a long gaze. There was tension there, warning signals puncturing my brain.

Was this what you were trying to tell me, Chai?

If demons were around, it would make sense why the messengers had acted strange. And if they were *still* worried, that meant the Fera hadn't left.

"Willow." I glanced at her. "We should search the area, in case those demons decided to wait for us to sleep."

"And Octavius?" she asked.

"I think he's under too much stress. Thanks to *someone*..." I glared upward, letting Alex know I was referring to him. "You pushed him too far, Alex."

Alex gave an indifferent grunt from my thoughts. *"We needed progress, not a speculation party. He was wasting time."*

"Regardless," I chewed, rubbing my temples. "I think Octavius needs a rest. Hunting Necrofera would only make him worse at this point."

Willow gave a morose nod. "I suppose our count of Reapers has fallen short, hasn't it?"

"Extremely." I grimaced. "We'll have to start the hunt now, and call back the others. You two ghosts, go with my vassals, Dalen and Vendy." Dalen's ghost, who'd returned to camp after I'd called him back alongside Vendy, floated beside me at the mention, saluting. Vendy's rabbit ears perked straight up as she saluted to the ghosts, one hand gripping the hilt of her Crystal sword that was sheathed at her hip. "Dalen, come, let's resurrect you again," I said. "We don't want the demons helping themselves to any souls—"

A string of obscenities made our heads whip to Ringëd, who was rushing back to camp with Octavius trailing him.

"Linus!" Ringëd bellowed, stamping to the goat-horned man. "I need your help!"

Willow and I exchanged uncertain glances, then hurried over to see what was wrong. Linus ceased his conversation with Prince Cayden and cocked an eyebrow at Ringëd, letting him know he had his full attention. "Help with what?"

Ringëd held a gold ring between his thumb and forefinger, and he thrust it into the goat's hooved-hand. The Runner's eyes were red, glassy and dangerously intense. "Tell me where she is!" he pleaded. "This ring came with the vines I gave her, it should help give a stronger vision— Where is Mika now?!"

Linus's eyes glazed, his Dream mark gleaming blue from his arm as we all waited in silence. The goat's fingers traced the ring, and after a long, stressful moment, he blinked back to reality.

"Oddly enough," Linus began in a soft hum. "She is in a wagon, where the moonlight is strong... She and her brother are just reaching the Golden Canyons that line the border of Tanderam Desert."

Ringëd cursed, turning on me. "We're going there *now*." He snatched his ring back from Linus's palm. "I'm taking her back."

He stormed off to swipe his duffle bag from the ground, slinging it over his shoulder and calling for Kurn to get in.

"Perhaps he's right," Alex considered from my thoughts. *"It's probably not safe here anymore regardless, what with demons stalking about."*

I nodded, glancing at Willow. "We'll leave tonight, then?"

"I think he's prepared to leave without us, otherwise," she muttered, pulling her white hair back. She tightened her ribbon and bell. "Funny, how hesitant he was when *you* wanted to leave right away. Now the tables seem to have turned, haven't they?"

I watched Ringëd snuff out the firepit with the last of the water pail. Kurrick lifted the wounded Reaper over his back, and Ana carried the warrior's swords dutifully. I looked back at Willow and smiled. "No. Now we *all* have a reason to fight."

25

TANDERAM PRISON

JAQ

This Gods damned sun blistered my bare shoulders, I could feel my scales cracking off again.

I heaved my hovering cart of copper ore one last foot and wheezed over my knees, peeling off the thick layer of snakeskin flaking off my shoulder and—

Crack!

A searing pain split my already bloody back, one of the guards' leather whips deciding to make friends again.

"I didn't tell ye to stop," the fuzzy guard snapped, hocking a glob of saliva in the sand-covered canyon.

My knees met the ground. *Death…* it felt like that last hit reopened some of the old scars.

Our assigned, blurry overseer—another viper named Lorak—made to reel in his whip again. Well, fuck him. I needed to catch my breath. Gods, my lungs were burning more than my scales.

I flinched when someone touched my shoulders.

Lilli's gentle voice hushed by my ear. "Come on. The day's almost done. Just make it through the last run."

I squinted at her blurry face. I was so used to it by now, I could pick it out from the rest of the fuzzy crowd. Her large black wings helped, too.

Snap!

The whip cracked over her shoulder, and I heard her yelp, but she clamped her teeth shut, drew her wings in tight, and bore through it as she went back to her own heavy cart behind me, that little owl kid pushing alongside her as we started forward again.

I heard Lorak biting into a pear he'd gotten for lunch today, chewing away and wiping at his mouth. Another guard crossed by and saluted him lazily, both exchanging their complaints of how long the day was stretching—

A scream ripped through, making even Lorak turn.

"Where is my sister?!" Someone hollered, his throat sounding raw and gritty.

They guy's face was too blurry to make out, but I saw a fuzz of black hair on his head, so I took it he was another Grimling. Must have been fresh blood.

I saw several guards closing in on him, one shoving him to the sand-ridden, canyon dirt and pinning the new guy's head down. His screams cracked along with his jaw against the rock. He wriggled and squirmed under the guards, then jerked when his ribs were kicked over and over. A sick groan sounded, followed by a yelping cry. Two lashings snapped over his back… then silence fell.

I could still hear him panting on the ground. Two guards took him by the arms and dragged him to where we were, and threw him down at our assigned overseer's feet.

"Got another one for ya, Lorak," one of the guards grunted. "Watch him good, ya hear? That one's got an arm on him that could throw a stone for miles if ya let him."

Lorak eyed the new guy like he was judging a feral dog show. "Any Hallows?"

"His file's clean, from what I saw."

"And a Grim cat…" Lorak paused to bite into his pear, then asked, "Reaper?"

"No badge, no bird," he reported, hefting his belt over his bulbous belly. "He hasn't popped up on their listings either, but we'll keep an eye out. And like I said, be careful with this one."

"He c'nt be worse than miss corpse-raiser." He flipped his head to Lilli, whose blurry head turned to me stiffly. "Caught the dingy Grimlette tryin' to raise a feral muskrat's bones yesterday, had it bite me right in the scales." He pointed to a dark blur on his nose, which I hoped was an ugly gash. The coward deserved it.

The other guard scratched his chin. "Should we take her to the lower cells?"

"I wudn't worry," he assured, muttering between chews of his pear. "She hasn't raised anythin' but little creepy crawlers. She looked ready to try for a shifter's corpse once, but the girl got sick and made a new paintin' on the rocks by the mines."

They shared a laugh. *Bloody bastards.*

The corpse they were talking about had been an old cell mate of ours. He was an older man, a goat named Viran. When he collapsed from fatigue, Lilli couldn't bring herself to raise him. To bring him back into such a horrible place; to be a slave the rest of his afterlife.

I didn't sleep that night. Something about hearing her sobbing in the corner kept my useless eyes wide open.

Lorak kicked the newcomer in the stomach. "Well, hop-to, Grim cat. Follow these three to drop off. If they like ye, maybe they'll fill ye in on what happens if ye break a rule. And if they *really* like ye, they'll tell ye what the rules are."

The newcomer shifted over the ground, groaning.

I gritted my teeth and helped the guy up, slinging his arm over my shoulder. "Come on, mate," I hissed, putting him in position next to me behind my hovering cart and moved forward. "Keep up with us. Ya came at a good time, we go back to the cells when the light's gone."

He tripped on a rock and caught himself on the cart, breathing hard as we passed over a roped bridge. "I-I need to find my sister. They separated us a-and…"

"Ya ain't gonna find her if you're chucked over the cliffs and swallowed by the sands." I tossed my head down to gesture to the roaring sand currents far, far below the bridge. They were always shifting and jerking around down there, daring us to jump.

Promising freedom.

The new guy's breathing started shaking. Then his blurry face turned to me. "H-hey… I know you."

My arms locked, panic stabbing.

"No," I growled, my fangs growing long, venom building hotly in my glands. "You don't."

Shit. The only reason Lilli and I were still alive was because no one knew who we were. If word got out how close we were to the Devouhs, they'd either kill us or… or I don't even want to know what else.

"Y-Yeah I do," he pushed, sounding relieved. "You were in my house in Brittleton. You took my little brother to help find my mom's soul."

I almost stumbled when I stepped off the bridge to the other plateau, gawking at him. "Wait. Your brother—ya mean Octavius?"

"That's him!" His voice sounded sore, cinching up. "That's my little brother…! I-I'm Neal. Oh, man, I can't believe you're here too—Bloods, does that mean Tavius… is-is he—?"

"He got away with the others," I hushed under my breath, glancing over a shoulder at the blurry Lorak and making sure he couldn't hear us. "I think. I don't know what happened after the war started… What in Death are you doing here?"

He ran a hand through his black hair. "They think we're Grimlings. So they torched our café and locked us up. I-I don't know what they did with Mika."

"She's a Pyrovoker, ain't she?" I asked.

He sounded confused about how I knew that. "Y-yeah… Did Tavius mention it?"

"Something like that," I muttered. Sounded like he didn't know about his Demon Queen ancestor. Probably better if I didn't tell him about her right this minute, though. I decided to stick with the more positive subjects. "They put all the dangerous inmates in the lower dungeons. Especially Evocators. The only reason *those* two haven't been taken there." I jerked my head toward Lilli and Oliver. "Is because Lorak doesn't think she has the stomach to raise anything dangerous, and the kid's just a Seer. If your fire-throwing sister is anywhere in here, my money's on the bottom cells."

He sounded relieved. "When do they let them out?"

I laughed. "When they're dead."

—A burst of scratchy caws wailed over the noise of workers, the sound of small, flapping wings brushing the dry air.

"LINE UP!" Lorak shouted at us, waving at another guard in the distance.

The other guard was carrying something fuzzy and dome-shaped. A black blur writhed within it, the sound of fluttering wings pushing the air again, screeching croaks blurting.

No.

Lorak cracked the whip over my back when I didn't move, and my legs rigidly marched forward. Lilli and Oliver joined me on my right, and Neal, confused, followed at my left.

We fell in line with the other hundreds of workers, forming wide blocks as we'd gotten used to doing for this *special event*.

Being six-foot-two would have helped me see over the packed crowd, but with my piss-poor vision, it didn't help worth a damn to see which crow was trapped in that cage.

Please, I prayed silently to the Mother Goddess, *don't let it be Bridge*.

My pulse beat the living Void out of my ribs, the bird screeching and croaking in panic. *Don't be Bridge. Don't be Bridge. Don't be Bridge. Dear Gods, don't be Bridge.*

My throat went dry. I should be used to this by now. I shouldn't be stressing out every time we do this, but Gods damn it, I kept remembering when Bridge first found me. And then remembered how she was lost with the others.

And worried she would come looking for me.

Someone squeezed my fingers, making me flinch. But I relaxed. It was only Lilli.

Her familiar blurry face looked at me, squeezed my fingers tighter, and nodded.

I blew out a relieved breath. She was my eyes, here. She knew what Bridge and her own crow, Dusk, looked like. If she said the bird in the cage wasn't them, then it wasn't them. I nodded back, shoulders lifting, and waited.

The guard holding the cage at the front paced unbearably slow, his boots crunching over the sandy plateau, his figure outlined in shimmering crimson as the setting sun dipped behind the golden canyons.

Then, in the silence, he stopped where he was and opened the cage. The crow screeched and tried to fly out, but the guard snatched the bird by the neck and lifted it high in the air.

He turned to the left half of the workers, displaying the bird; daring someone to come forth. Then he turned to the right half. He waited. He watched.

And snapped the crow's neck.

A shattering, howling scream pierced through the silence.

The guard stabbed a finger at the worker who wailed in an unseen agony, curled into his stomach and clutched his heart as his screams tore from his bleeding soul.

My heart cried at the wails. *It could have been me.* My eyes welled, hands shaking, but Lilli clutched my fingers hard and stifled the tremors. I caught her wiping at her eyes, cupping a free hand to her mouth.

Two guards dragged the screaming man out from the crowd. His legs had gone limp and every part of him was dripping as though he wanted to drain into the ground and soak into the cracks.

They hauled him toward the edge of the cliffs.

Not another one. Hate lurched wildly as I watched. I'm not losing another Brother to this damned Void-hole!

I shoved out of the block, sprinting after the guards and my Brother Reaper. I tackled one of them to the ground, straddled him and sank my fist into his face again and again and again and—

A plated foot broke one of my ribs from the side and shoved me off the man.

I curled into my stomach, the kicks tripling and whips *crack*ing my hands, my shins, my side… I don't even know how long it lasted, all I knew of the world was pain. And blood. So much blood…

"Get off him!" A tiny voice shouted over that nagging ring in my ears. "Get off him get off him!"

I squinted at the little brown blur kicking one of the guards—Lorak—in the shin and tugged at the guard's arm angrily. The blur had wings. *Oliver.*

"G… et back…" I wheezed, my jaw bruised and screaming painfully. One of the lashings had hit my cheek. Every syllable only stretched it open more. "Get… outta here…"

The kid kept to his thrashing. Lorak pushed the boy by his head and *shoved* him down. He raised his leather whip to the kid—

A pair of large, black wings flexed out like a shield and took the lashing in the boy's stead.

Lilli let out a single, strained squeal of pain, but swallowed it and wrapped her cut wings around Oliver. She held him as she choked back wail after wail with each lashing Lorak struck her spiny back with.

I laid there, sprawled on my side like a pathetic wad of snot, watching her blurry back drip redder and redder.

The guard finally stopped, spat on her, and yanked her up by the arm. I heard a bone snap under his grip.

He drew out a dagger from his belt and raised it to her face—

"Don't you fucking touch her!" I snarled and hurtled into Lorak, sinking my fangs into his scaled neck and letting my venom burn into his bloodstream.

Lorak grunted, pushed me off, and flared his own fangs at me. My venom didn't seem to do much to another viper. Damn this bastard—

A *zap* of electricity washed over me. Someone hit me from behind with a Shocksphere. I was forced to my stomach, twitching and writhing. When the shocks finally died down, four guards flipped me over and held down both my arms and legs.

Lorak loomed over me, his dagger flashing in the crimson sunlight, and he cut into my forehead.

Bloody Nira…!

My feet kicked under the guards' grips, screaming, the pain hot and searing as Lorak took his time to carve out each letter on my head, warm liquid draining into my eyes.

When he was finally done, the guards let me go, and I rolled to my side and vomited, my throat blistering from all the screaming.

Lilli, with Oliver encircled in her arms, knelt to me with a tender hand reaching for my chin. She carefully lifted my face and gasped softly. "Oh, Jaq…"

"W-what's it say…?" I asked, shaking.

She licked her lips, hesitating, then whispered, "Grimling."

MIKANI

"What did you do with my brother?!" I screamed at the guards as they dragged me to the bottom dungeons. "Get off me…! Neal! NEAL…!"

I wriggled, fingers stretching angrily and I tried to evoke my fire. The dampening gloves blocked the Hallows, my manacles too tight. "Get off me! where's my brother—!"

One of them slammed my head against the stone wall.

"Shut it," he grunted. "You should be thankful, Grimlette. You're getting your own little hole to burrow in, just like home."

Everything spun, my skull throbbing.

The lower dungeon walls were dripping with something… wet. The sandy floor was pooling, and even the prisoners were soaked. But it wasn't water. It was too thick and sticky, the dampening shoes on my feet sticking to the clear ooze. *Yinklît Gel?*

That was the gel they used on the dampening gloves. Was this whole floor drenched in it? Some of the inmates we passed started shouting, reaching out their grubby arms and whistling.

This is where they keep Evocators, I realized. *But most of these people aren't Grimish… and they definitely don't look like Reapers.*

I had a feeling these men weren't the chivalrous type.

Ringëd, I thought, nervous to watch so many beady eyes leer at me behind the bars. *Please get me out of here…*

I almost cried at the thought. Where *was* Ringëd? Did he know what happened?

The guards stopped at one cell and unlocked the door, telling the lone prisoner inside to stay against the far wall. They shoved me in, my still-shackled feet buckling as I stumbled to the sandy floor. They locked me in and stomped off, chatting as though nothing was wrong with the world.

The only light came from the dim lamps out in the hall. In the glow, I could barely make out my cellmate.

She was a white-haired girl, cream-skinned with cat ears. Squinting harder, though, I saw she *also* had bright, blue wings. There was a Death mark on her forehead. *A hybrid? For Shel's sake, are the Raiders counting all foreigners as enemies now?*

—I gasped when a thick, sticky mist shot from four valves at the corners of the ceiling, spraying us with Yinklît Gel. It lasted for a full two minutes, loud and high-pressured as it drenched us from head to foot. The same mist was spraying in the other cells.

When it finally stopped, I coughed, having inhaled some of it. "Does that, *cough!* happen a *Cough! Cough!* lot…?" I croaked to my cellmate.

The girl's cat ears folded down, her head cocking. "*Kegtcha lis beiv Cyulai?*"

My expression drained. "Oh, Bloods. You don't speak Landish, do you?"

Her brow furrowed, still not understanding. She licked her lips, trying again. "*Lis beiv Cyulai? Er tovt?*"

I groaned, head dropping. "Sorry, girl, but I have no idea what you're saying. If Ringëd were here, he could probably translate, but…"

I held back the sick sob that wanted to come up again. Ringëd wasn't here. But as soon as he figured out I was gone, he'd do everything he could to get me out, right? I just had to be strong for him… Just until he came.

I let the sob out anyway, holding my legs and quivering. *Just hurry, Ringëd*, I thought bitterly. *If you make me wait, I'm going to smack you so hard, you'll… you'll…*

I didn't know how to finish. So, instead, I just focused on one thought, concentrating as if he'd be able to hear it.

"Ringëd," I said, hoping that by some miracle his stupid prophetic Hallows would kick in and let him See me. "Please… *please* get me out of here."

26

FOREBODING

XAVIER

A bell jingled.
The sound was small and distant, yet it echoed as clear as a feral lark's song. Hssshhhaaauuuuwwww....

A soft hush came above, like sand plunking against glass. In the dimness, I could barely see a glimpse of an azure, opaque ceiling, which quivered and shook, loud scrapes crying from the other side.

Then there came furious lashes, squealing as if the claws of some crazed animal were being filed to stubs, the glassy ceiling splitting—

The ceiling shattered, a flood of black sand sprinkling in like soggy soot.

Yelping, I lunged back when the gelatinous sand poured over the floor and piled into a large mound at my feet.

Then the sands took shape. Two white eyes flickered within the black grains, its form fighting for clarity. It grew and shifted, stretching taller, longer, growing fangs until it became a colossal cobra. I drew a breath, thinking to holler, but the snake unhinged its jaw and cracked down like a whip.

I stumbled to my back and braced to be swallowed whole—

A hand seized my ankle and yanked me forward just as the sand-beast crashed on the mirrored floor in a dusty spray.

The man who reeled me in was antlered—ah, Jimmy!—and he shoved his hand forward, his palm glowing azure, and created a rippling barrier between us and the sand-cobra.

The beast hissed and screamed as it pounded at the bubble Jimmy had created around us, but it couldn't make a scratch.

"Bloody golems," the antlered Dreamcatcher muttered, keeping his glowing hand held to the protective bubble. "Guess Yulia's barrier was weakened after we switched shifts... You all right?"

"I-I..." I was still distracted by the nightmarish beast that scratched against the barrier. "What is that thing?"

"Noctis golem," grunted Jimmy. "Aspirre's got its own demons to worry about."

"Well, go on and kill it, then!" I said, shoving a hand at it urgently.

Jimmy snorted a laugh. "These things can't be killed. They can only be kept out. Just give it a minute to bore itself out, it'll shove off on its own."

It was a strain to concentrate on the elk with this hideous sand-creature still trying to break the barrier. But behind the screaming and grainy howls, something else was pricking my ears. Something quiet and gentle; a faint, crystal-like tinkling...

A blue blur caught my eye behind the golem. A shepherd's crook swung into view—a bell tied to the staff—and it hooked the golem round the neck.

The shifting creature gave a gurgled shriek, its grains forced to freeze into its current shape before the crook's wielder hurtled the beast away and out of sight into the black abyss. With the golem gone, I could now see who had sent it away.

It was a small child with azure hair and eyes.

The child's figure gave off a soft, blue radiance within the darkness.

Keep alert, Shadow Half...

The boy's whispers trilled like tumbling bells, his crook resting over his shoulder.

Many dangers follow... Those among your party cannot all be trusted...

The strangeness of his voice made my skin yield to a shiver. "What do you mean?" I called.

He said nothing more, then fizzled in a glitter of blue light as a fox took his place. I was left in awe, the beautiful creature's fur shimmering with rays of brilliant light as it trotted into the abyss, leaving Jimmy and me alone.

Jimmy gave me an odd look. "Who're you talking to?"

I was still entranced by the memory of the creature, my voice distant. "The child. The fox..."

"Did that golem get a chunk off you, Howllord?"

"He was there." I pointed to where the fox had left. "Just there."

Jimmy shook his head and sighed. "Well, I think that was a little too traumatic for you. Let's wake you up and change sleeping shifts with the others."

I started to protest, but Jimmy waved a glowing blue hand, and everything vanished.

"Yeah, that's where they are," Ringëd's voice hummed once I awoke inside the psyche of Alexander's mind. "They're camped there with everyone else. Got the whole city marked as Reaper territory."

Groggy, I looked round the abyss. The usual, circular window was above me.

After floating up to the window, I saw that Alex was looking at Officer Ringëd. My brother's arms were crossed, Octavius standing beside us. Ringëd's fingers were sliding over Octavius's Reaper badge with a sense of gravity, his brow furrowed low as he fiddled with the black, shield-shaped pin with silver letters that read 'Reaper'.

Confused, I called out. *"What's going on?"* My voice echoed in the psyche, catching Alexander's attention.

"I asked Ringëd to see what happened to our parents," Alex explained, scratching the stubble at his jaw which made a low, grating noise that I could hear from the void. "We heard Father had taken siege of Drinelle with the other Reapers, and a few southern towns have been taken over by rebellions against Galden. I wanted to clarify if those rumors were true."

Ringëd and Octavius regarded Alex curiously when he spoke, probably guessing that I was awake. They'd grown accustomed to our one-sided conversations, apparently.

"So, we're going to Drinelle?" I asked. *"Can we convince Mistress to storm Tanderam?"*

"My thoughts exactly," Alex agreed. "And with the towns below it being under the mercy of the revolution, the travel there should be easy enough. Luckily, the rebels are siding with us, thanks to Cayden. They won't raise Grim's flags and give up their territory, but they'll shelter us and give a clear path to the Golden Canyons."

He sounded hoarse, like his throat hadn't been wetted for some time. I pursed my lips. *"Have you... eaten? Slept?"*

"No," he sighed, rubbing his eyes and making my window darken. "I wanted at least one of us to stay awake. And there was no time for a meal."

"Well, I'm here now. Do you want me to take over and let you rest?"

His head shook. "I'll be fine. We're one measly town away from Drinelle. All we need to do is cross the wastelands between cities."

"How long will that take?"

"Perhaps a day, on foot. The railway won't be available, their route to Drinelle has been closed."

I searched the window's perimeter to see our surroundings. Alex seemed to be in a musky, open building. Straw cluttered the floor at his feet and flies zipped by his ears with waning, annoying buzzes. *"Where are we?"*

I didn't remember falling asleep here. Were we still in Riverstock? I couldn't tell. Wherever this was, I wasn't sure it was a secure place to hide from the Raiders. The walls weren't even walls, really. Just nailed, wooden planks with a tin roof.

The bottom right side of my window compressed upward, signaling that Alex was grinning. "We may have stumbled upon a rather convenient ride."

"And by 'stumbled upon'," Willow said behind us, making my brother turn to her. She was stroking the leathery, pockmarked skin of a Landragon's scrunched snout. "He means Prince Cayden thought of the idea. Apparently, some of the high-ranking Rockraiders have Landragons for fast-travel through the wastelands. They should cut our day's travel into a mere few hours' journey."

"*Excellent*," I laughed, watching as the long-eared dragon licked Willow's cheek with a thin tongue. That feral ferret of Ringëd's was scurrying over the creature's back, Kurn snickering playfully. *"But where did you find these stables?"*

Alex grimaced. "Well, that's the trouble. They're right behind the Eastern Riverstock Raider Station."

Ringëd grunted. "It's going to be hard getting these things out of here unnoticed. I'm just a Footrunner. We're not allowed to ride dragons."

"I've already taken care of that," Alex assured, clearing his throat. "Dalen? How goes progress?"

Our vassal's voice chimed in my thoughts almost instantly. *On our way back, Da'torr*, he said through our Necrovoker's connection. *We got what ya asked for.*

Alex sounded satisfied. "Good. Tell them to hurry. We don't wish to waste any more time."

Hey, they're hustlin' as much as they can. It ain't MY fault ya didn't resurrect me for this job.

"We need you unseen. Just do what you can. And don't get caught."

A snort came. *We're thieves 'n rebels, Da'torr. If we never got caught before, we ain't gonna start today. Have some faith in us, yeah?*

The communication line ended, and Alex leaned against the stable wall. "I suppose we just have to wait now." I murmured.

Octavius, who'd sat down at one corner of this small stable, stroked Shade from his lap.

"Where'd you send them, again?" he asked, Shade Two perched on his head with an entitled air about him.

Alex sat beside Octavius, folding his legs and rested his chin on one knee. "To the Raider's station. They're stealing armor for us to use as disguises."

Ringëd lifted an eyebrow. "You sure that'll work?"

"Well… No," Alex admitted. "But it's the best plan we have thus far."

Willow was still petting the Landragon's neck, making the creature sniff appreciatively. "There aren't enough dragons here for all of us," she said. "We can't *all* waltz out of here without notice. Even with uniforms."

Octavius glanced up at Ringëd. "We can get Ringëd to act like he's arresting some of us or whatever. We can have the Grim-haired people look like prisoners and the Landish-haired people take us out. If we need more Grimish people, we can get Her Highness to change their hair color."

Ringëd pulled out a pack of cigarettes and a lighter, burning himself a smoke. "Sure, why not? I've worked with Raiders before, I know how to act like one. All I have to do is think I'm above the law, and treat people like blood stains on their shiny, *taeux l'ïce* boots—"

"We're sorry to interrupt," a wispy voice cut in. "But we seem to have a bit of a problem."

Yulia had opened the stable door and walked in to meet us, her fox tail swishing and ears grown in concern. Jimmy followed behind her, his face set hard as he folded his arms. His long elk ears were also grown.

Alarmed, Alex rose. "What's wrong?"

"Did someone find us?" Willow asked, coming from around the dragon.

"No." Yulia glanced at Jimmy before answering. "It's the Reaper. Janson… He's been asleep since Octday last week, and still hasn't woken."

Willow's face scrawled with worry. "What day is it now?"

Jimmy answered, "Hexday. It's been eight whole days since he's been asleep. We've given him tonics that Ana made for him, but he isn't waking up. And that's not the only problem."

"Neither of us can find his dreams in Aspirre," Yulia finished. "There is nothing there, besides your own dreams. No other subconscious. We've searched night and day for even the faintest dream, but there has been nothing with Janson. It's as if he doesn't exist in Aspirre. As if… his soul is gone."

It was silent. Willow was the first to speak. "You mean he's died in his sleep already?"

Jimmy scratched between his antlers. "That's the only thing that makes sense. But see, that's where it gets weird. His ghost-vassals are still sticking around, right?"

Willow, Octavius and Alex nodded to confirm, since we were the only ones who could see Janson's vassals, who were probably staying at their master's side as usual. I didn't see Janson here with us, so I assumed he was in a different stall.

"Right," Jimmy continued. "Well, aren't Bloodpacts erased when the Necrovoker's soul is released?"

"When their *NecroSeams* are cut, eaten, or destroyed," Alex corrected. It was really a technicality. *My* soul had been released years ago, but that didn't stop my connection with Dalen and Vendy. Since my NecroSeam was still intact, we assumed that meant the Bloodpact wasn't void until something happened to the Seam.

"Right, whatever." Jimmy shook his head. "Well, since those ghosts are still hanging around, that means his soul is still here."

Ringëd, who'd been listening while working on his cigarette, raised a brow. "Then where's his subconscious? You said you couldn't find his dreams."

Yulia waved a hand. "Therein lies our concern. Are we sure this man is who he claims to be?"

"What are you suggesting?" Willow's tone guarded. "Sir Janson helped me a number of times when I first surfaced here. Are you saying we shouldn't trust him?"

"We're only saying something is strange." Yulia rubbed her delicate knuckles. "The messengers are constantly on edge around him, he sleeps yet doesn't dream, he does not respond to Ana's medicine normally... we don't know what to think."

Alex rubbed his chin. "Concerning the messengers' behavior, I think that is a simple territorial issue. Janson is a crow or raven shifter, and black birds have been known to act strangely around those shifts."

"But there is also the question of where *his* messenger is," Yulia pointed out, her angled eyes flicking to us. "Have you seen any unfamiliar black birds yet? Any that you *hadn't* found at the capital?"

Silence again.

"Perhaps..." Willow murmured, fiddling with the music watch around her neck. "Perhaps he's lost his messenger? The Raiders have been killing them on sight, and if he was captured before coming to us..."

It was a disheartening thought. None of us wanted to think of losing our own messengers—to have the Bond broken. That trauma, some say, can never quite be healed.

"I suppose that is a possibility," Yulia agreed, her voice almost a whisper. She bowed her head. "I hadn't thought of that... forgive me."

"I'll not hear any more of this." Willow's voice changed to a more commanding tenor. "He is our Brother. And he will be treated as such until you have actual proof to suspect him. Am I understood?"

Yulia and Jimmy bowed together. "Yes, my lady…"

JANSON

I pressed an ear to the stable wall to better hear the Reapers on the other side.

One of my ghostly vassals, Rossette, hummed broodingly to my right. "You seem to be attracting suspicion, *Da'torr*."

My second vassal, Nikolai, murmured to my left in broken Landish. "Maybe it be time you 'wake'?"

I kept my wings folded tight so I didn't make too much noise and clicked my tongue. "Those Dreamcatchers are becoming a problem. Maybe I should take care of them before they draw any more attention to us…"

I could wait until they were sleeping and stick my scythe in their ribs. *Would that be too obvious?* Damn it, that wouldn't work. That Bloody Seer could touch the corpses to See what happened to them. Should I kill him too? *No*, I decided, *if I don't want to blow my cover, I'll have to play it safe. Killing everyone wouldn't be smart.*

My stomach twisted. Nira, look at me—debating whether or not to murder people like it was as easy as planning a weekly schedule. *What have I become…?*

A monster, I reminded, sighing.

I still couldn't figure out where that second twin was. Mistress wasn't going to be happy. But *this* twin kept talking to himself as if his brother were right there. I wondered if they could communicate using their minds; sending messages, the way Necrovokers and vassals did?

Maybe the second twin IS dead, I considered. *And he's his brother's vassal?*

If that were true, then why was I still doing this 'fallen warrior' act Mistress insisted I play? I could just kill the last twin and be done with it. That's what she wanted in the end, wasn't it?

Then again, Mistress said to leave them alone until I knew for certain where the second brother was. If I killed this one and didn't have the other's head to bring back… I shivered. Mistress was quick to get over Lucrine's death, I didn't think she favored me even half as much. Not to mention, what she would do to Rosette and Nikolai…

"<What are you after, Dead Walker?>" a threatening croak rumbled overhead.

I glanced up, seeing that same raven from before was perched on the stall's ledge and staring down at me. I squinted up at it with my one eye. Wait, this wasn't the same bird. It had more feathers. It must have been that other one that follows the Howllord around.

"Get out of here!" I hissed.

"<Not until you state your purpose,>" it growled, black feathers rising in warning. "<Why go to such lengths to fool them? Why wait to strike?>"

"I said get out of here!"

A second, more tattered raven hobbled up to the wall, having climbed up with his talons and beak. "<They're preparing to leave, Mal. Has he given an answer?>"

"<None, still,>" he grumbled, turning and dipping his tail feathers. "<Have they begun to suspect?>"

A third, fourth and fifth bird flew beside them, and soon after, two ravens joined as well. *Great.* The Gods damned bird patrol.

"<The Dreamcatchers brought it up,>" the white-cheeked one announced. "<They're suspicious, but since they've got nothing to go by, they let it drop.>"

The raven next to him with the white diamond on its head gave the equivalent of a shrug. "<Don't sweat it, Shade. Since it was brought up, they'll keep a closer watch on him, I bet. Tavius will probably figure it out, with his Hallows going crazy and all. Just needs to stop whining over nothing.>"

The first raven, Shade, shot him an annoyed glare. "<It isn't nothing! Stop pretending you know what he's going through and go back to your own Reaper.>"

"<I don't have one yet.>" He fluttered an indifferent wing. "<I got locked in a box for a couple years after you left home. But now that I'm out, I'll get one. Tavius is *almost* my Reaper.>"

"<What does that mean?>"

"<Rats if I know. Just feels right, I guess.>"

"<That doesn't even… argh!>" Shade flapped hard. "<This is why I left the nest early! You always have to take my things, *Chwakchrih*!>"

"<Now wait a minute, I got a soldier name too, now.>"

"<Yeah, *Shade Two.* Congratulations. You've once again taken something of mine—>"

"<Both of you, focus,>" the twin ravens croaked in unison. "<We still have Sentient scum to deal with.>"

A female crow grunted from the wall beside them, her black feathers dull and puffing out. "<Y'alls Reapers are just bein' stupid. If Jaq wur here, he'd see raght through this dead thing no question.>"

"<Lilli would never tolerate such betrayal either,>" another female huffed, stretching her neck straight. "<She would see the danger, certainly!>"

The first female laughed. "<Lilli's a dumb primy-proper gal, she cun'nt see 'er way through a paper bag, Dusk.>"

Dusk gasped in outrage. "<Hold your country-stained tongue, Bridge! Lilli is the very model of an intelligent and loyal woman. If you and your *barbarian* Reaper can't understand true sophistication, that isn't our fault.>"

The two females began a flurry of annoying insults, and the younger, male crow off to the side sidled away nervously, murmuring the name 'Oliver' longingly. Shade and Shade Two started arguing again, and the twins screeched at them—

"<Enough!>" a sing-song voice cried over them all, reaching a frequency no normal black bird could give. A tiny, canary sized crow buzzed in front of them, looking disappointed.

"<Mal and Chai are correct,>" said the small crow. "<We must stay focused! We must work as an efficient murder, not a bunch of squabbling pigeons fighting over bread. We can't allow our Reapers to go unaware until it's too late. Willow is the most trusting. Unfortunately, she will not listen to me. She doesn't understand. None of them do. The only man capable of translating for us is the very demon we need eliminated.>"

One of the twin ravens—with more feathers—dipped his head. "<Jewel's right. Our primary goal should be to alert them by other means, since verbal communication has failed.>"

"<How're we gun do that?>" Bridge asked. "<Write them a dag'gum letter? I dun even know how'ta read. None 'a us do, raght?>"

"<Actually… I think I can,>" the tattered raven offered. "<I've been watching those Raiders scribble on paper for years. I haven't a clue how to pronounce any of it, but maybe if I research corresponding words that our Reapers often write down, and I found some materials, maybe I could…>"

"<We'll have to wait for now, Chai,>" his brother said. "<If we reach High Drinelle, we'll find what you need. In the meantime, Shade and Shade Two: our primary objective is to learn more shifter words to better communicate. The words 'demon' and 'bad' don't seem to be effective enough, they think we speak of the queen and her horde. Perhaps if we…>"

They kept croaking up there, planning, debating, conspiring right above my head. *Bloods, I need to get rid of those things.* I could snap their little necks and say the Raiders did it, couldn't I? I might actually have to, at this rate.

"Nile…"

My stomach twisted, remembering the crumpled crow in my hands, the utter hollowness…

N… no. No, I could never do that to someone else. Even if my cover might be at risk, I just…

More voices sounded on the other side of the wall, making me freeze. The rest of the party had returned, and they were getting ready to check on me before leaving.

I glanced at the two ghosts waiting for me to say something, Rosette and Nikolai looking worried.

"I guess there's nothing for it now," I said. "Time for me to 'wake up' from my little nap."

XAVIER

"Check it out!" Vendy exclaimed as she hopped into the stall and slung her sack of stolen goods on the straw floor with a clatter. "We got *loads* of stuff, *Da'torr*!"

Dalen's ghost phased through the wall after her in a grunt. "Yeah, their storage room was unattended for a while. We got to pinch a ton of goods."

"And armor!" Henry guffawed as he entered next and slammed down his bag of plate. "Gardener sow me, they've got some of the best alloys in there! Good, strong stuff. And there's plenty for everyone."

Prince Cayden came in laughing with his own bag, Linus at his side and lugging two on each shoulder. "I suppose if they weren't in need of it now," the crowned prince chuckled. "They won't mind if we take it for the remainder of the war, eh?"

The Teslers returned next with *several* sack-fulls of weapons, swords and axes and spears barely held in their arms.

"How in Void did you filch all this?" Alexander demanded of the Tesler siblings, incredulous but wearing a fiendish grin as he beheld the collection of plate and enemy garb Henry had acquired.

Carrie Tesler grunted. "We were arms thieves before this, Howllord. This ain't our first rodeo."

"I never thought I'd say this, but thank Bloods for your criminal background." Alex eagerly rummaged through the bounty of golden breastplates and mail, pulling out numerous brown tunics.

Everyone slipped on their guises, strapped their gauntlets, greaves, mail and helms tight, and prepared for departure.

The 'prisoners'—including Alexander and myself—slid on their stolen cloaks, in case anyone caught sight of our faces during the journey. Alex's face, especially, was plastered on nearly every wall in every city. Being the son of Lucas Devouh, the number one most wanted commander of Low Everland's army, made *us* just as equally wanted. We'd have to take care not to attract attention.

Alex pulled on his hood and turned to Willow. "We need a favor," he said. "You can change hair and eye color, can't you?"

Willow looked skeptical. "Yes."

"What about faces? Different noses or chins?"

"No. Only colors. And Evocator marks."

"The marks shouldn't be a problem, I think. But Xavier and I will need matching eyes. And some other hair color—brown, perhaps, that would suffice. Landish hair won't attract attention and our heterochromia is too notable."

She hummed, placing a hand at her hip. "Fair point. You'll need to wear something that touches your skin to make the illusion stay. I don't have the strength to keep it up. Here, I think I spied something in this pile…"

She sifted through the mound of stolen goods and plucked out a thin, golden choker. Her fingers gleamed azure for a moment, the illusion Hallows streaming around the necklace until the light was sucked into the metal. Willow then took a Raider badge from the pile, broke off the needle, and finished the Evocation by etching a circular sealing-mark at one of the balled ends of the choker.

She handed the item to Alex. "Try this on."

Alex slid the choker around his neck and picked up a shoulder-guard from the pile to examine himself in its reflective surface.

"Eerie," I breathed from the psyche, seeing our hair had become a light brown and our eyes were not, for once, mismatched. Now, both our eyes were blue. I couldn't find my usual, overlapping reflection because of it. *"Now that's a strange sight."*

"Strange indeed," Alex murmured. "Commendable craftsmanship, Willow. Hopefully, it'll be enough."

"Hopefully." She smiled wanly. "I'll have to do the same for myself—"

"He's awake!" Jimmy panted frantically, the Catcher rushing into the stall and urging us to follow. "The Reaper's awake!"

Does he mean Janson?

Surprised, Alex hurried after the elk, Willow at our side. We entered the stall next door and saw that Jimmy was right. Janson had awoken.

"Sir Janson!" Willow crouched beside the coughing Reaper on the ground and took his hand. "How are your wounds? Do you need more treatment?"

Janson reached a hand to his bald head, rubbing his temples. His ghostly vassals floated obediently beside him. "I'm fine," Janson croaked. "Just… hungry…"

Willow gave a sympathetic smile. "We'll find you something on the way out."

Janson's feathered brow furrowed. "'Out'? I… Where are we?"

"We're in Riverstock," Alex explained, leaning against a wooden post as Willow helped the Reaper up. "We're sneaking out in a prison cart and heading to High Drinelle, where our father and mother are."

Janson still looked confused. "'our'?"

Willow shook her head. "Never mind that. Let's just hurry and get you settled."

Kurrick and Alex heaved the Reaper over their shoulders, helping him to the wagon when Herrin and Rolen brought the hovering cart in, horses strapped on efficiently. When Janson was seated in the wagon, his two ghosts floated through the bars to stay at his side in silence. Such an odd pair of souls, they were... Even Kurrick and Ana seemed chatty by comparison. The whole time their *Shelic Da'torr* was asleep, they'd hardly said anything.

Octavius crawled in the wagon next, then Willow, followed by the Tesler siblings, then us. Kurrick guided his Landragon out of its stall by the reins with Ana at his side, and he helped her into the cart with us. Yulia and Vendy trailed her, marking the last of our 'prisoners' before Kurrick shut the wagon's gate behind us. There was no lock in case we had to break out in a hurry.

Our fake Raiders soon came with their dragons, and after making sure everyone had their hoods up, helms on, messengers—and ferret, in Ringëd's case—tucked beneath our cloaks, we moved out, the cart lurching forward toward the city gates and venturing into the wastelands toward High Drinelle.

As the red sun began to drip past the horizon, Alexander's lids fell heavy. A few moments of blackness engulfed my window from the psyche until I was forced out in a rush of breath.

I blinked, stretching my fingers to test control, the humid wind satisfyingly brushing my cheeks. "About Bloody time," I muttered, smiling as Chai perked on my lap and pushed his head against my stomach.

Mal had fallen asleep with the other messengers in their huddled murder, Kurn curled into a ball between them. Yulia and Carrie were sleeping as well, and Ana sat near the back of the wagon with her arms stretched through the bars, prodding the Landragon that Kurrick was saddled on while he rode beside her outside the wagon.

Ana looked to be holding a glass vial up to one of the dragon's lumped pockmarks. A yellow ooze was secreting from the pore, and she collected the substance in her vial, whispering to Kurrick about the creature's medicinal effects and how useful it would be for future injuries. Vendy lay sprawled in the center of the wagon, drooling in her sleep with ripping snores. Our accompanying ghosts were absent at the moment. Dalen had left the wagon to keep watch with Sir Janson's two ghosts, in case we ran into trouble and needed warning.

I sat back against the bars, the wet straw shifting under my feet when I pulled up a leg. It had rained here recently, the mud underneath us was still soggy.

"I thought he'd never let me out today," I said, stretching my neck with sharp *cracks*.

Willow took little time to sidle beside me and rested her head on my shoulder, yawning. "Neither did I... Is Alex asleep, then?"

"Yes. And if he's not careful, he'll make us sick if he keeps that up."

Across from me, Janson paused eating his bread and frowned. "I'm sorry Howllord, but... I thought *you* were Alex?"

I went rigid, remembering he could see our different eyes. But then, I was still wearing the choker with our disguise. My eyes weren't mismatched right now. They haven't been since Janson awoke. Bloods, he may not have even known we had heterochromia to begin with. And perhaps it was best it stayed that way.

"Have you had enough to eat, Sir Janson?" I redirected.

He still regarded me with suspicion, but seemed to understand I wasn't going to answer him. "Yes," he said. "It's enough. Thank you."

Octavius, on the other side of the wagon, cocked an eyebrow at the man's rings. "Didn't you have five rings before? There's only four now."

"I must have lost one while I was asleep." He gave a saddened hum. "But it's only a ring. I've lost... more than that, before..."

Silence swallowed the wagon, the whine of insects drowning the spacious, dry air, Vendy's cutting snores blurting inappropriately. We carried on through the wastelands in the new quietness, only hearing the horses' clopping hooves on the dirt and the Landragons' occasional crowing.

I was the one to speak next, daring a glance at Janson. "There is something we've wondered. We... haven't seen your messenger. We wondered if..."

Janson's expression fractured. His one, non-melted eye flashed with pain and he pulled away to hide the glaze welling there. "I..." he choked, breathing slow. "I *had*..."

His lungs quivered, and gradually, so gradually, his head dripped into his arms. He remained silent like that, shoulders slumped and quaking, until I barely heard him push out a whisper. "He's gone."

Not a soul dared move or speak. We watched the scarred Reaper sob into his hand, dignity abandoned. The heartbreak was infectious. I saw Willow wipe a tear from her cheek as her little crow nuzzled her jaw. Octavius cradled Shade from his lap. He even welcomed Shade Two's prodding beak from his shoulder.

I held to my own messenger. Chai's feathers fluffed in my arms, a soft coo coming from his throat. There was nothing more calming than feeling the proof of life there, so warm and tangible. I never in my life wanted to know what pain would come with Chai's absence. It took me so many years to find him, to free him from his imprisonment. If I lost him now... I pulled Chai to my chest until I could feel his heart beating against mine.

I felt enough time had passed to quietly ask the knight, "What was his name?"

Janson took some time to quell his sobs. When his breath steadied with a sharp inhale, he glanced out at the wastelands and croaked longingly. "Nile."

"Was it the Raiders?"

"No." His throat scratched, talons growing sharp. "It was that damned Sentient. I... I was one of the squads who went into Entrial Valley. I saw her. The Sentient. She was melting my face when Nile came to distract her and..."

He couldn't finish, and took a deep breath to start again. "I... don't know how I got out alive... All I have left are Rosette and Nikolai. It was a miracle they weren't eaten. If I'd lost them, I..."

My head bowed. "I'm sorry."

Janson let out a hard breath. "It's all because of that girl. That Gods damned Sentient. Someday, I'll rip out *her* heart and send her straight to Nira to be Cleansed."

Newly inspired, Willow wiped another tear and growled. "She's caused so much pain for all of us... So much destruction and death, ruined families, broken homes... She will see justice. I swear by my father, she'll Cleanse for it all."

She let her words die there, all of us glaring with our own vows burning alongside hers—

"Hold!" a woman's voice boomed ahead of our wagon. A troupe of Reapers had suddenly trotted toward us on horseback, blocking our path. The captain of the troupe pulled her stallion forward, her staved scythe gleaming at her feet threateningly. "Draw no further! You venture on Reaper territory. State your purpose or begone before we clap you in shackles."

A man beside her, perhaps her lieutenant, muttered to his captain in Grimish. "<Ysali, take a look at those uniforms. Those are Rockraider garments—>"

"<They are disguises!>" I called in Grimish from the wagon, throwing open the caged doors and leaping out.

Willow followed and trotted ahead of me, removing her illusion-disguise and letting her ashen hair flow in the breeze behind her. The Reapers gasped and leapt from their horses immediately, dropping a knee to Willow in respect.

"Your Highness Death!" the captain, Ysali, had lost her breath, stammering, "I-I-I hadn't known you were among this group...! Please, forgive our rudeness!"

Willow stood tall and put a hand at her waist. "I would hardly call proper protocol rude, Trixer. I commend your tenacity. But now, if we've already been stopped by a patrol unit, I take it we're near High Drinelle at last?"

"Indeed, your grace!" Ysali rose and mounted her stallion again, her troupe following suit. "Come, we'll escort you and your company safely. Is the High Howllord's son with you by chance?"

"I am," I said and came to Willow's side, pulling off my enchanted choker to remove my disguise and revealed my shadowy grey hair and heterochromic eyes. "We seek shelter with my parents."

The captain breathed a sigh of relief. "Oh, thank Death! Fangs Alice has been on our arses about finding you. Men, we're eating well tonight!"

The troupe cheered in delight, and we set off down the path with our new escorts.

27
REFUGE

~~~~

XAVIER

High Drinelle's enormous walls were dauntingly guarded. Reapers and rebels patrolled the high walls above and below, armed and plated, their noisy footfalls clattering here and there outside the torch-lit gate.

Our company followed our escorting Reapers through, abandoning the wagon and allowing a few rebel members to take our horses and Landragons to the stables.

I strode beside Willow through the cobbled streets, Grimish folk and rebels whispering as we passed. It was strange… Alexander and I have lived in Low Drinelle for most of our lives; our home was directly under our feet. I'd never known what *High* Drinelle was like. Now that we were here, I… *still* didn't know.

Sure, the flat-top buildings were vastly different from our pointed, spired roofs; the stones and wood were brown and red, whereas ours were black and grey; there weren't nearly as many cemeteries or statues of Nira and Death—but up here, the streets were teeming with Reapers. Even more so than in *Low* Drinelle.

Normally I would have found this odd, but given the war with Everland, it seemed to make perfect sense. Of course the Eyes would claim territory directly above his own home. Of course there would be troops of Reapers—and Grimish Footrunners—bustling everywhere.

These were not peaceful times.

We reached the manor where we were told my parents were housed, and our company was greeted by the head butler. However, captain Ysali suggested that Sir Janson stay at the Reaper Station for questioning regarding our travels and his account of what transpired among our party. Though he was reluctant,

Janson bid us farewell for now and went on his way. The black birds all seemed oddly calmer when he was gone.

The butler proceeded to take us to the second floor, but before we'd made it to the stairway—my mother stormed in.

A flurry of handmaidens shuffled out of her way as she *shoved* the butler aside and strode toward me.

"Mistress." I stood at attention, hands clasped behind my back as habit took control. "Here to report on the war—"

"Damn the report, thank Death you're alive!" She seized my ribs and crushed the wind from my lungs, startling me out of attention.

"You didn't call, you didn't write…!" Dear Gods, this usually ruthless woman sounded tearful. "Absolutely *no* word that you were alive! What were you thinking, staying out there without contact for so long?!"

"S… sorry, Mother…" I strained under her pincer-like grip, my back zippering with audible *pops*. "We ran into a few… complications…"

When she finally released me to dry her eyes, *Father* hurried through the corridors to meet us next. I thanked Death he didn't follow Mother's example, clasping my shoulder instead.

"Don't you ever make us worry like that again," he said. "We already went through one loss, what would we have done if…"

He breathed in deeply, barking at the lingering butler to fetch us new clothes and prepare us food and a bath. I glanced down at my ragged attire, Chai and Mal croaking at my bare, muddy feet as they greeted my parents' messengers, the proud Barrach and tiny Ethil.

Two familiar ghosts phased through the wall to our right then, Aiden and Nathaniel, my parents' vassals, laughing to greet us.

"Young Sirs!" Aiden called with a smile, his spectral wings flapping in silence. "If I'll be Ushar's surest arrow!"

Nathaniel made a motion to ruffle my hair, though the bear's translucent fingers couldn't disturb the strands. "Luck be on yer side, it looks like! What in Bloods took ye so long?"

I shook my head. "It's an exhaustingly tedious story."

Mother had finally composed herself and blotted her eyes with a kerchief. "Come, you can tell us what happened over dinner. Your father and I have already met with the Claws and Second Fangs regarding tactics today, so war strategy is done until tomor…"

She paused, spying our increased party members. She stared at Linus, Cayden—the rebel leader's face hidden in a Raider's helm—Jimmy and Ringëd. "Who are all these people?" she demanded.

"Friends," I explained. "They helped see us here safely."

She glanced from face to face, her brow puckering. "Where are Jaq and Lilli?"

We all fell silent.

"They..." I hesitated. "They were captured. They've been taken to Tanderam Prison. We were hoping you could help us form a rescue team?"

"Consider it done." Her wolf ears curled. "How dare they imprison my favorite student and Spirit daughter...!"

She puffed out her fury, but calmed in a breath and smoothed back her hair. "But that will have to wait for tomorrow. You all must be exhausted. Go and change, all of you. I expect to see you in the dining hall in an hour."

She stalked off, wiping her eyes again, and I sighed while following the others upstairs—

My father clapped a hand on my shoulder, stopping me. "Xavier..." he rumbled, "a moment?"

I stood at attention. "Yes, my lord?"

"Dash the formalities," he said softly. "I'm speaking as your father."

My brow furrowed. "Yes... Father?"

"I only wished to... Well, that is..." He coughed into a fist, his eyes darting away awkwardly. After a moment, he gave a defeated breath, and smiled. "It's good to see you."

The aged creases touching his eyes said something else. And damn it, if Alex had been awake to see it, he'd actually believe me when I told him later.

I realized Father was waiting for a reply. I offered a bemused smile. "Y... yes," I said. "And it's... good to see you, Father."

His lips drew into a line before he nodded and walked off, flustered but newly cheered.

I stared after him, grinning, then walked up the steps.

"My lord?" I asked Father once reaching the long dining table downstairs.

I was freshly bathed and shaven clean now, wearing a long white shirt and brown vest the servants had retrieved for me, though I had no idea whose clothes they were. But just when I'd started to relax, my nerves were shocked to full alert when I noticed with whom we were dining.

I pointed a befuddled finger at the figure who sat at the head of the table. "What is *he* doing here?"

High Roarlord Apsonald, Jaq's grandfather, furrowed his scaled brow at me. To his left sat a pair of other blond vipers, a man and woman, both of whom didn't look ecstatic to be here.

"What am *I* doing here?" Roarlord Apsonald echoed haughtily. "Is that any way to speak to your host?"

Ah. So this is HIS manor? I sank into my chair. But I'd thought his home was in New Aldamstria? Was this a summerhome of his? Glancing at the other pair of vipers, I saw the woman's eye twitch in annoyance. *No—it's HER manor. This must be Jaq's aunt.*

"Oh, er… forgive me, High Roarlord." I cleared my throat. "I was only surprised to see you."

"Surprised my tail," Apsonald snorted. "Accused and scrutinized in my daughter's own manor. Bah." He stabbed his sirloin with a fork, returning to his meal.

My father glared at me from the other end of the table, and I awkwardly coughed into a fist.

I caught Willow grinning across the table. Her long hair was draping over the lacquered floor, not tied up with her usual bell and butterfly ribbon. It was still damp from her recent bath, the flowery perfumes reaching my nostrils even from across the table. Her engagement-vines glittered from either side of her head. I'd nearly forgotten about those, she'd kept them in their box for weeks during the trek.

"High Roarlord?" Willow said, clearing her throat. "I don't mean to sound intrusive, but…Since you're here, does this mean you wish to help us? I expected you to be by King Galden's side, to be perfectly honest."

Apson gave a gruff snort. "Firstly, you should know I'm a head figure in the rebellion against the king. Land's Servant himself requested me to spy on Galden before I was ever appointed as his Hand."

"Oh," I said in surprise. "Strange, he hadn't mentioned that when we arrived."

Apsonald frowned at me. "Who hadn't?"

"Cay…" I stopped, not sure if the High Roarlord was aware who the rebel leader was. Just in case, I quickly amended. "Land's Servant. He came here with us."

Apson dropped his gilded utensils and hefted to his feet. "He's *alive?*"

"You… didn't know?"

"He just disappeared after the war started! No one's heard a thing!"

Chuckling sounded from the doorway in the back. Cayden was there, dressed as Land's Servant—having donned his plummed hat and mask—with Linus waiting beside him.

"Terribly sorry for losing contact, Apson," Cayden growled in his deeper, disguised voice. "I had to be sure the High Howllord didn't fall into any trouble with Galden's Raiders."

"Hah *ha!*" Apson bellowed and hurried over to clasp thrilled hands with the man. "You Bloody fool! Do you have any idea what it's like dealing with our soldiers during times like this without you?"

"I know—and I'm sorry, Apson," said Cayden, "But I hear you've done well so far. Word has it, the rebellions have been hugely successful in some cities. How goes progress with the rest?"

"It's slow," Apson admitted, ordering a butler to fix Linus and the Servant meals, and to bring two extra seats for them. "But we're getting there. As you can see, we've already taken control of Drinelle and the three cities just south of here. It isn't much, but it's proving most advantageous, since we've made an alliance with the Reapers. We share territory and men while they share imported clothes, arms, and food from Grim."

My father grunted at the end of the table. "And again, thank you for that. Though, I want to make perfectly clear that we *do not* believe your lost Relicblood is alive—it's madness, if you ask me—but I have to admit, we can't win this war without having some footing in this realm."

Prince Cayden gave a humble bow to my father. "My men are more than willing to help, High Howllord. It's the least we can do, since your sons will bring us our rightful king."

Both my father and mother glowered at me. "Isn't that what your latest bodyguards have been spouting?" Father asked. "And your vassal, and the Blacksmith?"

"And now the rebel leader?" Mother added, exasperated. "What have you been telling these people?"

I could only shake my head. The fatigue of today's journey was bogging down my spirits as well as my shoulders. "Nothing. They're all delusional."

Mother shot the Servant a narrow look. "And does he know about…?"

"Yes." I rubbed my heavy lids. "The goat over there already knew about us and told him—"

She slammed her hands on the table. "How many people are you going to tell?!"

"They didn't tell me anything, High Howless," Linus interrupted, taking his seat beside Cayden. He laced his fingers over the table and leaned his chin over them, his dreads tumbling over his goat horns, the beads clattering softly. "And I didn't mean to intrude. My prophetic Hallows is triggered at random, in their case. Normally, I would have kept their secret, but if they're to bring us our king, I thought it only sensible that my Lord Servant knew the situation. Who knows? Perhaps he can help fix their dilemma."

Cayden laughed. "And what a strange dilemma it is."

Roarlord Apson looked immensely confused, sitting back in his seat and rubbing his eyes. "My lord, what in Bloods' names are you talking about?"

Cayden patted the old viper's shoulder. "Perhaps I'll explain when things are normal again, Apson. I'd rather not impede on the High Howless's wishes any more than I already have."

Mother glared at him, but remained silent.

Apson pinched the rim of his nose. "Yes, well, regardless… My lord, I have a family crisis. I was hoping you could help?"

Cayden blinked behind his mask. "A crisis?"

"According to Howllord Lucas, my grandson has been captured and taken to Tanderam Prison. I've tried calling Galden earlier to convince him to free Jaqelle, but he nearly had me hanged for treason. He's been spending most of his time—and trust—with his Second Hand instead."

My father nodded. "And you say Roarlord Wales has been acting odd?"

"Extremely." Apson's eyes hardened. "He's been different, lately. Before, he was a rather passive man, a voice of reason when Galden wanted to declare outrageous laws. But lately, Wales has become more conniving and secretive, completely in concurrence with everything Galden comes up with—and has been suggesting his own ridiculous laws. He's like a completely different person. I'm worried he isn't the real Wales at all."

Mother lifted a delicate, grey brow. "Who else would he be?"

"Who knows? A demon in disguise? Much like what you claimed happened with your Death Princess there?" He flicked his eyes at Willow, who bristled.

"You're a fool if you believe that was me," Willow snarled from her seat. "I was with the Devouhs all that time. The stray Roaress with them in Galden's palace? That was my disguise."

He raised a mitigating hand. "I'm aware, Your Highness. Lord Lucas informed me. I meant no offence."

Father gave a long breath and sat taller. "Lord Apsonald—"

"Please, just Apson."

"Apson… Since you say you're against Galden, what do you plan to do now? Stay with us and declare your standing, or continue to survey him in the capital?"

"The latter would be wisest, I think. I will report here when I can, should any battle plans arise. For now, though, I'm afraid he already suspects me. I think it best I stay away from Drinelle as much as possible from now on. To be honest, Galden thinks I'm here under duress, trying to negotiate the release of my daughter and her husband."

The woman viper beside him shot Apson a peeved glare. "I will *not* leave my home with a bunch of Grimlings in it!" She declared shrilly. "It's ridiculous enough that we have to host them!" She shuddered in disgust. "Creepy little rodents…! Dirtying my furniture, my fine dishes, my *beds*—!"

"You will be silent, Helda!" Apson hissed. "This is not your decision, and you will not be leaving regardless. I don't need any more of my family to be held hostage by Galden. He already has Jaqelle. I'll not risk you as well."

"Better a hostage of the king than these shifty-eyed dirt crawl—"

"*Helda!*" Apson slammed a hand on the table, making everyone's dishes clatter, and I had to grab my drink before it fell over. The Roarlord's voice bubbled at his now stiff-backed daughter. "You will be *silent!*"

Her next words caught in her throat, petrified as her eyes fell to her untouched plate.

"—Erm," The head butler popped his head into the dining hall, cringing when all our gazes turned to him, and he cleared his throat. "E-erm, H-High Roarlord…?"

Apson's answer was gruff. "Yes?"

The butler ducked his head sheepishly. "Er, uhm, there are, er, some *guests* here asking for you…"

Apson's brow raised. "Guests? We're not expecting any…"

His eyes widened when a blonde, scaled woman stepped inside.

"I apologize for not calling earlier, Father," the blonde viper woman—Jaq's mother—huffed, striding inside with Jaq's black-haired father trailing her. "The High Howllord called us days ago explaining Jaqelle had gone missing. Howless Alice gave us permission to surface here, if we chose."

"Marcella…!" Apson may as well have grown wings on his feet, flying upright. He looked overjoyed and bewildered. So surprised, he didn't have a coherent greeting prepared. He decided an acceptable choice was: "You're here!"

She didn't give a response, and instead turned to me, glancing hurriedly round the table.

"If you're here, Alex," she deduced, not knowing that I wasn't Alex. Neither of Jaq's parents were aware of our situation. "Where is Jaqelle? He would be with you, wouldn't he?"

"Jaq…" I began, trying to word myself carefully. "He's alive. But he's been imprisoned."

Jaq's father cursed, looking to *my* father. "You're gonna get him out, right, Howllord?" the Grimish viper asked. "Ya can't leave him there to die…!"

Father rose to meet with them, giving an assured murmur. "We're gathering a rescue team as soon as possible, Yoric. Come, you and Marcella may stay with us. I'll ask the servants to settle you in. In the meantime, I suggest you…"

They, including Mother, walked out of the dining hall, and Jaq's aunt growled. "Whose home does he think this is?" she complained to her husband. "I don't want Marcella here! She's the one who chose to leave luxury to live among cave dwelling peasants—just because she had a worm-child doesn't mean she can come into *my* home and—!"

"That's enough, Helda!" Apson snapped, shutting her up. "You will welcome your sister into your home and keep your opinions to yourself!"

Helda crumbled, face red with resentment, but said nothing more. Her husband looked just as rigid, not daring to go against his father-in-law's wishes. Helda shoved her chair back and strutted out of the hall, dragging her cowardly husband with her.

Apson shook his head, sliding a scaled hand through his hair and turned to Cayden. "My Lord, I'm at a loss… Galden won't release Jaqelle—he won't even check the prison to see if he's still alive in there."

Cayden rubbed his chin. "I don't suppose you have any leverage against him?"

"Not right now. But given some time, we just might."

Cayden cocked an eyebrow. "How so?"

"You weren't the only one to disappear after the war started, my lord." Apson's voice lowered to a mutter. "It seems the crowned prince vanished as well. Galden is in a panic over it. If we could find Prince Cayden—alive, hopefully—we could make a trade offer to free Jaqelle and the Young Howllord's fiancée. But we don't know where the prince is, so until we…"

Cayden and Linus burst into laughter.

"What?" Apson asked, perplexed. "Have I said something?"

"Apson!" Cayden chortled with sly delight, pulling off his disguise to reveal his face. "You mad *genius!*"

Apson stilled. The color drained from his scales. "What… what in Land's name…?"

"Linus!" Cayden's head whipped to the goat, his grin wide and wicked. He held his mask and hat out. "Put these on, and tie me to a chair immediately! We're going to have a most amusing com call with my father…!"

The three rebels left the hall in a thrill. Well, Apson still looked numb with shock, but he followed Cayden and Linus rigidly, leaving the rest of us at the table.

"Well then," I said and set down my utensils. "As entertaining as that was, I think I've had enough excitement for one day. Or a few weeks. Or a whole damned month."

I left the table, Willow following with a scoff, and soon after came Octavius and Ringëd.

The four of us crossed the foyer and started up the stairs—until the master butler began shouting at the front door.

"For the last time…!" the butler grunted. "Commoners are not welcome! The High Howllord is not expecting anymore—!"

The door burst open, and in tumbled a ferret-eared man and a cat-eared girl.

"Holy Rin!" Ringëd cursed, trotting down the stairs in a hurry, his feral ferret scuttling at his feet to keep pace. "Uncle Lawson?"

Octavius followed close behind him. "Connie! You're all right!"

I called to the butler to allow them inside, and once the two newcomers brushed themselves off, Octavius embraced his plump sister.

"T-Tavius…!" the freckled girl, Connie, cried and buried her face in her older brother's chest. "They took Neal! And-and Mika…! And our house is gone, and—"

"I know, I know," Octavius hushed, "we're going to get them back."

Next to them, Ringëd patted his uncle's shoulder welcomingly. "Uncle, good to see you. Glad you made it out of town in time. I heard about all the trouble the Catchers are having… Guess you were looking out for Connie?"

"I was just heading out when she came hollering at my loft," his uncle explained. Ringëd's ferret crawled to the man's shoulder and huffed excitedly. Lawson went on, "We got out of there as soon as we could. Figured Drinelle was the safest place to be nowadays… oh, and she said your bride-to-be dropped these when she was locked up." He produced a long, velvet box and handed it to Ringëd.

Ringëd cracked it open to reveal a pair of golden engagement-vines. As he traced his fingers over the delicate chains, Ringëd's stare glazed over and his Dream mark lit from his shoulder, as though having a vision. I could swear his eyes began to well angrily. He snapped the box closed and shoved it in a pocket, nodding to his uncle. "Thanks. She'll be wanting these back when we get her out of there."

Connie sniffled and wiped her running nose as she glanced at Octavius, seeing Shade flap to Octavius's shoulder while Shade Two fluttered to his head.

One of Connie's cat ears flicked at the second raven. "You have *two* birds now?"

Octavius glared up at Shade Two. "Don't ask. Anyway, do you guys have somewhere to stay?"

Connie shook her head, giggling when Shade Two took a strand of her orange hair in his beak curiously. The raven dropped it in an indifferent croak and lost interest, settling back on Octavius's head comfortably.

"Right," Octavius sighed. "Well, uh, I guess Lawson can room with us. And you can stay with Willow, Connie—"

"No!" She clung to her brother. "I'm staying with you. Please. Everyone else is gone and…"

She started crying, and Octavius did his best to calm her. Eventually, he gave in. "All right, all right. We'll try and make room…" He glanced at me, apologetic. "Sorry, but is it okay if she stays with us? She's been through a lot…"

I made my way down the steps and crossed my arms. "I suppose it's fine. But you should be aware, Miss Connie, that you'll be in a room full of men you don't *all* know."

"I don't care!" She held Octavius's arm tighter and sniffled. "Octavius and Ringëd and Mr. Fleetfûrt will be there, right? I'm going to stick with them! Oh—uhm, if that's okay… Howllord…"

She gave her best attempt at a curtsy, trying to remember her manners. It was so awkward and clumsy that I couldn't help but smile. How cute.

"It's fine with me." I turned to the ruffled butler lingering off to the side. "Please inform my father that we're housing two more guests. Tell him they are friends of mine, and that I have vouched for them."

The butler bowed and went to do as asked, scuffing the floor in his hurry.

28

STALEMATE

~~~~~~~

MACARIUS

"You're sure of this, are you?" I questioned our young, generous informant who was fortunate enough to escape Drinelle when the Reapers invaded.

The poor viper's grease-stained skin blistered from weeks in the burdening sun, his breath a coarse wheeze and his eyes as red as his scales. I could see the venom dripping from this boy's fangs as surely as I felt the leather upholstery against my back.

"Aye," croaked the lad, his shaken voice swathed with horror. "I saw the high lord 'imself. Was shoutin' orders at the Bloody traitors that dun killed em Raiders. My Da... M-my Da din make it out…" His eyes leaked, and he rubbed at the tears with stubby, soot-coated hands.

"I'm terribly sorry for your loss," I hushed from my seat, flicking the guards two dismissing fingers. "Thank you for bringing this to His Majesty's attention. We'll keep you well guarded and like rewarded for your perils."

The guards escorted the sobbing boy out of the room. I waited until the door clicked closed before turning to the king who waited by the wall.

"Well?" I asked, fingers brushing my jaw ponderously. "Need there be more proof that Apson is out for your head, my lord?"

"You think he'd go so far…?" asked the blond king, pacing the lavender carpet and fiddling with the gold hoops that clattered from his wrists. He was a nervous wreck.

I shifted weight, the leather seat protesting with low groans, and sipped my red wine. "I cannot say for certain." I spied a black speck floating in my drink. Sniffing, sneering, I dipped a finger in the wine a rid it of the suspicious speck.

Disgusting place. Neverland may have had its flaws, but the scullery lads at least knew how to properly clean goblets. I had half a mind to call the Lady Lysandre here to give the women a proper beating.

The king, still fidgeting with those ringing hoops on his wrists, shuffled here and there past me, damn near wearing down the soles of his slippers. He couldn't see past my 'imposter' illusion. To him, my skin was *not* coated in scales, and my mouth did *not* have venom-filled fangs. I'd taken the image of High Roarlord Wales instead, the king's Second Hand.

The worrying man crossed me for the twentieth time when I sighed. "What sense is there in ruining your carpet, Sire? I'll admit, Apson's deceit is inexcusable, but it isn't worth such stress."

"But he called an hour ago to say he's returning from Drinelle!" cried the king, smearing his glittering, adorned fingers over his face helplessly. "He claimed negotiations were at a standstill with the Eyes! The Howllord would only release his daughter if *we* released the High Howless Lilliana and the other apprentice—Apson's *grandson*!"

My brow raised. "You're saying we have them captive?"

"It would seem so." Galden rubbed at his lids with a heavy thumb and forefinger. "The Howllord's son has declared it so. But the guards of Tanderam don't know *which* prisoners they are."

"I shall send men to clarify," I assured.

It would have to be Kael and Claude, I decided. I didn't have any faith in Roarlord Wales's incompetent servants, and I didn't trust Claude to keep his loyalty when I wasn't watching. Kael would have to go as well, to monitor him. That baker was a slippery ally, but a useful one if you could keep your grip tight enough.

"Even if they *are* there," the king growled, lion ears curling, "I won't let them out. Especially if I find this claim is true, and Apson is… is…"

I offered idly. "A traitor, my lord?"

He blew out a sneer. "How can he be? Nine years I've worked with the man—I called him my friend—I…!"

"It does seem rather out of character for him." I drawled. Not that I knew who in the five realms Apson had been before this, but judging from the king's reaction, he must have been a trustworthy fellow. Or so I assumed.

"But consider, Sire," I said, sipping my wine, "that he's been acting rather strangely as of late. One could say he's like a different person all of a sudden. I'm not even sure if he's the same man at all."

Galden scowled at me as though I'd told him the ocean waters were actually purple. "What do you mean?"

"Is it not possible Apson could be a demon in disguise?" I said. "You know of the Sentient Necrofera out there. They look and talk as we do. We would never know the difference."

The king's face cracked with fright. "A demon? My own Hand? That... that Bloody...!"

The king called for the guards and spouted orders to apprehend Apson upon his arrival, ordering an interrogation of the First Hand.

My lungs quivered with laughter, but I stifled it swiftly. Still, my smile couldn't be tamed. This was perhaps the easiest operation I'd executed yet.

Keeping back the noctis golems of Aspirre? Difficult. Staying hidden for five centuries from Dream while trapped in that timeless prison? Even more so. Keeping lit the fire that fueled Kael's rage? Exhaustibly trialing.

But this? This was a Gods damned farce.

If I'd known it'd be this simple, I would have killed the king and taken the crown with his image from the start. It's not as if I hadn't already assumed Wales's role that way, how much harder could it be?

The thought was tempting, but... then again, I needed Galden on the throne. Someone had to be the scapegoat who managed the tedious chore of warfare. Battle strategy was not my forte. Though I doubted it was Galden's, either... but I also needed Galden to distract the Reapers from the rest of the world's problems.

The com-screen blipped to life while the king was in the middle of ordering Apson's arrest, making both of us turn. The incoming number was unknown, and couldn't be displayed. Hesitant, Galden commanded the screen to accept the call.

"*Galden,*" a deep, scratching voice greeted, "*good evening... I thought I might have a few words with our false king?*"

Galden's mouth nearly unhinged itself, staring at the masked man with a wide-brimmed hat which cast his face in shadow. "Y...you...!"

Land's Servant? I gave an interested hum. He's never directly called the king...

Galden pointed a furious finger at the screen. "How dare you call here, you psychotic... You, you lunatic!"

"*And here I thought royalty had better manners,*" the Servant sighed, taking off his hat. There were curling goat horns sprouting from his head. "*But, then again, I suppose 'manners' have always escaped you... namely after you had my father beheaded.*"

Galden bristled. "Linolius! I Bloody knew it!"

The Servant laughed. "*Did you? Funny, I always took you for an idiot.*"

"I know why you've called, Servant! You think you've won now that your army of peasants has joined the dirt crawlers? Hah! I know your game. You think I'm intimidated by such pathetic efforts? You want me to surrender? I'll have you know that I have no intention of—"

"I suggest you stop there before you make even more of a fool of yourself. It's far too early to boast. Or, is it too late?"

The king's glare could have caused Shockdragons to puff into smoke. "What are you on about, Servant?"

"Where is your son, I wonder?"

Galden's retort died on his lips. He attempted a quick amendment. "He's... here with me. In the palace."

"A liar AND a coward? Tsk, tsk... you and I both know you have no idea where your son is."

Seeing my opportunity, I leaned toward the king to whisper in his ear, "Apson must have told him, my lord. None but *he* who knew the prince was missing, apart from us."

The king's lids narrowed, and he muttered back to me. "That Bloody traitor..."

"Now," the Servant continued. *"Here's a question for you: If the prince isn't with you, where do you suppose he is? Hm? I'll tell you a secret, Galden, but don't tell a soul... I know where he is. In fact, I think he'd like to say hello."*

The Servant moved the screen's view. There, bound to a chair and gagged with a black cloth was Prince Cayden. The prince struggled against his binds, gurgling from under the cloth tied around his mouth. He held a number of bruises and cuts while his blond hair was stringy and frazzled.

"Cayden...!" The king went pale as a ghost. "Release him, Servant, or I'll...!"

"Or you'll what?" the Servant challenged, moving the screen back to himself. *"Take him from me? That would be a sight. Your single army against two of ours?"*

"The Reapers haven't collected enough numbers to overpower us! I've constricted their growth here on the surface, and *your* little army isn't a match for my trained Raiders!"

"We'll see... but I have a better idea. You see, there are two Reapers in Tanderam Prison that the High Howllord wants back. A viper named Jaqelle—grandson of your First Hand—and a bat named Lilliana... who, as it so happens, is the fiancée of the Howllord's son. If you want your son back without bloodshed, perhaps we can make a better trade than what was suggested with Apson's daughter?"

"I will not make deals with rebels!"

"Think well before deciding, Galden," the Servant moved behind Prince Cayden, drawing out a knife and holding it to the prince's throat. *"This is, after all, your son we're negotiating for. The heir to your false crown..."*

Galden's brow beaded with sweat.

Clever, I commended in silence, an annoying admiration sprouting for the Servant. Galden was protective of his son. If he was going to crumble, it would be over this.

"My lord," I murmured. "It is a bluff. Who's to say they won't slit Cayden's throat after they have their friends? Say you want your half of the trade first, and then decide what to do with the Reapers afterward. You could always kill them later. The only thing that matters is your son's safe return."

"Y-yes!" Galden huffed, straightening as if he'd had the idea himself. "I want my son *before* I hand over anyone, Servant!"

"And say you'll only give back the viper," I whispered next. "The girl will be too useful as bait, if she's engaged to the Young Howllord."

Bait for me, at least. If Janson failed to find that missing twin, I needed a contingency plan. I could lure one of the twins to me with Lilliana, and the other twin would come to rescue his brother, perhaps…

Galden repeated my suggestion to the Servant, who scoffed. *"I'm afraid both packages must be delivered. And I'm not stupid enough to hand over my precious cargo so easily. If the original deal cannot be agreed upon, then I suppose I have no use for your son, and I'll kill him now—"*

"No! Wait…!" Galden was panicking, looking to me for help.

I shook my head, seeing that I would have to address the Servant myself. It seemed the king was too much of a coward.

"Lord Servant," I said, folding my arms behind my back. "I see that you are no fool, and have a firm understanding on negotiations. However, I advise you to not think myself so foolish either. Prince Cayden is too prized for you to dispose of so easily. You may be the commander of savage rebels, but I see you have more sense than to dispose of a 'precious cargo' so soon.

"You need the prince alive. And I know you will keep him that way until you've made use of him, because he is the *only* leverage you have against the king. My lord has made his demands for a trade, and unless you agree to them, we have no deal. Let us know when you've come to your senses. Good day, Lord Servant."

Before Galden could protest, I ended the call.

29

ROYAL OBLIGATIONS

~~~~~~~~~

WILLOW

I took a preparing breath, then blew it out in a nervous stream, one set of fingers tapping over my knuckles.

The stillness may as well have been a living creature all its own in the manor's conference chamber. Emptiness oozed from the indigo carpet; wafted off the ruby-papered walls and soaked the lacquered, wooden furniture in a strangling silence. I felt like a morsel being crushed inside a giant beast's throat, slipping farther and farther down to await my death in its abysmal belly.

I sat at the far end of the polished table with my hands cupped neatly over the silken, black fabric that draped over my body from neck to toes in subtle sheens of blue. It was a thin gown with sleeves that trailed past my fingers in lapping waves, the curling embroidery stitched with shimmering grey thread that patterned the garb with butterflies.

From my reflection in the glossy table, I watched as my solemn visage stared back at me, the silver engagement-vines glittering from either side of my hair. The com control panel was embedded into the wooden corner, and I spied it as I would a feral serpent.

It's been far too long. My stomach fluttered, but I reached for the controls in defiance. *It's necessary.*

Before I could change my mind, I dialed the appropriate number. The screen of projected light blipped into view over the far wall, churning within itself as I waited for someone to answer. Finally, someone did.

"Hello, Morice," I addressed in as regal a tone as I could produce.

The Master Servant had nearly dropped his handheld com in alarm. *"Y-y-y… Your Highness!"*

"I wish to speak with my father, Morice," I said softly.

"Y...yes!" Morice's eyes bulged. "Yes, right away!"

Just before putting me on hold, I heard the man let out a gleeful laugh. I waited patiently in the sapphire-lit room, counting the minutes on the wall clock and mentally rehearsing my lines. Then, as I was nigh seconds from surrendering to my cramping back muscles, Father flew into view.

"*Willow?!*" His colorless eyes were frantic, the Death King puffing hard. I guessed he'd run rather swiftly at the news. "*Thank the Gods—!*"

"I'm sorry, Father," I interrupted. The apology was overdue, so I wished to get it out of the way hastily. "I didn't intend to leave when I did. There were... circumstances that demanded it."

He exhaled gruffly and ran a hand through his short, ashen hair. "*So I heard... well, never mind that. I don't know if Lucas delivered my message, but please, you must listen to me. Do not return to the palace.*"

My previous preparations crumbled. "I'm sorry?"

"*Do not return,*" he repeated, his gaze sharpening. "*Your uncle convinced most of parliament to change the age minimum for Death's Duel. They demanded my immediate attendance for the vote. I... had no choice but to comply, Willow. If I refused, it would have made you seem weak. And with your absence, Yvan's claimed you're avoiding your responsibilities as future queen.*"

"That's preposterous!" I cried. "I admit, I was... nervous when Grandfather told me about the Duel, but I would have stayed and trained. I would have—"

"*I know, I know,*" he hushed. "*But the law has still changed in your uncle's favor. However, you shouldn't worry about your public image anymore. We've convinced the people that you left to help with the Necrofera crisis—they see this as a noble act, and one that the true heir would naturally do.*"

"Everyone has been parroting that here, also. I wonder, whose idea was the 'devoted princess' excuse anyway?"

"*Your mother's,*" he muttered, glancing sidelong as though wishing he'd thought of it first.

Cree...

The door groaned opened suddenly, making me turn. Xavier stepped inside, garbed in an ivory vest and champaign dress-shirt. He found me and crossed the carpet with silent steps.

"Ah, darling." He bent to wet my cheek with his lips. "There you are. Why, aren't you a vision this morning? Come, we've gathered everyone in the..."

Xavier stopped cold when he noticed my father's enlarged face on the screen. Then his spine splintered straight.

"*Death's head,*" Father whispered. "*That's him... isn't it?*"

"Er, Father." I pushed to my feet hurriedly. "I neglected to tell you... The real reason I left... it was to find Xavier." I snatched Xavier's petrified fingers, interlacing them with mine, and took a deep breath. "And I found him. Alive."

Father was Deathly still, his colorless gaze unmoving. *"I know."*

My prepared retort died on my lips. "You know?"

"Your mother told me." He leaned closer to his screen, scrutinizing Xavier's horror-stricken face. *"But to see him firsthand..."*

I stifled a wince when Xavier crushed the living Void out of my hand.

Bloods, he was panicking. Then again, I shouldn't be surprised. My father was the very man he'd spent the last six years taking pains to avoid at all costs. Perhaps I should have told him I was making this call earlier?

Father was silent for some time, staring at Xavier with incredulous, clear eyes. It took him a long while to find his voice again. *"Blood and bones... all this time, we thought you were dead. What happened that night, then? What became of you?"*

Xavier swallowed, like a feral deer facing down a coyote. "I'm... not... sure, Sire..." He struggled to keep his voice steady, sharpened teeth grinding and wolf ears draped to his neck. "I can't..."

"That assassin erased his memories," I explained, Xavier squirming under my fingers. I tightened my grip, hoping it would give him some reassurance. "That's what the man was doing that night—not destroying his soul."

"But what have you been doing all this time?" questioned my father. *"Where have you been?"*

"Xavier has been here on the surface," I lied, racing to fabricate a believable story, "washed ashore in Everland. He knew nothing of who he was for a long time... he didn't know where he'd come from, and didn't know where to return. He's finally remembering everything now that I've found him... and especially now that he and Alexander are together again."

To my satisfaction, Father seemed to buy it. *"Incredible..."*

I cleared my throat, turning to Xavier. "Could you tell the others I'll be down shortly? I've more business with my father to discuss."

Relieved, Xavier nodded and bowed to Father, taking his leave. He seemed to try with all his rigid might not to look rushed before closing the door after him.

Once alone, I released the breath I'd trapped and sank into my chair. "Now, Father." I sighed. "The reason I called was actually to tell you I wasn't coming back. Not anytime soon. I was surprised to hear you agree. But even after I rescue Lilli, I cannot abandon the war effort here. Everyone is looking to me as an omen of victory."

"I'm aware." Father shook his head to regain focus. *"And I understand. Pulling out would seem cowardly and affect the rest of the troops poorly. With two wars on our hands, we can't afford that. Keep to your duty as you see fit... your instincts seem to be in line with your mother's."* He cracked a grin. "You're thinking more like her by the minute. Although I was furious you left, I'm finding that that decision was best... Please be safe, Willow. Your mother and I love you."

Tears stung, and I willed them back. "And I love you both."

I forced myself to end the call. When the screen vanished, I wiped my eyes, inhaled, and left the conference chamber to join the others outside the streets of High Drinelle. Now was not the time to linger on sentiments, regardless.

Now was the time to march for Tanderam Prison.

HERRIN

The Dancing Desert waited at my toes, the flowing sands sifting in the wind and begging me to take the first step on its hot grains. There was so much mystery behind these currents... so much wonder to those solitary dunes—

Wait, was that a girl? Riding the sand currents?

Y-yeah! A girl was crossing the desert and heading straight for me! It looked like she was surfing the currents with her bare feet, snaking through the landscape like it was an every-day sport.

She wore a cheery, sunset-orange shirt with thin straps that hugged her collarbone, her slender legs paired with baggy white shorts that billowed behind her like sails, and big sunglasses hid her eyes. Her rust-orange hair was tied up in a tail and capped with a white visor, her fox ears perked and tail swishing at her legs. She looked like any other teenager I've seen around here. Except there were gold marriage-vines dangling from her head.

And she had a shiny crown.

When she surfed up to me, her hand gleamed blue, and the sand at her bare feet radiated with light, the grains freezing in mid-air to let her crouch down and inspect my face. She was clutching a thick book, but I couldn't read the title that was buried against her huge chest.

The girl lifted her sunglasses, sliding them between her glittering crown and raggedy visor. Now that I could see her face, she looked familiar... almost like... well, like the Death Princess, actually.

"Herrin Tesler?" *asked the rust-haired girl.*

I frowned. "Uh... yeah. Who are you?"

"Crysalette Sandist, Queen of Dreams," she answered, hopping off the frozen sand. She stretched, her bones popping. "Pleasure to meet you in person. Well, almost in person. Would that be considered 'out' of person, do you think?"

I stared at her.

She muttered, "I can see you're in a state of shock, so I shall skip the lengthy explanation and get right to the point: Anabelle tells me you're traveling with my granddaughter."

"Who's your..." I paused. "Willow Ember?"

"Precisely."

"But you can't be..." I scratched my feathered hair. "I mean, you look like her, sure, but you look... her age..."

"It's a drastically long and boring story," she said. "Now, I understand that you seek truth when in the face of false claims, Herrin Tesler. And I've brought you something to do just that."

She handed me the book she was holding, and I read the title.

"*The Choir?*" I asked. Why would she give me the religious text of Harmonism? "I've already read this."

"Not this version, I assure you," she giggled like a schoolgirl. "It was written during the lifetimes of the original Relic Children. My husband had taken the first copies away for a few thousand years, but I believe it's time to enlighten the world of the lost prophecy. I've chosen you to be one of those Enlighteners, Herrin Tesler. And I hope you will relay what you learn to Xavier and Alexander, in time. The Shadowblood must be made aware of their mission once Ana has declared the timing just. I trust you will do as instructed. Have a good morning."

From her pocket, she pulled out a single, azure orb. The orb brightened in her hand, and after sliding down her big sunglasses and touching the sphere to my forehead—

———✦———

Someone shook me awake, making me flinch in the library's cushioned chair. "Wh—what?!" I gasped. "Huh?"

"Sir?" the wrinkled librarian looked worried. "You're part of the High Howllord's party, aren't you?"

I blinked, glancing around. How long was I out? I found the window—it was bright and sunny, making me cringe. I jumped to my feet and collected the messy pile of books I'd scattered on the floor the night before.

I paused when I found a new book there. It was thicker than the rest, covered in dust and gnarled at the edges. It had that old-timey smell, like I should expect a swarm of moths to flutter out when I opened the cover.

I picked it up. *The Choir*.

My dream flooded back. That girl who looked like Willow—the Queen of Dreams...

What did she say about this book? She said it was a... a different version. The original version. Was all of that even real? Or did my subconscious make it up? I turned the thick book over, noting its ratty binding. I didn't remember picking this book up last night. I only saw it in my dream... Maybe I forgot I'd found it yesterday?

Shaking my head, I set it aside and scooped the rest of the books into a pile, shoving them in my small Storagebox. I didn't need to bring a religious text on a rescue trip.

The librarian looked alarmed to see me stuffing my Storagebox with the books. "S-sir!" he cried. "Those are the library's property—!"

"The High Howllord needs them!" I lied, shoving the last book into the box.

Now the only book left was *The Choir*. I stared at it, feeling I should take it with me. *But why did I need it?* It was just some stupid Harmonist book with a bunch of stories.

Still, that feeling didn't go away. It gripped my stomach, twisting until my fingertips were tracing the thick text's cover. *The original version...* My fingers made clean streaks through the dust. *Without any edits, without any censoring or alteration... a version no one from this era's probably read before...*

Biting my lip, I snatched the book and tucked it under my arm, then glanced at the librarian. "They haven't left yet, have they?"

The librarian rubbed his knuckles. "Well, no... but they're just about to depart—"

"Where?!"

"A-at the southern border! Near the stables—"

"Thanks!" I shoved past him and hurried out of the building.

I nearly got lost and had to ask for directions, but eventually found the entourage of caravans in time.

"Wait!" I called, seeing the Young Howllord in the back of one hovering coach, which was currently floating forward. "Wait! I'm coming, wait...!"

The Howllord saw me and ordered the caravan to stop.

"Herrin," he called, his weird eyes flicking past me. "And Dalen. Good, you both made it."

I glanced over my shoulder, but didn't see anything. I guessed Dalen's ghost was there. *How long had he been following me?* My head shook. *Doesn't matter.* I made it in time. I relaxed and slowed to a walk, hopping into the coach with the others.

The Howllord lifted an eyebrow when I sat down. "You look oddly excited." He said, sounding annoyed. Must have been Alexander. I was getting used to them switching now.

Alex leaned back and muttered, "Your other siblings elected to stay here. I would have thought you'd follow their example and read your books."

"I've always wanted to see the Dancing Desert with my own eyes," I explained. "Textbooks and geographical articles are nice, but it isn't the same. There's no way I'm going to miss seeing how the sand-currents react to the winds and document their patterns *in person*!"

"Hmm. All right, then." He cracked a grin and told the coachman to carry on.

The caravan started forward, taking us out of the city.

Excitement drumming, I pulled out *The Choir* from my arm and leafed through the pages. *Which parts are supposedly new? Are the older ones different also, or are they the same?*

Alex lifted an eyebrow at me. "*The Choir*? We didn't take you for a religious man, Herrin."

"It's a, er, commissioned read," I explained.

"Commissioned by whom?"

"Just… someone important." I wasn't about to say 'the Queen of Dreams', who may or may not have been a figment of my imagination. "They said there were different parts in this version, so I wanted to see what they were."

I figured the prelude was a good place to start.

Creation, the title read.

In ancient times, ere the shifters tread upon this soil, there roamed the human race. These strange new creatures were Father Shel's cherished creations, borne of the petals of his holy relic, the Blossom of Gold. These humans resembled not the animals which preceded them, yet the Gardener had hoped they, of all, would thrive within his sun-blessed land. Yet lo, a quandary sprouted: Despite his sacred spade and golden hands, he could do naught to sculpt their souls. In this, his wife succeeded, and hence did the Mother Seamstress mold proper souls for these new beings.

Yet ne'er had Nira beheld such creatures. Having naught a human soul in reserve, she infused the souls of departed animals. With time, the wild souls proved to change the humans in a most peculiar merging, and hence the shifters were borne unto Nirus. In scant ways, these morphing beings could change their form, yet with their e'er-shifting bodies came another quandary:

Their souls would slip from their vessels, leaving naught but a hollow shell behind.

Henceforth, Nira sought to stitch these shifters' spirits to their slippery forms, thus creating the NecroSeam—

I flipped ahead in the text, snorting. All right, so far it was the same as all the current renditions. I'll just skip to any new parts and—

I flipped to a new chapter, one that I didn't recognize. *The Legend of the Shadowblood.*

On the page was the picture of a man, grey-skinned with shadow grey hair and sapphire eyes. On both his hands were the black Crests of Nirus.

I nearly dropped the book. "Holy…!" Fumbling, I raised it up to compare it to the Howllord. Except for the mismatched eyes, it was *exactly* the same. "Holy Land…"

Alex looked concerned. "What?"

"I—n, nothing!" I pulled back the book before he could grab it, and flipped to the front pages. "I, er, was just wondering when this book was written."

"And when was that?"

I turned to the publication page and skimmed for a date. This whole thing was handwritten with pen and ink. Near the bottom of the page was the scripture date, marked:

The Choir, Edition I.

Scribed on the forty-eighth of Watermein, 0017 years After Bloods.

"… 0017 A.B," I mumbled.

He looked surprised. "You have a copy that old?"

"Apparently…" *But why,* I thought, eyes narrowing at Alex, *are* you *in here?*

30

DESERT DAYS

~~~~

`BIANCA

Stupid, stupid, stupid, stupid…!

The winds threw my hair in a tangled mess, my rabbit ears draped to my neck to muffle the deafening gale whistling past me.

Death, what was I doing up here? Stupid, stupid, *stupid*…!

The Culatian girl holding me by the ribs flapped us higher in the afternoon sky, using the wind currents to soar over the Golden Canyons with her scarlet wings. We'd found out her cat-jay friend was sent to Tanderam Prison. It was supposed to be a dangerous place to travel to, but I made a promise to Master Hendril to get this Sousül's friend home. I wasn't going to go back on my word. No matter *how* much I hated our method of travel.

By the sound of the swallow girl puffing above me, I was relieved to hear the Sousül was getting tired from the long flight, and I glanced up at her to jump at the opportunity. "You can set us down in the canyons and take a break!" I called over the wind.

The Sousül—Zyl—started losing altitude to prepare for a landing. Her emerald goggles gleamed in the sunlight, and she set us down on a plateau to rest, our legs swinging over the edge.

"We ees close, no?" Zyl asked and readjusted the un-strung bow and quiver strapped to her back.

She pulled out a crimson, glass ocarina from a pouch strapped to her belt and started twittering idle tunes. She did that a lot, to pass the time. It was nice, having music to distract us during this hectic trip.

There was something about this particular song, though. She played it a lot, and looked hypnotized whenever she wobbled and danced to it. I could swear I felt my stomach lurch on its own with the flighty tune.

"What song is that, anyway?" I asked, curious. "Is it common in Culatia?"

The Sousül paused mid-song, glancing up thoughtfully, her head wavering. "Not common," she said. "But ees favorite of mine. Ees called, *Prochtaet Astrabôv Mot Aero*. Winds of The Storm."

"Huh." I smiled. "I like it."

She grinned and kept playing the *Winds of The Storm*.

I reached into my Storagebox and pulled out a crinkled map of the Everland continent. "Well," I hummed. "Looks like we just reached the Golden Canyons. Tanderam Prison and its copper mines are somewhere on these plateaus…"

Zyl lowered her ocarina. "Ees good thing! When El ees the free one, I give her *big* fishes for eating! Salmon ees the favorite of her. Will like." She looked thoughtfully at me. "What you need for my thanks too, *Külleschkov*?"

I still wasn't sure what *külle-whatsit* meant, but she'd been calling me that since we left. I shook my head, rabbit ears folding down. "I don't need anything. I have my reward right here." I pulled out the Alchemy text Master Hendril gave me from my Storagebox, showing it to Zyl.

Zyl's face screwed up and she pushed down the book. "Book ees not for the fun! Book ees for the learning. Work time. Work time ees not now—now ees the holiday! Fun! Fun and work time not for the mixing."

One of my long ears flicked up. "I don't think I'd call breaking into a high-security prison fun."

Zyl snorted and waved a dismissive hand. "*You* not call fun, *Külleschkov*. Ees what you call… 'adventure'. Adventure ees fun. Well—*will* be fun, after we be getting *Prev'lae* of mine."

"What's *Prev'lae* mean?"

Zyl took a minute to think about that. "Ees, how you say… 'Aide'? One who helps another until they are older?"

"Oh. Right, nobles usually have that…"

That made me think about the twins. Jaq was technically their Aide, but he didn't want to be called that. Something about not wanting the responsibility attached to it. I sighed. *Guys… I hope you're okay.*

What if they were killed? Or, at best, imprisoned? Maybe I should look around the place after getting Zyl's Aide out? Just in case.

I pulled my knees to my chest and propped up my chin. I tried reading from the Alchemy text to clear my head, but I couldn't concentrate on tonic brewing right now. *Alex… Please be okay…*

Panic threatened to spike, but I pushed it down and scrunched my nose. *There's nothing you can do for anyone right now. Just get your mind off of it.* I forced myself to read the Alchemy text:

Editor's Note:

This is Edition V of the Lady Herdazicol's book of formulas and other Alchemical brews. Though the Alchemists' Guild has been long disbanded and its practices are neither commonly used nor relevant to today's economic and martial needs, the Lady Herdazicol's discoveries and innovative chemical compounds are still widely respected in the scientific and academic community.

I paused for a minute. *There was a guild for this?* Why did they disband? How could *any* form of chemistry and tonic brewing be considered 'irrelevant'? Bloody stupid. I'd bet my fluffy tail that politics were behind it. Maybe I could re-found it if I got enough members…

I flipped the page.

Author's Note: To my future incarnation…

I blinked. "What the…?"

To my future incarnation,

You will not remember our discoveries and experiments when next we're born. To combat this, I've comprised our formulas in one place so that we may continue our research and perhaps even improve upon it. I know not what new technologies your era's sciences hold, but I trust we will find ways to incorporate updated revisions to these practices, if able.

Post Script: If by chance we were to meet our ward, Anabelle, I would very much appreciate a due 'hello'. I expect she will still be around for some time. I wonder if Sir Kurrick is still stitched to her coattails, as it were?

Here's to the future,

The Lady Jilume Herdazicol.

I tapped a thumb over my forehead, scowling. "Anabelle…" I hummed. "I know that name. Wasn't that… Yeah! That was that lioness girl walking around with Alex and Xavier, back in the capital. One of their new 'bodyguards' or whatever…"

Was that the same Anabelle written on here? But, no, that didn't make sense… This book was from the 1800s. Some girl wouldn't be walking around in the 22nd century from that time. She'd have to be 300 years old or something… *But why make a note to a future incarnation about it?* Souls don't usually get recycled for… well, 300 years. *What in Bloods was wrong with this crazy Alchemist woman?*

Zyl put away her ocarina and hopped to her feet. "Break ees over! We go to El now."

I stifled a groan and put my book and the continental map away, then pushed to my feet. " You sure you're up for it, Sousül?" I brushed off the dirt from my shorts and small tail. "I know I'm not exactly as light as a feather."

She scoffed and adjusted her emerald goggles. "What you think, my wings not strong for you? Ees no problem, *Külleschkov*."

"What does that mean, anyway?"

She took a second to think, then said, "Stranger with kind heart. Ees friend not known long, but helps with great problem."

"Oh. Yeah, okay."

She wrapped her arms around my waist again and took flight, soaring over the canyons.

Her sleek hood had been blown down to show her scarlet-feathered hair, red eyes shielded by the glint of her goggles. I've seen Stormchaser goggles before, but hers were fancier than usual. They were framed with delicate, silver wires that curled and jolted around the lenses like lightning bolts, and were attached by rows of graceful chains crusted in rubies.

My mouth twisted, deciding it was about time to ask this. "What exactly are you and your, uhm, Aide doing in Everland?"

Zyl kept her gaze forward, focusing on her flying. "We ees finding someone," she said over the wind. "Someone with two-colors of eyes."

I paused. "Wait. Which two colors?"

"Blue and clear," she said. "There be two of these ones somewhere here. I see one on Screen. If one be here, that ees enough."

I rubbed my temples. *Are you kidding me?* "Why them?" I questioned. "What are they going to do for you?"

Her smile grew wide. "They ees also *Külleschkov*. They ees ones that can find my *Oltorofv*."

"Olto-what?"

Her nose scrunched, thinking. "Brother. My *Oltorofv* ees been the missing one for long time. Ees time to be finding him now."

"Oh... so these other, er, *külle-whatevers*... Do they even know your brother?"

"*Ye, ye, ye...* Maybe no. But they will be helping with me to find him. Ees what the... *ye, ye...* oracle tells to me."

"What oracle?"

"A wise one," she answered simply, giving a cough. "Ees best to changing subject now, yes—*Huew?!*"

A chained net shot out around us suddenly, squishing us together as the links slung around us and pulled tight at the top, held by three bronze-armored, winged men. *Footrunners!*

"You're in a restricted area!" one of the Runners yelled. "Resist, and we'll remove you through force!"

I blinked at them, the net making it hard to stay balanced, especially with Zyl's wings digging into my back. "H-hey!" We're just lost! We're, uhm, trying to get to Hensri down south!"

The first Runner looked suspicious. "Then why aren't you taking the designated route around the desert? Going straight through is dangerous."

"We're pressed for time!" I said, looking under my dangling feet and seeing we were just below a plateau. "Look, I'm a... a newly graduated Healer, I'm trying to get to a patient in Hensri."

"You can meet him the *right* way, doctor, slower or not—"

Zyl took a deep breath and, pushing out her hands, blew out a hard exhale upward. A powerful gust caught the Runners' wings and they were lifted higher against their will, the three giving startled yelps as Zyl's wind sent them scattering.

I stared in awe at Zyl. "Woah...! Is that Aero—?" The net was released and we dropped onto the plateau, my back aching on impact.

Zyl and I scrambled in the chained net, pulling on the links until we found the opened top and fumbled out—

I slipped over the plateau's ledge, screaming while hurtling down—but gagged when someone caught me from the narrow path below.

"Well, this is odd," a man's voice hummed. "I wasn't aware it could also rain *rabbits* on the surface."

My eyes cracked open an inch, and I found myself staring up at a hooded man holding me. The horse he sat on gave a soft snort and shook its head, one hoof scraping the rocky ground under us. I couldn't see the rider's face under his cloak and desert scarf, but there was a raven on his shoulder that cocked its head at me. *Reaper!*

"Oh, thank Nira for *you*!" My arms hooked around his neck, gasping out the panic in a burst of relief.

"M-Miss, will you please!" He shoved me back, and I stumbled off the horse in a puff of dirt. He brushed himself off, sounding exasperated. "Your appreciation is noted, but I am an engaged man, you should be aware. Personal space is preferred."

When I pushed myself up, Zyl flew down beside me, looking worried. "I sorry, *Külleschkov!*" She said hurriedly. "So sorry! I be forgetting you not have wings...!"

I shook my head, letting my pounding heart settle, and waved to the random guy on horseback. "It—it's fine, Zyl. This guy caught me."

The stranger pulled down his hood, wincing at the sunlight as he did. "Death, this sun is brighter than I thought." He held a hand over his eyes and pulled down the cloth covering his face, shaking a puff of sand out of his hair.

He was in his early twenties, with Grim-pale skin, black hair, angled sienna eyes... definitely a Howllord, since he was wearing a finely-pressed, white noble suit. And he obviously was not having a good day, with the way he rubbed his rear in a wince. He was saddled on a brown horse, bags and Storageboxes strapped to the saddle.

Shouts came from the sky, making Zyl and me flinch.

Those Runners were soaring their way to us, and flapped to the ground as Zyl and I ran behind the Grim stranger. The officers started at the sight of him, and it took the leading Runner a minute to collect himself before stepping forward.

"D-dirt crawler!" he spouted, pointing a Shotri at the stranger.

The Howllord lifted an insulted brow. "Excuse me?"

"Your kind aren't welcomed here! Either crawl back to your hole or face the dungeons!"

He took off his gloves and dumped out the sand that had found its way in.

"Inexcusable," he scoffed. "Had you any idea to whom you're speaking, you would walk away posthaste." His hands burst with blue fire, making the Runners step back. "I suggest you lower your arms before I have you roasted for such disrespect."

The other officers pulled out their Shotri. "That won't affect our shots! Just surrender, or we'll be forced to—"

Krrack-zap!

Zyl had clapped her hands together and pointed to the talking officer, using her Astravoking to send a bolt of lightning his way. The electricity sparked over his body, knocking him down and leaving him twitching uncontrollably.

Zyl stepped in front of the stranger and his horse, her hands sparking with zapping strings. "You be going now!" she barked to the remaining two Runners, her talons grown. "I no kill him, just knock out! But I *will* kill if have to!"

The Runners' gazes drifted from Zyl's sparking hands to the stranger's flaming ones. One bolted for it, and the other cursed, fumbling after his buddy while dragging his fallen friend on the ground. When they were gone, Zyl dismissed her Hallows, as did the stranger.

"Blasted Everlanders," the Howllord muttered, turning his horse by the reins to look at Zyl. He examined her expensive-looking clothes. "Well, thank you for the assistance, Sousül." He turned to me next. "And little rabbit. Since you seem to be better with the Landish language than your mistress, could you by chance direct me to Tanderam Prison? I'm afraid I've lost the path, and I'm admittedly terrible with directions. It's of the greatest importance that I hurry there."

One of my ears draped down. *Did he just call Zyl my 'mistress'?* What, did he think I was a servant?

"She's not my mistress," I corrected right off the bat. "She's my friend. And we're actually going to Tanderam, too. Here, I brought a map…"

"Splendid!" The Howllord perked. "I don't suppose you'd like to join me? In case more of those petulant Footrunners come to retaliate?"

"Oh… uh, sure. Sounds like a good idea."

"Wonderful." He heaved off the horse, touching down with careful steps and seethed while taking an awkwardly wide stance.

He handed the reins to me while rubbing his thighs. "Take after this creature, for me, hm? I've been riding for days, I can barely feel my legs anymore."

My stare flattened. "You wanted us to come with you so I can watch your horse?"

"Well." He slid off a boot to pour out the sand. "I also thought having a Pyrovoker *and* Astravoker would be more threatening."

"Oh. Good point…"

That reminded me. Didn't Zyl use Aerovoking when we were in that net? She must have been a Dual-Evocator. Why didn't she say anything about that during our traveling?

"Ees good idea!" Zyl answered him with an exuberant thump on the back, making him gasp. "And she ees the Healing one! Ees good to have if hurt."

Now the stranger eyed me like I had worth. It was an annoying look. "Is that so?" he asked. "Interesting…" He glanced back at Zyl. "And what is your name, Sousül?"

Her smile was fixed. "Zyl."

"Exotic… I am Matthiel Inion." He raised his chin. "I am the son of Matt*hew* Inion, the First Fangs of Low Neverland."

I frowned. "What the Bloods are you doing up here in the opposite Overcontinent?"

"Searching for my fiancée." He took out a pocket watch to look at the time. His brow furrowed though, and he shook the watch to knock out sand grains from the clockwork before giving up and putting it back with a scowl. "And I'm in a hurry. I was told by the High Howllord just last week that she left for these canyons mere hours before I arrived in High Drinelle. I have to catch up to her quickly. She's apparently begun a rescue mission for my Reaper Brothers in Tanderam."

"Oh." I threw a thumb at Zyl. "Well, we're going to Tanderam to bust out her friend. So I guess we're on the same page."

"Brilliant." Matthiel rubbed his eager hands together. "Shall we be off then, Miss Rabbit?"

"My name is Bian—uh, I mean... Dr. Florenne." *Bloods, that just rolls off the tongue, doesn't it?* I'd always dreamt of having people call me that officially. Downright giddy now, I pulled out my map. "Okay, if that's west, then... we need to go south."

Matthiel waved an encouraging hand to me. "Lead the way, Doctor."

I preened at that and nodded with confidence, strutting down the correct path and tugging the horse by the reins. Oh, I could *so* get used to this.

"And, er, Doctor?" He kept pace with me as his voice dropped to a low mutter. "While we're at it, do you happen to have any remedies for saddle sores...?"

31

PREPARATIONS

WILLOW

The clamor of stomping boots and shouted commands swelled outside the tent, the scraping of whetstones on steel singing in the millisecond gaps.

A glazed stew perfumed the tent as Alexander finished his bowl and set it at the corner of the foldable, wooden table, turning the lamp's knob to brighten the light over our map.

"What of ventilation?" inquired Alex, his eyes scanning the crude schematic our scouts had drawn after they'd returned days ago from Tanderam's perimeter outskirts. "Surely, the guards don't scour those tunnels?"

Trixer Ysali grunted at his side. "Would but they could, Howllord. From what I hear, the ventilation canals are barely large enough to fit feral rats."

I pushed my hands over the table, looming over the map. Stray strands of my ashen hair curled over it, my bell jingling from its ribbon. I gave a slow, nasally sigh. "There's no other option. The only entry points we can even hope to penetrate are those across the bridges."

"Then back to the original plan," Alex mumbled. "We've run out of time for an alternative. If we leave our campfires up and running any longer, someone is bound to notice. And we need that preemptive advantage."

I ran a finger over key points on the map, murmuring. "Sil Ysali, meet with the other Trixers and affirm that the original strategies are to be used. Divvy the teams among the bridge points, no fewer than ten bodies per station. Stealth is preferred, but should that be compromised, tell them to be prepared for anything."

Ysali saluted with a gauntleted fist to her chest. "As you wish, Your Highness." She bowed and left the tent, leaving Alexander and me alone.

I sank into a creaking chair, rolling back a shoulder while adjusting the gleaming, ribbed plate over my bicep. The armor was crafted with pure olium, my set uniquely decorated in intricate reliefs of prancing wolves and curling willow leaves. It had been a gift from my father, having been ordered and delivered to High Drinelle before we'd even arrived there to meet with Father Lucas. I supposed he had expected me to find the High Howllord sooner or later.

My glinting helm waited at one corner of the table, a slit running at the top half of the back, leaving room for my long hair to fall freely. Another unique feature for my plate, no doubt designed by Father. I remembered those times during my girlhood when he explained my hair was a symbol for the Grimish people, a means to invoke strength and pride.

I was Death, after all. And Death was a proud soul.

"Have you contacted the king?" asked Ale… no, Xavier had switched out now, his single blue eye was on the left. He wore his own glimmering plate, and while it wasn't as heavily decorated as my own, it was far from plain and certainly not simple.

"I have," I said, tightening the leather belts of my felt-padded greaves that were strapped to my calves. "He knows we move out tonight. Should we not return, or fail to contact him with results, he is to send a new militia in after us."

Xavier nodded, looking thoughtful for a moment. Then he said. "We meant to thank you, by the way. For keeping your promise…"

I cinched the straps tight around my thighs next, glancing up at him. "Which promise?"

"For staying silent," he clarified, clearing his throat behind a fist. "I'm… admittedly more than a little ashamed for hiding all this from you. If I'd known you'd be this accommodating—not to mention creative with the stories you tell him—I'd have come to find you sooner, and perhaps even…"

"You'd have done nothing differently, Xavier." I folded my arms over the table. "You couldn't even remember me, let alone whether or not I could be trusted with such a thing. You needn't be ashamed."

"But I am." He lowered into the seat across from me, laying a hand over mine. "Even more so, for forgetting my time with you at all. I know there's nothing I can do to make up for those years, but if by some chance there *was*…"

I sighed. "Just remember what you can, darling. We'll… discuss this after our friends are safe." I paused, an afterthought hitting me. "Though, I'd advise against getting killed and leaving me a second time. That would certainly not win my favor."

He let slip a laugh. "Duly noted—"

The tent flap was thrown open.

Xavier and I retracted our hands, but we must not have acted in time because the intruding knight blushed and gave a very low bow.

"I, er, I'm sorry, Your Highness," he said, flustered. "And High Howllord… I don't mean to, er, impose, but…"

I rose to my feet, pretending I didn't care that he'd seen me joining hands with, as far as he could tell, Alexander. "Are the preparations ready?" I asked.

The knight straightened, loosening his white cloak's collar. "Nearly, Your Grace. But another Brother has just come to the camp and is asking for you."

My brow raised. "Which Brother?"

"He says he's your, uhm…" His face turned bright red, looking at Xavier with a swallow. "Fiancé."

My brow furrowed. "What in Nirus are you…" I gasped, muscles locking. "Oh. Dear…"

"What?" Xavier's ripping tone made me wince. "What is he on about?"

"I, er… may have forgotten to call off an arrangement with someone before I surfaced." I gave a muffled cough. "Of the nuptial sort…"

Xavier's face crossed with the briefest pang of betrayal, but then he twisted his mouth, considering something. I wagered Alexander was speaking to him. After a moment, Xavier bobbed his head to both sides. "I see…" He said, still looking far from pleased, but kept his voice quiet and controlled. "And with whom was this arrangement made?"

"Well…" I stepped out of the tent while he followed. "I'm not sure if you remember him, but—"

"Dearest!" came an elated voice to my left. Before I could gasp, a pair of pale arms crushed me in a heartfelt grip. "Thank the Seamstress you're all right…!"

The surrounding campers turned in surprise when the newcomer swooped me down and brought his lips to mine—

A fist flew in and *cracked* the man's jaw, throwing him back and making him stumble.

"What in DEATH," Xavier barked, stepping in front of me with Bloody murder scrawled on his face. "Do you think you're doing with my betrothed?"

XAVIER

"Wait a moment…" My gaze narrowed at the sienna-eyed Howllord. His sharp face was annoyingly familiar. "Aren't you… Matthiel?"

"X… Xavier?" Matthiel's brow knitted. *Blast, that's right,* I remembered, *he was a Necrovoker—as well as a Pyrovoker, if I recall?* That's why he could tell the difference in my eyes. His voice cracked shrilly. "You're alive?"

The other Reapers gasped around us, all staring at me and murmuring fervently.

"*You damned idiot!*" Alex groaned from the psyche. *"Just tell them it's you! Make something up quickly, or you'll give us away!"*

I balled my hands and kept myself between Willow and Matthiel. "Ye... es," I told the intruding Howllord, whose wolf ears had grown, as had mine. "I'm alive."

Matthiel's face cracked with a mixture of amazement and dread. "But how did you survive?! Where did you come from?"

"That isn't your concern. The only thing you need to know is that I survived, and I'm here now."

"Then where is your brother?" he demanded. "The Devouhs told me *he* was here!"

"Alexander is resting," I lied. "He doesn't know I'm here. I've been watching him since he surfaced… and I've been, er, posing as him to gather information on the war."

This caused a wave of murmurs among the camp, all astounded and, to my confusion, excited. *Wonderful.* This sort of gossip would likely spread now, thanks to these nosy shifters…

"Now." My arms crossed and I glared at Matthiel. "Would you care to explain what you were doing with my betrothed?"

Matthiel's teeth gritted. "I hate to be the one to tell you, Xavier, but things have changed since you disappeared. Including Her Highness's affections."

I heard her groan behind me. I glanced back to catch her smearing a hand over her face.

"Her affections apparently haven't changed," I noted, "she only agreed to marry you because she thought I was dead." I paused, looking at Willow again for assurance.

She opened a hand in my direction in a confirming, albeit frustrated, gesture.

I turned back to Matthiel with more confidence. "And since I am *not* dead, our betrothal is still in effect. Which makes yours null and void. So if you'd be so kind as to *stay the Death away from her*, I'd be ever appreciative."

Matthiel reddened, scoffing. "Null and void? You never even asked for her hand in the first place! You were already given it without her consent!"

"Of course she consented to it. She wouldn't have left you in Grim otherwise."

"She only left because she learned of the demons here in Everland." He glowered nastily. "Don't be so conceited to think she came here for you."

My wolf ears curled. "Just keep your distance. If she wanted you, she'd say as much—"

"—Thank you, gentlemen," Willow chimed in flatly, pushing me aside. "It really takes the pressure off my shoulders to have you both speaking on my behalf."

She shot us both an annoyed glare, said nothing to me, then turned to Matthiel with hands on her hips. "Matthiel, you'll have to forgive me for being short. This isn't the time for a lengthy apology, and it's especially not the time for quarreling amongst Brothers. For this, I'll be quick."

She twisted back to me, prompting my spine to straighten.

"Xavier," she said, "I'm sorry I neglected to mention the new betrothal. Given all that's happened in the past few months, I don't think I need to explain myself when I say *it slipped my mind*."

I wasn't entirely sure why, but I bowed, my muscles seeming keen on it.

She spun on her heels to face Matthiel next, who stiffened into attention under her sharp gaze.

"Matthiel," she drawled, her arms crossing while her fingers drummed over her polished, silver gauntlets. She seemed in deep thought, conflicted with what to say. Eventually, she let out a long breath, her tone calming. "To you, I am most sorry. I should have renounced my acceptance the moment I learned Xavier was alive. But I didn't. And I'm truly sorry to recant my answer so unceremoniously here, and sorry that I have to at all. Though, you were correct that I, indeed, wasn't asked to accept my betrothal with Xavier... It was *I* who chose him. And it so happened that he'd chosen likewise. I'm telling you so you understand why I must say this..."

Matthiel's breath caught when she bowed to him, her voice soft and humble. "Please, forgive me. I am ever thankful for the offer, but I cannot in good conscience, nor true heartedness, accept your proposal. I have chosen my husband, for this life, and the next."

The surrounding crowd was in utter silence, their heiress still bowing before the stunned Howllord. I half expected Matthiel to sputter a protest, but he clicked his teeth shut and nodded slowly without a word. His sienna eyes had lost their luster, cheeks sagged and hollow.

She rose, and Matthiel was quick to kneel, making up for having been honored so completely. "Thank you, for your honesty..." It sounded painful for him to say. "But my forgiveness is unnecessary, my liege. You hold no blame for how the Goddess wills you to feel..."

She smiled, clasping his shoulder. "I'm glad to hear it. Now, dear soldier, our Brethren are being held in that fortress and it's long past time we retrieved them. We've wasted enough time. I hope you'll keep focused and join us in the mission?"

He shot up and saluted with a fist to his chest. "Of course, your grace."

"You'll find armor and other equipment in the barracks tents. If anything else is needed, I'm sure our Brothers and Sisters will be more than willing to help."

He bowed one last time, and left... But not before flicking me the darkest, reviling glare to ever be cast in the history of shifter-kind. The look was so curdled I'd likely have dropped dead, if only he could will it.

I relaxed when he was lost in the crowd, which went back to its bustling business.

My feet still hadn't moved when Willow craned back to me, jerking her head to the side, gesturing for me to approach. I hesitated, but stepped beside her. "Forgive me... for, er... that."

She hummed. "I suppose I'll excuse it. I can't say I wouldn't have done the same, if some other woman came and tried to steal you away from me. I'd want to rip out her throat."

I laughed, though uncertainly. "I hope you're exaggerating?"

"No," she said a bit too cheerfully, flashing me a devious smile. "I didn't say I would, just that I'd wish to. And no one said I couldn't threaten it."

"Ah..." I coughed into a fist. "Well, good thing you won't have to worry about it."

"Let's hope not," she sang with a smirk, walking off.

I half chuckled, half shuddered while starting after her—

Chai hobbled in front of my feet, nearly causing me to stumble. There was something in the raven's beak: a tattered piece of paper with a fountain pen.

I crouched and took the items, stroking Chai's head while taking a look. "What's this? A letter?" A set of three words were written there messily: *Wings. Reaper. Fake.* My brow furrowed. "Who wrote this?"

The raven screeched, fluttering his clipped wings.

It couldn't be... "Did *you* write this, Chai?"

I could swear he nodded, and a burst of pride sprouted in me, as if Chai's emotions were imposing on mine. I gawked at the raven. "You can write? But... why would you have to? Janson has been translating..."

Chai croaked angrily and took up the fountain pen with his beak, steadying the thing with a black talon as he struggled to scratch more letters onto the page. It was the most amazing thing.

When Chai was finished, he screeched and backed away from the page to let me read it. "'Lies,'" I said aloud.

"L... Lie-*s*," Chai repeated, testing the words himself. "*Lies.*"

"What lies? Janson's translations?"

Chai croaked wildly, hitting me with a burst of thrill through our Bond.

Alex mumbled from my head. *"Why would Janson lie about the translations?"*

"A grand question…" I glanced around the camp, catching Janson over by a firepit, drinking from a flask. My sight narrowed at him. "Chai obviously doesn't trust him. Neither do the other messengers. So… I don't know if *I* trust him."

"On that, we agree," Alex grunted. *"Though, our liege is convinced otherwise."*

Damn it, he was right. Willow trusted him—perhaps too much. *What if he'd fabricated that story about losing his messenger, so we wouldn't suspect him?* I picked up Chai and held him to my chest. "Thank you, Chai. We'll keep an eye on him. Don't worry."

Chai nuzzled my neck, relief and vindication streaming from our Bond as I went to find Willow.

OCTAVIUS

"You have to look after the others now," I remembered Dad saying the night he left us. Back then, he'd clasped a hand on my shoulder, his grip so tight it hurt. *"You and Mika. Keep them safe…"* And then he walked out. Just like that. Not a word after, no letter, no call, no warning…

Until the raid at the capital. I didn't tell Connie I'd seen him, either. What was I supposed to say? I still wasn't sure if he really *was*…

I smeared a hand over my face, reaching into a pouch strapped to my belt to fish out the two crumpled up pictures I always had on me. My family was in both photos, one with my mom, the other with my dad. I stared at Dad's face for a long minute, then let out a hard breath and got to my feet, going to get another tin of water, or Void, maybe some ale—

A Grimling snagged my wrist, pulling my hand to his face.

"You there!" the sienna-eyed guy rumbled. He looked pissed, and I saw he was wearing fancy, white clothes. Probably a Grimish noble. There was a black bird resting on his shoulder, which croaked at me as the Howllord sized me up. "Yes, you're the one. The Brother from the Screens, you traveled with the Death Princess, yes?"

"Uh." I tried prying my hand free, but he wouldn't let up. "I-I'm kind of busy…"

The Howllord gave an entitled *hmph*. "You have a new task! I'm in need of armor, so go and fetch me some plate and…"

He stopped cold after seeing the pictures I was holding in my captured hand. His already grey skin paled more. "What in Death…?" He ripped the picture from my fingers and shoved me aside, his eyes fixed on the image in a look of horror. "I don't believe it… Brother!" He thrust one of the photos in my face. "How do you know this man? This man here, with the yellow eyes?"

My brow furrowed. "That's my dad."

He made a disgusted, nasally sound and flinched away. "You're kin to that monster?!"

"I… wait, have you seen him?"

"Seen him?" he cried, tossing the photos and spat on them. "Good Gods, man, don't you know?"

32

BLOOD AND WATER

XAVIER

"All I'm saying," I argued to Willow, holding out the letter Chai had written. The raven was perched on my shoulder now, croaking urgently. "There might be something more to Janson. We should at least question him?"

"I thought I made it clear to Yulia and Jimmy that I didn't want to hear any more of this?" Willow snapped, her white fox ears growing. "It's amazing that Chai knows how to write, Xavier, but I'm sure he's been through a lot while in captivity. How do we know your raven hasn't developed a general distrust for others?"

Anger bristled my tone. "Are you saying Chai is biased?"

"I'm saying it's possible, yes."

"But think about it! Janson doesn't even have a messenger."

"He already told us it was killed."

"And if it was a lie?" I challenged.

She rolled her eyes. "It isn't."

"But how do you know? Look, even Jewel is upset with you." I gestured to the little crow hopping furiously over her white hair. "You can't tell me you don't feel her frustration?"

She bit her lip, staring at Janson, who was laughing with some of the other Brothers in camp. She shook her head, the bell in her hair jingling. "He helped me for the better part of a month, killing the demons when I first surfaced. We were alone many times. If he wanted to betray me, he could have done it at any time. And why would he want to? For what reason?"

Chai screeched and grabbed the paper from me, getting the pen again to write another word. Willow and I hovered over the raven, watching him scratch each letter with difficulty, biting one end of the pen with his beak and clutching the other in his talon. It was a balancing act for him, leaning on his cast for support. When he was finished, he hopped back to show us.

"'Black'," I read aloud, frowning. "What does that mean?"

"*Black*," Chai screeched and tried again, huffing with the pen as I read the next few words he wrote. "Er, that's not quite how you spell 'white', Chai… oh, now… er, 'black', you already wrote that one… 'fool'. Hm."

Willow cocked an eyebrow. "I believe that one says 'food'."

I scratched my nose as Chai began scribbling 'Black, black, black, black, black' for the remainder of the page. "You've got that one down, haven't you?"

Willow rolled her head back, giving me a pointed look. "Still think your messenger's little letters can be heeded? It looks as though he only knows a few words and wishes to make a show of it."

I sighed, crossing my arms. "I suppose it does look that way…"

"Now I'll not hear another word of this. Understand?"

I nodded grudgingly, conceding for the time being, and followed her through the camp.

Ahead, I found Vendy and Henry sitting round a firepit. Vendy had her tongue curled over her lips as she focused on sharpening her Spiritcrystal blade, and Henry was busy scarfing down a bowl of stew, nodding to me as I passed.

Outside a barrack's tent was the resurrected Dalen and his lanky younger brother, Herrin. The winged brothers were already dressed and armed with Shotri by the time Willow and I approached them. Dalen nodded to us in greeting, but Herrin didn't notice us. The teen was engrossed in the *Choir* book again.

Curious, I thought he wanted to study the 'sand currents' here? Had he forgotten? I read the title of his current chapter, leaning over his shoulder. "'The Children of the Relics'?" I asked.

Herrin flinched and *thunked* the book closed, hiding it behind his back. "Uh, H-Howllords…! We, uh, ready to go?"

"We are." I frowned, trying to see the book again. He shoved it down his breastplate as quick as a feral weasel. I hummed. "You're still on the first chapter? I thought by now you'd be done with it, Herrin."

"I finished it a few days ago." He rose, coughing. "I'm just, uh, re-reading to try and find some connections. This is a weird version. It's got a few extra stories that I've never heard of before."

"What stories?"

"I'll, uh… tell you about it after I'm done with the—"

Crack!

Pain splintered my jaw, a fist having flown so quick and heavy, I was thrown to the ground, dirt puffing in my wake. I clutched my burning face, befuddled, my gaze whipping round the new circle of startled faces staring down at me.

My wolf ears grew. "Who in the Bloody Void...!"

"You *bastard*."

My head snapped to Octavius.

Dearest Death! The man was the pure embodiment of livid. His eyes were glassy and red with tears, shaking fists clenched so tight his tanned knuckles were ivory, cat ears curled so far back I feared they may tear from his head.

"You knew...!" he accused, voice gravelly and tight. "This whole Gods damned time, you *knew*. My dad...!"

My shoulders locked. *Death*.

"When were you going to tell me?" he demanded, Shade screeching at his feet. "When were you going to tell me *my fucking dad* tried to kill you?"

I slowly pushed myself up, raising a pacifying hand. "N-now, calm down, Octavius... We were waiting for the proper time—"

"Proper time my ass!" He spat. "I'm not a kid. I'm not going to be patronized and 'protected', especially not by you."

My stomach twisted. "Octavius..."

"Piss off." He stormed away down the canyon paths.

I shouted after him. "Octavius...!"

He hollered a curse and disappeared round the bend.

"Gods damn it..." I hit a fist over my brow, irritated. "How did he find out?"

Alex growled from my thoughts. *"Perhaps you should ask that one."*

The crowd made way suddenly as Matthiel stalked through the crowd toward me, blabbering haughtily, "Xavier, I cannot believe you never told him!" He wagged a chiding finger. "He had a right to know what his father had done—!"

"You Bloody fool!" I threw aggravated hands in his direction, causing him to flinch back. "It wasn't your business to...! *Argh*! Bloody idiot, *idiot*..."

I stamped through the crowd, following after Octavius. This was *not* how I'd hoped to tell him. But damn me, I shouldn't have waited so long...

Trekking along the canyon's rocky pathways, I found Octavius crouched behind a boulder.

He was vomiting.

The retching hacks made me wince, but I waited until he was done, watching him slump against the boulder. I fell back beside him. "I see you're taking it well."

He wiped his mouth, spitting, but denied me any courteous acknowledgement. "Why didn't you tell me?" He demanded.

"I... well, I don't know," I admitted. A storm was approaching above, Tanderam Prison visible over the distant horizon. "I suppose I had hoped it wouldn't matter, after a time."

"What does that mean?"

I rocked my head to the side. How to word it? "Because," I said, "I didn't want you to think I'd distrust you for it."

"Don't you?" he grunted. "My dad tried to kill you. Shel, it's his Bloody fault you're even in this condition. And you..." His throat scratched. "You didn't tell me a Gods damn thing. Like you thought I might be like him, that I'd just snap one day and go on a psychotic murdering spree... Is that what you think?"

"Don't be ridiculous," I snorted, my plate-mail clattering as I folded my arms. "You're nothing like him. You're my Brother, Octavius. And I'm... sorry I neglected to tell you sooner. If I was trying to save you from anything, it was the worry that I would hold you accountable for what your father did. Which I don't."

He looked out at the fortress in the distance, his voice soft. "I just don't get it... he used to be good. Why is he doing this?"

I exhaled a stream of breath through my nose. "We may never know. He might have simply gone mad with grief when your mother died. Sorrow can consume us, if we drown ourselves in it... But we can't change the past, and *you* can't help what he chose to do."

He wiped his nose, cat ears curled back in resolve. "But... I can help fix it. Now I'm sure my dad is working with the Necrofera. With Cilia."

My brow knitted. "Why do you think that?"

"I saw him at the capital." His claws sharpened. "He was there, looking down at the demons... like he was surveying them. If he's working with the Necrofera, then I might have to..."

"We'll decide that later," I said, pausing. "But yes. As a Reaper, you'll be obligated to carry out the Laws of Death if your father has broken them. Let's hope apprehending him will be the first action. He will stand trial before the king first, and then his sentence will be decided."

Octavius only nodded, slumping. He looked miserable... Lost.

"You know..." I began, "despite what your father has done to me, I don't hate him."

He shot me a perplexed glance. "You don't?"

"Well, not anymore. I did at first. He'd ripped my life away from me, quite literally, but... what he must have endured, from the loss of your mother..." I leaned over a knee, gazing at the approaching storm and took in the gentle breeze lapping coolly at my neck. "There is a saying that we Nirians have. A phrase that we cherish: *Mu necros neschali yettek.*"

His brow crumpled. "What does that mean?"

I smiled. "*With death comes rebirth.* It's the maxim of Nira. The model of our faith. Most think the phrase simply means a soul's rebirth, when it is passed unto another vessel to start another life… but there is a more metaphorical meaning.

"A great change can mean the death of an old lifestyle, or an old belief, and the start of a new way of thinking—or a renewed way of living. I think the maxim applies to your father. With your mother's death came *his* as well—or, a part of him died. All that was left was hate, and that is what devoured his old self, leaving a shell of the man you once knew."

His eyes were glazed with thought, almost mourning.

I started again, more cheerful. "But, I believe there's still hope for his soul. Though his sins will be Cleansed by the Mother Goddess when his time comes, it will not be with anger. She will have sorrow and pity for him. It's the way of Nira. Her sadness for a soul's loss is stronger than Her hate for dishonor. He will be forgiven, in the Void. The Great Unknown will have a place for him, after his Cleansing."

Octavius dabbed at his eyes and looked out to the glowing fortress ahead.

I pushed off the boulder. "Come. We've spent enough time out here. If you wish to help make amends for his sins, why don't we start by taking back our friends?"

He nodded, muttering, "Sorry for clocking you earlier…"

I chuckled, rubbing the new welt my jaw fostered. "I can't say I didn't deserve it. Remarkable hit, by the way. I dare say Jaq will be famously impressed once we get him out of there."

A relenting grin tugged his lips at last, and he laughed, following me back to camp.

Willow and Matthiel were waiting where I'd left them—as was, to my surprise, a rabbit girl.

Alex yanked me into the psyche to take my place. "Bianca…!" He rushed for her, flinging his arms round her and crushed the living Void out of her ribs.

"A—*K-khaugh!*—Alex?" Bianca gasped, arms trapped at her sides and voice cinched tight under his relieved grasp. "You *are*… here…!"

He held fast, his breath leaking away with a new ease that he hadn't displayed in weeks. "Thank the Goddess… With the way things have been, I thought you'd…"

"*You realize you've gained quite an audience?*" I said from the psyche.

He found a number of campers staring at him, and grew rigid. He quickly ripped apart from Bianca. "I'm... *Km-hmm* I'm glad you're all right. Yes."

"Me too." She latched right back to him, squeezing his ribs and forcing delighted chuckles from his throat.

She smiled briefly, but her expression soon soured, and she let him go—

Thwack!

She smacked him upside the head, demanding, "What the Death is wrong with you? I tried calling a thousand times! Do you have any idea how worried I was?"

He rubbed his new sore spot tenderly. "We ran into some trouble... Wait, what are you doing here in the first place?"

"Helping someone." Bianca gestured to a Culatian girl behind her, whose face was scrawled with shock to see us. "Her friend was taken to Tanderam, so we're trying to bust her out."

Alex scrunched his brow. "That's what we're about to do for Jaq."

"Jaq's in there?" She gasped.

"Hopefully after tonight, he won't be—"

"Ees wolf boy!" the Culatian girl exclaimed, pushing past Bianca to stare wide-eyed at us. She had rose-red eyes, the same hue as her scarlet feathers. "*Halla'ech Skrii*! Ees you really?! Ke, ke, ke, two color of the eyes and everything...!"

She snatched Alexander's hand and shook it eagerly. "I can no be believing! I look so long, *Külleschkov*! So long for *you*!"

From his uncertain tone, it seemed Alexander shared my bewilderment. "And you are...?"

Beside us, Willow let out a shocked breath. "Zylveia?" Willow stepped closer to better see the Culatian girl's face. "*Zylveia Skrii'etey? Hozen tu?*"

The bird shifter finally seemed to recognize Willow, and pointed at her with her mouth dropping in amazement. "*Willow Ember?! Yebe hozen tu?!*"

They babbled in that same gibberish for a while, until Alex shot a hand up to stop them. "Ladies? I don't think anyone else knows what's going on."

"Yes," Matthiel agreed impatiently. "You know this Sousül, Your Grace?"

Willow's glance turned askew at us. "None of you recognize her? Why, this is..."

"*Tovt, tovt, tovt!*" The girl jabbered in Culatian, flailing her hands wildly to stop Willow. She spoke fervently in Culatian now, my ears ringing from how fast her tongue was moving.

Soon, Willow cleared her throat and tried again. "Er, very well... This is... Zyl. She's an... acquaintance of mine. Apparently, her friend is in Tanderam also. She's coming with us into the prison. Trust me, she'll only help us with the rescue. She may be a great asset."

Bianca puffed up her chest. "If she's going, then so am I! Jaq better not be hurt in there."

Alex gave the rabbit a sharp glare. "You're not going anywhere. *We're* getting Jaq. You're staying here."

She let out a pompous laugh. "Like you're going to do anything to stop me? You can never have enough field Medics. Come on, Zyl, let's go find us some armor." She went to her Culatian friend and started off.

Matthiel snapped his fingers. "Armor! Yes, right." He hurried after them, demanding they find him a set of plate as well.

Alex gave a heavy sigh, not sounding happy. But with the lower part of my window darkening, I caught the hint of a grin as he stared after the rabbit.

Willow noticed Alexander had switched out, and chided, "Alex! What are you doing out?"

His brow furrowed. "Taking my turn?"

"Oh, no you don't. Xavier told everyone that he just popped into camp, out of the grey. He has to stay out until a convenient excuse makes him 'leave' later."

"I can pose as him instead." I saw his gaze flick back to Bianca. "It's not like anyone else can see our change in eyes."

"Everyone here has soul-seeing masks, Alex," she reminded. "And Matthiel is a Necrovoker as well. You're only lucky you weren't facing him just now. Does Matthiel, the master of spilling secrets—as he'd just does with Octavius—seem like the type to keep silent about such things?"

Alex thought about it, stealing one last glance at Bianca, then sighed and grudgingly forced himself inside, kicking me out to take his place.

Willow turned about and marched forward. "I thought so. Now come with me, Xavier. You and I have troops to rally."

We stood at the edge of the canyon's path, staring out at the fortress, the prison aglow with torchlight in the distant night.

Prince Cayden, disguised as the rebellion's leader in his plumed hat and mask, folded his arms and growled low. "This will not be an easy task."

"There are so many guards down there," I murmured, noting the dots of torchlight pacing the perimeter. "Can we really force our way in?"

Willow gave a thoughtful hum. "Perhaps. But we happen to have someone who can give us the upper hand in this weather."

"Do we?" Linus questioned beside Cayden, his dreads tumbling over a shoulder as his head cocked curiously. His Dream mark gleamed from his shoulder, and his eyes went stale as a vision came to him. "Ah. How very convenient..."

"What's convenient?" I asked. "Who do we have?"

I flinched when the sound of flapping wings puffed behind me. That scarlet-feathered, Culatian girl was there. As was Bianca. Then everyone else appeared around the trail's bend, followed by the troops who were armed and prepared for battle, Reapers and rebels—under the command of Cayden—alike.

Willow spun to face the knights, her voice loud and brimming with a commanding tenor.

"Brothers and Sisters," she began, every ear hanging on her echoing words. "Tonight, we take back our own. Our friends, our Brethren, our Dreamcatcher allies—and those Everlandish citizens who have suffered for their beliefs and loyalties to the lost Relicblood of Land."

Enthused cheers replied, and she waited for them to die down before continuing.

"Though it may seem we stand alone, supported by no one but ourselves during this doubled war, I am pleased to tell you our fortunes have changed. Tonight, I am not the *only* Relicblood among you."

There was a murmur of confusion with that. Willow turned to the Culatian girl beside her. The bird gave a complying, albeit hesitant, nod and stepped forward.

"My name ees Zylveia Skrii'etey," the scarlet swallow said—and threw off her cloak to reveal the crowned Sky mark on her right shoulder. "I am Sky Princess of Culatia."

Gasps roared through the company, the murmurs rising. The Sky Princess waited until their voices faded before speaking again. "Everland king take knight of my father's," she said in broken Landish. "She ees Stormchaser of great skill. She ees dearest friend to me, and I not pleased with king for taking her. In this war, Grim and Aspirre be having allies with Culatia!"

She shot a pointed finger to the rolling storm clouds, her hands glowing with red light as she evoked her Hallows and brought heavy rain down upon us.

The crack of thunder ignited our roaring cheers.

33

KIN

~~~~~~~~

MIKANI

Hsssssssssss...!

The routine spritz of Yinklît gel sprayed from the tubes in the ceiling.

I was used to them now. Not that it made my shitty situation any better. I was still in chains, these annoying gloves and shoes were still strapped on, I was still drenched in this cold gel, still stuck in this cell with a cat-jay hybrid who didn't speak Landish, and still—as always—whispering to myself, hoping Ringëd could hear me in a vision.

I had no idea how long it'd been since I'd seen him. Since I'd seen *anyone* except this Culatian girl. Day and night meant nothing in here—and there was nothing to do but sleep, wake up, eat whatever slop they brought down, cry your eyes out, have an imaginary conversation with your boyfriend, and sleep some more. Rinse and repeat. Was I going to die in here?

"Ringëd?" I sighed, leaning against the bars of the cell. "Do you remember that time I was framed for arson? And you were still looking for an apprenticeship, but helped prove I didn't do it?"

Course, Mika, I imagined him saying, *May as well have been our first date.*

I sniffed, wiping my nose. "I remember thinking you were just a dumb kid poking his nose where it didn't belong."

I imagined him laughing. *And I remember thinking you were a psychotic sociopath with serious bloodlust.*

"Yeah, well... if I could go back, I'd smack some sense into me. If it wasn't for you, I'd have been *here* back then... so thanks, I guess..."

No reply came to mind. What would he have actually said to that?

Bloods, look at me! I've gone crazy! I slammed my hands on the sticky bars, angry, miserable... crying.

"I want to go home, Ringëd," I sniffled, wiping my nose, even though my arm was soaked in gel anyway. "I want to see you again… Bloods, what if I forget what you look like and…! And Gods damn it, I want some Bloody *cake*—!"

"Cilia…?"

I yelped and jerked my head up. A man was suddenly standing over me behind the bars, his yellow eyes glinting in the torch light.

"D…" I blinked, my skin crawling. "Dad…?"

Oh, Gods, I really am crazy! I smacked my head hard, shaking it hysterically. "No, no, no, no, no…!" I shoved my hands over my grown cat ears, rocking back and forth and muttering to myself, "He's not real! He's not real! *He's not real—*"

"Cilia," the phantom breathed again, gripping the bars as his voice shook. "It can't be…"

Wait, I squinted in the small flicker of firelight. *He's too young to be Dad.* He looked my age.

The man's yellow eyes faded when he studied me more, crestfallen. "No… you must be one of *his* children…" He gave a heavy breath, squeezing the bars. Then he noticed the half-finished bowl of slop at my feet. That was the 'food' the guards gave us every morning. We only got one ration a day, and it was disgusting, but what else did we have to eat?

C-Clack!

Dad's doppelganger picked up my bowl of slop and replaced it with his own food: a tray of delicious-smelling, genuine, *real* food.

Holy Bloods! I dove for it, ripping the slab of juicy meat with my sharpened teeth, grease draining down my lips.

The guy just sat there, staring at me with those yellow eyes, watching me eat. *Weirdo…*

When I finally got a hold of myself, half the meat already finished, I wiped my mouth. "Look man," I puffed. "Thanks for the food, but can you stop *staring*?"

He looked at me like I'd grown wings right then and there. He took a minute to answer, forcing a breath. "What?"

"You're staring." I waved a hand at him. "Like, *a lot*. You're creeping me out."

Black cat ears grew from his head, folding down. "I… didn't mean…" He glanced away and whispered, "I'm sorry…"

I snorted and ripped another chunk of meat with my teeth, chewing as I asked, "Whaff yur name?"

"Kael," he said. It was so soft, I barely heard it.

I swallowed. "You got a last name with that, Kael?"

He hesitated. "I believe we share that name."

"… What, Treble?"

He nodded.

What the Void? "So, you're some kind of relative?"

"We are kin, yes." He put down the bowl of slop, looking excited now that we were talking.

"Uh huh." I wiped some juice off my chin. "Guess that explains why you look like my dad. So what are you? Cousin? Uncle?"

He gave a glum chuckle that echoed in the dungeon. "Farther than that, unfortunately."

My brow furrowed. "Great uncle?"

"Farther."

"Dude. How *old* are you?"

A grin crossed his face. "Physically? Perhaps twenty-seven. That's not an easy question."

"What's not easy about it?"

He ignored that with a sigh, then gave me a curious look. "What is your name?"

I tore off another piece of meat. "Mikani."

"Mikani," he whispered to himself in awe. "That was my mother's name… Amazing…"

"Right… So, uh…" I left the rest of the meat on the tray and slid it toward my hybrid cellmate, who's cat ears perked and blue wings fluttered before tearing into it herself. I looked back at the guy. "You don't look like a guard, so what are you doing down here?"

He blinked, probably not realizing he hadn't explain that. "My friend requested that I come to clarify a few prisoners' identities," he said.

"And was I one of those prisoners?"

He gave an admitting shrug. "No."

"So why'd you stop here and give me your food?"

He folded a knee and laced his fingers over it, resting his chin there longingly. "You remind me of someone. Someone I haven't seen for… a very long time."

"Uh huh. And that is…?"

He smiled, honey-yellow eyes glazing. "My wife."

I only now noticed the gold wedding ring on his finger, and the glint of a marriage-stud on his left ear. "Oh," I mumbled. "So, where's she at?"

His cheer drained, cat ears folding down again. "By now, she's with Nira…"

Oh. A widower…

He gave a dismal sigh and rose to his feet. "I must see to other concerns," he said, giving an old-fashioned bow. "It was… a pleasure to speak with you, lady Mikani. Thank you."

With that, he turned and walked off.

Kael, huh? He was weird all right, but I felt for him. I should count my blessings anyway. I thought I was alone here. It was relieving to find a relative—albeit one I didn't know I'd had. But hey. I'd take what I could get, if it meant not having to talk to myself anymore—

"He gone?" Came a guard's voices around the corner.

I jumped when he and another guard shuffled up to my cell, their sleaze so thick I could cut it with a rusty spoon.

"Yeah, he's gone," said the second guard, licking his lips and eyeing me. "This the one?"

"That's the one."

A bag of Mel beads was exchanged.

Land...

The first guard unlocked the door. "All right, remember: don't take off the gloves and shoes. Keep her shackles on. If she's down here, then she's dangerous. Other than that, it's fair game."

The door swung open with a ringing squeak.

I stumbled against the wall next to my Culatian cell-mate. A quick look at her said she was scared as Void too—

The first guard grabbed her by her clipped wings, and she screamed in gibberish, the guy dragging her out...

Leaving me alone with the second guard.

I shuffled along the wall, igniting my fire and spewing a stream of curses when these Gods damned gloves stifled it. My cat ears curled, and I hissed at him. "Breathe on me, and I tear out your neck...!"

"It's all right, little cat," he hushed, raising his hands in a calming motion—

He lunged and grabbed my shackled hands, keeping me from clocking him in the face. I hissed and kicked when he smeared his grubby fingers over my sticky collarbone, his claw ripping my tunic down the middle. The slug kissed my neck, his slobbering tongue wriggling like some starved water snake.

He shoved his hip against mine, pinning me to the wall, and I screamed—

His weight fell away suddenly. Then the guy sputtered out a gasp. Clawed fingers were wrapped around his throat from behind, and he was yanked to his feet.

Kael had come back.

His yellow eyes burned hot with anger, and he thrust the man's head against the wall, his skull giving a loud *crack* as black, jagged veins sprouted from Kael's fingers. The veins spidered over the man's skin, making him shriek in agony until the blackness absorbed into his bloodstream. The guard's skin *burned* away, like it was rotting from the inside.

Then he went limp, giving a lifeless sigh. Kael dropped the blackened corpse to the floor and spit in disgust.

He looked at me. Flushed.

I followed his eyes, trailing down my... *crap!*

I blushed and pulled my ripped tunic together for cover.

Kael kept staring, but not at my chest. He was fixated on my face. The guy looked conflicted, like he was debating something in silence.

Then he stepped forward, knelt, and hushed, "Come quickly. There will be more, once they find him. I... I wish to help. If you'll allow?"

I peeked at the dead guard, his head stained with blood and fleshy burns in his cheeks, eyes emptily staring at me. *He has Dad's infection Hallows.* If I was getting out of here alive—if I was going to see Ringëd again—it'd be with him.

"Um," I said, "*Yeah.*"

His shoulders slacked with relief, and he gently scooped me up and rushed out of the cell.

LILLI

I shivered, huddled in the corner with Jaq. It was so *cold...*

Jaq did what he could to keep me warm, using his scaled skin as a blanket of heat, but it only did so much. Neal held onto Oliver, the boy's face wet and red.

Breathing was painful, the air squeezing my shriveled lungs. The moldy cell was swaying, and... *why was the floor rushing up—?*

Jaq fastened his grip around me, forcing the floor to tumble back to its proper place.

"Stay with me," he rasped, alarmed. *What did that mean? H-how did I look, to make him sound panicked?*

He lifted me from the floor, my head feeling airy and light. I barely noticed my cheek had hit his chest. *Why was it so cold...?*

"We need to get her out of here," Jaq said to Neal from the other corner. "She's not going to last another night."

Neal cursed, and I blearily glanced at him, my vision swimming when he slammed his fists on the bars. "Hey!" Neal shouted. "Guards! Someone! We need a Healer, or...!"

The murmuring voices of other inmates came in a roar from their cells.

"Another one's going—"

"—Poor dear—"

"—That makes twelve since—"

"—I heard Gorun's daughter went just yesterday, from that same bug—"

I squeezed my eyes shut, the voices bouncing nauseatingly.

"... should be in this level," a new voice caught my grown bat ears, clattering footfalls reverberating. "If they ain't here, then you gotta tell High Roarlord Wales we ain't got 'em."

I felt Jaq's fingers tense over my shoulder, and my stinging lids cracked open by slits.

Through my blurred vision, I found four guards peering into our cell. They were escorted by a Grimish man...

With yellow eyes.

"Dad?" Neal gasped beside me.

My head snapped to him, ignoring the following dizziness. *What* had he just said?

"No way," Neal whispered. "Dad?"

The Grimish man lifted his gaze. Then his eyes splintered. "Neal?" He clutched the bars, his voice trembling. "*Neal?*"

"ey." One of the guards sounded suspicious. "What's goin' on..."

The Grimish man shoved his hand over the guard's throat, and black veins crept over him like plant roots digging into soil. The guard's cheeks *disintegrated*, burning away and turning black, some of his bones poking through the skin.

The disfigured guard dropped after his throat was released. The other guards made shouts of surprise, readying their spears—

The man shoved his black, infected hands over their chests, and one by one, they dropped like flies, veins surging from their skin.

The Grimish man—the assassin from so long ago—swiftly took a dead guard's key-ring and unlocked our door, throwing it open with a furious glare at Neal.

"Out," he rumbled. "*Now.*"

34

STORMING THE FORTRESS

~~~~

XAVIER

Rain washed over the canyons, drowning our company's plated footfalls.

The looming, cylindrical prison was far larger than what we'd spied from our camp. Ribbed bridges made of wood surrounded the towering figure, stacked every few floors by support beams stretching from the previous bridge, save for the bottom bridges which were set into the sandy floor of the chasms with an intricate, sturdy foundation. Each bridge was manned by blocks of men whom I could barely see pacing the suspended walkways in the dense fog and rain. They were only visible by their bobbing lanterns.

With a clap of thunder and a series of shuddering lights from above, I peered round my shielding boulder, watching the first cluster of guards at the head of our bridge.

It was a strain to see them in the dense fog, but then, I supposed it would likewise dampen our own figures from their view. Our Sky Princess was giving us an advantage up there somewhere. At least, I *assumed* she was still up there. The Archer knew I couldn't see a damn thing in the storm.

Our squad's current targets were four patrolling guards at the head of our bridge. They were huddled round a small circle they'd drawn in the wet sand, a pile of Mel beads scattered round it as they drank from their tankards and cheered on the two feral lizards that were battling in the makeshift arena.

I hummed. "Boredom seems abundant here. Yet another advantage."

I glanced at Willow. She was peering round the other side of the boulder, assessing the situation for herself, the rain pattering against her polished armor and open helm. A short moment later, she gave hand signals to our Dreamcatchers who hid behind a dead tree trunk nearest to the guards.

Jimmy nodded first and waltzed over to the distracted men, clasping two of them on the shoulders. "Feisty little guys, uh?"

The guards glanced at him once. Twice. By the time they thought to jolt, Jimmy's hands gleamed with azure light and the two men in his hold collapsed at his feet, sleeping.

Their two comrades made to go after him, but Yulia strode beside them and brushed her glowing-blue fingers over their jaws, sending them to the ground to slumber soundly.

Willow grunted. "Clear."

She moved out, and I followed close behind her. As did, to my annoyance, Matthiel Inion. His passing glares weren't missed by me, and I doubted that slight shove onto the bridge had been due to ill footing.

Vendy stayed close at my back, keeping her Spiritcrystal blade sheathed to keep its natural glow hidden for now, and Henry stayed by her side. Dalen and Herrin flew quietly over our heads, and farther behind, Octavius kept pace with Ringëd. Bianca was to his left, wearing black leather armor that matched our Dreamcatchers' garb.

I kept an even trot behind Willow, who made a point to keep her gaze firmly affixed ahead of her, chin raised stiffly, never daring to gaze over the edge of the bridge.

I couldn't help my grin. *Lovely Death, just look at her.* Over a hundred feet from the shifting sands beneath us, and still she charges ahead like a true queen, ignoring the fear I knew simmered under that façade. Nira, it had my blood pumping, giving my feet an extra kick while I followed the fiery steps of my hallowed liege—of my bride—along the bridge.

Hers was the true face of courage.

Ahead, orange dots swelled in the fog, growing as we moved forward. Willow halted and raised a fist over her shoulder, signaling the rest of us to hold.

Death drew out her scythe.

I plucked one of my short-handled blades, and took out the Shotri at my hip. A quick glance over my shoulder showed me the others had done the same. Bianca had a small dagger strapped to her waist, but she kept it sheathed and held her Shotri with rattling fingers, her rabbit ears draped. There was a clear flash of fright burdening her face. The poor girl was straining to keep her weapon from dropping.

I felt Alex wanting to switch. Of course he did. I allowed it, watching from the psyche as he tucked his Shotri away and reached for Bianca's tremoring hands. Bianca flinched under his calming fingers, but he kept them squeezed tight around hers.

"You'll be all right," he hushed softly. "Just stay close to us."

She swallowed, but nodded timidly. Then he exhaled a short breath and released her, turning forward.

The orange dots grew larger.

Willow crouched at the front, cocking back her glowing scythe and crept for the approaching men—

Laughter erupted behind us.

Alex whipped his gaze at Ringëd. The madman had begun chuckling hysterically.

"W—what the—*Oscha*...!" the human snorted, laughing with more fervor while squirming awkwardly.

Willow cursed, regaining Alexander's attention. The orange lights were bobbing now, questioning voices sounding within the fog.

Alex glared back at Ringëd. "Shut the Void up, Human."

"I-I can't—something's in my—!" A furry head popped up from beneath his breastplate.

"*Kurn?*" Ringëd hissed at his pet ferret, which gave curious snickers as it sniffed the rain-sodden air from under the man's chin. "I thought I told you to stay with—!"

"*oy!*"

Alex snapped forward again. The guards had come, no longer shrouded by the fog. They were drawing their swords, Shotri firing in rapid bursts.

"Down!" Alex shouted as a Shocksphere whistled past his ear. He shoved Bianca's head down to avoid it also. The sphere shattered yards behind her, and she screamed, the electric bolts exploding when they caught the rain in a blinding flash.

From the psyche, I growled. *"Their voltage is lethal."*

"So is ours!" replied Alex, sweeping back an arm to shield Bianca from another barrage of Spheres. He took aim with his Shotri and pulled the trigger with a heavy *bang*!

The barrel's smoke was smothered by the rain, and not long after firing, Alex's sphere shattered over the helmed head of the guard.

Sparks zapped and burst about the man's head, his scream desperate as he yanked off his helmet—melted skin peeling off.

The bridge was now flickering with sparks and ringing with clashing metal. I could barely see anything from the psyche, Alexander's gaze moving too erratically to make anything out. Between avoiding the torrents of Spheres and keeping Bianca out of danger, Alex couldn't decide where to keep his attention.

Of the short glimpses I caught of the skies, I found the other rib-like bridges flashing with sparks as well. The other teams had moved in. Some had pushed ahead of us, others were farther behind.

Alex looked left to where Willow was—

The princess blocked an overhead strike with her staff and was pushed back by the blow. Her foot slipped from the ledge of the bridge, the wooden railing splintered, and she let out a yelp as she dipped—

I lunged out of the psyche, rain crashing over me once touch returned in a flash, and snatched her wrist. I yanked her back to the bridge's steady surface, and she collapsed to her plated knees, letting out a shuddered wheeze while keeping a vice-grip on my arms.

"Too high," she panted, repeating the mantra like a madwoman. "Too high, too high, too high…"

"Don't think about it!" I shouted. *So much for her well-kept calmness.* "Keep to the center!"

She sucked in a few breaths, looking up at me. Her eyes blazed. "Move!" She bellowed, taking up her scythe and shoved me aside, swinging her crooked blade up in an arc.

It hooked into the stomach of a guard, whose sword had been raised where my head used to be.

The man's eyes dimmed, blood rushing from his stomach where Willow's blade was wedged.

I stared up at her, shocked. "Willow… You've just…"

Pain wrenching her face, she heaved her scythe upward through his sternum and ripped into his chest, where a sharp *snap* sounded faintly over the surrounding clamor. She tore out her weapon and let the body collapse, the man's soul gleaming pale and translucent before her.

She stood tall, gazing at the new spirit with swelling lamentation. "Find our camp further into the canyons," she said. I couldn't tell if the rain had spattered her eyes or if she was in tears. "We have Necrovokers who will keep you safe. Nira be with you."

She weaved the specter a violet, temporary NecroSeam and tied him to his body, resurrecting him. After a bemused moment, the man regarded his newly living vessel shakily. Then his feet were forced to walk down the opposite end of the bridge when Willow waved her violet-streaming hand.

She shut her eyes, inhaled, and looked down at me. "Are you hurt?"

"I'm… fine," I said, pushing to my feet and re-gripping my Shotri and single scythe blade. I hesitated. "Will you be all right? This was your first… well…"

"*Mu thechat necros yettek.*" She stomped onward over the bridge. "With war comes death."

She charged back into the mass of struggling figures, keeping to the center of the bridge.

The prison halls were total chaos.

Sirens blared, shouts and screams bounced from the walls as we hurried through the corridors, weaving and turning, crossing arms with the guards, blood spurting freely as we passed cell upon cell with our Brothers and Sisters.

Willow and Matthiel took the liberty of freeing the prisoners by melting the locks on the doors with their Pyrovoking. Vendy and Henry reshaped the metal bars apart with their Terravoking. Herrin and Dalen used traditional, non-Evocating methods with thieves' picks.

Once our allies were freed, Willow gave instruction on where the prisoners were to escape: a rendezvous squad was waiting a few floors below to shepherd the prisoners out.

We passed other squads in the halls, all of us working frantically to free the prisoners.

But damn it all, where is Jaq—?

I slammed into someone, forced back to the floor. I pulled off my helm and rubbed my forehead where I'd been hit, glaring at whoever had run into me.

My anger evaporated.

"Jaq!" I cried in surprise. But I drew back, seeing whom he was keeping secured in his arms.

Alex hushed from my thoughts. *"Lilli?"*

Gods, she looked a hair's breath away from death. Her already-pale skin was blanched and shining in a cold sweat, red rings puffing round her dark eyelids, cheeks hollowed, limbs shaking. I was fairly certain she was unconscious.

"Guys?" Jaq sounded unsure, squinting his black eyes. "No Bloody way…! Is that actually you or am I hearing things?"

"Yes, it's us," I affirmed, clasping a hand on Lilli's brow. "Bloods, she's freezing."

Willow came from behind me, spying Lilli, and gasped.

"Lilli!" She flew to her Aide, putting away her scythe to relieve the shivering body from Jaq's arms, keeping Lilli's folded wings tucked gently under her hold. Willow was in tears. "Blessed Nira, what have they done…?"

"Out of my way!" Bianca shoved me aside, fishing into her medical satchel with several clinking vials rattling inside. She checked Lilli's pulse at her neck, cursing, then felt along her lymph nodes, felt her cheek and brow temperature with her fingers, cursed again, then pried open Lilli's heavy lids to shine a penlight in her eyes, and cursed a third time.

"She needs to be treated immediately," Bianca assessed. "Her pulse is weak, and she needs fluids. Your Highness, keep hold of her. Your Pyrovoker's heat will help warm her. Her iron levels are probably low as Void."

Willow nodded, still in tears, and led the way out.

I grabbed Jaq's arm and pulled him along. "Come on, stay with… us…" *Hang on*, I thought, catching something on Jaq's face, *what is that on his brow?* I lifted away his greasy, sandy bangs.

"Gods, Jaq!" I almost tripped, staring in horror at a scar carved into his scales. It read *GRIMLING* in large, blood-caked letters. "What happened?"

Jaq swatted my hand away from his face. "It's nothing."

"Nothing?" I cried. "Death, Jaq, how is that—"

"Mate, we're running out of a Gods damned prison with guards and prisoners scattered amuck, and *I can't see.*"

"Ah—ah, right!" I fumbled to produce Jaq's glasses from the pouch clipped to my belt, sliding the square frames over Jaq's nose. "You dropped these at the capital."

Jaq blinked, adjusting his cracked glasses. It seemed he couldn't believe they were actually there.

"*Finally!*" He looked at me with more clarity through the cracked lenses, regarding me with an impressed frown. "Nice plate. Do I get any?"

"Come out alive and you'll get a better set than us."

He grinned. "Damn right—"

Octavius gave a startled gasp behind us, making our group skid to a halt.

"Lil' bro!" A tall man, looking much like Octavius, laughed brightly, hugging him from behind and lifting him off his feet. "Land, am I glad to see you!"

"N-Neal…?" Octavius wheezed as his older brother crushed his ribs. "Dude, put me down!"

Neal complied, letting Octavius drop and puff for air. The older brother hit his arm. "Took you long enough! What have you been doing this whole time, you Bloody slacker? I've been stuck in here for weeks."

Octavius gave him a flat look. "Would you rather I didn't come to bust your cocky ass out, Neal?"

He grinned and slid his hands behind his head. "Wouldn't have mattered. A certain someone already beat you to it." Neal tossed his head back, gesturing for him to look toward the corner.

I looked as well, but only found a cat eared, winged girl standing there, befuddled as she gazed upon our company's faces.

—The Sky Princess shoved me aside. "El!"

"Zyl!" cried the hybrid girl, the two rushing into a tearful embrace, jabbering with wavering voices in Culatian. The owl boy was lingering at their legs, rubbing his watering eyes.

Then I noticed someone else there, in the corner. A slumped figure waited in the shadows, lingering just shy of the light... A glint of yellow eyes flashed in the lamplight.

Every bone in my miserable body hollowed.

It can't be...

The siren's wails dampened, shouts dimmed... the only sound I could hear was my pounding heart. I stared into the yellow eyes of the man who had plagued my nightmares for six Gods damned years.

At last, I brooded in silence, my teeth sharpening. *The time has come.*

35

A HAUNTED PAST

～～～

XAVIER

My veins twisted painfully, hands yielding to a tremor.
This was it. Face to face with my killer again. Six years it's been. Six years I've waited. Part of me had hoped this day would never come. But in the end, I knew it must, eventually.

And I was *not* prepared.

"Dad…" Octavius stepped to my side and drew out his glowing blue sickle. His voice swelled with hurt. "You have things to answer for."

The father's pained gaze moved to his son. His voice was coarse like sand. "I know, Tavius… And you'll get answers. I promise. But we have to leave now."

I flinched back when the monster stepped forward. Octavius blocked his father's way, keeping himself wedged between me and that *thing*.

"No, Dad!" he growled. "Not until you tell me one Bloody thing!" Octavius glanced back at me, cat ears grown. Then he turned back to his father. "Where did you go, after you left? Did you go to the Death Palace? Did you kill all those people, those *kids*…" He was shaking, throat trembling. "Did you kill my friend?"

The beast said nothing, then his brazen eyes flicked to me.

My pulse jumped, nightmares flooding back—me, clinging for life to that Gods forsaken cliff, fear spearing my eardrums, his fingers squeezing my throat—

He stepped into the lamplight. Then once more, toward me.

I ripped out my scythes. "Don't…!"

He stopped, towering over me, stooped down…

… and gave a gentle embrace.

"I'm sorry…" he whispered.

Shock froze my limbs; stilled my weapons. *What?*

"I thought… I thought he…" He sounded on the verge of tears. "I couldn't do anything. I'm sorry…" He drew back, clutching my shoulders, his yellow eyes glistening. "You shouldn't have come. He'll kill you, if he finds us. And if your brother's here, he'll kill him, too."

I *shoved* him back, finally finding my voice. "W-what… what are you saying? You were the one who…"

"Kael was the one at the cliff," he said. "When I heard he'd killed you, I… I did what I could. To make sure he didn't know about your brother."

I glared at him, fury pricking my voice. "A trick…"

"Bloody Void—look at me, Howllord!" He hit his chest hard, teeth sharpening. "I'm getting old! Your killer was the same damn age that you are now—would I have been that young less than a Bloody decade ago?"

I hesitated, scrutinizing his face. There *were* wrinkles prevalent, now that he was so close and in the light of the lantern. This man was in his mid-forties at best. *He… WAS rather young, back then*, I thought. *Could he have aged so much in such a short time?* It was possible, I considered. But not plausible.

Alex murmured from my thoughts. *"The man I saw that night was indeed this old."*

I whispered back. "But the man *I* saw wasn't…"

"Then… there were two men?"

Death, my head was spinning. I shut my lids, breath coarse. What was happening? This man… this was Octavius's father. Both his sons didn't question it. He had infection Hallows, he looked so much like that monster…

Yet, doubt was festering. Nira, what was wrong with me?

Answers. My jaw clenched. I needed answers. "Kael," I said, wolf ears pinned back indignantly. "You said… Kael… was at the cliffs that night?"

His shoulders slacked in relief. "Yes."

"Then what is your name?"

"I'm Claude." He smiled, the scraggly hairs at his jaw pulling with his lips. A new calm had washed over him, as if a great weight had been lifted from his shrouded soul. His eyes began to well. "Bloods, I… I never thought I'd have a chance to say that to you, you know. And you must have been the one to get Tavius out of that cage in Brittleton, weren't you? Shel, I can't thank you enough."

My brow knitted desperately. "Cage?"

"I'll explain later." The father, Claude, looked over his shoulder, then threw his head to the side in a gesture. "Come on. One of the bridges out of here is this way."

He hurried in front, waving us on.

I wasn't the only one to stay in place. Only Neal had no reluctance following him. I caught Octavius's gaze, his attention dueling against my face and his father's retreating back.

"W-well?" he asked me. "What do you want to do?"

He was leaving the choice to me?

I craned back to the others, Willow looking just as puzzled as I. The chaos in the halls was still bustling above and below us, some of the escaped inmates and straggling guards rushing past our corridor. The clamor of battle rang with metal on metal screams.

"Blast it all…" I snarled, wolf ears flicking, and my legs spurred after Claude. "I will get to the bottom of this!"

OCTAVIUS

What the Void is going on?

I glared at Dad's back, watching him run alongside Neal, the two of them talking hurriedly like nothing had changed.

But *everything* had changed. Didn't Neal get it?

"Where're your sisters?" Dad asked him, panting.

"Mika's in here somewhere," answered Neal. "I don't know about Connie."

Next to me, Ringëd piped up. "Connie's in Drinelle with my uncle! Do you know where Mika is in here, Neal?"

Neal twisted back to him and shrugged. "Void if I know. I've only been on one damn level."

Dad looked back and saw Ringëd, then laughed. "Ringëd! Well, if it isn't my favorite feral human. Long time no see, pal."

Ringëd looked just as suspicious as I felt. "Claude," he grunted in a greeting, keeping pace with our herd. He apparently didn't have anything else to say to him.

"I take it you're here for Mika?" Dad asked.

Ringëd muttered flatly. "Obviously."

Dad squinted at him. "You two married yet?"

"After this," Ringëd's voice scratched, Kurn snickering from his shoulder, "We're damn well going to be."

I snorted. "Finally."

Bloods, I was so confused. *How am I supposed to feel about Dad? Should I believe him about whoever the Void else he was talking about, or—?*

Someone screamed behind me, a girl's scream. I dug my heels into the stone floor, twisting.

An oak-skinned girl with blue wings was being pulled by the neck from behind. A guard was choking her as he dragged her back at sword point.

Bloods!

I hooked around and slammed my sickle into the guy's side, where his armor was bare. He gave a grunt, then loosened his grip around the girl and fell on his back—my sickle sliding out. Its glow was dampened by the red dripping from it.

My stomach lurched as I looked over the guard, feeling sick. His eyes were still open, glazed and empty.

I forced myself to look up—away from the corpse—and checked over the winged girl.

... the winged girl with *cat ears*.

Her hair was a Grimlette's shade of snowy white, matching those shivering ears and the Death mark on her forehead. Her lemon eyes blinked at me, snowflake lashes fluttering twice.

"Uh." I forgot what I was going to say. Bloods, she was cute... She had small freckles dusting her creamy nose and cheeks, cool tattoos of yellow ringlets trailing from the side of her neck to her left shoulder.

But those *eyes*...

"Are... are you with us?" I asked, flushing. I hadn't been paying attention to all the people joining our team, it was possible she'd jumped in while I wasn't looking.

She stared at me. "*Re?*"

My brow scrunched, and I waved a hand in front of her face, feeling for any head injuries. The 'static' feedback didn't alert to anything wrong up there.

"Are you okay?" I asked.

She kept staring, one of her cat ears flicking. "*Re?*"

"She no speak Landish, Grim cat," Princess Zylveia muttered and shoved me aside with a sharp flap of her scarlet wing, looping her arm around the hybrid girl. "Thank you much to be helping my El, but we need go now, yes?"

"Uh..." I looked away in a blush—looked at the corpse. Shel, the sickness came back. I shoved the dead man out of mind and ran after the two winged girls. "U-um, right!"

We rounded out to an opening exit, a bridge stretched from the building to the plateaus in the distance, soaked wet from the still-pouring rain. Above, below, and to our sides were the other ribbed bridges, all of which were being used by our Reapers and the freed inmates.

Dad trotted to a stop in front of the bridge—grabbed Neal and me by the shoulder and pushed us onto the bridge. "Hurry and go!" he said. "I'll meet you after Ringëd and I find your sister—"

"Dad?"

We all whirled. Standing in the rain just at the exit was... holy Bloods, this guy looks just like Dad! But... but younger.

And wrapped in his arms was my sister.

36

DESPERATE MEASURES

~~~~

XAVIER

"Mika…!" I heard Ringëd cry, shoving me aside to rush for the woman; the one who looked eerily like our stalking demon queen. "*Min Yujannît, zarrash Oscha…!*"

Miss Mikani's cat ears jerked straight up. "Ringëd!" She leapt out of the stranger's hold, fumbling with the chains on her ankles. She tripped and slammed into Ringëd and sent him tumbling onto his back.

"Where have you been, you *idiot*?!" She was sobbing, kissing him desperately. "Didn't you See any of my messages?"

"All of them." Ringëd sat up and brushed a hand through her hair. He was in tears himself, his voice fracturing. "I came as fast as I could. *Min Yujannît… Bezrït. Bezrït mauén…*"

I watched them in the rain, my heart weeping warmly as he murmured that all would be well. All she could do was choke and bury her head in his chest.

Then I noticed that feral ferret, Kurn, crawl out from Ringëd's armor, dragging out a slender box with him.

Mika's eyes splintered at the box, and she immediately snatched it up. "Give me those!" With trembling, shackled hands, she opened it and took out the gold engagement-vines, clipping them to her hair and pressed herself against Ringëd's chest once more. "I am *never* taking these off."

Despite himself, Ringëd laughed.

The man who'd brought Mika never took his eyes off her. He lingered in the shadows. *Wait a moment.* His figure was obscured in the darkness, but now that I looked closer…

"I… see you'll be well cared for," he said, sounding dismayed as he watched her.

A crack of lightning streaked across the sky, lighting the night. My veins iced. The man was visible for only a second, but it was long enough.

It was *him*.

I craned my gaze to Claude. *He* hadn't moved from my side. *So, there ARE two men.*

The monster's gaze snapped to me. "Nira be damned," he whispered, his glare turning murderous and flicking to Willow at my other side. "The princess *and* the Shadow?"

I backed away, keeping Willow and the unconscious Lilli in her arms behind me. "You're the one from that night, then?" I asked. "At the cliffs?"

"You really are a slippery one, aren't you?" His hands sprouted with black Hallows. "I'll have to do a more thorough job... And I can find this apparent 'twin' of yours afterward, to complete the set. How nice of you to bring the Death Princess along. She'll make a fair gift to Macarius."

Willow scoffed behind me, keeping Lilli cradled firmly in her arms and paying the downpour no heed. "I will not be going anywhere. You're outnumbered this time. Surrender now and face my father under trial for your crimes."

He spat at the ground. "It is your father who ought to stand trial. You know naught what cruelty your ancestors dealt, and you've naught to make amends for them. It is only by divine providence that I meet you here with the Shadowblood."

I glared at him. "The... what?"

Herrin, who had just finished unshackling Mikani, paused. "Did he just say the Shadow—?"

A winged blur soared down between us and the man, the newcomer's black feathers stretching outward.

It was Trixer Janson. His scythe blade was pointed threateningly at the killer's chest.

"Stay back!" the crow-shifter snarled, his two vassals obediently rushing to his side. "You won't touch anyone tonight!"

The beast's sight narrowed at Janson.

Claude stepped around Janson, glaring at his younger doppelganger. "Tell Macarius I'm done," said the father, his hand crawling with black, poisonous veins. "If either of you come anywhere near my kids again, I'll kill you both. Blood or not."

"Claude," warned the man, his tone oddly... hurt. "Do not do this. Please..."

"Save the world on your own time, Kael. Leave us out of it."

My brow knitted. What on Nirus were they on about?

Kael set his jaw, stepping back. He flicked his eyes at me, then Willow, then at the rest of our company... He ended on Mikani, his face flashing with pain.

"Very well..." His whisper was barely heard under the squall. He snarled at me. "We will meet again, Shadowblood. Your Highness Death... Lady Mikani." To Mika, he gave a low, noble bow, murmuring, "Farewell..."

He vanished inside.

"Bastard!" I growled, stepping after him. I didn't know what he meant by this... this *Shadowblood*, but I'd be damned if he was getting away this time—!

"Leave him!" Willow barked.

I gaped at her. "*Leave him*? After everything he..." Shouting guards made me pause. "Damn it all!"

Everyone darted across the bridge, and I was the last to sprint behind them. Halfway across—

BRRR-POW!

A deafening burst exploded behind me. I spun in time to watch as licking flames plumed out from an enormous, glass globe that shattered over the bridge. The wood *cracked* under my feet.

I heard Willow scream, "Xavier—!"

The bridge vanished from under me.

I hurtled down the dark chasm, the cold gale shrieking past my grown wolf ears.

A flash of lightning lit the several ribbed bridges of the prison, flying upward like a giant beast's bones—which disappeared behind the canyon wall.

Over the wind, I could hear a sloshing, grainy sound. When a new flash brightened my view below, I found the ground rushing up at me was... *slithering*? I gasped the last of my breath as the winding sands *splashed* upward, catching my legs and pulling me into its currents.

The grains were wet and heavy, pelting me as each wave folded over my head and turned me wherever it willed. I floundered in the strange ocean, spitting up sand and blinking grains, knowing the weight of it would crush me if I didn't find steady land soon—

My back hit something hard, making me cough. I'd landed on a jagged rock embedded in the ground, unyielding to the current. I clung to it, my hands slipping from the wet grains, but managed to keep a secure grip for now. A flash of light illuminated the chasms, and I saw I wasn't holding onto a rock.

It was the skeleton of an aged Stonedragon. I'd taken refuge on a ten-foot fang in its opened jaw.

When the light faded, I threw my head up, trying to see the cliffs overhead, but couldn't find anything in the blackness. The rain was dissipating, though. *Was that Zylveia's work?*

Then I realized: that's what we needed! Someone with wings!

"Dalen!" I hollered over the thrashing desert, bracing as a grainy wave slammed me against the skull. "Dalen, are you there?!"

The connection line fuzzed in my thoughts, our vassal answering. *Here, Da'torr.* He was panting, probably flying above somewhere. *Where are you?*

"We dropped below!" I spat sand out of my mouth. "We're stuck in the desert's currents!"

Where exactly?

"I'm... I'm not sure!"

A grimace sounded. *Hold tight. I'm looking.*

The connection ended.

Another string of light flashed from the clouds, and I stared into the dragon's hollow throat, holding my breath as a wave lapped over my head, nearly prying me from the dragon's tooth.

"Let me try something," Alex voiced from the psyche. *"It's a slim shot Dalen will find us. We need to get higher."*

"And how are we supposed to do that?" I yelled.

His response was to tug at my soul, signaling he wanted to switch. *Fine.* I kept my grip firm on the tooth, then took a deep breath before tumbling into the psyche, relieved to be rid of the feeling of stinging sand.

From the void's window, I watched Alexander gasp and choke, spitting up the sand blowing into his throat and eyes. "Death!"

"You asked for it," I chided from the psyche. *"Now what's your idea?"*

"This!" He inhaled a deep breath and held it in his lungs, then evoked his Hallows into the tooth we held. Purple light gleamed from his hands and sank into the bone, trailing toward the rest of the skull. Alex's vision rumbled.

Then the dragon *moved.*

37

THE UNDEAD GIANT

WILLOW

I paced the perimeter of our camp's medical tent, cupping a hand over my mouth to stifle the cry that threatened to rise.

Useless! Utterly useless!

First Xavier and Alexander disappeared in the Dancing Desert, and now Lilli was being swarmed by doctors and medics. I was told to wait outside. And of course I was. Because, like with the twins being lost, I was Gods damned *useless*.

"Willow?" a small voice whispered behind me, making me whirl.

It was Miss Ana. She'd been in the group that was treating Lilli.

My limbs locked. "Is she all right?"

"She is stable," the lioness whispered, her round ears flicking. "Lady Bianca's and my Hallows were enough to quicken the effects of the medication. The infections have lessened on her back, but it will take time to heal completely—"

I hugged the wonderful woman. "Thank you! Thank you…! Can I see her now?"

She hesitated, a bit taken aback by my reaction. "She is resting, at the moment. Perhaps when she awakens, you may have your time with her. I must stress that once she recovers, we will have to restrain her wings. We cannot risk the skin on her back stretching and opening the stitches, so please be sure she doesn't try and remove the straps we fastened to her."

"I'll be sure to. Thank you, truly…" I paused when an afterthought hit me. "Why Ana, where is Kurrick? I scarcely see him leave your side."

She nodded to the camp's outskirts. "He is keeping guard with some of the knights. He fears a raid may ensue after our success."

"He needn't worry about that. We destroyed all the roped bridges surrounding our camp, and our allied Terravokers made sure to entrap us with walls to hide within."

Ana smiled. "That is good to hear. Still, he fears. It is simply in his…"

A faint rumbling shook the camp.

Everyone ceased their work to turn when another tremor ruptured from the west. I stepped forward, trying to see past the jutting rocks surrounding our camp in the distance. "What was that?"

Another tremble shook the ground. It wasn't a powerful tremor from where we were standing, but it was enough to cause concern.

Shouts came from the barracks, and I saw two of Prince Cayden's scouts had rushed over, panting while reporting whatever was going on to the masked prince by the campfire.

I strode brusquely with Ana to meet the rebel leader. "What's happened?"

I couldn't see Cayden's face under the mask and cloth, but his rasping tone hinted at urgency. "Tanderam men. They're trying to break through the walls we've built."

"More Terravokers?" I guessed.

"Just one, as far as the scouts could tell. Plus around two hundred men waiting on the other side of a makeshift bridge. There are two massive cannons. They're shooting Flameglobes, largest I've ever heard of."

I cocked an eyebrow. "Any Shockglobes that size?"

"Only one. And they've already used it to make the biggest dent in our defenses. All they have left is fire."

I rolled my eyes with a hard sigh. "Well, as devastating as this new weapon might have been to another army, they've come ill equipped for *us*. Come, gather the squads. Cay—er, *Servant* and Ana, I think you two can handle our enemy's lone Terravoker. I'll take care of the flames, perhaps with… ah, Matthiel!"

The Howllord had just stepped out of a tent to see what the rumblings were about. When I'd called him, he came quickly, asking, "What's happening?"

"Our defenses are being attacked," I said. "One Terravoker. A couple hundred soldiers." My lips rolled into a smirk. "And new weaponized canons with enormous Flameglobes."

He snorted. "Is that all?"

"Pathetic, I know." I slid my shoulder guards from around my head and set them aside, beginning to untie the leather strings of my other plates. Matthiel followed my example. Metal would be an ill idea in this fight. If they were using fire, best to go armor free to avoid cooking underneath, should we be engulfed in flames. For Pyrovokers, we were safer going as we were.

After I slid off my gauntlets and stepped out of my boots, I ran toward the ruptures with Matthiel at my side.

Finally! I preened to myself after we were yards away from the wall. *A task I can be of use for—!*

Something *cracked* in the night like stone splitting metal, followed by terrified shrieks from the other side of the wall. Something crumbled, more screams sounded, another echoing *crack* followed by tremors...

And the wall fractured.

MATTHIEL

Mournful Nira!

Her Highness and I quickly leapt back, the stone barrier deteriorating from the center piece by piece, making way for a ten-foot-long, boney claw that scratched away the debris.

The wall fell to nothing, and I found myself staring up at the enormous, toothy, horned skeleton of a colossal dragon. The terrifying thing must have been thirty stories tall!

The fierce skull stared down at Her Highness and me with empty eye sockets, making little sound other than the clatter of lose, grinding bones that were only connected at the joints by purplish, stringy light.

I sputtered. "W-what in Death?"

"It couldn't be..." Her Highness squinted at the gigantic skull, calling up, "Alexander?"

—Alexander's grey-haired head popped into view over the dragon's brow.

"Saw you had a bit of a pest problem!" he hollered. "Thought I'd clean it up for you!"

What in Bloody Death!

I wasn't the only one gaping. With my now grown wolf ears, I could hear campers murmuring disbelieving prayers. Some thought they'd had too many spirits. Bloods, *I* thought I'd had too many spirits, and I was as sober as a chaste priest.

That thing was enormous! How could one man take command of something that gigantic? Look at the bastard, propping his elbows on the skull's crown with that childish grin, like it was barely an afterthought!

"Alexander," Her Highness chided, as if this ridiculous, impressive sight was the most mundane event she's ever witnessed. "Stop fooling around and come down here!"

"What?" Alexander hollered as his beast lowered its massive head to the dirt—rumbling the ground at my feet and causing me to stumble—and curled its tail around itself like a snoozing hound. Alex dismissed his Hallows and hopped off to meet Her Highness. "Can't I keep it?"

"Keep it if you like, but tell your brother he ought to break his habit of falling over cliffs," she said. "Once was enough for me. Two is downright irresponsible."

I pushed off the dirt, brushing myself off, still staring wide-eyed at him. "Alexander?"

Alex hummed, only now noticing me. "What?"

"How in the five realms did you do *that*?" I demanded, stalking to the curled-up beast. It was now only a pile of bones. I clasped the skull and evoked my death Hallows, letting the magic sink in… Bloods, this was exhausting…!

The skull shook a measly bit before laying still once more in a hushed rumble.

"This thing is enormous!" I spun on Alexander. "It must be the equivalent of a hundred corpses—maybe *three* hundred! The world record for a Necrovoker is *fifty*!"

Alexander snorted, but stifled it quickly, frowning. "Oh. You're serious?"

"Why would I not be serious?!"

"Well, someone ought to update that. I passed that number when I was… oh, how long was it? … Really? Sixteen, apparently."

"I… but how…" I stopped suddenly, realizing something. "Hang on. Where is Xavier?"

Her Highness swiftly explained, "Didn't I tell you? Xavier came back to camp a short while ago. Alexander was the only one left missing." She stole a glance at the resting dragon skeleton and shook her head. "Well, Alex, I suppose you've made me irrelevant again. Did you take *all* the Raiders out?"

"Most," he admitted. His mood drained at the reminder, remorse sinking his shoulders. He shook it off. "Some ran off to the prison. They'll bring more, I'm sure."

Her Highness nodded. "Well, now that all of us are present, we can move out before reinforcements arrive."

Alexander grunted his agreement and resurrected the dragon once more. I staggeringly followed them and his ground-shaking, boney pet back to camp.

Madness! I had to trot to keep up, falling behind to gawk at the massive beast. *Utter madness…!*

WILLOW

Alex set the bone pile outside the medical tent, about to follow me inside to see Lilli—but Jaq and the Treble family caught our attention. I followed as

Alex went to Jaq, who was still holding onto the winged boy, whose head was now occupied by a small crow.

Alexander glared at the engraving of 'Grimling' on the viper's head, his teeth sharpening. "Your head, Jaq. Why did they give you that?"

Jaq rubbed the scabs, glancing at the tent where Lilli was resting. "I wasn't gonna let them do it to *her*."

There was a long pause, then Alex gripped the viper's arm. "Thank you. For watching over her."

"Yeah," he grunted, then headed into the tent with the owl boy.

I began to follow him, wanting to check on my Aide myself, but Alex gave a confused breath behind me. "What's all this?"

I spun round, searching for what he was talking about. "Oh," I gasped, seeing something surprising with the Treble family.

Everyone's messengers seemed to have come back. Jewel was at my shoulder, Mal had alighted on Alex's arm, Chai hobbled at his feet, Shade was on Octavius's head... but Shade Two, for once, was *not* clinging to Octavius.

The extra raven was perched on *Neal's* shoulder, relishing the cheery strokes he offered.

I crossed my arms with a chuckle. "I suppose that explains it?"

"Yeah." Octavius shrugged brightly. "Definitely makes sense. He's just as cocky as you, Neal."

Neal was enjoying an excited beak-rub on his cheek, laughing. "This little guy's awesome. What's his name?"

Alex's head wavered. "We've been calling him Shade Two, but it's your choice. He's your messenger now."

"Cool." Neal glanced up in thought for a moment, then smirked. "I'll call him Ace. What do you think, little guy? You like that?"

Ace croaked his approval, his clipped wings fluttering.

The family laughed and congratulated him, and I grabbed Alexander's arm to pull him away. I thought it was more appropriate to let them celebrate as a family. Whatever had happened with their father, they seemed to have forgiven him... though Octavius, especially, still looked skeptical.

I couldn't say my reservations were put to rest either. But there had undoubtedly been two men in Tanderam. I still wasn't certain how Claude was involved in the assassination those years ago, but that second man, this *Kael*...

My teeth threatened to sharpen. Kael was the one at the cliffs. He was the man I saw, six years ago, tossing my love into the ocean. If Claude represented anything, it was answers to all my questions—answers that I hoped would bring the true fiend to justice.

I led Alexander into the tent, wading through the other patient beds until we reached the place Lilli was resting. Jaq and the little boy, Oliver, stood at one side while Alex and I took our places across from them.

I sank onto the mattress, cupping Lilli's cold face. "How are you feeling, dear?"

She was only half awake, her eyes bleary and drifting over all of us. "I'm... thirsty..."

Bianca came with a canteen, helping Lilli sit upright to drink from it. "That's a good sign," the doctor assured, touching Lilli's brow and seeming pleased. "You'll need to keep up your fluids as we move. Just sit tight, we're packing everything up. We'll move you to a comfortable wagon when we're ready. For now, take it easy and let the drugs take effect, for the pain."

Lilli nodded sleepily and was lowered back down, her eyes gliding up at Alexander. She clasped a limp hand to his fingers.

"Alex?" She asked. I noticed he tensed at the touch, even more so when she squeezed tighter. "Thank you... for coming... I-I didn't know if you would..."

Alex seemed confused. "Why in Death would you think I wouldn't?"

"Well, you..." She yawned. "You still haven't given me... my vines, so... *mnhmnnn...*"

Her grip slacked from Alexander's fingers, and she dozed off.

I sighed. The aforementioned drugs must have made her a tad loopy. I chuckled and tucked one of her stray locks behind her ear.

"Vines?" Bianca clipped suddenly, making me start. The rabbit's face was scrawled with shock as she stared at Alex. "Why would she want you to give her vines?"

His shoulders locked. "Well... it's just..."

"Are you engaged?"

He hesitated, looking away.

The hollowness that sagged her cheeks made everything click for me. *Oh, dear.*

I saw the glint of tears well in her eyes before she turned on her heels... and stormed off.

38

WHILE WE'RE YOUNG

XAVIER

"Thank you all for joining us on this blessed occasion," Willow addressed to the crowd of soldiers. Her azure gaze swept the many faces that offered her their full attention. "It is often the darker times that remind us what we hold dear, and that the brighter moments are spent with those we love. As was so with Mikani Treble and Ringëd Fleetfûrt."

The bride and groom were blinking through joyous tears, their fingers intertwined at the center of the crowd, the light of the firepit flickering bright and warm behind them. Willow flipped a page in the *Choir* book she held, borrowed from Herrin for this abrupt, but overdue occasion. The moment our scouts had announced us clear of dangerous territory, the couple had asked Willow to hold their union right away. Even I had to agree that, perhaps, a cheerful occasion was necessary now more than ever.

"Through trial and suffering," Willow said, "they lived through the horrors of war, yet stand before us now… Unified. And stronger than they ever imagined."

I broke my gaze when the ferret in my hands squirmed. Kurn had been given to me for the time being. Obviously, Ringëd was busy. But I was finding this pet to be… slippery.

Chai watched from my feet, his head cocking up at his fellow feral and bobbing his head, eager to climb up. He tried to flutter his wings, but his feathers still hadn't grown back. He hopped about, but soon gave up in a croaking huff.

"In the text of the Gods," Willow continued at the center of the gathering, her finger placed on the correct passage of the *Choir*. "It tells of the union between the Mother of Death and the Father of Life. When the first form of life was born upon Nirus' soil, Shel was hence created. And once that life form's time did end, Nira arose to usher its soul to the Great Unknown. Legend has it, the two newly created Gods were not always the lovers we know Them as today.

"At first, Shel could not understand Nira's obsession with death. He thought it a disgrace to ignore the glory of life and look only toward the end. But likewise, Nira thought it dishonorable for Shel to cast away his gaze from death and ignore the inevitable. For the longest time, it is said the two could not stand the others' presence… until both saw the beauty of either perspective. They discovered that without life, death means little to us, and it is because of death that life is so precious.

"It is due to this understanding that the two still persevere as husband and wife today. Their love has been told and written for thousands of years, unfaltering and everlasting. That is because, as They teach, love is not simply looking through the window of the other's mind, but of exploring *with* them outside the glass."

She paused to flip the page, looking at Ringëd. "Now, I ask that you please present the groom's ring and marriage stud."

Ringëd nudged Neal beside him. The groomsman jerked upright and held out the velvet box containing the specified items. Ringëd took the box and presented it to Willow, who nodded and set down the *Choir* text to hold the items. She first picked up the gold ring and lifted it for all to see.

"The ring," Willow said, "symbolizes the unity betwixt the Mother and Father. The shape of a circle has no true beginning, nor a true end. It is whole, always and forever."

She gave the ring to Mikani. "With this ring, Mikani Valerie Treble, do you give the promise of eternal love, through life and afterlife, with your soul, body and mind, until your spirit returns to the Goddess, to Ringëd Lület Fleetfûrt?"

Mika grasped the groom's hand and slipped the ring on his ring finger. "I do."

Willow took out the marriage stud. "And will you promise him a marriage filled with thrill and unfettered care by striking his ear with your mark, as Ushar strikes his arrows in the storms above?"

"I… will…" Mika hesitated at that one, giving Willow a cautious glance. "We don't have the tool for piercings, though…"

Willow smiled and evoked her fire Hallows with a finger, turning the earring's sharp needle over the flame to sterilize it. "We will manage without it. That is, if he is willing?"

Ringëd seemed to pale a bit, but set his jaw. "Y-yeah. Fine with me."

Mika took the sterilized earring and then placed a lemon wedge behind Ringëd's earlobe to use as a soft backing for the needle. Mika tried not to cringe when piercing the needle through Ringëd's ear, spearing the lemon wedge out the back. Ringëd seethed out a pained breath for a brief moment, but soon collected himself and managed to flash a smile at his bride.

Willow clipped the back end of the earring to secure it, and they resumed their previous stance, Ringëd raising a hand to his newly weighted ear. I couldn't tell if he was fascinated or still bearing the sting.

"And now," Willow went on. "Please present the marriage jewel for the bride."

Octavius was holding that box, and nervously thrust it out for Ringëd to grab. The groom took the diamond droplet, and Willow cleared her throat. "The marriage vines represent both of your lives, which is why they remain separated when engaged. But now, this moment is the time your lives converge and become a single path, connected by this day—and this jewel. Do you, Ringëd Lület Fleetfûrt, give this diamond centerpiece in promise to give your love through life and afterlife, as a single, united path, and to walk by her side every step with your soul, body and mind, until your spirit returns to the Goddess, to Mikani Valerie Treble?"

Ringëd stepped up to connect Mika's vines at her brow, placing the diamond droplet at the center. His breath was wistful. "You bet your ass I do."

Laughter rippled through the crowd, and Willow picked up a bowl of water that had been waiting at her feet, chuckling. "And as the final ritual, I ask that both join hands and wet them in the waters so that Rin may bless you both on your journey together, so that it may be filled with beauty and grace in even the darkest hours."

They clasped hands and dipped them in the bowl. Once their fingers were withdrawn, Willow set down the bowl and smiled. "And with that, I proudly pronounce you husband and wife. May the Gods bring you peace and glory. *Nira kemn begna myel gharreyl la lochen.*"

Cheers erupted, Linus and Zylveia bursting into music with a lute and ocarina, other campers having brought instruments for leisure. Prince Cayden, still disguised as Land's Servant, had taken up a fiddle, the crowd dancing round the jigging newlyweds as frothing mugs and peppered kabobs were passed round.

I grabbed myself one of the mugs and *three* kabobs, laughing while Jaq looped an arm through mine and wheeled me about, plucking the mug and kabobs from my fingers—then he shoved me into Willow.

She chuckled as we both stumbled back, her white hair swaying, and she dropped the *Choir* book when I pulled her into an impulsive dance. In the midst of our circling, I caught a glimpse of Herrin rushing to the fallen book, brushing it of dirt and sighing in great relief. *Sorry, Herrin.*

The song came to an end and another began. Dizzy from all the twirling, I slowed my dance with Willow, keeping our hands connected, chuckling.

"What do you think, darling?" I asked, combing my fingers through her ashen hair, her engagement-vines glittering. "Shall we have dancing at our wedding?"

She smiled. "I do hope so."

Memories flitted, so many dances we'd shared before, so much cheer… so many smiles she would cast me, just like this one. I brushed my fingers over her blazing cheek, leaning closer, feeling her breath on my lips…

"Don't."

I started—joy tearing so suddenly, I could hear it rip. That voice had come from my thoughts.

Willow looked dismayed, cupping my face. "Had you forgotten?"

Forgotten…

My hands balled; my *borrowed* hands. Borrowed skin, borrowed fingers, borrowed heart…

I pulled my gaze from her stunning, icy eyes, and shoved through the ignorant campers.

The pain, at least, was *mine* to claim.

39

NEVERLAND'S HEIRESS

SYREEN

THE NEVERLAND CONTINENT

Ah, that satisfying sound: metal plunging into muscle.

How strange, though, there came resurfaced memories that I once thought forgotten. Quite unexpected. Nostalgia bloomed from the depths of my heart, remembering the thrilling boar hunts my sisters and I would conduct in the forests so long ago... Which, I supposed, was a fitting memory for this momentous occasion.

The cool, red mist flecked my cheek as I slid the blade from my sister, Liara's, eye, saving me from the heat before her body fell at my feet with an ungraceful thump.

Cheers roared from the arena's surrounding benches.

I sheathed my weapon, waving with a victorious smile before pulling off my golden gauntlets.

The gold-dressed queen approached, crossing the grassy field with a laurel of green ivy and yellow blossoms in her hands. I knelt with my fists on one knee as she kissed my brow and laid the laurel over my crown.

"Rise, beloved daughter," she said in her light, gentle voice, smooth as the softest silk and warm as a babe swathed in coal-heated linen. "You've fought masterfully. I'd always hoped you, of the three, would be the victor."

"Thank you, Majesty." I pushed to my feet, pride pumping hot in my veins.

She gipped my hand to raise it to the crowd, announcing, "The last remaining heiress stands before you! Her Highness Syreen has proven superior over her late sisters. Ladies and Lords, I give you your future queen!"

Adoring shouts erupted, my smile fixed between pants. At last. At long *last*. My dream was unfolding before my very eyes… and it was everything I'd hoped.

The queen dropped my hand and waved for me to follow her, which I rightly obeyed, my armor clattering noisily, contrasting her quiet, lithe steps and the calm ruffle of her shimmering gown.

She and I waved at the adoring Roaresses and their husbands as they tossed petals of every flower and color, a beautiful sprinkle raining upon our heads. I breathed in the mixing scents, basking in the glory and sunlight.

Only when we left the arena and were in the royal hovering coach did the queen speak. "Congratulations, Syreen, on your accomplishment." She smiled tenderly, her hands poised in her lap. "You've grown to be a fine young woman. My star pupil."

"Thank you, your grace." I bowed my head.

"Please." She took my hand. "You're now my heiress. My last and strongest daughter. You may at last call me your mother, for you've brought me no shame, unlike your sisters."

My heart swelled, lion ears folding down in awe. "Thank you… Mother."

Such joy it brought, to allow the word to pass my lips. Tears began to sting, but I commanded them into submission. I would *not* ruin this glorious moment by showing weakness in her presence.

"Now, my dear." She released my hand, reclaiming her original posture. "You are sixteen, are you not?"

"Yes, your gr… Mother."

She nodded, considering. "The proper age to choose your consorts. Tell me, have you any men in mind?"

"I admit I haven't devoted the time."

"Well, you have free reign to choose, as heiress. Any capable bachelors may be your claim, and any number of them, should you wish. It is often wise to birth offspring of different seeds while you're still fertile, to maximize the competition between daughters. Only the one with the strongest genes can succeed you. It was proven today, as the man who sired you apparently had the strongest genes of my own consorts."

I bowed. "I will search the kingdom for any such candidates, Mother."

"Tell me who and where once you decide, and I shall write the decree that very moment. Only the best, for my heiress."

I beamed, the air tasting sweeter through the open windows of the carriage, trees a more luscious green and the sky seeming a brighter blue. *Mother, devoting all these gifts to me? Only me?* It was an honor I'd dreamt of in my youth. Until now, my sisters and I were treated as tenants in the palace, kept at a distance and promised reward of her love if we found success… That promise, it seemed, was no lie. And I soaked up every succulent moment.

"In the meantime," Mother went on, breaking me of my revere. "I will send you a few of my own picks, whom I think may suit you. Feel free to either accept or reject them. I don't know your preferences, so I will start with a wide range and go from there. How does this sound, dearest daughter?"

"It sounds like a grand idea, Mother," I said. "Thank you."

The carriage came to a sudden stop, and I whirled to the window, seeing a messenger woman had trotted up beside us, saluting with two fingers crossed horizontally over her chest.

"Gardener bless the forests, Your Majesty," said the messenger. "Pardon the interruption, but a letter was sent for you. The headmistress of the Hexin School requests an audience with her eminence."

Mother peered out the open frame and took the letter, thanking the messenger, who blushed.

"The headmistress, mm?" Mother hummed, opening the letter's seal and scanning it. When she'd finished, she handed the letter back to the messenger. "Thank you. But tell the headmistress that she needn't bother with formal post. She is welcome to contact my direct line whenever she pleases."

The woman bowed. "Yes, your grace."

Mother waited until she was well away before sighing, still gazing out the frame. "Syreen."

I straightened, lion ears flicking at attention.

Mother inhaled a soft breath, seeming to enjoy the floral scents that clung to the spotted light as the horses pulled us into the palace courtyard. Rows upon rows of cherry blossoms decorated the bloated trees, feral sparrows twittering in a delightful lilt as we passed.

It was some time before Mother continued her thought. "You are my heiress now. As such, I think it appropriate you attend certain meetings with me, for your education."

"Yes, Mother."

The coach stopped, and a servant man came to help us out. Mother went on as we walked through the fruitful gardens together. "I am meeting with an old friend tonight. She will be dining with us, and I expect you at my side when the meal begins. Take this time to bathe and dress appropriately."

"Appropriately, Mother?"

She nodded, her eyes lifting to the sky. "As an heiress would."

She seemed troubled, looking at the approaching storm clouds that threatened to smother the innocent blue.

"Mother?" I asked when she fell silent.

She narrowed her eyes at the clouds, her voice a grim purr. "Culatia seems to have arrived early this year. And with it, their storms."

The nimbus formations were scattered in the distance. One of the patches, which I knew to be one of the floating islands, was close to our city. The wind was picking up as we watched, ruffling my cropped, honey-golden hair.

The island itself was far enough off that it wouldn't block the sun from us for days to come, but the storm would no doubt shield the moon tonight.

"An omen, perhaps," Mother sneered, turning toward the ivy-dressed palace. "Ushar taunts us with His son's descendant. Better that his illness takes him quickly and leaves His islands without a Relicblood of their own. It would do Culatia some good to rule for themselves. Even the Stormchasers down here could advance more without tying themselves to ancient souls that are too old to learn what the new times offer."

I hadn't dedicated much thought to such ramblings, but now that she broached the subject, I understood her concerns. Sky's Relicblood in particular never made any sense to me. Ushar, the God of Sky, was a dragon. *Yet his son was a swallow?* Every other God was the same shift as their Relic Child. Shel's son, Land, had been a lion before his descendant was killed and my ancestors took over Neverland. Ocean was a Seadragon, like Rin. Iri and his son, Dream, were foxes. Death was a wolf, like her mother, Nira...

But Sky? A swallow? Bah. There was something dishonest going on in Culatia, and the root of it was surely the Relicbloods themselves. Perhaps Mother was right. It would do them good to break away from the tyranny. Only prosperity would follow, as it did with the Land realm. You need only look about the land to understand, full of luscious greens and vibrant colors, fertile soil and blissful citizens...

Well, blissful save for those ill-hearted rebels. Nothing could bring those madwomen happiness, except my Mother's head on a pike. Foolish bitches. They were a plague in the minds of Neverland's good people. I once asked Mother why she hadn't seemed concerned about the resistance, but she merely patted my cheek and said they were so few in number that it wasn't an issue. For her safety, I hoped she was correct.

The guards saluted us as we entered the palace's large, marble foyer, and we nodded in kind to the women, moving onward.

Thunk!

We paused before turning the corner, hearing wooden bangs echo through the corridor.

Thunk!

Ku-thunk, thunk, thunk!

Confused, we rounded the wall to see the source of the noise, and Mother bristled.

"Hugh!" Her voice was shrill, yet hushed at my younger brother. "What in our ancestor's name do you think you're doing?"

Hugh ceased hitting the carved, oakwood lion with a practice sword, the blond boy blushing and hiding the weapon behind his back. A golden glow shined from his hidden hands, the Land mark under his open collar gleaming, and I saw the wooden blade shrink its height a few inches. It didn't shrink much further. Hugh may have strong Hallows for a boy, but that wasn't too impressive a feat in itself.

Needless to say, his plan to hide his offense failed, because neither Mother nor I were fooled.

Her usually calm composure cracked a good fraction, making the tan boy pale in fright and turn to run—

Mother snagged the fourteen-year old's hair and yanked him to a stop. "No you don't, young man! Give me that sword."

She pried it from his grip, still clutching the boy's hair. She handed me the weapon. "Take this dangerous thing away from him before he hurts himself—or some*thing*."

She took his chin and pulled his face out, forcing him to face the oakwood statue that now housed many dents. "Do you see what your reckless playing has done to this fine work of art?"

"I-I'm sorry, Mother!" Hugh was shaking.

I used to envy how the sons could always call her Mother. Only daughters needed to earn that privilege. But now that *I* earned it myself, I saw why it was necessary. If I hadn't had that reward to look forward to, I may not have trained as hard as I had to defeat my sisters. How wise Mother was proving...

Hugh struggled under her grip, but Mother's backhand *smacked* his face so strongly, Hugh was thrown back a foot. He tripped on his ankles and stumbled to his rear.

Mother stared down her nose at him, snorting. "Your weapons are the pruning clippers, like a good young man wields, without complaint. Now I suggest you retrieve them and fight your real enemy: stray stems in the rose bushes."

Hugh's glare was hot and wet, resentment burning in his whisper. "There are men who fight *demons*..."

—*Smack!*

She struck him again, harder, releasing a cry from his lips.

"No son of mine is going to kneel before a Relicblood!" she sneered coldly. "And I thought I made it clear that I didn't want to hear another word of this Reaper business again? It's not as if they'd take you now, anyway."

"Yes they would!" He tried to keep his voice from quivering, but his throat released a small tremor. "I read how they take anyone with a messenger—"

"You *read*?" She was furious now, lion ears grown and curling. "Boys have no business *reading*. Who taught you such feminine things?"

He shut his mouth, and my legs went rigid. Truthfully, it was *I* who taught him to read. Hugh was my beloved brother—my *full* brother, the only one who shared my same father. The other four were my half-kin, whose fathers were my mother's other consorts. Those men were still alive, but my sire died of illness two years ago. Hugh was all I had left to remember him by... and Shel, but the boy was growing to look more like him each day.

Mother shoved him on his back, brushing the wrinkles out of her skirt. "I'll not hear of this *reading* nonsense again. Nor of this talk of Reapers. Am I understood?"

Hugh spilled silent tears, sitting up over his knees and glaring daggers at her. She spun away, smoothing back her hair as her tone lowered. "No matter. The Reapers won't take you. I had that dirty beast disposed of yesterday."

Hugh's breath ceased, horror stricken. "Lady Lilac...?"

Mother grimaced. "You only had that thing for a week and you already named it? Bah. No matter... Syreen snapped its neck last morning."

I crumbled when Hugh shot me a sharp, betrayed stare, his eyes rimmed red.

Mother then turned to me, her face calm and smile returned. "Make sure he doesn't get his soft hands on that again." She nodded to the wooden sword in my hands. "And do be sure to arrive for dinner on time, to meet with our guests, my heiress. Rest well."

With that, she strutted past Hugh, not giving him a second glance, and left the two of us in the corridor alone. Once she was gone, Hugh pushed to his feet and ran at me in a rage, shoving me back.

"How could you?!" he cried, hitting me with more force than I expected of a boy his age. "How could you...! Lady Lilac was the only thing that gave me purpose! The only thing that I... I felt whole with...! I loved her and you killed...!"

He collapsed into my armored chest, sobbing. I hushed him, cradling his dear head. "Be still, little brother... It... will be all right."

"You don't understand!" His voice was tight with despair, refusing to remove his face from my breastplate. "I wouldn't have served the Death King. I wouldn't have. I just wanted to keep Lilac... But you..."

"Come." I led him through the hall toward the stairs, glancing over my shoulder to be sure no guards followed us. "There is something I think you ought to see."

I walked him up to my chambers, shutting the doors behind me and secured the latch.

"Now, you mustn't tell Mother," I warned, going to my closet. I pulled out something dome-shaped that was hidden under a curtain. His nose scrunched at it, and he gasped when I peeled off the cloth.

"Lady Lilac!" He hugged the wicker cage, the crow inside cawing delightedly and rubbing its beak through the bars to nuzzle Hugh's cheek. "She's alive?"

I chuckled at his precious smile, the one that could melt even the coldest of hearts. "Mother asked me to kill her… but I know what happens when the Bond is broken. I've heard terrible things, from the Death Knights in town. I could never put you through such pain, dearest brother. Her life is my gift to you."

He set down the cage and squeezed my ribs, his grip surprisingly crushing under my armor. "Thank you, Sy!" He held tighter. "Thank you!"

I ruffled his blond hair. "You're most welcome. But I'm afraid she'll have to stay here, in my chambers. Since you share a room with our half-brothers, there is a risk at least one will tell Mother. Then she'd have *both* our necks."

He crouched before the cage, poking in a finger to scratch his messenger's head. "Not yours… you are the heiress now. Punishment will be less severe than anything she'd exact on me."

"Do you think so?"

"Most certainly." His gaze moved to the wooden sword I'd discarded on the bed. He ran his fingers over the smooth lacquer, his expression darkening. "I'm caught with a practice blade, and am told my place is in the gardens. I'm told it's improper for a young man to read, and that it won't attract any Roaresses to ask so many questions as I do. I receive a messenger that would otherwise make me a knight of *something* instead of a handsome seed-producer, and its life is immediately threatened.

"But you—*and* our late sisters—rarely received more than a slap on the wrist if a rule was broken. And then you were promised glory and honor, if you obeyed. We sons are promised no such future, regardless of what we do."

I watched him sadly, pursing my lips. Then I came over and picked up the sword, using my Arborvoking to shrink it down, keeping its heavy weight as I condensed it into the shape of a beautiful rose, using a claw to etch in a sealing mark on the stem and locked the Hallows in.

I handed it to Hugh. "Keep up your practicing. The sealing mark will let you change its form without straining your Hallows."

He took the rose, bemused, and tested the sealing mark by pressing a thumb against it. The flower shifted into the sword in a golden glitter and morphed back to the flower after he pressed it again and gazed up at me. "Really?"

"When I have sons of my own, I want them to know how to protect themselves, as well as being handsome seed-producers." I winked. "But might I suggest *not* training in the palace halls, where Mother and the servants can see you?"

He beamed, gripping the rose and embraced me once more. "I love you, Sy."

"And I love you." I hugged him back, kissing his crown. "Anything for my dearest little brother."

A knock came at the door.

I quickly covered the cage with Lady Lilac inside and hid her in the closet, then went to open the door.

My personal handmaid, Helen, came striding in with a basket full of gowns, the cheer stretching her impeccable smile. "Congratulation, Your Highness!" Helen sang. "I heard of your victory! Bloods, the whole kingdom has, I imagine! *Kh-hmm*, now, you're expected to attend dinner with the queen in an important meet…"

She stopped when noticing Hugh standing by the foot of my bed. "Oh. Prince Hugh, hello. Come to praise your blood-sister as well, eh?" She had nothing but adoration for the boy, balancing the basket against her hip to pat his soft cheek. "So cute, you are. But best be off, your sister has much to prepare for."

She shooed Hugh out the door before shutting it after him with a foot, looking me over. "My, that tournament sullied your complexion. Come, let's wash the unworthy's blood off. Mustn't offend the queen and her guests, eh?"

Once nightfall burdened the land, I was cleaned and dressed in gold silks with yellow blossoms braided in my hair. I wore the heiress's tiara of gold wire and amethyst jewels. Helen had left to tell the queen I was ready and would be down soon.

While I had time to myself in my chambers, I went to the large window that led to the terrace, watching the rain pelt the glass in a hushing applause. The soft rumble of thunder came, a flash bringing light to the darkness.

An omen, Mother had said.

The tremble of explosions quaking my stomach seemed to prove the merit in her words. There was something sinister in the wind. Where the showers would normally feel like a blessing, providing our crops and beautiful forests hydration, this one brought with it a menacing howl. One that clattered the shutters and screamed by the windows like a band of monstrous Necrofera.

The gales were so violent, I even spotted a pair of Nimdragons playing outside my terrace. They were cloudy creatures, with gossamer skin glistening like mist in the flashes of light. Though usually known to be gentle, even domesticated in Culatia, they only came out for the heaviest showers. Their abundance measured the storm's severity, in a way. But Nimdragons only cared for the rain. And were it simply rain out there now, I would think nothing of it. But the powerful bolts of lightning that splintered the clouds had me fearful of the real danger the Sky realm had to offer:

Shockdragons.

They were enormous flyers that wove through the clouds, stirring up the harshest storms... Only the Sky Knights have ever tamed them successfully, as far as I'd known. But they weren't always able to stop the destruction the electric beasts left behind. This night felt fit for one of them, and Hugh's screeching crow in my closet seemed to agree.

I went to the bird's wicker cage and hushed it. "Not so loud, Lady. I helped you once, but I cannot guarantee your safety a second time."

The crow calmed at my touch, if only a little. She responded better to Hugh. *Oh, what will become of my brother?* Could he truly stay here and be content with *having* the messenger? *Or will the promise of knighthood entice him too far?*

I wrung my hands, staring at my reflection in the darkened window. If Mother still treats him the way she does, the latter will be inevitable. *But then, if I were queen, would he stay?*

I jumped when a knock pounded at my door. Quickly hiding Lady Lilac, I called for the interrupter to enter.

A servant boy I didn't recognize peeked his head inside.

"Uhm, your grace?" he said. He held a tray of tea in his hands, accompanied by a plate of pastries and an enormous vase of a colorful bouquet. "The kitchen staff has brought you a gift, for your victory."

"Ah, how wonderful!" I allowed him entry with a wave. "Set it on the nightstand, please."

He bowed and came in, setting down his items as directed. He was young, perhaps only a year older than I. I watched the lion-tailed boy fill my cup and set the cakes aside, admiring his sharp features and somewhat muscular build. It was odd to see such strength on a man, even under a servant's loose uniform. Odd, and strangely alluring...

He turned to leave, but I stopped him. "One more thing, if you don't mind?"

He looked back, stiffening slightly. "Y... yes, Your Highness?"

I motioned to my gown. "An opinion? What say you? Is it too much?"

He blinked, not having expected the question. "It... er, is appropriate for an heiress, your grace."

"Oh, good. Yes. For an heiress…"

He bowed again and turned to leave, but I laid a hand on his shoulder to stop him once more. "Just one more thing."

He swallowed audibly, inching his head to me and seeming unnerved that my face had come so near. "Y… yes, Highness?"

"What is your name?"

"Jacob, your grace."

"Tell me, Jacob. Why haven't I seen your like in the palace before?"

"I work the kitchens, my lady. I'm the scullery boy. They don't often allow me to roam the halls. They only sent me up now because I've just turned eighteen and they think me old enough."

Two years my senior, then. Older than I expected, but not by much. My excitement was wetting now. "Well, Jacob," I purred in his ear, my hand running from his shoulder to his arm. "I think you're old enough for… other things, as well. You see, now that I'm the heiress, I've been told I may begin choosing… consorts."

He went cold under my touch.

I gripped the muscle bulging from his bicep. "You have quite a figure, dear Jacob… Not a common one, either. I suppose lifting crates of pantry stock and dishes has its perks, mm?"

He shuddered when my breath brushed his neck. The shy thing tried to shuffle away, but I tightened my grip. "Why the hurry, dear Jacob?"

His blush was precious. "I… er, really should be heading back to my mistresses…"

"They will pardon you, on my order. Why don't you come and sit?" I pulled him to the bed and sat him down, setting a knee between his legs as I wrapped my arms round his neck.

"Y-your tea, Highness," he squeaked like a mouse. "It'll get cold…"

"Never mind the tea. You see, Jacob, I've decided that I want my daughters to have only the strongest genes. And you may just have such genes. You'd give me powerful children, I should think. It would be an honor for you…"

He gulped, leaning away as his voice cracked. "I… I must stress that the tea shouldn't be left to cool, your grace…!"

"Playing coy," I chuckled softly. "Have you ever been with a woman, Jacob?"

"I, er, really think you should try the tea! I hear it's a special brew! Delicious, and…!"

I shoved him down, straddling his hips. He yelped and twisted, wriggling under me and tried to crawl away. I nearly had a better hold of the weasel, but he suddenly reached into his long sleeve and—

He pulled out a knife, slashing it over my face.

I jerked back in a scream, and he fumbled off the bed as I clutched my bleeding cheek, dumbfounded. "How... how *dare* you...?!" I glared at the boy holding the blade, his grip and posture suddenly steady and determined.

The frightened boy who'd once quaked under my hold had vanished. In his place was a man with a purpose, his expression hard and tone unfaltering as he said, "You should have accepted your tea and cakes, Your Highness. Now I can't guarantee this will end pretty."

It dawned on me. This was no 'congratulatory gift' from the kitchens. This was an assassination. Had the tea been poisoned—?

He slashed for me again and I lurched away, knocking over the table, kettle and pastries toppling in a noisy mess. He stabbed for my chest, but I dodged and rolled away, hurrying to my sword, which was sheathed against the wall by the terrace window.

A bolt of light cracked outside as I withdrew my steel, coming at the assassin with a heaving thrust. He ducked and retreated back a step, lunging away from a second strike before cursing under his breath and rushing out the door.

"Stop!" I shouted, running out to the hall. "Guards! Stop him! Guards...!"

My breath crumbled when I found him throwing open a new door and barging inside.

It was the princes' chambers.

"Hugh...!" I rushed over, no time to wait for the guardswomen. Pulling open the doors, I found the assassin already had his bait set.

While my four, useless half-brothers sat quivering in fright in their beds, Hugh stood in the center of the room, his throat kissed by the man's knife, a drop of red trickling. The assassin was hunched behind the boy.

"Not too quickly, Highness," he warned in a guttural click, lion tail swishing at his feet. I noticed Hugh's hands move behind him, holding a wooden rose. "Best we put that blade down, eh? Wouldn't want to hurt the precious flower here..."

The man's eyes bulged, his breath cutting off. He'd stopped moving, and eyes rolled up... until his back hit the floor and I saw the hilt of a wooden sword skewered through his chest.

Hugh spun to look at his kill, shaking. "L... leave...!" he panted, his lungs sounding constricted. "My sister...! Alone...!"

Hugh collapsed to his knees and started hacking, spitting up vomit.

I dropped my blade and scooped him up. "Thank the stars!" I kissed his crown, grasp tightening to stifle his quivering.

I wanted to keep him there, to console him, to calm his nerves that still seemed shocked and sick... *but what if that wasn't the only assassin?*

And what if I hadn't been the only target?

"Hugh." I drew back the crying boy. "Come. We must warn Mother, in case there are more."

He trembled, but nodded, letting me take his hand as I picked up my sword and led us down the hall. Mother's room was upstairs on the third floor. When we reached her chambers, I shoved open the door.

Mother's body lay strewn across the floor. A cup of tea had spilled beside her hand.

I didn't have to go near to know she was dead.

I also didn't have to think long before I realized it meant that I, as the heiress... was now queen.

Hours later, the town Reapers came to escort the corpses of the assassin and my mother away. Their Seams were to be cut before a funeral was held.

I now sat on the throne, staring blankly at my feet. Hugh sat cross legged on the floor beside me. He held his wooden rose, staring at the blood spatters with a nauseated grimace. Still, he didn't loosen his fingers from the stem.

"What did he want?" asked Hugh, having finally regained his composure after being sick a few hundred times. "Who would want to kill us?"

My voice was gruff. "The resistance. They've plotted to kill Mother since she was crowned... they must have been waiting for her daughters to fight amongst themselves before targeting the winner." My claws were already sharp, and they gripped the throne until the wood splintered.

Hugh said nothing more, tucking his knees to his chest and pressing his face against them.

Squeeee....

The throne room's doors opened, my handmaid looking inside. "Your High... majesty? There are guests here. They'd come for..." Her face flushed with grief, bowing when I waved my acceptance.

She stepped out as two figures stepped in, both dressed in glistening violet gowns with gold, floral designs that sparkled in the lamplight above.

One was a girl, looking a few years my senior, dark skinned with smooth scales and brown hair. She came and knelt, bowing in silence.

The second woman was perhaps nearing forty, but with the same scales and brown hair as the girl. I guessed they were mother and daughter. The mother's eyes were red from tears, which she was still drying with a kerchief when she knelt beside her daughter.

"Your Majesty," said the older woman, dabbing at her eyes and taking a moment to calm her voice. "My greatest sympathies. Your mother was a dear friend…"

Her throat tightened, apologizing in a whisper as she wiped away more tears. Her daughter didn't lift her gaze from the floor, still kneeling.

I raised a hand to them. "Please, dear friends, rise. My mother spoke fondly of you, Roaress…"

"Lysandre," she said, she and the girl lifting to their feet. "I am Lanyce Lysandre. And this is my daughter, Genevieve."

Genevieve only nodded.

Her mother, Lanyce, went on. "We had business to discuss with Her Majesty. But I suppose that title now belongs to you… I will understand if tonight's meeting is postponed."

"My mother thought it imperative that I attend your meeting," I said. "I fear a cancelation would bring her shame. Come Hugh, let us dine with our guests. We can discuss the contents of this gathering over a warm meal."

They nodded as I rose from the throne. Hugh hurried to his feet, falling into step behind me as I led the way out to the halls.

Roaress Lysandre sounded uncertain. "Erm, Your Majesty? I doubt a boy will be too keen on politics. Perhaps he should wait elsewhere while—"

"My brother nearly had his throat slit by an assassin tonight," I clipped, though delicately. "He is not to leave my sight."

She staggered. "Oh… Very well…"

I glanced down to see Hugh had trotted to my side, gripping his wooden rose with white knuckles. My gaze craned back to the Roaress and her silent daughter, pausing. "I hear you're a headmistress of a school?" I asked.

Lanyce gave a wan smile. "Indeed. We are an old establishment. My second husband's ancestors founded it in the late sixteenth century."

"And what business did my mother have with your school, if I may ask?"

"Most of Neverland's queens have conducted business with our school. The education of our children and young women are a key function to our economic success. It's our school's belief that an educated woman means one less uninformed member of the resistance."

My mood darkened. "Then I suppose you do Shel's work. I don't know what those rebels think they'll achieve. It's not as if Land's Relicblood will pop into existence out of the blue."

"Unfortunately," she sighed. "They believe precisely that. They've even been more relentless as of late... and I think I know the reason."

She produced a folded piece of parchment from her robe's pocket and handed it to me. I smoothed it out before inspecting the inked drawing and letters with a scrutinizing eye.

Depicted were two men, perhaps a few years my senior, but young enough to be notable bachelors. They were Grim-born, judging from their chalky, pale faces and grey hair, handsome noses and square jawlines. Wolf ears had been sketched at either side of their heads and, most peculiarly, their eyes were mismatched, one painted with blue watercolors and the other left empty and milky-white.

Below the portraits was a symbol: three black diamonds fanned upward in a tri-leaf shape. The crest of Nirus. And below this read, *The Shadowblood Emerges—Land's Heir soon follows! They are the key. Join us for the coming Day of Revival!*

"The Shadowblood?" I asked, brow knitting as I studied the parchment again. "Who are they?"

"We've looked into this after seeing these posted throughout town. They are a high lord's sons from Grim. They were the twins that were separated for a time, after one was thought dead. Now it seems the other is alive."

"You sound as if they're known here."

Her head wavered. "The story was a big one when the reports first aired. Though, I imagine you were quite a young sprout at the time. The years have caused most of our memories to wane."

"And what do these Grimlings have to do with the fictional 'lost Heir'? The poster makes it seem as though they'll bring him back."

"That's what the revolution believes. I'm still not sure how it correlates exactly, but I've heard rumors of clergymen preaching new sermons during Songday congregations about it. I can't make heads or tails of it, to speak true. Our school has even undergone attacks from the rebellion over it. I came here hoping to find help... but it seems the palace has its own complications to worry after."

"Yes..." I murmured. "But the rebels must cease their terrorism on *all* accounts..."

What was the protocol for such a subject? What was to be done? Oh, if only Mother had taught me the ways of a queen before I became one...

But then, who's to say I had to follow the footsteps of previous women? I was my own ruler, with my own ideas. No one said I couldn't make decisions for myself. *I* was the queen, after all.

I straightened, inspired anew, and shifted my tone to a more refined, confident song. "I will send for extra Leaflite guards and Footrunners to your school, Roaress Lysandre. For the safety of your staff and students. It is most important that our educational system stands strong, as well as our castle."

She looked overjoyed by this. "Thank you, Majesty…! Truly, it's a great relief."

I lifted the poster again, peering over the portraits of the Grimish brothers. "As for this Shadowblood business…" I considered. "If they're overseas, there doesn't seem to be much to do, is there?"

Her head shook solemnly. "Last we heard, they were seen in the Everland continent. The locals have taken to calling one of them 'he who rides the undead giant'."

I frowned. "Why such a strange name?"

"Word has it, he's taken control of a Stonedragon's corpse. They say the twins are exemplary Necrovokers. Perhaps the strongest of their kind, it's being speculated."

"Strongest of their kind…" I rolled the words over my tongue, a certain thrill coming with it. *I wonder…* "You say they're in Everland?" I asked.

"Yes, fighting the war. They've just demolished the most heavily guarded prison in the deserts."

"And they're against that lumbering king, I presume?"

"Of course."

I nodded, a grin tugging my lips as I stared at the parchment. "I think there's been a misunderstanding with these two. Those against Everland's king cannot be on the wrong side, I should think."

She didn't seem to understand. "Majesty?"

"I'll send them a message," I concluded. "An invitation. We can bring them to our side and may even win the hearts of the terrorists hiding in our cities. They seem to honor these two with some regard. This paper may well be correct: They are the key. The key to bridging the gap in our fair country. And who knows?" I purred, turning forward to continue toward the dining hall. "With their help, I dare say we may get the better of that weakling king and take back Everland for ourselves."

And I, came the afterthought. *May have found two worthy candidates as my consorts.*

40
DO NOT ANNOY THE ALCHEMIST

~~~~~~~~

BIANCA

EVERLAND CONTINENT

Our wagon lurched, gliding over a huge rock in the desert and knocking me out of my chair, my groping fingers nearly tearing out El's feathers.

Her Highness Sky, Zylveia, pulled me upright. "You being the hurt one, *Külleschkov?*" she asked.

I fanned a flippant hand, rubbing my sore rear. "I'm fine, thanks… Miss El, give me your wing again, please?"

Zylveia translated for me, speaking in Culatian, and the cat-jay hybrid did as asked. I gently ran a hand down her pale-blue feathers again, examining the clipped stems. She winced at the slightest touch.

"It's slow," I hummed. "But they're growing back normally."

Zyl translated again, and El's face flushed with relief.

Poor girl. She must have been scared they were permanently damaged. I don't know what in Death those Rockraiders did to her and the others in that prison, but *everyone* we rescued had similar scars, brand marks, carvings…

Carvings. My rabbit ears dropped, stomach burning. *Like Jaq's forehead.* Those bastards used Jaq's scales like a damned woodworking project, cutting the word *Grimling* on his brow for everyone to see. Not even my remedy Hallows could heal those scars. I've *always* healed Jaq's injuries, even when we were kids. I'm a Bloody doctor now, but all I can do is give him some creams and hope he gets an illusion to hide the scars. For all my studying, I'm still Gods damned useless…

I sighed and went to the small desk bolted to the spacious buggy. It wasn't *that* big, but it was enough to fit me and a few patients at one time. The other doctors in our caravan had their own 'clinic wagons', but there weren't many of us to begin with. *Bloods, when we get to High Drinelle, I hope I can stretch my legs again.*

On the desk, that giant Alchemist text Master Hendril had given me gathered sand-dust. Death, I hadn't had time to read any of it. After I left the capital with Zyl, it's been non-stop traveling, and then the prison break at Tanderam with Jaq and Lilli, who's apparently Alex's fiancée...

My ear twitched. *That Bloody IDIOT.*

I snorted and pulled the Alchemy text over, flipping to the forward page and reading that weird message at the end of the author's note again.

... If by chance we were to meet our ward, Anabelle, I would very much appreciate a due 'hello'. I expect she will still be around for some time. I wonder if Sir Kurrick is still stitched to her coattails, as it were?

"Anabelle..." I hummed and lifted the window curtain in front of my desk.

Outside, Ana rode on a red mare, her walnut hair bouncing over her shoulders as her lion ears flicked and glinted her looped earring in the sunlight. She rode beside that warrior of hers, two huge broadswords strapped to his back. I grumbled suspiciously, "*And* Kurrick..."

No way they're the same people. They had the same names, but this book was written three hundred years ago. People can't live that long... well, except maybe the King of Dreams. Legend said *he* was over two-thousand. Maybe they learned how he did it? They did say King Dream sent them to find the twins in the first place.

The coachman outside hollered for the horses to stop, and my long ears perked, the wagon slowing. The buggy steadied and halted, and I peeked out the window, squinting at the sunlight. We'd arrived at some little village. Stone buildings squatted on the glittering sand of the desert, a few dozen locals staring at our caravan of soldiers and freed prisoners with wary glances.

Zylveia peeled back the curtain to look beside me. "Where we being?"

"Don't know," I said, unlatching the window to poke my head outside, "but it looks like we're stopping to rest."

I went to the little desk at the side of the wagon, closing the Alchemy text and pushing it aside in another sigh. With another stop, there were sure to be new patients, like usual. I needed my desk cleaned and my focus undeterred. *Am I ever going to find time to read that book?*

As expected, the door's curtain flapped open... Though, unexpectedly, Octavius stepped in.

"Miss Bianca?" Octavius asked, pulling down his beige face wrap and patting his sand-ridden pants. He shook out the grains in his black hair, rubbing his reddened eyes.

Behind me, El gasped, suddenly stiff as bones in her seat.

I stretched my arms up, leaning back in my chair. "You don't have to call me miss, you know."

"Oh… uh, sorry." He looked flustered, coughing like he'd swallowed dust.

"The wrap wasn't enough for that sandstorm this morning?" I guessed, pulling open a drawer. I plucked out a jar of cough syrup and a tiny bottle of eye drops, sloshing them in a gesture. "For your eyes, you should try and find some goggles, like what Zyl has. See if this village sells them."

He took the bottle and jar, flushing. "R-right…"

He stood there, lingering. Before we lapsed into an awkward silence, I asked, "What else?"

"Well, um… Xavier wanted to know if you had anymore aloe. Said he can barely move up there."

I grimaced, knowing he meant up on Alex's stupid bone dragon. Boys. They never think before acting on an impulse driven by their inner six-year-old.

"*Xavier wanted*, my ass." I reached under the desk, finding my satchel and rummaged through the clinking vials. "Alex is the only one who can control bones. They'd be down here and landed already if Xavier was out."

Octavius shrugged. "He thought you'd be more likely to give him the salve if you thought it was Xavier asking."

"I figured that, since he sent you to get it. Tell him he's Bloody lucky I'm not swapping it with cooking oil." I pulled out the jar I wanted and tossed it to him, along with two other bottles filled with capsules. "One of those is for Lilli's lash wounds, if she's run out. I don't want her to miss a day, in case they get infected again."

As much as it hurt to say *her* name, I wasn't about to let her suffer… I didn't exactly know what happened to her and Jaq in Tanderam, but their scars said enough. And damn me, even though she literally *stole* Alex from me, I couldn't let her be in pain from something so horrible.

Octavius collected the medication in turn, but his brow furrowed at the third bottle. "What's this one for?"

"For headaches," I explained in a sigh, folding my arms behind my head and leaning back to look at the wagon's creaky, wooden ceiling. "And muscle cramps. Alex must be killing his back, sitting on a skull all day for the past few weeks. Serves him right anyway, the idiot… But it's not fair to make Xavier suffer for it."

Octavius scratched his head. "Right. So, uh… Alex hasn't really said what's up with you guys, so can I ask—"

"No."

His head ducked. "Uh, right. Sorry. I'll, uh... I'll just... yeah." He made a break for the exit.

"*O-oy...!*" El called suddenly.

Octavius glanced at her. El blushed, waving at him with the smallest smile. "*Ha... Halloow...*"

It took him a second to realize she was finished, and he waved back in a confused grin. "Uh, hi. I guess?" He left, rubbing his neck.

When the curtain flapped closed, El swooned. *"El beiv fö baböl!"* A drunken blush flushed her cheeks. *"Yebe baböl fö El!"*

Zyl laughed, the Sky Princess offering a toothy grin while gripping her Aide's giddy fingers. *"El roch zetzet? Ke, ke, ke—re öl mot heft?"*

El's face bunched up, her tone draining. *"Ö... Ye, ye... tovt pravofv."*

Zyl turned to me, switching to Landish. "What cat boy's name, eh? The one just here?"

"Octavius," I said propping my chin up with a fist.

El preened. "Oco-*tay*-vii..."

She giggled, the two babbling in their weird tongue.

Hmm.

My stomach growled. Did I eat today? Maybe now was a good time since we were finally in a village. Leaving the two girls to their gossip, I pushed to my feet and stepped out, stretching an arm across my chest and squinted at the sunlight.

The village was tiny. Dried up, five-foot weeds sprouted from cracks in the ground and tossed in the breeze, sand coating most of the surface. I guessed the locals were on the rebellion's side, since I saw a few people bow in reverence to Land's Servant down a ways.

Who is that guy, anyway? The rebellion leader never took off the mask, so I'd never seen his face. Why did he bother hiding if his army was already in an open war with the monarchy?

My long ears picked up some of the locals' whisperings. They were scared, stupefied, and downright overwhelmed by 'he who rides the undead giant'.

I glared at Alex near the back of the caravan—

An enormous *crash* vibrated the ground when Alex's bone dragon collapsed in the back, so strong that I almost lost my balance, several Reapers and rebels gasping as they staggered at the rolling tremors that followed.

After Alex's colossus of bones had settled on the sand, which puffed with dirt and dust around those giant ivory trunks, Alex slid off the skull, wincing. He took the salve of aloe from Octavius, unscrewing the lid and seething while liberally applying the gel to his bright-red skin.

My nose scrunched. *Serves him right.* It was his own fault for not wearing a shirt and then baking up there all afternoon. Sweltering heat or not, it was stupid. Grimlings weren't built for UV rays. Not the way the Everlanders were.

My stomach groaned again. Back on task, I scanned the few buildings to find a place to eat. There was a grand total of eleven structures, not counting the residential blocks around us. Not much to choose from. I found one place spewing smoke from a tin pipe at the roof, a number of our traveling pack coming out with meat-stuffed flour wraps. I scowled, but headed over, hoping they had something for vegetarians.

"Excuse me!" A voice clipped.

I paused mid-step, my rabbit ear flicking toward the front of the caravan.

"Those are *not* your belongings to rummage through, sir!" It was a man's voice, shrill and cracked, as if his throat hadn't tasted water in days. A crowd of rebels formed around the noise, and even some Reapers went to see what was going on.

"I demand that you put that back at—careful with those texts!" I heard a tumble of what sounded like books dropping to the ground. He let out a wounded cry, attracting more Reapers to the scene.

I know that voice!

I trotted over but leapt back when a crow soared past my face. I watched it screech and perch on a nearby Reaper's shoulder, who cried joyfully while cradling the bird. There were more black birds returning to their Reapers, the knights praying thanks to the Goddess for their lost companions.

"You have no right!" a woman puffed beside the first man, obscured by the crowd of rebels. "Look there, you see? We're delivering these messengers to Drinelle, not capturing more. And will you please take care with those beakers! We've little of those supplies left as it is, and…!"

"Roaress Tonya?" I called, pushing through the cluster to see the newcomers. "Master Hendril?"

The elderly couples' heads snapped to me, Master Hendril taking in a coarse breath. "Bianca! My, but… w-what are you doing here?"

I hurried over, hugging him in a laugh. "I'm with the Reapers here! I did as you asked and freed the hybrid, Master, and my friends were at the same place."

He chuckled. "Wonderful, wonderful! *Khm-hmm! Khum!* … s-sorry, dear… I don't suppose you… well, we had to reroute our trip after the trains to Drinelle were shut down, and carrying a full load of birds slowed our horses. We've been crossing this desert and ran out of water yesterday morning…"

I smiled. "No problem. Come on, I'll find what you need."

"Oh, thank Shel!" He and Tonya hefted their heavy packs, following me—

One of the rebels stopped them with a spear. "You haven't been cleared yet," the soldier grunted.

I waved him off. "I clear them."

"You don't clear anyone," snapped the rebel. "We're at war, miss. No one is granted entry until we've checked every belonging. Lord Servant's orders."

"—What are my orders?"

The rebel leader himself had come to check the ruckus, his face wrapped in one of those desert scarves. "Dr. Florenne." The tall man peered down at me behind his mask. "Do you know these two?"

I nodded, blushing. *He knows my name?* Alex and Xavier must have told him. "This is my Master Healer and his wife," I explained. "They served as doctors and messenger care staff in the old Reaper District at the capital."

Dr. Hendril bowed. "Lord Servant! Erm, we don't mean to intrude, but you see, we escaped the capital hoping to… well, that is, if you'll accept…"

His wife shoved him aside. "We wish to join the cause, sir! My husband and I wouldn't have crossed the desert alone while smuggling all these messengers if we wanted to serve that tyrannical king."

By his tone, I could imagine the Servant smiling. "Oh, brilliant. We're always happy to accept new recruits. Doctors are especially needed." He threw his head at the guarding rebel who'd stopped us earlier. "Thank you for the good work. We can never be too careful. But Dr. Florenne is with the High Howllords' company. If she speaks in confidence of a suspected party, I'm granting them permission of entry from now on."

The guard grunted and lifted his spear, saluting. "Yes, sir. Apologies, doctor."

He got a squinting glare from Master Hendril when the two walked through, following me as the Servant went to the back of the caravan.

I grinned after him. *What a weirdo.* But Nira, was I glad to have him on our side.

I took Master Hendril and his wife to the tiny eatery, buying their meals and drinks. Bloods, they were thirsty. They guzzled the canteens of water until they were coughing it back up, then chugged it down again. They collapsed onto the rickety, wooden table when I sat down, and I had to lift my plate of cooked lizard—*ew*, but it was the only thing they had here besides roasted viper, and imagining eating Jaq's semi-distant cousin was a serious *no*—to keep it from launching off.

They let their luggage drop to the sandy ground and puffed for breath.

"Bloods," Hendril wiped the sweat from his burnt forehead, scratching between his goat horns. "I was beginning to think we'd die out there! What luck you were here."

"And with the Servant, no less." Tonya sounded impressed, chugging her canteen again.

Hendril took off his glasses to flick off sandy grains. "So." He smiled. "You found the *Sousül's* friend, eh?"

"Yep." I grinned, glancing at the road to find Zyl and El sharing their own crispy, roasted lizards and running around like a pair of hyperactive kids. "And she's... kind of more than a *Sousül*."

"What do you mean?"

"I mean, I should be thanking you with more than just a meal and some water. You helped boost my status with Culatian royalty, Master."

He and Tonya stared bug-eyed at me. I laughed. "I know, right? I didn't find out till Her Highness Willow recognized her."

"You met two Relicbloods in one month?" Tonya questioned.

I shrugged. "One was already with my friends when I ran into them. Her Highness Death's Aide was in Tanderam, too. I... actually helped treat her, after the jailbreak."

That reminder stabbed at my conscience, feeling sick. It wasn't that I'd helped Alex's fiancée. I would have treated her anyway, but it was more the reminder of *learning* Alex had gotten engaged to someone else while I was gone... like he'd forgotten all about his proposal to *me* the day I left Grim...

My stomach knotted, not so hungry anymore, and I shoved away my plate of charred reptiles.

Master Hendril pushed up his glasses, his fatherly voice humming. "Is something wrong?"

I glared bitterly at Lilli on the other side of the road. That little owl boy clung to her fingers, dragging her around. She chuckled under her parasol, kneeling to scoop up some sand and blew it off her palm in a glittering puff. The kid marveled at that, demanding her to do it again.

No, I thought miserably, sinking in my seat and rested my chin on the table, *Nothing's wrong. I lost Alex to someone better. If anything, it's... right.*

"Master Hendril," I began, keeping those thoughts to myself. I wasn't going to bother him with stupid stuff. Besides, there was something I wanted to talk with him about. "Have you ever felt like you wanted to do more than just healing?"

This had them both staring curiously at me, and Hendril pressed, "Such as?"

"It's just..." I lifted my head off the table, scratching an itch on my chin where a splinter had stuck. "I helped a lot of people. I patched them up, administered the proper medication to help the sick, I even directed a few of the Medics with an entire tent of patients."

"It sounds to me like all went well," observed Hendril.

"Yeah. It really did. But in the middle of it all, I felt like... like something was missing. Like there was more I could do, to actually..."

Tonya asked, "To what, dear?"

I glanced at my lap, whispering, "To fight. I don't know why, but I want to go out there and help that way, too. Back there, when I saw what they did to Jaq, what they carved on his head... I wanted to hurt whoever did it. I want to hurt anyone who hurts my friends." Guilt curdled like a sick lump in my throat. "What kind of Healer wants that? What does that make me?"

Hendril took a calm breath through his nose, his voice quiet. "It makes you a shifter being. We all want justice for those who threaten our loved ones." He reached over the table and gripped my fingers, smiling his old, wrinkled smile. "Don't think yourself a monster for having perfectly rational feelings. It's also possible those thoughts are simply a phase, and will pass soon."

My head shook. "No. I love Healing, and I loved helping all those people, but I felt something deeper than that. There was something hollow." I pressed a hand to my chest. "It clicked, up there in the canyons. Even though I liked the medical work, my new title as a doctor, the new authority you gave me..." I slipped my hand out of his. "You always said to follow what my heart told me. That my soul knows what path it wants. And I thought I knew what it wanted back then, but now, it's telling me I haven't reached it yet."

His nod was slow, listening intently. "And what does it say now?"

"I don't know," I admitted. "But I'm close. I feel it. I think it might be related to my work, I'm just not sure how, exactly."

He stroked his beard with great thought, quiet for some time. So quiet, I was starting to worry. *Is he angry?* Did I offend him by basically throwing all his training in the dirt?

"Bianca," he finally said.

I froze at the thick tone, rabbit ears dropping. "Yes?"

"How much have you read of that text I gave you?"

I frowned. *The Alchemy text?* "Just the forward... with the war, there hasn't really been time."

"Yes, of course..." He mulled over a thought. "I think I know what's wrong. There have been Healers who've described what you're going through, in their bibliographies. In fact, one in particular wrote exactly what you've just told me, nearly verbatim. Her name was the lady Jilume Provauge Gabriella Herdazicol."

One rabbit ear lifted. "The author of the Alchemy text?"

"Indeed." He sighed, drumming his fingers on the table. "The lady Jilume was said to be a fair Healer and renowned doctor. But her time treating patients was short, as she longed for something different. She strayed from her Healing duties one day and sought a different doctorate. She went on to found a specialized type of tonic brewing. And these concoctions were not used for Healing. They were used more for… well, the opposite, most times."

No way! "That's Alchemy? You think I can do that?"

He chuckled. "Of course you can. The very reason I took you in as my ward was for your talent in tonics. You're a chemist at heart, my dear, what you make with it is up to you. It was a skill you possessed prior to any training… but Lady Jilume's study has been long banned. Its art has been lost for centuries, with most of the world's wartime affairs piddled down. There hasn't been a need for it… until now, I think. *I* have neither the skill nor knowledge to revive it, though. It takes much experimenting, going 'off the books', so to speak. But that is something you, often to my frustration…" He grinned. "Have an inherent habit of doing."

I was perched on the edge of my chair. "You think I can bring it back? Re-found the study?"

"If anyone can, I do believe you would," he considered.

My smile was insatiable now. Just thinking of exploring a new, *banned* study of tonics was making me giddy. Me, re-founding a lost study!

"All right!" I said, a smirk tugging my lips as I picked up one of the lizards on my plate and bit off its tail, too lost in my daydreams to notice the disgusting crunch it made between my teeth. "I'll be a new Alchemist!"

41
FAMILY REUNION

~~~~~~

XAVIER

My ears rang, a bell jingling in the abyss—then he was there.
    A small child, skin glowing with blue light, sat suspended before me. His glittering, long robes fell below him, stiff and stationary in this windless, empty terrain of nothingness.
    The child stared at me, His wide, azure eyes peering into the darkest recesses of my mind. Upon his shoulders was a shepherd's crook, a bell jingling at its hooked end. He was so... so beautiful...

> Lest they drown with folly of past...
> The present light shall guide them in...

His voice bounced in my skull, as if speaking through my thoughts rather than vocalizing with his lips.

> Future winds must clothe the mast...
> Toward the hollow dreamers' din...

He lifted His crook, bell ringing.

> North nor south, nor east take fast...
> what you seek lies within the absence...

He swept His crook to the west. A tiny beacon rippled with blue light in the distance. It was so far...

Isle of Emeralds, the kingdom with grace…
And home of one loved by Rin…

The beacon pulled toward us—or were we flying toward it? The light grew larger and larger, crossing the continent of Everland and gliding overseas, the wide expanse of sloshing waves lapping under our floating feet, as if the world was spinning beneath us.

Then it halted. Below us was an island, a Marincian province. I braced as an untouching wind rushed past, the island hurtling upward, and I passed through buildings as easy as taking a breath, walls and floors and ceilings mere phantoms on my skin—

I ended in a clinic. There was a patient on an isolated bed, in a hidden room. A curtain shielded all but his hands and legs. An orange haired, cat eared doctor strode into the room, disappearing behind the curtain and murmuring to the slumbering patient. Though his upper body was hidden, I could see his lax, spindly fingers, his limbs thin as bones…

And below his knuckles was a tri-leaf of three, black diamonds.

Morning light slammed through my retinas, and I gasped awake.

No, it hadn't been *my* retinas, it had been Alexander's. I was in the psyche.

"Wh… w-what was…" Bloods, I didn't have any physical limbs, but my soul itself was shaking.

My window blinked, Alexander's voice shivering. "Did… D-did you hear?"

"*I saw.*" My thoughts tumbled in a blur. "*I-I saw… me.*" A thrill quivered out my lips. "West. I'm to the west—on a Marincian island, I…!"

Alex lurched up, and I saw through the window that he was still riding the gigantic bone dragon of his through cobblestone streets. We had apparently arrived in High Drinelle at last.

"A Marincian island…" Alex's vision narrowed. "Like the one where Dr. Hendril had seen Sirra-Lynn?"

"What was the name of that island?"

"I don't remember… But." He had his colossus slow to a stop, its skull lowering to the ground, and he hopped off. "Luckily, Hendril himself is with us."

I laughed. "*Then we must find him!*"

"Immediately." Alex stomped through the streets of High Drinelle and its glittering, gold buildings—

"Daddy!"

Alex spun at the joyous shriek.

The Trebles were clustered across the road. Octavius and Neal stood beside Mikani and Ringëd, their smiles tearful as their youngest, cat-eared sister clung to her father's neck. Miss Connaline grabbed him so suddenly that she'd accidentally pulled them both to their knees, weeping freely as Claude pressed her close to his chest, their sobs filling the quietness that had sucked the air dry.

Jaq trotted beside me, puffing. "What happened?" He wiped sweat from his scaled brow. "I heard a scream."

Alex folded his arms and tossed his head toward Claude and his daughter. "Family reunion."

Jaq found them, his expression softening. He held a touched hand to his chest. "Death... That's damn near the sweetest thing I ever—*haughk!*"

Jaq choked on a gasp when his lungs were crushed from behind.

"There ya are, kiddo!" laughed a middle-aged, black-haired man—Jaq's father. "Knew ya'd fight your way out!"

Jaq sputtered under his father's grasp, baffled. "D-Da?! What in Death are you doing on the surface?!"

His blonde mother shoved her husband out of the way as she came to embrace her son, her eyes misting. "We heard you were missing so we-we had to come ourselves! Oh, thank Shel you're all right...!"

Alex chuckled, stepping aside to give them room. "I'll... let you all catch up—*oh!*"

She snatched Alex by the neck and squeezed him next. "Oh no you don't, Howllord!" she chided. I heard a faint *pop* from Alexander's spine as her grip tightened. "You're not getting away that easily. Not until we've thanked you properly for getting him out of there."

Jaq sighed, ruffling his sandy hair as he dropped his peasant persona. "Mother, please. You intend to suffocate him?"

She released Alex, dabbing at her eyes. Once composed, she laid a hand on her son's arm. "You aren't hurt? No scratches, no wounds?"

Jaq nervously turned the ring on his finger and glanced at us. I knew that ring held an illusion, the one Willow had given him to hide the *Grimling* scar on his forehead. And I knew that curdling look of his meant *shut your damn mouth*.

Alex pointedly glanced away and pretended to be distracted with something else.

"NO!" A shriek wailed across the street. "NO—DADDY!"

Alex whirled. That had come from the Treble's youngest daughter.

A crowd had formed, obscuring us from most of the scene, but I managed to catch a glimpse of Claude being shoved to the cobblestones, his limbs twitching and spewing electric bolts. He'd been hit with a Shocksphere.

A team of Reapers came next, swiftly clapping Claude in shackles and dampening gloves, strapping on similar shoes as well. Claude's jaw scraped the ground, his cat ears flicking every which way in bewildered panic.

"*Daddy!*" Connie screamed again, pulled back by Octavius when a wall of armed Reapers and Footrunners surrounded their father. She hiccupped, blubbering incoherently.

"Decided you'd hidden long enough?" My mother's voice chewed from the crowd of soldiers that had formed around Claude.

They made a path as Mother strode over, in full armor, her helm's visor shut and wolf ears curled. She knelt to inspect Claude, yanking his head up by his hair and scrutinizing his face through the visor's slits.

Her throat rumbled in satisfaction. "Remember me, *demon?* You killed my son. But look at you now." She chuckled darkly, dropping his head to the stones and rising, spitting on him. She turned to the soldiers holding his chains. "I would see this beast rot in the cage he belongs in."

Alex shoved his way through the confused spectators. "Mistress!" he shouted. "Stop! What are you doing?"

She glanced at us and raised her visor, displaying her pleased smile. "Ah, boys. I'm glad you're here to see this monster finally brought to justice."

Father came behind her, also in armor but with no helm, and held himself high with immense pride. "It seems he'd hidden among your entourage on your journey back."

"He wasn't hiding," countered Alex, waving briskly toward Claude. "He was returning *with* us."

"Then it seems he escaped his bonds," Mother commented. "But we're handling it now."

"I—no, Mistress, he wasn't—"

"I want him questioned," she commanded of the Reapers hauling Claude to his wobbling feet.

Two men held either of Claude's arm, and the others cautiously kept an eye, and their scythes, aimed at him. They started to move out—

"You'll not take him a step further!" a new, feminine voice bellowed.

The men staggered at the outburst, shocked when they found the source. Mother cocked an eyebrow at the Death Princess, who'd pushed her way to us. She was not pleased.

"Release him," Willow barked, stepping toward my mother. "This is not the man you seek. Unlock his chains."

"With all due respect, Your Highness," Mother growled. "Your father is the one I take orders from. And secondly, I'm afraid this is, indeed, the man we seek."

"He is not," Alex disagreed and caught Mother's wrist. I felt him wanting to switch with me. "We know he isn't. Let *him* tell you."

The pull on my soul grew stronger, and I hurried to take my cue, swapping places with him, my fingers still gripped around Mother's thin wrist. I glared at her, tone firm yet beseeching. "Mistress, you must listen. Please. Claude isn't who you think. There is another man still out there running free. Willow and I, of all people, would know. This is a mistake—"

"No," Claude suddenly sighed, his breath heavy and tongue sounding numb. His lip was split, cheek bruised where it'd scraped the stones.

Claude looked upon his terrified children, at Willow, then glanced at me with pained, yellow eyes. "I've done things. Things I'm not proud of… I… deserve this." He met my mother's gaze. "And I have information you need to hear."

42

THE TRUTH

~~~~~~

CLAUDE

SIX YEARS PRIOR

I waded through the bustling shifters, meeting the standard protocols of shoving anyone in my way aside as they likewise did for me.

A few shouts at a reckless airboarder here, a sidestep from a pissing feral there, a snickering fest at the poor tourist who didn't notice the shitting seagull on the lamppost, and I was a block away from the market.

I checked the crumpled list in my hand, squinting at the small print. It was my own handwriting, but Land, I could barely make it out. *Were my eyes already checking out?* I wasn't even fifty yet, this stuff wasn't supposed to happen to young people.

"Twenty pounds of sugar," I read aloud in a mutter to myself, hefting the small hovering cart with my groceries. "Check. twelve dozen eggs—check. Fifteen pounds of chocolate—check. Nine sacks of flour…"

No check. That'd be next, then.

I sniffed and stuffed the list in my pocket, tugging the hovering cart along behind me.

The autumn winds were picking up, and the few trees scattered around were taking on bright colors. Except for the palm trees. Their wide fronds were only just starting to yellow at the finger-like tips.

It looked like everyone was getting ready for Death's Festival, which was coming up in a few weeks. Some merchants were selling pumpkins imported from Grim, and Void, there were even some Grimlings walking around under parasols, probably fresh from the Surfacing Port over in the geysers just north of here—

"*Hwuaou…!*" a voice gasped overhead, followed by a winded grunt and a *crash* as my cart was busted from a new weight.

I heard a groan come from the broken cart and saw a tuft of black hair and cat ears under the mounds of scattered sugar.

My own cat ears grew. "Damn it, Octavius!" I barked, storming over. "What have I told you about keeping off of those Bloody roofs? I thought I made it clear…"

The young man opened his bleary eyes. They were as yellow as honey. Not green as limes. *Not Octavius, then.*

"Macar…?" The kid croaked, and I could feel static running through his head with my Infeciovoking. It felt like malnutrition. He wasn't a skinny thing, but it was almost like his brain had been sapped of important nutrients.

He stared at me, and I stared back. Then the light in his eyes faded and his head *puffed* back into the pile of sugar, cat ears receding. He was out cold.

What in Bloods?

I scanned the skies, but didn't see any platforms nearby that he could have leapt from. And all the winged shifters who could have tossed him off were a good few blocks away. *Where did he come from?*

A crowd was starting to form and some of the local merchants hurried over. When the ones I knew saw it was me, they kept a safe distance as usual. They knew about my infection Hallows, and although they liked me well enough to do business with me, they still couldn't help but take some… precautions.

"What happened, Claude?" The jeweler, Mr. Hafner, shouted over. He was a nice guy, but was still sure to stay outside the safety bubble everyone had made around me. "Is your son all right?"

I checked over the unconscious cat in my cart. His shoulder-length hair was slick with grease, stubble just starting to grow at his jaw. He didn't look a day over twenty. But Bloods, did he look familiar. Almost too familiar… like one of my old photos come to life.

"He's not one of mine," I said. "I think."

I was pretty damn sure Mikani was my first kid. This guy looked about her age. *Maybe I had a nephew?* No, I didn't have any siblings. *An estranged cousin?* Wait, no aunts or uncles either.

Well, that was beside the point. I hefted the broken cart, thankful it was still intact enough to lug around.

"I'm, uh…" I began and looked at Mr. Hafner. "I'm going to take him to Sirra. See if she can treat him. Maybe wake him up."

Hafner nodded, still looking worried as I gripped the cart's two wooden handles and hauled the new baggage back to the café. Land, this guy was heavier than a new bundle of feral grouper pulled fresh from the fisher's market.

When I got home, I shoved open the doors and pulled him inside. Thankfully, there weren't any customers. I'd closed the place so I could prepare for Mika and Ringëd's surprise engagement party tomorrow. *Gods, was it already that time? When did my little girl grow up so quick?*

I heaved the unconscious, possible-relative out of the cart and slung him onto a table.

"Honey?" I called up the stairs by the back corner. "You home? Could use your help down here!"

The floorboards upstairs creaked, and Sirra yelled down, "Did you find what you needed for the cake?"

"Not exactly! Picked up a, uh… well, I don't know what to call him!"

"Oh, not another feral cat!" She stormed down the stairs. "I finally got Connie to let go of the last one! You know that thing argued with me for hours about who owned the damn bar counter, and I don't… Oh, Gods!"

She saw the young man passed out on the table and rushed beside me. "Is he all… Wait." Her brow knitted, looking at me. "Why does he look like you?"

"Maybe *he* can tell us." I ran an inspecting hand over the guy, feeling the static to detect what was wrong with him. "He isn't hurt too bad. Just a few bruises from the fall and some malnutrition… Feels like he's starving. Dehydrated. Let's get him some food and water."

She was already on her way to the kitchen in the backroom. "I'll see what I can find, you keep an eye on him. I should have some smelling salts somewhere in the cupboards. Let's see if we can't wake him up—"

"Augh…" came a disoriented groan from the guy. He clasped a hand over his eyes. "Will you snuff out some of those damned candles…?"

Sirra came hurrying back as he peered between his fingers and honed in on our faces. "What in Death's sorrowed name?" He seemed to sober more, then bolted upright off the table. "Macar?! Macar…!"

His legs wobbled and he almost face planted right there, but Sirra and I held him steady.

"Careful," I warned, letting him sit back on the table to catch his ragged breath. "I don't know if you fell from a stray piece of Culatia, or if you just popped into existence, but it'd probably be a good idea not to move around too much."

He squinted at me, wincing at the light again. "Where am I? Where's Macar?"

"Only found you," I said. "But we'll worry about that later. Look, my wife's going to take good care of you. She's a doctor."

"So am I." He rubbed his eyes. "Why is everything so bright? Did you weave a Bloody sun in here?"

"That's not the sun, pal. And most people complain that it's too dim in here. We only got 40 watt metaglobes in those sockets."

"40… what?" He glanced up at the lights, skeptical. Then he swept his head around the rest of the place. "I've never been here," he mumbled, more to himself.

"You got that right," I muttered.

"Is this a new building? I've never seen one woven to look like a place of dining… why bother? You can't eat in Aspirre."

"News flash, buddy: you're not in Aspirre."

He stared at me like I'd told him sparrows didn't fly. "I'm… not?"

"Nope." I knocked on the table. *Thunk, thunk, thunk.* "Solid reality, right here. No dreams."

He blanked out for a good minute, thinking. Then he pushed off the table and dragged his feet to the door, pulling it open to the let the sea breeze roll over him. He took in a breath, gazing out at the setting sun now dipping under the watery horizon.

"I'm… free?" he whispered, then shuddered with small chuckles, wrapping his arms over his stomach like he'd be sick. "I'm free."

I watched him with a squinted eye. "You feeling okay?"

"What year is it?" he asked.

Sirra and I looked at each other. Then she answered him, "2096."

"209… 20?" He fell back against the doorframe with a heavy *thud*. "Nira below… five hundred…"

He stood there in silence… then wandered outside. It didn't look like he was paying much attention to where he was going. His bare feet seemed to pull the rest of him with them, vibrating the boardwalk.

I went after him. "Hey, wait a minute. Let me check your head before you starting walking off."

He stopped and gripped the wooden railing, staring at the city past the beach. His eyes were following a hovering coach that was making its way across the street. "Five hundred…" he whispered. "So many years gone… It's all so… different."

I tried to see what he was talking about, but all I could find was that same hover-coach. "Different how?" I asked.

"The buildings," he murmured. "They seek to pierce the clouds, as if to climb straight to Culatia. And the horses carry wheel-less carts upon their backs, carriages which fly above the ground. To think, that outlandish invention become so commonplace…"

He twisted back to look at the setting sun, breathing deep. "And yet dawn still stands to steal one's breath... Macar, my friend, there are simply some things you cannot weave in your realm..."

I set a hand against his forehead, checking for any warning 'prickles'. "Feels like you need some hydration, pal. Come on, I'll get you some food too."

He clutched his stomach. "I... thank you. Yes. That would be wise, I think. I won't find Macar if I collapse."

"There you go." I patted his back, leading him inside. "Now you're making sense."

Sirra pulled out a chair for him, and I helped him lower down.

"Let me get you a menu," I offered. "Don't worry about the price. It's on the house."

He started looking around the place, frowning. "I suppose... you own this eatery?"

"Sure do." I swiped the disc-shaped remote from the bar counter, clicking on the vision-screen by the wall. A laugh track blared to life from the speakers. It was one of those comedy shows that customers usually liked—

He bolted out of his seat at the distorted laughing, fumbling behind his chair. "Death's hallowed head...!"

"Sorry, sorry." I dialed back the volume, handing him the remote. "It's not my favorite, either. Go ahead and change it to whatever you want."

"Change it?" He stared at the remote in his hand, then at the screen, then back at me. "What do you mean?"

"Bloody kids, don't you know how to use old tech anymore?" I sighed and pushed the channel button to demonstrate for him.

When the screen blipped to a new opera show, he jumped back. Hesitant, he clicked the button himself. The screen blipped to a romance drama, and a disbelieving laugh escaped him. He kept on clicking that button, scrolling all the way through the list of the ten channels we had. He stopped at the news station and craned back to me with a splitting smile. "This is amazing!"

I thumped his back. "Have fun."

"This must take its power from the vision-gems our miners had discovered... Can they see us as well?" He pointed to the news anchors. "They don't seem to acknowledge us. When last I used a vision-gem, we could see and speak to whomever held the other fragment. But we had to glance at the rock itself. How did you magnify it in such a way?"

Sirra sidled next to me and muttered, "How hard did he hit his head?"

I shrugged, rubbing the stubble at my chin. "Hey, uh, why don't you sit back down? Let me do some scans real quick, make sure you don't have a concussion."

He held a hand to his temple, then said, "I do not."

"Why don't I double check? Trust me, I have a way of telling what's going on inside if something's acting screwy."

He flipped through the round of channels again. "Thank you, but I am fine. My inner ear has undergone some trauma, my cornea has a minor scratch, but it is shallow and will heal itself with time. At this moment, I'm not as concerned for myself as I am for your wife's illne…"

He stopped. Sirra and I stiffened.

Silence choked the room, and he turned and flushed, his black cat ears growing from his head. "Oh," he said. "I'm… sorry. I thought you were aware."

My own cat ears came, curling back. "We were. But I'd damn well like to know how you were, too."

He bowed respectfully. "Please. Forgive me. The static is often too loud to ignore."

Static?

My lids narrowed. "You're an Infeciovoker?"

He nodded.

"Shel Almighty, another one?" I cupped my mouth. "How… where did you come from?"

"I came from Grim," he said matter-of-factly. "Though, it's been some time since I've been home. I migrated to the surface to find work. Macar claims I still have a bit of an accent, but I can't hear it myself…" He trailed off, staring at the wall where a bunch of our family photos hung.

"Blood and bones," he whispered, moving to one picture in particular. It was an old shot of Octavius when he was six, holding up a bucket of collected shells he'd found on the shore. The guy lightly touched his fingertips over the glass, whispering, "Caleb…?"

"That's my son," I explained, throwing a thumb at the more recent picture of Octavius sweeping the kitchen with his brother. "Well, one of them. He's got our Hallows, too, but it's not as developed yet."

"Amazing," he murmured. "He looks so much like my own son…" He stopped, head craning back to me. "Sorry, but did you say 'our' Hallows?"

"Infeciovoker." I waved to myself, grinning. "My son and I have the element."

"Someone else survived the hunts?" He ran a thoughtful hand through his greasy, shaggy hair. "Death… Does your son know of your wife's… well…"

Sirra and I exchanged a hollow look, and I sighed. "We tell him he's just feeling a bad migraine. He's never run into that kind of feedback before, so he doesn't have anything to relate it to."

He nodded solemnly. "Still… I wasn't expecting anyone with our element to be left standing. I was sure they'd all been wiped out, based on the dreams back then. Could Caleb have survived…?"

He scanned the photos again. Most of them were taken here in the café; some were more recent than others. He brushed a finger over one that showed Mika pulling out her latest confectionary creation beside me. It was her last apprenticeship test. Which she passed.

"It can't be…" His tone wavered with grief, and I could have sworn his eyes were welling now. "She looks so much like her…"

"What did you say your name was again?" I asked.

He blinked and straightened. "Ah, yes, forgive me. I am Dr. Kael Lorien Treble. Former head surgeon of Everland's royal clinic."

I laughed. *I Bloody knew it.*

"Claude Treble," I said, shaking his hand. "I'll be damned. Where in Void has this side of the family been hiding?"

"Family…" He looked awed, gripping my hand tight. "My kin. And her's…" A smile pulled his lips into a crooked curl. "My son survived. Our line was carried on." Revelation flared in his eyes. "My kin…! You can aid me on my mission. Our family will find justice together…!"

Justice? "Huh?" I scratched my head. "What kind of—"

The door burst open. Seawater sloshed onto the floor as a scraggly newcomer stumbled his way in.

"Excuse…" He coughed up water and peeled off the strips of seaweed that clung to him. "Excuse me…! I… I saw your light from outside, and hoped you could…" The soggy snake noticed Kael from under his water-spattered glasses. "Kael! Thank the Gods…! Blast, but my vision is hindered, I'm seeing two of you."

"Macar!" Kael went to the snake, waving an inspecting hand over the guy. "Your vision hasn't changed, my friend. Dear Claude is my descendant."

"Descendant?" I frowned, watching Kael inspect Macar. "I think you mean *uncle*. Or something."

Kael chuckled. "I am far too old to be your uncle."

"I meant *I* was your… wait. Too old—?"

"Death, Macar!" Kael cursed, his hand stopping over a large gash in the snake's arm. "You've gotten careless over the years. Was this the golems' doing?"

"It's only this much, at least." Macar's sigh was heavy as I came over to help Kael lift the guy by the arms and set him on a table.

Kael's tone took a grim turn. "I suppose you're right… it could have been much worse. I can't believe how many there were this time. We've never been so surrounded."

"Surrounded by what?" I asked, seeing Sirra run upstairs, probably getting a first aid kit.

Macar's tan scales were pretty pale, and I could feel the static of bacteria festering from his cut. I wasn't a doctor, but even I knew if he wasn't treated it could be bad later.

"The noctis golems," explained Kael, ripping off a piece of his already ragged sleeve to wrap around Macar's wound. He cinched it tight to hold back the bleeding. "They are the demons of Aspirre."

I gave a low laugh. "Aspirre doesn't have demons. Just the ones we dream up."

Macar hacked into a hand and shook his head. "You damned plane-walkers. Your ignorance will be the death of you all someday."

He went into a coughing fit, and Kael held him steady when he almost fell off the table.

"Be still, Macar." Kael turned to me, his brows arching. "I must apologize. It seems being trapped in the pseudo-physical plane for so long has sapped a good amount of nutrients."

"You were…" I rubbed my eyes. "Wait, you think you were trapped in Aspirre?"

He started more scans on Macar. "We do not think, Kin of Kael. It is an infuriating fact, one that we were reminded of every aching moment of walking through that empty void of nothingness."

Sirra came back down with a stitching needle and a thick, black thread. Before she could even get near the patient, though, Kael thanked her and took the stuff himself, doing his own prep work.

He started by sterilizing the cut with an alcoholic swab, readied the thread and needle, and Macar gave a stiff grunt when it was laced through his skin. Kael's fingers seemed to act on their own, quick and efficient, but he didn't seem to be paying much attention to the procedure.

I leaned against a nearby table and scratched my neck. "So, er… for argument's sake, how can you get trapped in Aspirre? You mean just a really long dream?"

"Physically entrapped," Macar growled between pained yelps. "Spirit and body, locked away in that timeless prison for *Gods* know how long."

"Uh huh." I perked an eyebrow. "And uh, how would that happen, exactly?"

"It's a skill only one man possesses," Macar spat. "And he can be, to put it politely, a self-righteous *prick*."

Kael finished his stitching and tied off the thread, cutting the end with sharpened teeth. He grumbled. "Dream's soul will be left to rot after we're done with the Death King. Of that I swear, Macar."

"Ah, yes." Macar's smile curdled, rubbing his hands. "Now that we're free, it's time to prepare for Sanctuary. What year is it, then?"

"2096," answered Kael. "It has been five hundred years."

Macar cursed. "Five hundred... Too long. Far too long... but no matter. We know the Land Bloodline is out of the way, at least. We've only four left."

I had to stop them there. "What in Void are you talking about?" I demanded.

Kael took my shoulder, his tone rising eagerly. "Descendant, you can aid us! Bring our line justice!"

"Justice from what?"

"The Relicbloods," he said, emotion scratching his voice.

My nerves started flaring. I did *not* like where this was going. "What do you have against the Relicbloods?"

Kael went to the wall of photos again, staring at Mikani's picture. "They took away my family. My wife... she was slaughtered. *Butchered* in my own home... and all because I failed an already doomed surgery on Land King Adam's wife."

Ah. Yep. Time to clock out.

I shifted my stance, waving for Sirra to back away as Kael's growl ripped through his throat. "That monster, that murdering *fiend*..." He spun to face me, his fists shaking. "The other Bloodlines were there! They *defended* the beast! Those who aid a murderer are wrought with corruption themselves. They are the stain I left festering in the world before Macar and I were sealed away." His sneer twisted into a smile. "But now, we are free. And as my kin, the injustice that was brought unto me is extended to you. Those with our Hallows, I'd imagine, won't be easily matched in this era. Not with our kind hunted to near extinction and forgotten."

I stared at him. "Right... look pal, that's fine and all if you have a death wish, but I'm fine where I am. Go and get yourself killed by the Relicbloods on your own time."

Kael retracted, looking like I'd slapped him. "But this crime against our family must be answered for!"

"First off," I chewed, barely keeping my voice contained. "This 'crime' involves you. I didn't know your wife, if she exists, and I have my own family right here. We're doing fine. The Relicbloods haven't done us any—"

"It was by my seed that your family even exists!" he snarled, slamming his hands on the table. "My seed, and her womb! As your ancestors, you must respect all we have given you! Without us, you would not *be*!"

I held up my hands, waving them in a calming motion. "O-o-o-okay, buddy, I think it's about time you left."

"Claude, please! You must at least consider—"

"Get out of my house. Now."

Kael glared Bloody murder at me, the silence getting thick. I gritted my teeth and prepared to summon my infection Hallows if he tried anything.

"Is this truly your answer...?" asked Kael in a low, hostile rumble. "You choose to ignore your ancestor's suffering?"

I had my Hallows evoke, palms crawling with black veins, my cat ears curled in warning. Worst case, I figured I could try and erase his memory so he'd forget all about us.

"... Very well..." His posture slacked, though resentfully. "It was at least a pleasure to meet you, Descendant... Perhaps... we will meet again."

"I'd rather not." I kept my Hallows up in case it was a front.

His cat ears folded to his neck. He stared at me a final time before turning to the door and walking past his friend. "Come, Macar," he hissed. "It seems we are alone..."

Macarius stayed where he was, his eyes slitting at me. Then he stalked up. "Mr. Treble. You don't understand what's at stake. If you value the lives of your family, as you claim, then you must hear what is to come if the Relicbloods aren't stopped."

"Are you deaf?" I spat. "I'm not going anywhere."

"You must," he pressed. "The slaughter that is to come, the impending horror that haunts our world..." His voice dropped to a terrified whisper. "Everything is hanging in the balance. And it will be the Relicbloods that keep the pendulum swinging toward Nirus' end."

"Right," I muttered. "Nice speech. Now get out."

He glowered at me, his fangs growing in his mouth. "You've shut us out before hearing the explanation... a willful fool, you are. Perhaps then, what you need is some... motivation."

I frowned when his chocolate eyes glided past me. Turning around, I saw what he was staring at.

"Sirra," I hissed, waving her back. "Get upstairs."

Sirra's feet stayed planted behind me, her orange cat ears folded down. She shook her head.

I chewed on a curse. "Damn it, Sirra, get up—"

"Good evening, my lady," Macar purred, bowing to her. An azure Dream mark started gleaming at his chest under his thin, silken robes—and the man suddenly split into two. Then a phantom stepped out of him, like mist drawing from his pores and shaping into a mimicking figure that now stood beside him.

A Somniovoker? I didn't know much about that Hallows, but I'd heard they can make little 'copies' of themselves. I guessed that wasn't a joke Ringëd made up.

The phantom walked toward Sirra.

My wife gripped a nearby chair when the copy approached her, the thing giving a creepy, calculated smile. "Forgive the informality, my lady," the thing said. "I fear your husband may suspect me of foul play if I approach as my physical self."

"Can't say I blame him," she muttered, her teeth sharpening.

I barked at the original man. "Get that thing away from her!"

"Oh, don't make such a fuss," the original chuckled. "Copies cannot touch anything. Merely observe."

"If you don't get rid of it, I'll do it myself!" I lunged for the phantom, infection Hallows flaming with black veins from my fingers—

My hand phased through without contact. Like touching air. "What the Void...?"

The copy stared dead-eyed at me. "Again: we merely observe. We cannot touch, nor can we *be* touched, let alone poisoned. Bloody fool."

The original came to stand beside the copy. They looked the Gods damned same. The expression, the posture, the voice... It was getting hard to tell which was which.

"Madam," one said to Sirra, "If you would allow, I wish to have a few words alone with your husband? Will you permit me to steal him away for a few moments? I assure you, my only aim is negotiation."

"I'm not going anywhere," I spat. "Get away from my wife."

The original's tongue clicked. "Pity. I'm afraid we cannot leave until our case has been properly considered..."

"Fine—then let's talk. Outside. Out of my house."

His lips curled into a wider smile. "Grand. I should, however, request to leave my copy here to watch after your wife. Only for surveillance, of course, I've shown you well enough the phantoms can do no physical contact with anyone. It's necessary, you see... Kael and I cannot risk having the local authorities sent for us so early during our first day of freedom."

"Whatever. Just get out."

Macar walked to the door where Kael was waiting, leaving his copy behind. I followed after the original. No way in Void was I going to turn my back on this psychotic—

Sirra let out a shriek, and I whirled. The 'copy' had grappled her from behind. Solid. Physical. And wickedly satisfied.

"It seems Kael's intellect has been diluted through your bloodline," Macar mused, drawing back Sirra's orange hair, her tan neck exposed and dangerously close to the cobra's fangs. "A shame. Truly. But your Hallows is still far too useful for us to ignore. Now, about my aforementioned negotiation. Here is my offer..."

He *sank* his fangs into Sirra's neck.

She screamed and dropped to the floor, writhing in pain.

"SIRRA!" I scrambled for her. "No, no, no, no, no…!" I could feel the painful static surging through her. It was rapidly destroying her cells.

Sirra clasped a golden-glowing hand to her neck, trying to use her remedy Hallows to counteract the venom, but she shuddered and cried that she needed antivenom from the clinic. I cursed and scooped her up—

The snake stepped in my way, towering over me.

"Now." Macar's arms folded behind his back. Sirra's blood dripped from his lips as he glanced at the wall of family photos. "What a happy bunch… My offer is simple: Should you aid us, I will spare your children from the same fate as your wife."

"You get anywhere near my kids and they'll set your ass on fire!" I roared.

"You assume they'd be able to tell the difference between me…" His image suddenly flitted and morphed into… Me? I was now looking up at yellow eyes, watching my own lips curling as the thing kept talking. "And you? Or even one of them?"

He morphed again, this time looking like Octavius. Shel Almighty, it looked just like the kid.

Octavius's lips moved, but the voice was still Macar. "Luring one of them would be child's play." His original look came back in a few, flittering seconds. "And all it would take is one, little prick… or perhaps a more direct method? A dagger to the ribs? A blade to the throat?"

My breath was heavy, Sirra's heart hammering under my grip. "Who are you?!" I demanded.

"You may call me…" Macar paused, considering. Then his lips curled. "The Lightcaster. And I thank you for your noble service to Nirus, Descendant of Kael. I suspect your name will be written into history for all to revere."

He started for the door at a leisure pace, humming. "Now… I will give you time to grieve. And even time to prepare a funeral and reaping ceremony. But after which, I expect you to be ready for our journey. Good day, Mr. Treble. It was a… *pleasure* meeting you."

He stepped out without a final glance, and Kael just stood by the door. My supposed *ancestor* didn't say a damn thing to me.

"Please…" My voice cracked, Sirra's pulse fading under me. "You can't…"

He turned to the shore outside, breathing deep, and I barely heard him whisper, "I am… sorry…"

He left after the snake, not looking back.

43

A CHANCE FOR REDEMPTION

~~~~~

XAVIER

"Macarius did as promised." Claude leaned against the cell bars and wiped the grime from his brow. "He waited three days until her funeral, came that night... and I left. Twice a year, he went to take pictures of my kids, to let me know he was still keeping track of them. If I hadn't found Octavius in the capital—and Neal and Mika in that prison—I'd still think they were being watched."

Everyone let his echoes die in the dungeon, the silence as thick as the damp heat in the torchlight. The only sound left came from the dripping ceiling over Claude's head.

I was leaned against the molded wall, my arms folded as I gave my parents a critical glare. The king's Eyes and First Fangs were front and center of the shackled prisoner, their stares hard and scrutinizing.

The Trebles were absorbing their father's tale with grown cat ears. Ringëd, beside his new wife, let out a soft curse. Connaline sat on the disheveled floor by her father's cell, her legs folded to her chest and crying softly. Octavius and Neal were smoldering above her.

Willow let out a heartbroken sigh beside me, gripping my fingers and dabbed at tears. On the other side of me was Lilli, who better withheld her anxiety and kept her hands delicately cupped before her, bat wings folded respectfully—though still rigid—behind her.

Jaq sat hunched on a rickety bench, propping up his chin with overlapping fists as he waited for someone to break the silence.

Octavius took the initiative. "Mom didn't die of her sickness?"

"No." Claude rested his head against the bars. "Granted, we didn't have much time left with her to begin with. But it was still too early."

"That *bastard*..." Neal's claws dug into his arm. He either didn't care or didn't notice the blood drawing from the pricks. "I'll kill him. I swear to Land, I'll..."

"Don't," warned Claude. "As long as he has his guard dog around, Macarius won't be easy to hunt. I've tried. If you want him, you'll have to get rid of Kael first."

I noticed my parents were standing quiet for some time. It was Father who spoke first. "And you say Kael was the assassin? The one responsible for my son's attempted murder?"

"Yeah. But I can't say I'm scott-free there either... I was there that night, in Grim. I thought I could go under Macar's radar and get Her Highness out of there before Kael had a chance to show up, but..." He threw his head toward Lilli. "I ended up following the decoy."

Mother's fingers drummed on her arm. "Two Infeciovokers, there at the same time? The odds are astoundingly unbelievable..." She flicked her gaze at me. "But you saw the other man yourself?"

"He was at Tanderam," I said. "Younger than Claude. He was more near our age, by the look of him."

Claude gave a dark chuckle, his shackles rattling. "Not even close."

Willow twisted her long strands ponderously. "So, Kael simply seeks revenge for his wife?"

Claude tilted his head. "That's the gist of it."

Willow looked ill. "I... I can't believe the last King of Land would have done something as disgusting as *butchering* someone... Whoever she was, Kael must have been devastated to hold that rage for so long."

"I'm still not sure I believe all of it, to be honest." Claude shrugged. "But Kael's dead set on killing the Relicbloods. The guy's obsessed. Said he still dreams of the night he found Cilia in pieces—"

"—*Cilia?*" I blurted. But I hadn't been the only one to interrupt. The entirety of our team had jolted to attention, shock painting our faces.

Mikani, however, merely hummed and tapped a finger to her lips. "Hey, I know that name. He said it once, in the prison. Kael said I looked like her."

Octavius let out a shivering laugh. "I'll bet. I thought she was *you* when I first saw her."

Claude jumped in a start—*thunking* his head on the cell bars and winced painfully. "W-wait, wait, *wait*! What do you mean when you first *saw* her?"

Octavius shrugged. "Cilia's been stalking us since we first left Brittleton. Every time we think she's gone, she pops back up again like crabgrass."

Jaq's tongue clicked on the bench. "Well, *this* story gets weirder by the minute, huh?"

"If Cilia is his wife," I began, glancing at Willow. "Then his story seems legitimate after all. He *is* as old as he claims."

Willow nodded broodingly. "And it *is* possible to be physically brought into Aspirre. That's how my grandfather Dream has lived so long."

"The Void are you saying?" Claude demanded. "You think Cilia's alive?"

Willow scowled. "Just the opposite. She's the Necrofera queen who's been causing us immeasurable grief."

Octavius added, "And she's been trying to 'collect me'. Wants the family back together or some crap like that since I apparently remind her of her son—"

"Caleb," Claude finished with a wild grin. "Land, I don't believe it… *She's* who Macar's been making deals with while we're gone?" He couldn't stop chuckling now, rubbing his hands. "Oh, this is too good! Well, that settles it. We show Kael that Cilia's still out here walking around, and his little revenge scheme should dissolve on the spot. Then Macar won't have his damned bodyguard and we bring him down. War's over."

"Maybe the demon war," Jaq grunted. "It probably wouldn't do anything for the war against Everland."

Mother, who'd been listening intently in silence with Father, tapped a nail to her teeth in thought. "Still, it would relieve some pressure if one war was taken care of."

Connaline sniffled from the floor, wiping an arm under her runny nose. "Can you let him go now? Dad didn't do anything."

My father glanced at the plump girl, then at me. He sighed and pulled out his com, calling for the prison guard who was waiting on the upper floor. "Send the keys."

I heard a fuzzed affirmation from the com before he put it away and the sounds of footfalls echoed from up the steps. A rebel member came to join us, unlocking the cell and Claude's shackles before retiring back upstairs.

Claude hefted to his feet, his children already at his side as he looked at my father. "Thank you."

Father turned to the stairs in a gruff sigh. "I take my sons' word on this matter heavily, Mr. Treble. You ought to be thanking him. And I you, for giving us the details we need to bring down the assassin responsible for my son's disappearance… We will begin planning. There is, apparently, much work ahead of us."

He and Mother left, Father flashing me a short glance before disappearing up the steps. *I leave him to you*, the look said.

When the last of their footfalls faded, I pushed off the wall and went to Claude. "There's still something I don't understand," I said. "Macarius told you he was something called the 'Lightcaster'?"

Claude shrugged. "Search me what it means."

"I think... I may have heard that somewhere before." *Perhaps in a dream? I couldn't quite remember. It was just so familiar...*

Claude scratched at his scruffy neck. "You got me, Howllord. They say stuff like that a lot. 'The Lightcaster' and 'The Shadow...'" He stopped himself, looking about. "Wait. Where's your brother? There was something else I wanted to talk to you both about."

I rubbed my neck. "I'll... relay the message."

"No, I need both of you here for this. It's important."

"Er... how important, exactly?"

"Life and death. *Your* deaths. I think it has something to do with the whole reason Macarius is doing this."

I glanced at the grimy ceiling uncertainly, murmuring to Alex. "Well?"

"Just tell him," Alex called from my thoughts. *"I've heard of this Lightcaster also, somewhere. I want to know what it means."*

I nodded, referring back to the now confused Claude. "Mr. Treble, regarding my brother and I... you should be aware of a few... *difficulties*. But we can't speak in front of so large a crowd."

Ringëd sighed and gripped his wife's hand. "Mika, you better go. I'll meet up with you later."

She looked suspicious. "Why?"

"Because it's really not your business. Sorry, honey. Take Connie and Neal with you, too."

"Neal can stay," Octavius contradicted. "I mean, if he's going to be a Reaper with all of us, then he should probably know too, right?"

I glanced at Neal, cocking an eyebrow. "Do you also plan to apprentice under our parents, Neal?"

He gave me a flat look. "Uh. *Yeah?* Diplomatic immunity sounds awesome."

"Then, I suppose we'll have Mistress conduct an exam... In the meantime, Miss Mikan—I mean, *Mrs. Fleetfürt*—and Miss Connaline, I'll have to ask you both to leave, please. This is a private matter."

They offered baffled looks, but complied nonetheless, and soon left up the steps. Neal and Mr. Treble were staring bewildered at me, and I ran a fretting hand through my hair. "For lack of knowing where to start, I'll just say now: *I am not physically... well, here.*"

Silence. Then Neal snorted. "Could have fooled me."

"I have," I said. "And I most humbly apologize. There would be consequences if certain parties knew."

"Knew what?" pressed Claude.

I held a hand to my chest. "This body isn't my own. I'm only... borrowing it, after a fashion." Alex reeled me in to take his turn, clearing his throat. "... From me."

I watched from the psyche's window as Claude jumped back, his stare fixed on our eyes. "What in Land?"

"What?" Neal squinted at us, straining to look harder. "What happened?"

Alex folded his arms. "Neal, you don't have soul-sight like your father, so you won't be able to see the difference. To make a very long story short, I'm sharing my vessel with Xavier's soul."

Claude stared beguiled at us. "But how?"

I came back out and explained as best I could, having already exhausted the story. Recounting the events was a breeze by now.

"We aren't certain how we ended up this way," I finished. "We can only assume Kael had torn out my soul with his Infeciovoking."

"No way," Claude contradicted, his head shaking vigorously and crossing his hands. "No way in Void can Kael do that. He'd be using that all the damn time if he had that kind of Evocation."

My brow furrowed. "You're sure?"

"Howllord, *I* have his Hallows." He lifted his hand and displayed small tendrils of black veins that slithered out from his palm. "We can't do anything like that. Trust me. It wasn't Kael who did this to you. If I had to guess..." He nodded to me. "I'd say *you* did it yourself."

I paused. "Me?"

"With the soul half of your split Hallows," he said, "I can't think of anyone more likely. Your brother can play around with a giant dragon corpse, so you pulling out a living soul doesn't seem so impossible after that."

I cupped a hand over my mouth. "I... hadn't thought..." *Was it possible? Had I done this to myself? To Alex...?*

Neal shifted his weight. "I don't get it. If you're sharing a body, what happened to yours? Or, his? Whatever."

I muttered absently, "We believe we've narrowed down where it could be. But we need to speak with Dr. Hendril to find it."

Claude's brow knitted. "Why?"

"According to him, Mr. Treble, someone on a certain island spoke whispers of a recovered boy who matched my description." I clasped his shoulder. "And that someone was your wife."

44

TACTICS AND TORTURE

~~~~~

APSON

Pain flared in my hand, the iron mallet smashing another fractured finger and forced my teeth to clamp on my gagging cloth. My screams tasted of dusty thread and stale sweat.

My torturer wasn't a stranger. Many a time had I worked with Eric Bouldrueck and watched him use his cruel tools on the sordid prisoners who had the misfortune of being thrown down here in the palace dungeons... And now, after I was arrested the moment I'd stepped foot on the royal grounds again nearly a fortnight ago, I was one such misfortunate.

I hadn't a clue what fate had befallen the rebellion. I only prayed Jaqelle was safe with the Devouhs now.

Bouldrueck wiped his brow with his gloved fingers, though it did little to remove his porous glisten. The torch was above his head, adding more heat to the sweltering cellar.

As he readied his next tool, he grumbled, "I don't know why you bother with silence, Roarlord."

There was something odd about his voice. It was different than I remembered, slightly higher; not as smoky. Perhaps my hearing had been muddled from the head bludgeoning earlier?

He inspected a syringe in the torchlight, squinting as he raised a finger to the bridge of his nose and pushed up imaginary spectacles. Though I could swear there were no eyeglasses, I still heard the faintest *chink* with the touch.

"We already know you're the rebellion's general," Bouldrueck said. He flicked the syringe and the liquid in the vial quivered. He nodded to the left, where six bodies were piled in a disheveled heap over the hay. They looked as though they'd been rotting away for weeks. If he expected me to recognize them, he would be sorely disappointed. The rats had already made a meal of their faces.

"We captured several of your men earlier this month," he hummed in a gloating song. "Four of the six sang the same tune. Though for what it's worth, the last two said nothing. At least you'd found a few men worth having, eh?"

"They could have... been lying," I croaked, my throat burning with the words. Water had been scarce down here.

"We thought of that." A thin spray squirted from the syringe. His tone was too pleasant. "But then, we met a number of shifters who'd escaped from Drinelle. You were witnessed clasping hands with Lucas Devouh, and were heard giving orders to the rebels. I'm sorry to say, Apson, but the incriminating evidence is far too overwhelming."

He didn't sound sorry to say it. Not with that smile.

I growled. "If you wish for me... to tell you where the prince is, *I'm* sorry... to say you won't be so fortunate..."

"Oh, I don't need to know where he is." He took my arm and aimed the syringe. I'd been starved to exhaustion over the weeks, I hadn't the strength to rip away. "Now, let's try and get it right this time..."

He pushed the needle through my scales, and I bit down a wince as the hot liquid rushed into my blood.

—*Cl-CLACK!*

There came a loud, metal clatter at the front suddenly. Then light spilled through the now opened door. It was the flickering fire of a new torch.

A voice I didn't recognize called out. "High Lord... Wales?"

"Ah!" Bouldrueck withdrew the syringe to greet the newcomer. "Kael. Good, you've returned."

A brown-haired man stepped forward, his yellow eyes narrowing at Bouldrueck. "A new form? Again?"

The torturer shrugged. "I've grown rather bored of the last one."

"And have you killed this one as well?" The man, Kael, had an accusing tone.

Bouldrueck waved a flippant hand. "He was a stubborn thorn. Better off dead than making our ends more difficult to acquire."

"Was it necessary? The more you strike off, the emptier this king's court will be. Don't you feel you're treading on dangerous territory?"

Bouldrueck drummed his fingers on his folded arms, considering it. "You think me spreading myself thin, do you?"

"I think you're indulging impulses... What's all this?" The stranger frowned, then glanced at the syringe on the small table Bouldrueck had brought down with him. "Blast, Macar, what have I told you about playing doctor while I'm away?"

Ma...car? The room was beginning to churn, my lids feeling heavy and waxed. I didn't know what he'd injected me with, but it must have been taking effect. The firelight danced in whimsical, blurred streaks.

I shook my head, blinking to try and sober. There was something strange going on. My attention threatened to slip away, but I transfixed my glare on the two men, sure there was something gravely important here.

Despite being called by a different name, Bouldrueck gave Kael a smile. "I think I've finally gotten used to finding the correct vein, as you've shown. Perhaps with time, I'll make a fair surgeon?"

"You'll be lucky if you make a fair nurse." Kael knelt beside me, and I flinched away when he reached for my arm. But he didn't touch my skin. He merely hovered a hand over it. Then his head craned up at Bouldrueck. "Why haven't you sealed the insertion point?"

Bouldrueck shrugged. "I didn't see a need."

"It's standard procedure."

"I'd hardly call the circumstances 'standard'."

"At least tell me you sterilized the needle beforehand this time?"

Bouldrueck's fingers snapped. "I knew I'd forgotten something."

Kael sighed, giving a hollow chuckle. "Death, Macar. I've seen *custodians* drug patients better than this. A masterful weaver of dreams you may be, my friend, but you're a piss-poor surgeon as I ever saw. You'll end up killing him instead of keeping him delirious."

"He'll meet the block this afternoon, regardless. The king is set on this one's beheading even if we don't get a confession."

"Then why are you down here looking like the king's hired torturer?"

His smile widened. "Passing the time with a bit of entertainment. Would you like a try? It's rather fun."

To my immense relief, Kael's disgusted grimace was answer enough.

Bouldrueck lowered into a foldable, wooden chair and plucked off a silver ring he'd worn around his little finger. Then he... changed. *Or was it my bleary sight that was changing him?* Bouldrueck's balding head suddenly flared with brown locks that had thin blond streaks running down his now scaly jaw. He was suddenly wearing spectacles, and long fangs were visible in his mouth when he gave a yawn.

"Well," said the man who had just moments ago been Bouldrueck. He sounded more at ease as he leaned back in his seat, the chair creaking under him. He looked years younger, and much leaner. The new snake pushed up his eyeglasses. "I've already drugged him well enough, I should think. You can do away with your disguised hair, Kael."

Sitting back on the floor in front of me, Kael rubbed two fingers over his brown strands in thought. "I'd... rather leave it, for now."

The snake snorted. "No one's going to come down to this disgusting place. You won't be seen."

"Forgive me for taking caution while walking through a city whose people wish to see all Grimlings hanged."

"You could give it a dye," he muttered. "Be done with it. Then you wouldn't have to wear an extra ring, or risk losing it."

"I..." Kael hesitated, then blew out a resolute breath. "No. It is my heritage. I am proud to be Grimish."

"And yet you want to kill its monarch?"

Kael's teeth sharpened. "It is not the fault of the caves that those ruling them are kin of monsters."

The snake gave a low, musing chuckle. "Heritage. A noble excuse... It sounds familiar. Who'd said that before? I could swear, the very same speech came from a certain someone..."

Kael grew silent.

"Ah." Macar clapped his hands softly. "That's right. I do believe you stole that line from her?"

Kael only shifted his legs, staring at the floor. Then he took in a breath and removed the ring on his right index finger.

I had trouble focusing on his face, and leaned a shoulder against the nearby wall as I watched Kael's brown hair bleed black.

"Macar," Kael whispered, his eyes watering. "Do you think... Nira has brought her back?"

The snake frowned. "What do you mean?"

"It's been so long, since..." He swallowed. "Her soul... the Goddess must have deemed it time to return her soul by now? For all we know, she is walking the streets in a new vessel as we speak."

"If she were," rumbled the snake, scratching a nail at a crumbling spot in the stone wall near him. "We would have met her by now. She is gone, Kael. Adam made damn sure of that."

I noticed Kael's lips twitch, whispering. "I know. But in Tanderam..."

The snake perked. "Ah, yes! The prison. Well, go on, tell me the news. Were the bat girl and viper there, after all?"

Kael's figure spun in front of me as the fire streaked and blurred. I was sure he hadn't moved, but with my bleary vision, he seemed to be gliding every which way. It was enough to make me ill.

"They were there, yes." Kael's answer was dimming in my ears. "That is, they *were*. Reapers stormed the prison and took them while I was there. Others were released as well."

The snake's muffled tone was a blurb, but I thought it sounded angry. "How many?"

"Three-fourths, roughly."

A curse from the snake. His colors had changed to a purplish hue, patterned like mist that twirled and wafted over his scales... *fascinating*...

"And," I heard Kael's fading voice linger and ring, and I shut my lids for just a moment... "The Shadowblood made an appearance."

I was jolted awake when the snake nearly toppled the chair. "*What?*" he hissed. "Both halves?"

"Just one," corrected Kael. "Your demon spy was still with them. The crow-shifter. He claimed he had orders to keep the boy alive—orders, I'm guessing, that were issued by whomever this queen is that you keep mentioning. I assumed that meant the second twin still hadn't been found."

"Damn it... Then I suppose it's a blessing you waited. I want both heads brought to me—understand? I will take no more chances. This is the world's survival we're dealing with. Removing one half of Dream's destructive champion won't guarantee Nirus's doom has ended."

"I understand," Kael sighed. "And... Claude has left us."

My ears rang when the snake gave another enraged snarl. "Excuse me?"

"He found his children there, in Tanderam. He freed them and left with the Reapers."

"Why didn't you kill him?! He could jeopardize everything—!"

"I will not kill my kin, Macar!" Kael roared. "They are my blood! Mine and... Cilia's..."

Kael slumped back in the straw, which was looking more like needles by the minute, his gaze distant and misty. "One of Claude's daughters," he whispered. "She looked like her, Macar. *Exactly* like her. How could I bring harm to someone who resembles her so?"

Macar massaged his temples, groaning. "Kael, Cilia is dead. Your descendants are *not* her, regardless of how they may look. You said yourself no woman could replace your wife."

"But what if it *is* her?" he asked. "It's past the proper time her soul would have been reborn. This one is from a different era, yes, but I've spoken with her. She is so much like..."

The snake's face contorted in revulsion. "Get a hold of yourself, man. She is your descendant. A relative. What do you expect to do even if it was her soul? The way you speak, it sounds disturbingly incestuous."

"I wouldn't…" He inhaled, then ran his fingers through his hair. "It is enough to see her alive again. And this one is already with another. I… could not rip her away from the life she's lived without me." His gaze smoldered. "But I can ensure her survival this time. If the End draws near, then the ones who will bring it must be destroyed. Before they take her from me again."

The snake's lips drew into a grin. "A noble deed, my friend… romantic, in a deranged sort of way, I suppose." He cracked his knuckles. "Enough of that, for now. At least tell me there was *some* good news from this disaster at Tanderam?"

"Well…" Kael hesitated. "I'm not sure if you'd consider it *good* news, but… it seems the missing Sky Princess has joined the Reapers."

The snake perked. "The crowned princess? Zylveia?"

"Yes."

"Oh, this could be to our advantage! I can take a little holiday from the 'Wales' role and take over a similar position in Culatia… I hear the Sky King is fatally ill. I'm sure rational thought is beyond him. He must rely heavily on his advisors… But how to spin it? A war with the Reapers may be a bit of a stretch, but he hates the *Ocean* King with a passion, doesn't he? Perhaps we can… Kael? Are you listening?"

Kael's head snapped up, regaining focus. "Hm? Oh. Yes… will you want me to stay here and oversee Galden?"

He plucked a pebble from the crumbling wall, inspecting it in thought. "Yes, I think that would be wise. I'll infuse Wales's image to your wedding band—"

"*No.*" Kael's cat ears grew and curled back, jerking his hand away to protect the ring. "I want no magic tainting it. Find me something else to put his image in, I don't care how many meaningless bands weigh down my fingers."

The snake glared, then sniffed and rose to his feet. "Fine. If you insist on being difficult, I'll take time out of my busy schedule to search for a new ring. You're a selfish idiot sometimes, Kael, and I…"

The colors dimmed into blackness, their voices fading into nothing as I fell into a groggy slumber.

45

A FRESH LEAD

XAVIER

"Sirra-Lynn?" Dr. Hendril shuffled through a mountain of beakers beside the clinic room's sink, bending to pull out several more vials from his luggage. "Well, I'm still not sure it was even her. These old eyes aren't what they used to be."

I laced my fingers over the counter. "As of late, we've gathered some... new intel that suggests otherwise, doctor. I can't stress how important finding her is for us, and even more so, I'd think, for her husband."

Claude sat behind me with cat ears perked in our direction, now dressed in a cleaner attire after his bail.

He briefly broke his gaze to glare at Neal and Ringëd, who were releasing their stress with a 'well needed smoke'. Claude scowled at the two and covered his nose with a hand, but returned his attention to the busy doctor without protest.

Octavius unconsciously mimicked his father's posture. He, too, was hunched by the door and covering his nose and mouth. *Was it the 'static' they were always on about?*

Jaq waited in a different corner, the viper scratching his forehead, possibly to itch at the hidden scars as he watched the doctor fiddle with the cluster of glass beakers, ceramic jars and wooden bottles.

Willow sat poised beside me, eagerly leaning forward, not wanting to miss a word of the discussion. Lilli had left us before arriving. The owl boy had demanded her attention after we left the dungeon. He was strangely attached to her.

"I suppose," Hendril sighed, ceasing his unpacking to stroke his wiry beard in thought. "If you really want the details…"

The door squeaked.

A rabbit-eared figured froze behind a crack in the door, looking as though she'd been caught stealing sweets at a bakery.

"Bianca?" I called.

She cursed, then pushed the door open and stepped inside, shutting it behind her.

"Sorry," she mumbled, stuffing her hands in her ivory coat pockets. "I, uh, overheard you guys talking about Sirra-Lynn and thought it might be important."

I grinned. "Oh, it is. Probably better that you're here for this, in fact... So, *Km-hmm*, doctor?" I turned to Doctor Hendril. "What was the island's name?"

The doctor snapped his fingers. "Ah, yes, right... It was a place to the west, called Mochelle Krép."

From the corner, Ringëd flicked the ash off his cigarette, perking. "Hey, I know that place," he said. "It's near my hometown."

I stared at Ringëd, pausing. "Hang on. Your home?" *Blast, that's right.* Ringëd was Marincian. "Your home..." I began, rolling the word in my thoughts. "Hang on—Ringëd. *Rin-gëd...* It means *one who Rin loves*, doesn't it?"

The human cocked an eyebrow. "Uh, yeah. Why?"

"'Home of one loved by Rin'..."

Alex grunted from the psyche. *"The riddle."*

I tossed a hurried hand at Ringëd. "Ringëd, your home—what was it called again?"

Ringëd scratched his neck. "Y'ahmelle Nayû."

I laughed. "Emerald Isle!"

"*Isle of Emeralds,*" Alex recited from the riddle yet again.

I rose in a thrill, nodding to Hendril. "Thank you, doctor. You've been a great help."

Ringëd followed close behind when I went out the door. "Wait a damn minute," the Runner protested. "Why all the questions about my island?"

I smiled over a shoulder. "That's where my body is. And it's where we're going next—"

"Jaq!"

The nurses in the halls were shoved aside, Jaq's father barreling through, panting over his knees. "Jaq, ya gotta come with me. Your ma's not doin' good right now, not good at all."

Jaq, startled, went to his father. "What happened?"

"It's your grandad!" he said. "He's bein' executed!"

JAQ

I sped ahead of Da, clumsily bouncing off Reapers and refugees scattered around the cramped bazaar.

The mass had stopped to look at the large screens fixed in the store windows in the markets, all tuned in to the same live reporting.

Bloody Death!

My boots slid to a stop, puffing up dirt—and I crashed like a boulder into a Grimish girl, throwing her back a good two feet.

I barely noticed it was Lilli, keeping my eyes stuck to the screens. I heard Oliver somewhere next to her, asking what was wrong. She murmured something to the kid, but I wasn't paying attention.

On the screens was Grandad.

The old man looked damn near as weak and pale as a Grimling, beaten like he'd been tortured for weeks. His head was placed on a wooden block, his neck stretched under the looming, rusty guillotine. A masked man kept a hand on the lever, his head turned at the crowned man who stood at the stage's podium.

King Galden was holding up a scroll and announcing a list of crimes to the surrounding crowd.

"*... siding with Land's Servant and joining the treasonous rebels against my family.*" His tone rose with each accentuated syllable. "*Endangering my wife, my children, the very kingdom and its proud people...*"

Someone came panting next to me. It was Prince Cayden, who had to readjust his mask and covering hat. He didn't put much care in the disguise this time, one of his lion ears sticking out as he stared wide eyed at the screen and whispered, "Apson...?"

King Galden went on with the charges. "*...Allying with the demon-summoning Reapers...*"

"What's happening?" Kurrick demanded when he stormed up to us next, Ana clinging to his scabbards, horrified.

"*... abandoning your duties as my First Hand...*"

Da grabbed my shoulder and shoved me forward. "Jaq, come on! Your Ma—"

"R, right!" I hustled back on track, Prince Cayden following us as we crossed the long yard up the hill. I didn't wait for the guards to open the gate before shoving it open myself.

Bridge swooped down to follow me through the courtyard, cawing urgently. My shoes screeched when I hung a sharp right, Da now taking the lead into one of the expansive rooms, where I could hear Galden's voice fuzzing from inside.

"*... a disgrace to the honor you've been given. How do you plea to these charges, Roarlord Apsonald?*"

I burst in with Da and Cayden, gasping for breath and startling Mother and Aunt Helda.

I kept my eyes on the screen, watching as Grandad spat a dark glob at the ground, blearily answering, *"Guilty."*

The crowd around them rippled with disgust, and in a sore, cottony chuckle, Grandad went on. *"To piss with this rubbish... You're naught more than a shepherd, Galden. Directing sheep in their pins with your feral collies, feeding slop to keep them distracted and happy, adding but a sprinkle of fear, playing on preexisting assumptions..."*

The king sniffed and rolled up the scroll. *"You think these shifters fools? Simpletons who cannot think for themselves?"* He chuckled. *"Is it a wonder they've come to see your sentence carried with proud spirits?"*

The crowd was a flurry of angry shouts, shoes and rocks flying onto the stage, a number of them hitting Grandad.

Galden sidled away from the projectiles. *"What you mistake for foolishness, Apson, is the peoples' faith."*

Grandad's jaw took a sharp hit, and his tongue sounded numb. *"You can stop this..."*

"I could, yes. It is my right to choose whether men live or die." His tone waxed viciously. *"Once, Apson, I called you a friend. It is... nothing short of disgusting to see what you've become. Shel take mercy on your damned soul."*

Another shower of stones rained down on Grandad. He wheezed. *"Mine is not the soul which needs mercy... you've stolen the crown from the Life Father's son. A plague consume your spirit... All hail the thief of thrones..."*

Galden bristled, cocking back a leg to kick him, but instead took a long, dreary breath and turned to the crowd. *"Please, stay your stones. This venomous worm will meet his sentence under justice's blade... but now, I speak directly to Land's Servant."*

I saw Prince Cayden's exposed lion ear twitch at the mention.

"Your general's life, I cannot preserve. For his soul, however..." From the scabbard at his belt, Galden pulled out a radiant, glowing sword, the blade smooth and pristine. *"I could make an exception."*

I knew that faint blue light anywhere. It was the same glow my chain-scythe gave off, but it was brighter. Much brighter. *Spiritcrystal.* Spit me sideways, that was *pure* Spiritcrystal.

Galden threw his head at the executioner, and the masked guard thrust down the lever and sent the guillotine's blade down.

Mother and Aunt Helda screamed on impact. The sound of the chop wasn't picked up by the speakers, having been drowned by the cheering crowd, but our view was clear enough to see the crimson aftermath on the blade. Grandad's neck was still attached at one end, breathing. It took a second slice to clear the rest.

Galden slipped on an eye-mask before he raised his glowing sword. *"Land's Servant. Howllord Lucas... you know for what I barter."* The sword was brought over Grandad, the blade fizzling through his back and arched its way out, as smooth as cutting nothing at all.

A white mist rose from the body, the translucent figure taking shape. I lifted my glasses for a second, the specter vanishing until I slid the lenses over my eyes again.

Damn it. Gods damn it.

Grandad's ghost looked delirious when he first stumbled out of his body. Under Grimish customs, the Reaper who'd performed the cutting ceremony would take this time to comfort the detached soul. Take their hand, keep them steady with crystal-woven gloves to touch their wispy fingers, tell them it's all right, that they were safe and cared for...

Shit on all that here. The minute the ghost's white eyes found lucidity, the executioner came behind him and clapped his wrists in glowing shackles.

My fists were shaking by the time Galden pushed up his eye-mask and looked Grandad up and down, sniffing. *"Death suits you well, Apson."*

"I suspect it would look far more fetching on you, Sire." There was poison in the last word, the ghost's fangs flexing.

Galden's brow furrowed, not hearing any of it. *"Ah, may as well hold your tongue. I only have the sight aspect."* He tapped the mask and smiled, turning to the audience again. *"This man's soul is my prisoner until you return my son. Cayden is not to be harmed, if you wish your precious general to be out of the Necrofera's bellies. I expect a hasty compliance."*

Cayden smashed a fist at the wall, screaming.

Everyone was either crying or pacing the floor testily... I just stood there.

Grandad...

My feet glided out the door on their own. I wandered the halls and walked outside, dropping onto a step. I stared at the city's horizon, my stomach twisting. It hurt to move, so I didn't bother.

"Papa?" Oliver came up the stairs and tugged on my shirt, his clipped wings twitching feverishly. "Papa? What's the matter? Everyone keeps sayin' someone got 'ecksa-cue-bed'."

Lilli came up the steps next, scooping him up. "Oliver, *hush!*" She wrapped her leather wings around him, shielding his face from me. She met my gaze carefully. "I'm sorry... I told him not to come, but he flew off and..."

I grunted. "It's fine."

She bit her lip. "Will you be all right?"

"I... Yeah. Yeah, I just." I sucked in a sharp breath. "I need a minute."

I stood up and walked past them, not giving the guards at the gate a word of acknowledgment as I shoved open the entrance and stalked into town.

46
SEPARATE WAYS

~~~~~

XAVIER

Silence smothered the clinic room, cheers and gleeful hollers piercing my grown wolf ears from the screen.

My limbs were numb. *With what, though? Shock? Anger...? How was I to feel about something like this?*

I was pulled into the psyche, the sensations of touch vanishing as Alexander took control in the physical plane.

From the psyche's lonely window, I watched Alexander lift a heavy finger and tap the engraved rune on the vision-screen's wall mount. The projected light blipped into nothingness and the cheers cut off mid-chant.

All that was heard was the soft hum of low-wattage metaglobes and the muffled bustling of doctors and nurses roaming about the hospital on the other side of the door.

I pushed out a dead-toned whisper from the psyche. *"Death..."*

Alex drew in a long, deep breath, and exhaled. Then he stormed out to the hall.

Bianca followed close at his side. She paused for a second, as did Alex, then both exchanged a scowl and stomped down the hall at a hastened pace.

"I'm guessing Jaq's mom is at the manor?" Bianca asked, keeping her hostile tone contained.

Alex jerked open the hospital door leading outside, the two shuffling out to the chattering, crowded street. "When last we heard, yes," explained Alex. "It's a place to start, at least."

She nodded, her rabbit ears draped down her neck.

We flagged down a hovering coach and sped to the manor. When we reached the gates, the guards recognized Alexander and let us through without question.

We found Lilli sitting on the front steps with little Oliver, her leathery wings draped depressively over the stairway.

Bianca staggered next to us at the sight of her, but ground her teeth and kept pace when Alex reached the bat.

"Have you seen Jaq?" he asked.

Lilli's expression drained. "He's... taking time to reflect."

"Where?"

She shook her head. "He went into the city when last I saw."

Alex pivoted and started back the way we came, but Lilli seized his arm, stopping him. "Don't," she said, her voice soft. "I think he wishes to be alone."

"Is that what he said?" Alex growled.

Lilli paused, brow scrunching. "Well, no..."

Bianca snorted. "Then how would you know?"

"It only... seemed that way, I suppose. He looked the way *I* had felt when my mother..." She bit her delicate lip, rubbing her knuckles.

Bianca crossed her arms and cocked a questioning eyebrow at us. Alex kicked at a loose stone in the pathway and rumbled. "Fine... we'll assume he'll come back when he's ready. But in the meantime."

He strode past Lilli, she and Bianca following hurriedly to keep pace, and went inside the manor.

Alex headed straight for the timid butler who waited with fidgeting hands in the foyer, my brother barking, "Where is my father?"

The butler pointed down the hall in a squeak. "L-last room on the left, High Howl—"

Alex stalked in that direction. The girls' footfalls echoed behind us. Alex threw open the indicated door, finding Father and Mother turning away from the vision-screen on the wall to look at us. Prince Cayden was there as well, his plumed hat and covering mask foregone.

"Master." Alex's breath was ragged. "Have you a plan?"

Father's thick brow creased hauntingly low. "It's hardly been ten minutes since the broadcast, Alexander—"

"But you do intend to retrieve his soul?" he demanded. "You don't mean to leave him condemned to a Fera's stomach?"

Cayden's teeth were already sharp. "Of course we're damn well getting his soul out of there. The question is how we'll do it."

"Could you pretend to turn yourself in?" asked Alex. The girls came to either side of him and shifted uncomfortably at the suggestion. "Drop the disguise and say Land's Servant agreed to the trade?"

Cayden's eyes sullied. "I can't trust my father to keep his end of the bargain. And even if he did, I've no way of *touching* Apson's ghost. Nor could I lug his body out of there without a Necrovoker accompanying me. Not to mention, said Necrovoker may very well not make it out himself the moment my father has his hands on me."

"Unless," Mother considered, tapping a chipped nail over the lacquered wood of the table. "We have a Dreamcatcher produce a phantom copy and pretend to be the escorting Necrovoker... the real Raiser could sneak in unnoticed afterward and retrieve the Roarlord's soul and body. This way, there is no chance of the phantom copy being harmed."

"Perhaps Yulia or Jimmy could offer the decoy," said Alex. "And Xavier and I can be the Necrovokers—"

"—No."

Alex spun on his heels.

Jaq had suddenly appeared under the open doorframe.

Alex frowned at the viper. "No?"

"You already pulled a prison break getting *us* out." He threw his chin toward Lilli, shoving his hands in his breeches' pockets. "And besides. You just figured out where Xavier's body is."

Father straightened at that, shock striking his aged features. "You've what?"

I told Alexander I wished to switch, and once in control, I addressed Father. "My body is on a Marincian province." I turned to Jaq, tone growing stern. "Which is *far* from here, and away from any danger. Your grandfather's soul, on the other hand, is right in the midst of enemy territory and being robbed of his due afterlife."

"Yeah." Jaq's fangs were growing long in his mouth, tongue slitting as his scales took on a rougher texture. "And he doesn't deserve that. He's a son of a bitch sometimes, but Gods damn it, he doesn't deserve what they're doing to him."

"So, we must get him back."

"Not you. Not us." His gaze flicked to my father. "Master Lucas. You'll bring him to Grim by the end of this?"

Father nodded, though rigidly. "I owe him a life debt, as do many of our men. To abandon him would bring me dishonor in Nira's eyes."

"Good," Jaq grunted, stabbing a finger at me next. "You and me? We're going to that island and getting your body back."

I staggered. "But we can't just..."

"No arguing. Not with this. We've spent too many years waiting to get you both back to normal, and I'll be damned if you kill Alex before you get there. Especially while trying to save a man I've spent most of my life resenting." His black eyes staled, voice quieting. "I want to help Grandad. He's still family, still my blood. But you and Alex have been more family to me than he ever was, and if I ditched you for him, I'd be one shitty guy."

I stared at him, beguiled. "I can't ask you to do this."

"Don't have to." He crossed his arms. "I'm going to drag your ass over to that island and smack *both* of ya for being idiots when we get there."

My grin was sour. "All right... It's a deal."

Bianca snorted and put fists at her sides. "And you know I'm sure as Bloods coming. We've been waiting way too long for this."

I grinned. "All right, then. We leave for Y'ahmelle Nayû as soon as... Er, Lilli?" I frowned at the bat. "Didn't you come in with the child?"

Lilli blinked, searching round the room. "Oliver?" She bolted out to the hall, her voice echoing. "Oliver...!"

OLIVER

I flapped through the town's streets, not going too high like Mama wanted, since my feathers weren't completely grown back yet.

They were gonna look for me soon. That vision was clear. Super clear. As clear as... as... something *really* clear. I might get in trouble for it later, but this was important, I think. I had a *really* good feeling this was important.

Linus was going to be sad if he made the 'clearest' choice soon. And Auntie Ana wouldn't make it. Linus needed to go with the fainter choice. He wasn't going to like it... but he had to do it. I had to show him both options so he knew what was gonna happen. If I could just find that dummy...

I didn't know where he was right now, but I knew where he *would* be, in a few minutes. I mean, *maybe* a few minutes. Maybe it already happened... *what year was it again?*

I slowed down and sat on a lamppost, squinting at my hands. My fingers were still little. So, the rest of me was probably still little, too. I grumbled, nose scrunching at my hands. I could'a sworn I was caught up with the bigger me by now. My fingers were longer just yesterday... or was that another vision?

I groaned, flexing my *little* wings and took off again. Clover cawed to my right—uh, left?—and followed me, her black wings flapping hard to keep up.

"When am I gonna be big?" I muttered to the crow. "I mean, *really* be big? I already lived like, a bazillion years in the *after* parts. When are the *before* parts gonna be over?"

She rumbled a caw that felt like a question.

My wings were getting tired, so I slowed down and landed, running instead. I got to the right road and stopped at a trash can, puffing. *Did I make it in time?*

I waited for about five minutes, getting on my toes and keeping an eye out for Linus. *Did he already run by—?*

I almost fell over when someone's long legs bumped into me.

"Oh—" Linus's eyes popped open at me, like just getting out of a vision he'd been stuck in. He blinked a couple times, scratching his long dreads. "Oliver. So sorry, didn't see you there—"

"Don't," I said, panting.

His face screwed up. "Don't what?"

"Don't go with Cayden. Go with Uncle Alex and Xavier."

He glared, looking mad. "I've made my choice, little one. I won't abandon my friend a second time."

He walked past me, but I grabbed the hem of his shirt and pulled as hard as I could. "No! Don't!"

"I know the risks." He kept moving forward, dragging me with him when I dug in my heels. "You may know the years ahead, but you cannot comprehend what mistakes I left behind. I'll not make such mistakes again."

"There won't be any more'ta make if ya go with him!"

He waited for that one, craning down at me. "I... don't care what happens to me."

"Not you." I stamped a foot, staring at him in a squint to tell him I was *serious*. "Look. I know, okay?"

His eyebrows went up. "Know what, exactly?"

"I know you, um..." My ears got hot. "I just know stuff. Stuff you say to him... when he dies."

I saw him get really stiff, like he forgot how to move. I stretched up to touch his face. "He takes a sword for you. To save you. Look, I'll show you..."

He was one of the only people who could See the visions with me. So, I showed him what I Saw. His eyes went blank for a minute, watching with me. Then he started crying. It was just a little water rolling down his cheek, though, getting my fingers wet. He didn't make any sound.

"And if I don't go...?" He was quiet.

"He's okay if you don't," I huffed, taking my hand away from his face. "You gotta go with Uncle Alex and Xavier, okay? Cayden's gonna be all right, but Miss Ana won't be, without you. She's gonna need you."

He didn't say anything for a while. I saw another drop leak from his eye before he wiped it and took in a breath. "Gods help me," he whispered, then he exhaled. "Thank you, little one..."

I grinned wide, putting fists over my hips. "Good. I gotta get back to Mama now. But don't forget, okay?"

I waved goodbye and ran back to the giant house where I'd left Mama, my wings too tired to fly. Bloods, I hoped she wasn't mad.

47

OUT OF HIDING

~~~~~~

CILIA

"Curious," I hummed, feeling the Mark I had placed in that bird travel farther west. My leg swung idly over the branch I laid upon, and I stared at the night sky. "So far away from Reaper territory, yet still he hesitates."

Something was amiss. *Perhaps the twins are still among other Death Knights? Surely, my little bird wouldn't disobey a direct order?* No, my Mark wouldn't allow that. He must be waiting. "Or perhaps he's reverted back to his old Reaper ways…"

I rolled onto my stomach to peer down at my other commanding Sentient. The Healer was waiting by a rock below my perch, and cringed when catching my eyes.

"Maveric," I called. "Gather those sticky mongrels. We're going to make certain our bird follows through with his mission."

Maveric nodded glumly, walking off to do as asked.

"Ah," a different voice mused to the left. "What's all this?"

I scanned the barren terrain, seeing Macarius was there by the shallow cave. Well, his *copy* was there. It phased through one of the skeletal monstrosities that leapt for him. He looked pleased today, his smile twisted and scheming. "Both brothers have been spotted, then?"

I sat upright and crossed my arms. "It would seem so. Where have you been? It's been some time since your last copy left. You're unsettlingly cheery."

"I am taking care of a business endeavor in the Sky realm. Oh, that king is in a sorry state, as well as his kingdom! He has no idea his daughter is working with the Reapers, it's the perfect opportunity to… oh, never mind, the intricacies will bore you. Now, the Shadowblood: where are they?"

"They've just arrived in Brittleton, I believe. Janson has informed me they're heading for a little island called Y'ahmelle Nayû,"

I hopped down from the tree to meet the copy. "I was ready to gather some underlings and go there myself. I can call for a few water-dwelling beasts to take me. Not worrying after weather and breathing can certainly shorten the time, so I believe I can arrive before them."

"Good, good. Keep track, stay in touch with our crow. I will send more copies with you, after each uses up its time."

I hesitated, a knot tightening my chest. "Macarius... I was hoping your *original* would show himself again."

He regarded me with a puzzled expression. "Why?"

"*Cilia...*" My cat ears draped to my neck, his gentle voice rippling in my memory. "*Forgive me...*"

I drew in a breath. "I have yet to receive more... rewards."

The cobra stared at me like I was an idiot. "Are you still on about that voice, Cilia?"

"It's the reason I've stayed alive so long." Five hundred years of hearing my name whispered—sobbed—begging my forgiveness... *Forgiveness for what?* Centuries of questions, gnawing at my sanity for so, so achingly long... and their answers were miraculously at my fingertips.

At *his* fingertips.

"I think..." I swallowed, my throat drying for the first time in a very, very long while. "I think it was my husband. Or perhaps a lover?"

"You were a whore for the better half of your life," Macarius reminded. "You had many lovers. You can include myself in that infinite list."

"Clients aren't to be counted." My cat ears grew and curled. "And my son—if I had a son, I must have known the father?"

He smeared an exhausted hand over his face, sighing. "Cilia, rid us of the Shadowblood, I will give you your answers. But not before."

"But I only wish to know if—"

"*Not before*," he hissed, his fangs unfolding. "This is Nirus's future we are protecting. I assume you yourself wish not to perish with the rest of us in this crumbling world?"

My gaze lowered to the dirt. "No."

"Then I'll not hear of this voice idiocy until those End bringers are dead at my feet. Both of them. At once. I shall *not* find the second walking about again." His tone declared he was finished with me.

I turned, grumbling. "Very well..." I strutted off as the copy left in the opposite direction. *I suppose I'm off to the western seas, eh?*

That was dangerous territory, even for me. I hadn't traveled outside my own domain in so long... *who ruled the west again? Was it the ice-woman or the demon shark?* Oh, I could never remember who reigned which parts of the Bloody ocean.

Nothing for it now. If going there meant remembering *his* voice, it was worth facing another Ancient. Still, best to avoid detection. If I couldn't, well...

I prayed the Gods be on my side, for once.

48

SETTING SAIL

XAVIER

The ship's bell gonged in the breeze, sails catching wind as a salty spray of seawater slushed against the bow.

Alex tipped his wide hat forward to cast his face, and falsely-orange hair, in shadow, making sure his vest collar was pulled up and veiling his bristly cheeks.

The other passengers of the ship were busy with happy chatter, ignoring us as we surveyed the crew. The familiar faces of Janson and Linus came into view near the back rails; Willow and Lilli were disguised with Landish hair and pretending to play with little Oliver; Jaq, Octavius, Neal and Herrin were in the cabin, presumably taking care of the unseen staff, along with our ghostly vassal, Dalen. Matthiel and Mr. Treble were out on the deck with us, along with Ringëd and Mikani. The three new Footrunners onboard were *our* men—Prince Cayden had his rebel agents within some of his father's military—so stowing away had been simple. Hopefully if things went well, this next part—

"A'ight, lads 'n lassies!" Bellowed our appointed commander—my father's resurrected vassal, Nathaniel—from the upper deck. "It be time ye turned yer pretty gazers this way!"

Startled, the passengers turned. Then they fell Deathly quiet.

Nathaniel had a rapier to the captain's throat.

Vendy had drawn her Crystal blade beside him, her rabbit ears folded back and her face wrenched in a comical, menacing expression. Her uncle Henry wasn't present; he had volunteered to join Prince Cayden in rescuing Jaq's grandfather instead.

The sight of Nathaniel's blade against the captain's throat caused a stir and screams broke when our disguised men—Alexander included—pulled out their weapons. Shotri, swords and scythes were held toward the common people, and we corralled them to the edges of the ship.

Nathaniel inspected the status of our mutiny, and with a satisfied snort, he shoved the captain down to the lower deck, the man crashing on the floorboards with a winded *ka-thunk!*

"Grow yer ears 'n listen right!" Nathaniel barked, idly turning the blade in his hands. "This be our ship, now. 'fraid yer little trip southward ain't to our likin'. We be on a different route, and ye can all find another boat yonder, after the coastguards pick ye up round this way."

He hopped off the rail and landed next to the frightened captain, waving his rapier in the air. "Now get to the dinghies, mates! Go on—all 'a ye! Help'll come right enough. We just need the ship. No one need be hurt."

Our crew herded the passengers and staff onto the dinghies, and when they were all floating beside the ship in frightened groups, Nathaniel thanked them for their cooperation and turned the ship around at the helm.

Alex hurried up the wooden steps to meet him, patting the bear's back with a wide grin while slipping off the ring Willow had infused our disguise into. "Brilliant, Nathaniel. Now, to Y'ahmelle Nayû?"

"Aye," Nathaniel turned the ship westward, peering at the compass he'd brought along. "But ye best be watchin' me steer this girl one 'o these days, eh? Me master ain't here, 'n me resurrection only lasts another seventeen days, without 'im. Won't be fer another two weeks till we be getting' to that island."

A boyish laugh fluttered above us as Aiden, our mother's winged vassal, flapped to the railing next to us. "Two weeks?" Aiden mocked, the robin's goggle lenses glinting in the sunlight. "I should hope sooner than that! The island isn't so far off. I'll have the strongest winds blowing at those sails for the remainder of my resurrection—*one* week, at most."

Nathaniel scowled at the bird. "Even the strongest winds ain't fast enough fer that, feather-head. It'll help good, but yer Aerovokin' ain't *that* great."

Aiden's wings gave a defiant flap. "I feel a bet coming on, Nathaniel. I say fifteen days, no more."

"Name yer wager."

"Loser takes on the winner's scouting duties for a month."

"Hmm… a'ight, done." Nathaniel rubbed his black beard, stealing Alexander's hat and placed it on his own head, his eyes brightening with interest. "Any more 'n fifteen days, 'n *you'll* be watchin' fer assassins in the kitchens all day. Now get yer feather-tail up there 'n give us some gusts!"

With a chuckle, Aiden flew to the skies, summoning his Aerovoking to blow against the sails, the many dangling ropes swaying and the masts groaning.

Alexander crossed his arms, looking at Nathaniel. "I'm glad Father sent you with us. We don't know the first thing about sailing."

"I know ye don't, lads." Nathaniel ruffled Alexander's hair. "Don't ye worry none. I'll get ye to Y'ahmelle Nayû sure 'nough. 'Specially since yer old man talked ye outta bringing yer giant pet with ye."

Alex grumbled ruefully at that. Father had indeed convinced him to leave his bone dragon puppet behind. It was argued that the sheer weight of the skull alone would sink the ship. Alex had protested that it was merely a theory and not fact, but when Father mentioned it would *at best* slow our travel and delay us from finding my body, Alex changed his tune.

Nathaniel breathed in deeply, lifting his square face to the open skies as a new calm honeyed his voice. "Too long," he sighed, smiling. "Been too long, since I be getting' me sea-legs back."

Alex folded his arms on the wooden rail and watched the waves lap in a rhythmic lull. "How long has it been for you?"

Nathaniel stroked his scraggly beard, his bear ears folding down sadly from under the plumed hat. He was still staring at the blue skies. "I can't rightly 'member, lads. Hundred years? Hundreds? I tell ye, 'tis a crime to be on land so long. I lived by the seas, and died by them. The Marincian Reapers picked me corpse up and reaped me NecroSeam fast enough a'fore I could rot, but then I got slammed into them wee little caves..."

He glanced at us briefly, shrugging an apology. "No offense. Ye Grimlings be content with yer tunnels and ceilings, but me?"

Nathaniel shook his head in a dramatic frown, then leapt onto the railing with his chest pulled high and his arms stretched wide, his long, ruffled sleeves flapping in the wind as he sucked in a deep breath and released it in an overjoyed laugh. "Bloods, did I miss the smells 'o fish and salt, the breeze on me back and the spray o' foam in the mornin' waters."

His laughter dwindled to a pleased chuckle, and he stepped down from the rail, grabbing the helm with one thick hand while his other gripped a nearby rope. He sighed dreamily. "Aye, I used to spend night after night lookin' up at the stars, chartin' the next course, explorin' island after island, soakin' up sun and stars alike."

"But Nathaniel," Alex began, the top of my window in the psyche bowing as he knit his brow. "Aren't *you* Grimish? Your hair..."

The corner of his lips cracked a grin and he slid a hand through his black strands from under his hat. "Aye, I was born in the caves, just as you were. Couldn't stand the tight space, never could. 'Tis hard to be a claustrophobic Grimling." He winked. "I left when I was a lad, younger than the both 'o ye. The

Surfacin' Ports weren't as nice and fancy as they are these days, but they were just as quick. My first step on surface land was the greatest moment 'o me life..."

He spit at the floor and waved us off. "Aw, 'nough 'o that, lads, go on. Why don't ye go settle yerselves in? Make sure ye get something in that stomach 'a yers."

Alex grinned, seeing that the glint in Nathaniel's eyes had grown distant and focused on the horizon. We left the captain to his duties and nostalgia.

Alex went to the lower deck and stopped to overlook the bobbing waves of the lively ocean, leaning over the rail and taking a deep breath of the salty, sea air.

"Well," he said. "We're nearly there."

I smiled thinly from the psyche. *"Nearly. But won't it be strange? Not able to talk like this anymore?"*

"Strange?" He pushed off the rail. "We'll be talking face to face. As it was before. For once, it will be... right."

"It will be right..." I tested the words curiously. *"It's been too long to remember what that was like."*

"Far too long," he agreed.

Willow suddenly skipped beside him and crushed the air from his lungs. "Can you believe this?" She laughed with delight. "In a matter of weeks, you'll be yourselves again. We'll have Xavier back!"

He pried her off, grumbling. "Yes... and I look forward to having personal space again."

I pushed myself out of the psyche to take control, the ocean breeze brushing my face. I clasped Willow's hand in a chuckle. "Soon, darling," I said wistfully. "I'll see you with my own eyes again."

She squeezed my fingers, her smile glowing. "Not soon enough."

She laughed and strode to the upper deck, peering over the expansive horizon and speaking with our captain.

I sighed and walked out to the deck, the sunlight hot on my cheeks as I lifted my chin, wind licking my hair wildly—

"...have not been told to do so!" I heard Kurrick growl from across the deck, breaking my attention. "We cannot tell them anything until it has been finalized!"

"B-but we're right there!" Herrin's voice clipped next.

I narrowed an eye. *What are they on about this time?*

I walked out, finding Kurrick was harassing the poor scholar. The scarred warrior towered over Herrin, the bird clutching his *Choir* book like it was a precious tome as his voice shuddered. "S-shouldn't they at least know a little before—?"

"I have not given permission to inform them," Kurrick snarled, yanking Herrin up by his collar. The lion's sharpened teeth ground. "I still have yet to believe they will be of *any* use, after this. I have watched long enough, and still have not seen a speck of what is written."

Herrin swallowed. "But Miss Ana said—"

"Ana is too optimistic for her own good. She will accept anything Dream and Crysalette say, without question. I am not swayed so easily—I require proof. And I have seen none."

I cleared my throat, stalking up to Kurrick. "Bullying the bookworm, Kurrick?" I cocked an eyebrow. "How brave. Is there any docile soul you won't threaten to mince into little pieces?"

Kurrick tossed Herrin aside, the bird stumbling to the floor. Kurrick's lion tail swished at his feet. "Not if they threaten my mission. And should *you* jeopardize it, I'll not make an exception."

My eyes rolled, and I heard Alex snort from the psyche. I went to help Herrin to his feet. "Yes, your *mission*," I drawled. "Bringing back the lost heir of Land, wasn't it?"

His expression wasn't amused, his silence answer enough for me.

"And you still think Alex and I are going to do that for you, don't you?"

"*I* never believed so," he corrected. "And I still do not. Your skill has yet to show itself, and I am growing impatient. Look at you—even excluding your outrageous handicap, you were never able to hold a single, *whole* element of Hallows. It's beyond discouraging."

Herrin's face grew some down-feathers, anger boiling in his glare. "What if they just haven't used that skill yet?" Herrin shouted. "They just… just need the right motivation, is all!"

"Motivation, eh?" Kurrick drew out a knife and grabbed my shirt collar. "Very well, Enlightener: let us give them motivation. Do something to amaze me, wolf twins. Prove me wrong… or I will bring this worthless hunt to its misery."

I tensed when the lunatic raised his blade to my throat, the metal cold against my skin.

"K-Kurrick…" I kept a cautious tenor. "Put it away."

"Not before you show me your supposed skill."

"I—we don't have… We've already told you we can't take you to your lost king."

"That is not what concerns me. Show me that you are worth my time."

"What the Death do you want from us? We don't have any—"

"You've supposedly used your skill once to rip your soul away from your vessel," he growled. "Do it again."

That shut me up. I stammered. "I... I don't know how."

His lids turned to slits. "Then how do you expect to *replace* your soul when we reach your vessel?"

I felt the warmth drain from my face. "I... don't know—"

Kurrick *cracked* the hilt against my temple, and everything went black.

"... the Void is wrong with you?" I heard Alex shouting when I came to, his voice bouncing from every direction. I'd woken up in the psyche. Alex must have been forced out.

He now thrashed in the sea beside the looming ship, his vision bobbing in the water.

"If I hadn't been in there," he bellowed up at Kurrick, who stared down at us from the edge of the ship. "You would have let him drown!"

Kurrick sneered, then stomped away, his heavy boots pounding the deck's floorboards as he left Herrin standing there in a panic.

"I, um!" the scholar stammered, setting aside his book and flapped down to us, "I-I'll get you out!"

Alex reached for Herrin's scrawny arms, but his grip slipped, then again on the second try, then the third.

Alex spit seawater from his mouth. "For the love of—!"

Plip!

Alex and Herrin froze when a light lapping sounded from the water around them.

Plip... plip... plip...

A long, slender body began to circle Alex in the water, its back wavering with a translucent-green fin. It looked like an eel, waving in a hypnotic circle around Alexander's rigid head.

The creature slithered from the water and wrapped its smooth, serpentine body around Alexander's flinching arm. The creature's head poked out of the water, and it stretched up to *snatch* Herrin's wrist, wrapping itself round it and sticking to him with its suction-cup coated underbelly.

It was a thin thing, as long as Alexander's arm and as thick as two fingers, its leathery skin a deep bluish color with a beautiful green sheen that glittered against the sunlight. It had deep violet eyes with slitted pupils, and it blinked at Alex, its snake-like head cocking. I could swear it was smiling.

Herrin and Alex froze. The creature opened its gummy, toothless mouth and gave a pleasant *Aaahn*, its grip tightening round both their arms.

Alex's tone was nervous. "Herrin?"

Herrin swallowed, his wings flapping stiffly. "Y-yeah?"

"What *is* that?"

"*Aaahn!*" went the excited creature. "*Aaahn! Aaahn!*"

Herrin was slack-jawed, inching his face closer to examine the thing. "I… I think it's a Bindragon," he said, fascinated.

"A what?" muttered Alex.

"A Bindragon." Herrin held his free fingers to the little thing, laughing when its head stretched out and rubbed lovingly against his palm in appreciative nickers. "They're one of the Ocean realm's dragons. Supposedly, their suckers secrete a sticky oil that give them a crazy good grip, which lets them pull off barnacles from rocks and bows of a ship to eat… Bloods, I read about them, but I didn't think the pictures were the *actual* size."

"All right," Alex chewed, shaking his arm, which in turn shook Herrin's wrist as the dragon kept them stuck together. "And what is it doing, exactly?"

"It looks like it's helping us out," Herrin observed, licking his lips. "Let's see…"

Herrin flapped harder, easing a flailing Alex out of the water, his clothes soaked through and dripping. Alex had lost a boot.

Somehow, even with Herrin's fingers open and hovering over Alexander's arm, the Bindragon kept a firm hold of the two, lashing them together as if sewn to their skin.

Herrin lifted us over the deck, gently lowering to—

Ffw-pah-pah-pah!

The Bindragon popped off in soft sucking sounds, and Alex thumped to the deck, coughing when his back hit the floorboards.

Alex rolled over and pushed to his feet, grumbling as he shook himself and glanced at his one, shoeless foot.

Herrin touched down next to him, chuckling as the Bindragon wrapped around his arm. "Thanks, little guy," Herrin said and held his arm out to the deck's railing.

"*Aaahn!*" cried the dragon. It slithered off of Herrin's arm and crawled to the railing. Then it hopped off and dove into the sea with a tiny *splish!*

Alex shed his soaked vest and wrung it out, water raining down his feet. "Strange little thing," he muttered. His gaze swept round the deck. "And, to no one's surprise, Kurrick seems to have disappeared. Bloody lunatic, almost drowning us…" He spit a glob of salt water that had dripped from his hair into his mouth and shook his head to dry his hair. "What does he think he's going to get out of that?"

I was silent in the psyche, sighing. As brutish as Kurrick had been, he'd had at least one fair point.

How *was* I going to return my soul when we retrieved my vessel?

49
ROTTEN REGRETS

~~~~~

JANSON

Sunrays filtered through the round window in my cabin, hitting my eyes as "sleep" slipped away. Not that demons really slept. We *remembered*... at least, we remembered what was left of our memories.

I lay on the bolted cot and stared at the wood-plank ceiling while the ship rocked in a calming rhythm, seagulls crying outside.

"Rossette?" I called softly. "Nikolai?"

I found the ghosts hovering by the door. Rossette answered. "Yes, *Da'torr*?"

"Have I ever been out at sea?" I asked.

Nikolai spoke this time. "No, *Da'torr*."

I hummed, thoughtful as I stroked my feathered goatee. "I like it."

They chuckled. It sounded odd to hear them laugh. *Had they done it once since I'd Changed?* I swung my legs over the cot, sighing. "I'm sorry... For what I've done. What I'm doing. Neither of you should have to share this burden."

Rossette floated to me and laid a translucent hand on my leg. "It isn't your fault. We know it would be different, had you a choice."

Nikolai nodded his agreement.

Still, it didn't lighten the heavy ball of guilt. "Your afterlives are in constant danger because of me," I said, ashamed. "Because of what I couldn't do." My insides churned with the waves, faintly remembering my own scythe, shoved into my chest cavity, the shock and numbing burn as I tried to rip it over my Seam... *But she'd gotten there first.*

And Nile... My *Nile*...

A wave of agony slammed through me, stinging my lids as that festering, hollow pit clawed at my chest. The chasm flared where my Bond had been sewn by the Seamstress, the bond that tied me to Nile... *the Bond that used to tie us together.*

But Nile was dead. I remembered holding him in my hands, his neck bent the wrong way, his black eyes stale, his blood soaking my fingers...

"*Da'torr,*" Nikolai's ghost began gently. "It not fault of you."

"But it *is,*" I hit the cot's post with a fist. "Nikolai, when I first made the Pact with you, I promised you a second chance at life. This isn't the life you should be stuck with! I don't deserve to be called your *Da'torr...!*"

Nikolai's finned ears flicked from his head. "*Da'torr.*" His tone was morose. "Demon girl be ze reason for zis. Not *Da'torr.* I eez... proud, to be with you."

"As am I," whispered Rossette, gliding onto the cot beside me. Her long, feathered hair fell to her shoulders, spectral wings tucking tight to her back as she folded one leg to her chest, the other swinging off the edge. "I cannot speak for dear Nikolai, but I've had many a Necrovoker *Da'torr* in my afterlife. There are a number of whom I regretted making the Pact with. You are not one of them."

My eyes started to water, and I managed a laugh. "Then you must be mad—"

Something shocked my nerves stiff. I jolted upright, gasping. The air seemed to grow colder. *Freezing.* From deep in my stomach, terror sprouted, and I started panting.

"*Da'torr?*" Nikolai asked, concerned. "What wrong?"

I lifted off the cot, feeling like I was twenty pounds heavier, and scrambled to the window. There were only waves... Just waves, just ocean, for miles and miles... and yet...

"Something's out there." The words rang low and haunted. "Something's watching."

What was this feeling...? Like claws scraping my insides, terror gripping my blackened blood and spreading to my muscles like an infection. Every part of me wanted to run; wanted to hide, to curl on the floor and cower. My hands were shaking. *Why in Bloods was this familiar...?*

I gasped for breath, my lungs shuddering. Then I remembered what it was. I'd felt this before, many times. But only near Mistress... yet, Mistress wasn't here. At least, I couldn't feel her. Her... *weight* was different. Just as terrifying, but different, like a whole other flavor.

Were there others like Mistress? I gazed out to the sea, searching the waters for the source of fear that rattled my veins. I saw nothing. The weight of their presence was there though, and it was strong— A knock came at the door, making me jump.

"Sir Janson?" a woman's voice called. It was Her Highness. "Have you woken?"

I stole another glance at the empty sea, swallowing the thick clot of fear. Whatever was out there would have to wait. I still had an act to keep up.

She knocked again, and I threw on a cloak that was hanging on the wall, lifting the cowl over my scarred face before I went to open the latch. The Death Princess's smile was blissful this morning. Or it *was*, until she looked at me and staggered back, the bell tied to her ashen hair jingling.

"Are you well?" she asked. "You look sickly..."

The dark Weight pressing my soul burned, but I balled my hands and forced a smile. "Just tired, Your Highness... what brings you here?"

Her cheer returned, hands cupping behind her with barely contained excitement. "Our captain tells us we should reach land sometime after nightfall," she said. "He wished for the passengers to prepare for docking, when the time comes."

"Ah..." I kept what I hoped was a peaceful demeanor. It was an ungodly strain to seem relaxed. Every muscle and tendon tightened in terrified shudders, the urge to cower rising steadily. The Weight wouldn't leave. "That's... wonderful news. Thank you for letting me know."

"Also." She held out a fist, looking apologetic. "I'm sorry I hadn't thought to give you one of these sooner... I'd made one for Jaq and Lilli, but hadn't considered you might want one as well."

She opened her fingers to reveal a silver ring. There was a sealing mark etched on the outside surface. I picked up the ring, turning it in examination. "Is this... an illusion?" I asked.

"It will hide your scars," she explained, hesitating before reaching for my face and slowly pulled down my cowl. "So you won't have to shield your face from everyone you meet."

I stared at her, then at the ring, and slipped it on a free finger. Her smile told me it had worked, and I rubbed the right side of my face; the darkened side, where my eye was sealed shut. I still felt the risen lines of burn scars under my palm. *Of course I did... illusions were only a visual change. Just a mask to hide what horrors lay underneath.*

I walked past her to look at a picture that hung on the wall in the hallway. I wasn't interested in the picture itself, I wanted to see my reflection in the glass. My breath fell at the sight. My eye was still closed, but it looked more natural. There was no ugly scar melted over the lid. There was no ugly scar *anywhere*. Just smooth, untouched skin... the way it was before my death.

I touched that side of my face again, still feeling the bumps and webbed lines, but not seeing any of it in my reflection. Macarius had given me rings enchanted with illusions before, but they were only meant to make me seem wounded and trustworthy... he didn't care about hiding my shame.

My one good eye was blinded suddenly, tears welling. "Thank you," I whispered, drying my eye. "Thank you..."

She took my hand, her gaze full of warmth. "It was the least I could do. You helped me so much when I first stumbled here on the surface. And you lost even more because of it... If there is anything more I can do to ease your pain, please, don't wait to let me know."

She touched my cheek, the scarred side, and smiled. Her heat left my face when her fingers withdrew, and I watched her go to the next cabin to inform Ringëd and his wife of the upcoming docking.

The wife's green eyes flicked at me for a moment, and I shuddered. That woman was the splitting image of my mistress. Except her hair was darker, along with her skin. But that face, those eyes... I shivered again. If not for her black pupils, I would have thought Mistress had followed me onto the ship. *Why did they look so alike? What did it mean—?*

A pulse rippled through my soul, the Weight returning furiously. It was heavier now, making my knees sink to the floor.

Her Highness spun, seeing me curled, and hurried over. "Sir Janson? What is it?"

My breath came out in sputters. I clutched my lurching stomach. "S... seasick..."

She helped me to my feet and led me back to my cabin, where Rossette and Nikolai's ghosts were waiting. She set me on the cot.

"Wait right here," she said, walking out. "I'll retrieve one of our doctors."

When she shut the door, I grunted, the Weight pressing harder and harder, until it pulled me to the floor again, as if to yank me through the floorboards and cut out my stomach. *What... was this... pain...?!*

Then, suddenly, my head began to burn. Something writhed inside my brain, slithering like a worm under my skull.

Whatever it was, it dulled the Weight in my stomach, the air feeling lighter. The slithering burn in my head quelled whatever had been pulling me down. The burn must have been Mistress's Mark. She once said it made me *hers*, and *hers* alone...

But then, what else was out there? And what in the Gods names did it want?

My head splintered in pain again, a familiar ring grating my ears. *Little bird...* Mistress's haunting voice sang in my thoughts, an incessant whine resonating. *I hope you're still committing...?*

That slithering knot in my skull pulsed mercilessly. "Y... yes," I seethed against the pounding ache. "Yes, Mistress..."

I'm so glad, she purred. *I was so excited, I decided to see the game for myself. I look forward to seeing you again, my little bird… we can play together soon…*

The ringing vanished along with her voice, and I sputtered out a breath. *Death.* I panted over my knees. *These damned demons won't let me be.*

50
IT'S NEVER THAT EASY

XAVIER

I felt it—the cold burst of static that tugged under my ribs. My pressing hand radiated violet light, which pooled over the grey hairs warming my bare chest and seeped into my pores like a layer of thin, smoky ice.

I breathed in slowly, drowning the creaking floorboards that moaned in our private cabin, the waves lurching in a hypnotic sway as our ship drifted through the crisp, evening seawater.

This wasn't the first time I'd felt this cold grip. I'd had the whole ride to test this foreign Evocation and I was sure this was the right one; the one that would return my soul to its proper vessel. But there was still the next step to take. Just a quick pull outward, and theoretically, I would drag my soul out of Alexander, NecroSeam and all. *Theoretically.*

Jaq's head craned over the edge of the bunk above me, folding his arms. "Ya actually gonna do it this time?" he asked dully.

I dismissed my Hallows and stared at my hand, sighing. "What will happen if it works? How am I to put myself back without a vessel to channel the magic?"

"Can't you just... walk back in?" Jaq suggested with a cocked eyebrow.

Chai croaked from the bedpost beside me, and I reached over to stroke his tattered feathers. "There's no telling if it will be that simple," I explained. "I don't want to make a mistake that can't be fixed."

"*Da'torr?*" Two spectral heads fuzzed through the wall: the feather-haired Dalen and the rabbit-eared Vendy. Our vassals scowled at us, and Vendy muttered, "Are ya tryin' that stupid trick again?"

"'Cus it keeps pulling us on the inside in *weird* ways," Dalen added in a shudder, "and we don't like it."

I leaned back on the bed, my arms holding me up. "Sorry. I'm getting anxious... It's nightfall and Nathanial thinks we'll reach land within the hour." I smeared a hand over my face. "And I'm not ready. Damn me, I'm just not ready."

"It will work," Alex encouraged from the psyche, the words tumbling through my head in time with the swaying ship. *"Wait until we find your vessel if you must, but it will work once we get there."*

"Bloods, do I hope so," I sighed.

Dalen's and Vendy's ghost floated through the wall completely, Dalen tucking his translucent wings behind him. "It's gonna be weird when you're separated," he said. "You tuggin' at your Seam is already rattlin' us around, what's it gonna be like when both of ya are givin' us different orders?"

"Oh!" Vendy lifted an informative finger. "I actually had that happen once with them! Nothing major happens or anything, but what we figured out is that the most *recent* command cancels out the older one. Pretty easy—"

Brrip—brrip—brrip!

My com chirped from the desk. I scooped it up and answered the incoming call, noting that it was my mother.

"Honored Fangs," I greeted, saluting with a fist to my chest. "Grand timing. We've nearly arrived at Y'ahmelle Nayû."

Mother grunted from the screen of light, one grey wolf ear circling to the side. *"I'm glad to hear... I'm calling to assign you two new tasks, once you've finished this one."*

My brow knitted. "Two tasks?"

"I've just received a call from the servant of Neverland's new queen," she explained, ponderously tapping a nail to her chin, *"It seems the new queen has heard of the Reapers' struggles against Galden and wishes to offer aid."*

"Does she?" I asked, curious about this 'new' queen. I hadn't known of a new crowning. It must have been recent. "What is she asking for in exchange?"

"Her servant wouldn't say," Mother muttered, annoyed. *"She claimed the queen would only disclose such things in person. But given that your father and I are busy with the effort here, she had accepted my compromise to send you in my stead... Though, oddly,"* she drawled, an eye squinting at me from the screen, *"she is expecting both of you."*

I blinked. "Both? Not only Alex?"

"So it seems," she agreed, her tone suspicious. *"I don't know where she received her information, but she thinks both of you are on your way."*

"Hopefully with luck, we will be."

She sighed, closing her eyes. *"Indeed..."* For a moment, I thought she was ripe to expound on that, but she cleared her throat and stayed on topic. *"Now,* that is only the first new task. Before you make your way to Neverland, I would have you detour to Marincia's capital."

I frowned. "Why?"

"If Neverland's queen is offering us military aid, there is a fair chance the Ocean King will offer the same." She jabbed a finger at the screen. "But were I you, I would have the Death Princess handle those negotiations. Relicblood to Relicblood, as it were. I do not want the Ocean King thinking us a disorganized bunch of cross-eyed pups. Understand?"

I saluted again. "Yes, Honored Fangs. We'll depart the moment our current task is seen through." I added in a grin, "And by Death, we'll see it through."

She cracked a pleased smirk, chuckling. "That's what I like to hear, soldier. And please. Contact your father and I when you do?"

I nodded, and she ended the call.

Shouts suddenly came from overhead. It sounded like Nathaniel, his heavy footsteps thunderous. He wasn't calling out warnings, by the sound of it. He was laughing jovially. I went to the door and stepped out as the others followed me to the outer deck.

"There we are!" Nathaniel guffawed when I spotted him at the helm above us, the breeze ruffling the large man's black hair. He was looking out at the horizon through a brass spyglass, and nudged Aiden in the ribs beside him. "Y'ahmelle Nayû. *Seventeen* days of voyage. I win, feather head."

Aiden took the spyglass with a click of his tongue. "Damn it all."

"Teach ye to question a seasoned sailor," Nathaniel preened, his bearded lips curling into a smirk. "T'aint no one better to navigate these seas than me."

"Ah, yes, how could I forget?" Aiden quipped. "You were quite the *ship merchant* when you were alive, weren't you?"

Nathaniel had a suspicious spark in his eye. "What's yer tone about, fluff-fer-brains?"

"Oh, I'm just prattling." Aiden laced his fingers and cupped the back of his head. "Though, you really ought to remember: I was still around when you were alive."

"Ye said ye was dead by then?"

"Oh, I was. But I'd been bound to my first *Da'torr* and brought to the surface." His voice turned mischievous. "I *had* thought you looked familiar when *Da'torr* Lucas brought you in… And now I've finally remembered why. Does *The Terror at Port Riffcult* ring a bell?"

Nathaniel stiffened, prompting a chuckle from Aiden. "Thought so!" Aiden clapped his hands. "What you didn't know was that my *first* master died there. That very night. I only caught a short glimpse of you then, but I distinctly remember the face of the legendary Captain Bl—*gleght!*"

Nathaniel grabbed the bird's throat, his other hand bursting into flames as the bear evoked his fire Hallows, the smell of burnt flesh permeating. *"Shut yer Gods damned mouth, storm-rat,"* rumbled Nathaniel.

Aiden's laughter intensified, though it was choked under the bear-shifter's grip. "N-now, now…!" Aiden's voice tightened under his fellow vassal's fingers, dropping the spyglass with a *thunk* as he reached up to try and wrench away Nathaniel's arms. It was a contest of strength that he wouldn't win. "Why the hos…tility? Two hundred years was… so long ago! We're… comrades now! Through and through!"

"If I catch that beak 'a yers squawkin'a word to *Da'torr*, I'm gon'ta tear out yer insides 'n shove 'em down yer throat like chicken feed! Ye hear me, birdie? 'N when yer resurrected again, me thinks I'll rip off yer…!"

While the details of Aiden's future disembowelments were extrapolated, and Dalen's and Vendy's ghosts floated up to try and calm them, I felt a tug at my soul. Alexander wanted to switch. I allowed him outside as I was dragged into the psyche, the cool wind vanishing from my face. The ship was sucked away and replaced with blackness, save for the window that was Alexander's view.

I watched as he climbed to the upper deck where the two were quarreling and he snatched the spyglass Aiden had dropped. He lifted the glass to an eye, and my window's view was amplified. Only the dark, lapping waters were visible, spraying in the breeze and glistening under the silver moonlight. There were storm clouds brewing from the west, creeping toward us as the sounds of our sails snapped and whipped, the winds picking up. Alexander swept the spyglass across the horizon, my brother hurrying to find the piece of land Nathaniel had mentioned.

"There!" I called. The lens froze in place, and in the distance was a blooming, quivering light. *"It must be a lighthouse,"* I said.

"Finally." His tone was anxious, his gaze lingering on the flickering, orange beacon.

Jaq's footfalls clunked up the steps then, and we found the viper making his way toward us. "Find it?" asked Jaq, taking the spyglass to see for himself. "Where?"

Alex pointed, squeezing our friend's shoulder. "Just there. That beacon."

Jaq whistled, the eyepiece softly *clink*ing against his spectacles. "Bloods, it's small. How far is it?"

Alex turned to the squabbling vassals, making them cease their banter, though Nathaniel was still strangling Aiden. "How long until we reach the shore?" called Alex.

Nathaniel kept hold of Aiden's throat and absently glanced at the horizon, thinking. "Me thinks half an hour, or…" He trailed off, looking at the hand wrapped around Aiden's neck. I noticed even from the psyche that his fingers were growing morbidly pale, veins bulging from under his thinning skin. Aiden also seemed to notice the bear's sagging face, his *own* head looking more skeletal as his feathers began to molt like he was sickly.

Nathaniel grumbled. "Bloody Death."

He and Aiden deteriorated to bones, which clattered against the floorboards. When their bodies decayed, their ghosts were released and floating on either side of the helm.

"Damn," Nathaniel cursed. "Resurrection's done. Say lads, can ye take the helm fer me?"

Alex trotted over and gripped the wheel. Then he hesitated. "So, er… how exactly do you use this?"

Nathaniel's specter motioned to pat us on the back, but his hand fuzzed through without contact. The ghost didn't seem to notice, nor mind, and laughed. "Wide stance there, lads, square with yer shoulders. See, the helm controls the ship's rudder at the stern, so ye want to be sure to…"

Nathaniel gave us instructions and Alex did his best to follow, but every foreign term Nathaniel spit out was lost in context. I couldn't remember half the words he used, let alone knew their meanings. We Grimlings were a peoples bound to caverns all our lives. What little sailing we'd experienced was in Grim's straits, whose waters were freezing and whose tides were far more piteous compared to these surface waves.

"…That be why I had all a ye runnin' about tyin' up the sails, climbin' the masts and all," Nathaniel continued with his lesson.

Alex was focused on keeping the wheel steady, but flicked his eyes at the vassal. "And scrubbing the deck for hours on end?" he asked.

Nathaniel motioned to swat our back again, phasing through a second time. "We don't want any 'a ye slippin', now do we?"

Dalen's ghost crossed his arms to our left. "Ya look like you're havin' fun, *Da'torr*."

"It is fun," Alex agreed in a chuckle. "Xavier, you should try this—"

"—Bloods, look at this mess!" Lilli clipped from the steps.

She and Willow ascended to join us, both dressed in loose trousers, laced boots and rather drab tunics, no doubt borrowed from the many abandoned trunks that the original passengers had left behind when we hijacked the ship.

Willow had lazily bundled her hair with the ribbon and bell. There were countless ashen strands sticking out in a frayed tangle along her back, but she neither seemed to notice nor care. For now, she was concerned about the pile of bones clustered at Alexander's feet. The princess knelt to a splintered femur, her Death mark gleaming and hands glowing with a black and purple light that surrounded the bone. She drew back her hand in a pulling motion, but was met with no reaction.

"Whose vessels are these?" she asked. "I can't stir them… are they vassals?"

Aiden's ghost hovered in front of her and gave a bow. "Those bones are ours, Highness. Sorry for the clutter, our resurrections have ended."

Lilli scowled at the tangled skeletons, then glared at us in disapproval. Alex had his hands on the helm, but shrugged. Without bothering to ask permission, she strutted over and snatched two of the four Storagecoffins that were fastened to Alexander's belt. She'd taken the empty ones, which had been beside Dalen's and Vendy's shrunken corpses in the remaining coffins.

"How irresponsible," she muttered, walking back beside Willow. She bent to help collect the bones by hand. "A good number of these pieces could slide overboard in the coming storm, Alex. Don't you remember the gale a few nights ago?"

Alex leaned an elbow on the helm and threw a thumb over at Jaq. "I remember him vomiting on us all night."

Jaq glared. "You weren't lookin' any less green, ya cocky bastard."

"He's right, *Da'torr*," Vendy agreed in a snort. "Ya were kissin' a bucket for most of the storm, too."

"Disgusting," Lilli scoffed and lifted what looked like a tiny finger bone from the floorboards. She stared at it intently, her nose scrunching.

Nathaniel's ghost came over with narrow lids. "What was that, missy?"

Lilli's bat wings tightened, glancing up at the offended specter, then she fanned a hurried hand over her collarbone. "Oh! Not this." She waved the small bone and shook her head. "It's all this talk of coughing up bodily fluids. It's making *me* queasy… is this piece yours, then? It's difficult to tell in this mess."

"Aye." Nathaniel sounded more at ease now. "That one be mine."

She set the finger bone aside to separate it from the rest of the pile. She and Willow continued to work with the two ghosts to discern which piece belonged to whom. It was a long, tedious task, what with the number of pieces the average shifter possessed. Normally, it would take a mere minute to complete this with death Hallows. But if they were vassals of another Necrovoker, well, who could tell how long it would take by hand?

The cabin door squealed open from the deck below, and Zyl's spritely cheers blurted. "Ees land! Land, land!" She came flapping out and Alex and I watched her perch on the rail down there, putting a flattened hand at her brow as if it would help her see better in the dark. "Ah! Small speck be land?"

El ran to see for herself, the hybrid's blue-and-white wings fluttering. She mimicked Zyl's pose and gazed out at the horizon.

"*Kcheftpa!*" El sang excitedly, wings lifting along with her toes. "*Glittey! Luli luli...!*"

"We found land?" Octavius asked after peeking his head out from the door next.

Neal shoved him from behind to clear the way and trotted to the rail in a thrilled laugh. "Finally!"

Octavius muttered something I couldn't hear and looked about the deck, his eyes stopping at us from our place at the helm. "Aw, what?" He went up the steps, exasperated. "How long have you been steering? Do the rest of us get..."

His breath flew out of him when he saw the pile of bones the girls were rummaging through at his feet. He drew back. "The Void is this?"

Alex's hand came into view from my window as he waved at Octavius encouragingly. "A minor issue, it's being tended to. Did you wish to try the wheel?"

Octavius's stare was glued to the skeletal heap. "Uh... yeah..."

Alex stepped back in an offering gesture and Octavius tiptoed around the bones, taking the helm. Alex nodded for Nathaniel's ghost to come over. "Nathaniel, I'll help the girls finish. Why don't you instruct Octavius?"

The ghost floated over to give Octavius the lesson, but Jaq interjected that he'd been waiting longer. The two fought for the wheel and Neal soon ran up after seeing what they were doing. He wanted a turn as well. They all ended up sharing different hand-grips, muttering curses and battling for elbow space.

Alex shook his head, leaving them to figure it out and went to crouch beside Willow and Lilli with the clutter of bones. He began gathering the ivory pieces, swiftly dropping them into the separate Storagecoffins sitting on the floorboards. In a matter of minutes, the skeletons were stored in their rightful coffins, though in a rather disorganized fashion. He took the newly filled containers and strapped them onto his belt once more for safekeeping. We were to return them to Master and Mistress when next we saw them.

Herrin stepped out to the deck then, his wings fidgeting eagerly. "Did I hear right? We found land?"

"We did." Alex pushed to his feet and descended the steps to meet the lanky scholar. "Are the others awake?"

Herrin shrugged. "Don't know. I went straight for the door."

Alex's eyes drifted to the thick, leather-bound *Choir* book Herrin had tucked under his arm, and he hummed. "Do you *sleep* with that thing in hand?"

Herrin's freckled cheeks flushed, holding the book close to his chest. "It… it's a really old text. Super fragile. I want to make sure it stays in good condition for when I return it."

"Return it to whom?"

Herrin glanced sidelong at the ocean. "The… person who gave it to me?"

Alex sighed and shifted his weight. "When do we hear what all the fuss is about with that thing? You said it had new stories?"

"Technically, *old* stories." His expression brightened as he lifted the tattered thing. "This is one of the *original* editions of the *Choir*. Everything we've read from our era has been watered down, edited, and censored to the point that the history we've been taught was completely rewritten to fit the new versions. This…"

Herrin stared in awe at the cover, his voice quivering with thrill. "This answered almost every question I had on the Relicbloods' history. There were so many holes in those stupid renditions, too many biased views… no one knew what happened to the original versions. Everyone assumed they were so old that they deteriorated. But they were hidden, the whole damned time." He smirked wickedly. "And I have one. I Bloody *have* one. I wonder if she'll let me keep it…"

Alex's brow furrowed. "She?"

"Oh, the, uh, person who lent it to me."

"And she asked to remain anonymous, I take it?"

Herrin licked his lips. "Well, no… she actually didn't give me much to go by—*hey!*"

Alex swiped the book and flipped through the pages curiously. "Where do the extra sections come in? Or is the whole thing different?"

"D-don't!" Herrin reached for the text, but Alex swerved and swept it away. "Give it back…!"

Alex muttered and flipped another page, squinting in the lamplight by the wall. "You keep blabbering on about how amazing this book is, I want a look myself."

"You can't!" His voice fractured a note. "I mean, you—you might get the pages wet! Look, just give it back, it's not even mine…!"

Alex sidestepped the teenager again, turning to a new page. "You'll get it back. I only want to see what you've been… on about…"

Alex ceased his flipping at a bookmarked chapter labeled: *The Legend of the Shadowblood*. He lifted the book to his nose. "What in Death?"

From the psyche, I saw the page held some sort of drawing. A very *familiar* drawing.

Filled with watercolor paints and outlined in grey ink was a grey-haired young man with sapphire eyes, a black tri-leaf of diamonds on the backs of both hands.

It was the Crest of Nirus. The same mark my brother and I were born with.

Herrin jerked the book out of my brother's stiffened fingers and thumped it shut. He cringed when Alex gave him a haunted look. "Herrin?" Alex began, breaking the silence. "How old did you say that book was?"

Herrin swallowed. "Two... thousand, or so...?"

"Then why did that drawing look like... well, like..."

Herrin shrank away. "There m-might be something you guys should know..."

Alex growled. "And *what* is that?"

Herrin bit his lip, taking a deep breath. "Okay, so... you know how I mentioned it had parts of history that were missing? There's kind of, sort of, maybe something that mentions... *you*..."

"Death's Head there is." Alex snorted. "Is that what all this is about? The drawing? Is that the reason King Dream's been pushing people onto us?"

Herrin coughed into a fist. "Yes and no?"

"The Death does that... who gave you this book, Herrin? I swear to Bloods, if Dream was behind this again—"

"He wasn't," Herrin assured, but shrank even further. "It was his wife..."

Alex kicked the wall, causing the lamplight to quiver. "For the love of...! I'm really starting to hate that family... Herrin?" He shot the bird a testy glare. "What *exactly* does that book say?"

"You should wait until you're both back to normal..."

"Now Herrin."

"O-okay!" he squeaked, shakily opening the book. "Uhm, so there's this... *theory*, we'll call it..." The breath caught in his throat when a shadow loomed over us.

Kurrick stood there, livid in the dim lamplight. The warrior jerked the book out of Herrin's fingers and flung it over his shoulder with such force, it launched past the ship's railing and *splashed* into the ocean.

"No!" Herrin screamed and rushed to fly after it, disappearing under the bow.

"Bloody pest," Kurrick snarled. He stabbed a finger at us. "You. You do not receive answers until I approve it."

Alex ground his teeth, wolf ears growing. "And when will that be, O Lord of Everyone's Gods' Damned Business?"

Kurrick glowered at us, then strode to the upper deck. Alex hustled after him.

"Kurrick!" Alex trotted up the steps and slid in front of the warrior, startling the others, who still hovered around the helm. "Your 'lost heir' isn't the only reason you started following us, is it? What are you not telling us? Why is Dream sending people to us with promises we can't fulfill?"

"Because Dream has far too much confidence in you," he said, his teeth sharpening. "Confidence that you are undeserving of."

"Bloody Death..." Alex massaged his temple. "Can you go a single sentence without the cryptic bullshit? And for another thing, whatever your expectations of us are, we obviously didn't set them ourselves."

He stared hard at us, perhaps considering. "True; expectations were brought on by another. But they are there, regardless. Too much responsibility rests on them, and if you cannot meet the demands, then I must find someone who will better provide that protection for Anabelle."

Alex paused. He craned to look past Kurrick, seeing Miss Ana had come out from the cabin and had crouched beside a drenched-looking Herrin on the lower deck. The bird was grieving over his ruined book, some pages so soaked they'd shredded out of the binding altogether and sopped into a disheveled mess on the floor.

"Anabelle?" Alex echoed, turning back to the warrior. "You're looking for someone to protect your servant girl—?"

"Kurrick," a small voice whispered from the steps. Ana had come to the upper deck to meet us. Her crimson eyes were disappointed, brown lion ears folded. Her voice was gentle, yet scolding. "For what reason had you destroyed our Enlightener's holy text?"

Kurrick kept his back to her, scowling at his feet. "It was not yet time to..."

"I will decide when it's time. It is not for you to assess. You had no right to cause grief for our Enlightener. Apologize at once."

Kurrick bristled. "I do not owe an apology to that craven—"

"Kurrick," she hushed. "That was not a request."

He lingered for a moment, his fists tight at his sides. Then grudgingly, he marched past her and down the steps. Bloody Void, the brute *kneeled* before Herrin.

"Forgive me... Enlightener." Kurrick chewed on the words, his glower so dark the flickering lamp could barely brighten it. "It was not my place to disrespect you. I shall... request a replacement from Her Majesty Dream, if you desire..."

Herrin squirmed. Even *he* seemed at a loss for words, as the rest of us were.

Alex leaned closer to Ana, murmuring. "How did you get him to do that?"

She gazed sadly at Kurrick. "I am sorry for his behavior. He often struggles with diplomacy. It is an ongoing obstacle he has yet to master... Though,

I suspect his recent stress stems from the ticking moments that pass by us each day. It must be bearing down his poor soul. His duties seem to be the only thing he… cares for now…" She pried her eyes from him, her face sagged with hurt.

Alex hesitated. "Miss Ana… What was in that book?"

Ana sighed and lowered her gaze. When she glanced at us again, she—

Froze.

Ana's feet glided her to the railing, and she stared at the glowing beacon of the steadily growing island. Her voice was hollow. "Smoke…?"

Alex moved beside her to look himself. Yes, she was right. Black smoke curled from the island in the closing distance, light blooming within the darkness, the beacon raging in the night.

But it was no beacon. It was no lighthouse. Bloods be good, Y'ahmelle Nayû was in flames.

51

UP IN FLAMES

~~~~~~~

XAVIER

Alex gripped the rail, horrified by the blazing city in the distance. "What's happened…?"

"*No…!*" I watched the glowing fire from the psyche, the smoke thickening as the storm winds billowed. I tore my hand through the portal, a flurry of ripples spreading over the discus, and leapt out to take Alexander's place. The spiced wind licked my face the moment all senses came rushing back, but my focus latched on the island. "No, no, no, no, *no!*"

The cabin door behind us burst open, and Ringëd came panting outside. He was covered in sweat, his azure Dream mark shining from his shoulder.

"*Teivelle…!*" he bellowed. His heavy heels thumped up the steps, shoving me aside to watch the flames. "*Teivelle! Tooven…! Tu irann! Tu irann…!*"

His Dream mark gleamed brighter, his eyes glazed in tears as he fell to his knees, sobbing. Mikani came from the cabin, rushing to her husband. "Ringëd?" Her hand quivered as she touched his back. "What's wrong?"

"*Min Teivelle!*" he yelled at the burning docks. "*Min Tooven…! Cesset… cesset rollglëce…*"

He was only speaking in that tongue now, his mind elsewhere. Mikani shook him, but he wouldn't stop his foreign chattering. She gave him a sharp slap. "Ringëd, knock it off! I can't understand you!" He collapsed into her bosom, sniveling like a scared child as he held her tight, still babbling.

The ghosts floated over to watch him, and Willow's eyes began to water, a hand held to her mouth. Though his voice was strained and gasping, I caught enough of Ringëd's Marincian blubbering to understand him. My fists balled.

"How…?" I whispered. "We're so far from Everland…"

Mikani was still panicked, looking to me for help. "What is he saying?"

"His mother and father are fleeing for their lives," I said, hushed. "The city's been overrun…"

"With Necrofera," Linus finished, suddenly coming from behind her. The goat's own Dream mark was shining, his eyes staring out at the flames. "It's a slaughter… an absolute slaughter. Their queen is there. The Pyrovoker."

"Why is *she* here?" I demanded.

"She must have known we were coming," growled Alex from the psyche.

"How?!" I slammed a fist on the rail. "Why does this keep happening? So close—we're *so Bloody close*…! We finally get this far and…!"

I hit the rail again, shaking. Somewhere on that burning island was my body. A body that would soon be dead, by the looks of it. Dead with however many others lay strewn across the streets.

Linus crouched beside Ringëd and clapped a hand on the human's shoulder. "Your parents are safe, Ringëd," Linus said. "They are with the survivors, who fled to a storm shelter underground. We can find them there."

Ringëd looked bleary eyed at the goat. "You're sure?"

"Yes. I'm Seeing them now. They're praying to Rin with the others… but there are very few survivors."

I grabbed Linus's arm. "And… my body? Am *I* there? Am I still alive?"

Linus's eyes drifted for a moment, his Dream mark gleaming at my touch. He let out a relieved breath. "Yes. You've been moved with the rest of them. Alive."

I bent over my knees and puffed out the terror. "Thank the Gods!"

"But the Fera may find the shelter, if nothing is done soon," Linus said. "There are too many entrances that aren't well hidden."

Ringëd shoved to his feet, wiping his eyes with a ratty sleeve. "Then let's go. I have to get my parents out of here. I know the shelter you're talking about, there's another entrance near the shoals to the east—"

A shrill scream cut him off.

It was Oliver, who'd sprinted outside and tripped up the steps. The child's face was drenched in tears and snot as the Dream mark on his neck gleamed. The owl fumbled back to his feet and went to hug Lilli's leg. "M-Mama!" he wailed, wings twitching with fright. "We gotta dive! Mr. Treble won't listen—tell him we *gotta*!"

Claude, who I assumed had been watching over the boy, came huffing after him from the cabin. "Land, kid, will you slow down? What is going…" He froze, seeing the island.

The others filed out to see what the noise was about. Zyl and El withdrew their strung bows, and Bianca shoved through the doorway.

"Holy Death," Bianca whispered, trotting to Jaq, who stood by the rail with a hand clasped to his mouth.

Matthiel ran out next, bumping into Zyl. He rubbed his nose and blinked, baffled, but when his gaze caught the devastation, he couldn't pry his legs from the floorboards. "Sorrowed Nira…!" Matthiel gasped. "What's happened?"

I felt Alex wanting to take over, and he dragged me inside the psyche. I watched as he reached for the two Storagecoffins on his belt. "Dalen, Vendy, we want you resurrected before we land. We can't revive Aiden or Nathaniel, but the less exposed spirits we have to look after, the better—"

SKRIRIRIRIRIRIRIRIRI!!

The shriek made us cringe, and the boat lurched. It was a challenge to keep a stable footing, everyone dodging crates and tables that slid across the deck. Everyone hurried to cling to whatever they could find, Alex seizing a thick rope dangling from the masts.

One by one, skeletal beasts emerged from the sea and crawled onto our boat. Fishtails flopped and slithered with tar-like ichor, finned ears dripping sickeningly. The things scurried for us, bringing water onto the slippery deck. Their tails transformed into dislocated legs as they rose, skulls cracking in unnatural angles.

"Everyone fall behind us!" Alex roared, plucking the scythe-spheres from his neck. The Fera shrieked and lunged for us, and we braced with our weapons drawn—

Kcrrrach-zap!

Everyone screamed, though the Fera hadn't struck. They'd stopped in their tracks and backed away the moment we were brought to our knees, an electric shock sparking over the water at our feet. The shocks spidered up our party's limbs, forcing them to drop their weapons…

Except Zyl. The bolts didn't seem to affect the Sky Princess, and she aimed her arrow at the crowd of demons, craning back to us in a panic. "What wrong?" Zyl panted, sweeping her aim over the horde.

Of course, I thought, remembering Zyl was an Astravoker. I'd nearly forgotten those with her Hallows couldn't be electrocuted. *But WHY are we being electrocuted? And how?*

Zyl yelped—and a frozen gust swept over her. Ice began to coat her wings, the frost wrapping her limbs, her bow and arrow encased in a rigid, lopsided block. She tried to move, electricity spewing from her hand within the ice, but only a tiny fracture came.

Alex grunted, trying to turn his head, but the movement was restricted with a sharp *zap!*

He strained to reach his scythes, cried out in pain, arm retracting at his sides. "What is this?" He demanded.

Then, from his peripherals, I saw the blurry, green-winged figure of Rosette. Janson's Astravoking vassal. Her hands were sparking with the electric bolts that paralyzed us now, touching the water that pooled on the deck.

"Rosette?" Alex's brow furrowed, then twitched from the static. "What are you d-d-doing?"

Rosette's eyes welled, her green wings bowing solemnly. "Obeying orders."

"Orders?" Willow echoed behind us, incredulous. "Janson wouldn't tell you to do this!"

"I'm sorry," came Janson's voice above us. The Trixer touched down to join his vassal. His lone pupil, once a normal black, was now glowing and white, shining in the darkness. "I'm out of time." His voice quaked. "My queen has come."

There was silence. Alex stared at the man's glowing pupil. I cursed from the psyche. *"Is this what Chai was trying to tell us?"*

Alex's wolf ears curled back. "Gods damn it… We were right. There *was* something wrong with you."

"How long?" Willow's voice cracked behind us. "How long have you been Changed?"

Janson rolled back a shoulder, glancing away. He gave no answer.

"But then…" I heard her breath shudder, Jewel twittering behind us. *"You were the Sentient following me since Timberail…? You weren't helping me?"*

Janson's head bowed, staring at a ring wrapped on his finger. Hesitating, he slid the ring off, the scars on his face returning, and whispered, "I'm sorry."

"Traitor," Alex snarled. "You aren't our Brother. Even when dead, we wouldn't side with those beasts—"

"There are things about the Necrofera you don't understand, Clean One," he sneered, his glare sharpening. "I can't drag my feet anymore. Where is your brother, Howllord?"

Bolts sparked Alex's neck when he tried to move. "What does Cilia want with us?"

Janson snapped his fingers at Rosette. She increased voltage on Alexander's static. Alex screamed, and after a few seconds of intense shocking, Janson had his vassal pause.

"Where is your brother?" he asked again. The *traitor* looked round the deck, his one eye set in a nasty scowl. "He should have been here… Everyone else is." He kicked the cabin wall with a sharp *crack*, screaming, "Why are you never in the same place?!"

Alex's glare slitted, silent.

Janson turned to the shadows. "Nikolai!"

His Marincian vassal meekly stepped into the light. "*Da'torr...?*"

"See if anyone's in the cabin and bring them out! Find the brother!"

Nikolai sighed, his head bowed. From his scaled hands spewed fogging ice, which crystalized as he summoned his Glaciavoking, creating a spear of ice.

Nikolai gripped his icy staff and started toward the cabin door, but he hesitated, twisting back to Janson. "*Da'torr...*" Nikolai began, "you no have to do this. We can—"

"I won't let her shove either of you down my throat!" Janson roared, his skin flickering with black sludge, his one good eye wide and wild. "*Find him!*"

Nikolai jolted at the command, his limbs forced to life, and he stumbled into the cabin.

"You're not going to find him," Alex spat. "We can't be seen together."

Janson glared, turning to his winged vassal. "Rosette."

Alex screamed when the electric shocks increased again, forcing him back to the floor. He rolled on his side, fighting against the sparks, but the bolts rose again and brought a crackled yell from him.

"Stop...!" I heard Willow shriek behind us. "Please, stop! What you ask for is impossible!"

Alex's torture ceased. My brother's gasps shuddered—and I was suddenly dragged out of the psyche, my throat sore and dry, muscles exhausted. Alex murmured a faint apology from my head as I uncurled myself, coughing over the flooded hardwood. It was hard as Void to swallow.

When I lifted my dizzy head, I was surprised I could move again. Then I noticed Janson wasn't looking at me. Willow was still locked in place from the bolts, like the others.

"Please," Willow begged, sparks snapping from her shoulder when she tried to move. "They *can't* be seen together. It's impossible."

"Why?" Janson demanded. "I've seen both of them walking around this ship. I know they're both here."

Willow's tone turned vicious, her fox ears curling back in a growl. "You know so little... Cilia will only get half of what she wants. You deserve whatever punishment she gives you."

Janson's fists balled, a snarl rumbling. Then his gaze dropped to me, and he blinked. "What in Death...?" He started toward me. "Your eyes changed..."

Damn it! I scuttled away, reaching for the scythes Alex had dropped—

The electric bolts returned twofold, and my muscles tightened. I curled into an agonizing ball, gasping in pain.

Janson loomed over me. "I could have sworn they were just..."

I could feel Alex tugging at my soul urgently, wanting to switch. *But if we changed now...* I focused all my will power to keep him in the psyche, bearing through the resulting migraines. Switching a second time in front of Janson would give ourselves away faster... Even though I wished to Death to be rid of the pain.

"You..." I seethed, my jaw aching. "You weren't... paying attention..."

Janson's lids narrowed. "I wonder..." He drew out his staved scythe, aiming the crook at my lowered neck. "What will happen when I cut open this one? How many souls will come out?" Janson lifted the blade and threw it down.

—a large *crash* came from the sea when an enormous wave washed over the deck, and with the water came a man's hurtling figure. The stranger swooped onto the ship and slammed shoulder-first into Janson, who toppled to the floor in a startled clatter. The newcomer had his back to me, silhouetted shoulders hefting as he rose from his crouch.

My eyes strained in the dim moonlight, our lamp having been snuffed from the wave. I noticed an odd, ghostly glow radiated from the long trident in the stranger's hand. It was from that faint gleam that I could see the terror contorting Janson's face as he gazed upon the newcomer.

Janson shook on the floor, scrambling back with a tight voice. "N-n-no...!" He flipped to his stomach and scampered on all fours, his wings going limp, looking like a heavy weight was pulling him down. He dropped to his elbows and knees in a sudden wail, but still he crawled toward the railing. "Please... please...!"

He choked off and gave a piercing screech, throwing up his head and clutched his temples. He squeezed so tight, his talons dug into his skin and dripped with blackened blood.

"Stop...!" Janson was sobbing now, roaring, "Let me go...! To Void with you Gods damned beasts! I don't belong to any—!"

The stranger plunged his trident into Janson's head.

Janson shrieked and squirmed while pinned to the floor, his head leaking black ink. He flailed under the stranger desperately. The surrounding, smaller beasts scurried overboard in fright, vanishing with many splashes into the sea.

We were all released from Rosette's paralyzing sparks when she dropped her hands with a gasp, then took flight and rushed for the stranger pinning down her *Da'torr*.

"Stay back!" Janson managed to scream at her, thrusting a taloned hand toward her. "Keep away! He... he's like *her*...!"

The new man was tall and lean, with finned, navy-blue hair that waved down to his shoulders. His bare back was coated in scars, appendages pointed with sharp, shark-like fins fused to his skin. From the deck's rail, a thin, serpentine creature slithered onto the man's arm and wrapped round his bicep, giving a soft, "*Aaahn!*"

I blinked at the creature, recognizing it. *The Bindragon? From weeks ago? Did it belong to this man...? Then*, I realized, *has this stranger been following us?*

"What have we here, Aahn?" rasped the man, his voice a deep, gritty twang wavering with a subtle Marincian accent. "It seems the newborn threatens to break my rule."

The Bindragon gave a carefree *Aaahn* from his bicep, its head cocking. The man's spindly legs bent over Janson. Then he dug his fingers *into* the Sentient's brow.

Janson wailed when the shark-man ripped out a black piece of sludge and stared at it musingly, turning the squirming ooze between his fingers.

"Ah. Cilia's Mark." His accent flowed smoothly like spoken water. "I should have guessed."

Janson lay still on the floor, his head pinned by the trident, blinking dumbly. The newcomer rose and strode to the edge of the ship. He held up the sludge. "Poor tidings, Queen Cilia of Everland. This is Demon King Hecrûshou, of Marincia's western seas. I am displeased to inform you that you've crossed my territory and have broken our treaty. Be ready, Cilia. Your Cleansing awaits."

He tossed the ink blot into the waves and turned to us, his white pupils blazing in the night.

The shark man's face was traced in scars along his high cheekbones and sharp chin, and his white pupils gleamed in the darkness as he plucked his glowing trident out of Janson's head.

"So, little newborn," the Sentient hummed, his Bindragon, Aahn, curling from his bicep to peek at Janson curiously. "How does freedom feel?"

"F... Free...?" Janson quivered and reached a hand to his brow, falling quiet. He seemed to be listening for something. "She's gone..." Janson started laughing, pushing to his feet and rushed over to embrace Rosette. "She's Bloody *gone!* Nikolai, return! We've been—"

Willow and I blocked his path, our newly retrieved weapons shoved at his throat.

"Brother Janson," Willow growled, her scythe's crook wrapping around his neck. "You've broken countless laws of our realm, as well as gone against our creed. Your betrayal has written your sentence."

"Now, now," the other Sentient demurred, striding to us. "The newborn had no control of himself. That sentence is hardly fair without a trial, don't you think, Aahn?"

"*Aaahn!*" cried the Bindragon, as though agreeing. "*Aaahn! Aaahn!*"

Matthiel, Jaq and Lilli came forward to block his way, scythes glowing at the beast's slender throat.

"Fera aren't granted a trial," Matthiel sneered. "They're only to be exterminated and sent to Nira."

The shark sighed—and darted around them in a blur, swatting Willow's scythe away, and snatched Janson by his neck collar.

"You Reapers have always had a biased view on justice." The shark set Janson down and propped his trident on his shoulder. "You refuse to accept there are some of us who do not crave souls."

My brow furrowed, looking at the others behind me. I was met with equally confused gazes. Save for Zyl, who was too busy jabbering in Culatian to El—who was using her Pyrovoking to thaw the ice over the Sky Princess's limbs.

"But you're a demon," I protested. "All you care about is gaining power."

"That is merely a means by which to *get* what we care about," he snorted. "It is a tool. Not our primary objective."

Willow kept her scythe steady in front of her. "Then what do Sentients seek?"

"What do the living seek?" He held up his hands, palms raised to the sky. "Does any shifter share personal goals with another? Not always. It is the same for the Necrofera."

Willow sounded impatient now. "Then what is *your* objective?"

He dug the butt of his glowing trident into the hardwood, and Aahn slithered down his arm to wrap around the staff instead. "To exterminate the demons who break my law. I am Hecrûshou, Lord of the rotten beasts who live in these waters. I have no tolerance for those who kill innocents. I only accept the consumption of criminals. Eating souls of the clean hearted is strictly prohibited in my domain. All who disobey are eliminated, or, in the case of a Sentient, brought to trial. Such as *this* newborn will be."

He turned to Janson, humming while studying the crow. "Well, little newborn, I find myself in a bit of a predicament. Cilia has broken the treaty we'd arranged a few centuries prior and crossed my lands to kill and feast. She seems to have built a little army, and she and I are of equal power. Killing her will not be simple. I will need assistance. Though, I doubt there is much you can do, being so terribly weak… but I think your pet corpses may be useful. Will you aid me in killing your former mistress?" He held his trident to Janson's chest. "Or be Cleansed by the Mother Goddess?"

Janson's face darkened, and hardly a second passed before he answered, "You can do with me as you will after we kill the bitch."

The shark grinned, set down his trident and turned to us. "Good answer. Now, as for you all: I couldn't help but overhear you need safe passage to a particular shelter on the island."

He hopped overboard, then a large wave lifted from the sea, allowing him to step waist-deep inside. His hands were glowing green as his emerald Ocean mark brightened on his bare chest.

"*An Aquavoker*," Alex murmured from my thoughts.

Once his legs were submerged in the water, they fused together and created a smooth, wavering shark tail, and he gestured for us to follow. "Come along. I expect you all to protect the people of the island. The Marincian Reapers are not faring well against her."

Willow's grip tightened on her scythe beside me. "Do you expect us to trust a Sentient?"

"No." He waved his glowing-green hands—and an enormous wave rose behind the ship, towering, looming, wavering as if it were a colossal creature with a mind of its own, poised to strike. "I expect you to trust Cilia *less*."

He brought his hands down, and the massive wave thrust against the ship, all of us screaming as we were hurtled toward land.

CILIA

A small piece of black sludge slithered over the beach to my foot. It crawled up my leg, to my waist and finally my torso before making its way to my brow, where it sank through the pores. A familiar voice hit my mind with a message of death.

My face crinkled, muttering, "Hecrûshou."

Macarius's phantom-copy raised an eyebrow beside me, turning away from the burning village. "What was that?"

"Hecrûshou has come for me. I'd hoped it would be the weaker boy..." My cat ears grew and curled back. "Damn that fish. This changes things."

Macarius frowned. "Whom do you speak of exactly?"

"Hecrûshou is the Demon King of the western seas," I explained in a growl. "We're in his territory."

"There are other royal Fera?" He seemed more curious than concerned. Foolish, in these circumstances. But then, I supposed *he* had nothing to fear. Macarius wasn't physically here to begin with.

"There aren't many of us," I admitted. "Only nine, last I was aware."

His arms folded, looking fascinated. "I'll have to ask you about those other monarchs later... Will this Hecrûshou be a problem?"

"A great problem. I've met him quite a few times. He's an odd one, but powerful. We were killed around the same era. He's just as old, and just as strong."

"Do you think you can take care of him?"

My claws drew. "I suppose we'll find out. We at least have the advantage of an army with us... Maveric." My gaze shot to the Sentient Healer, who cowered at my glare. "Prepare the beasts. We're about to see if I've shoved enough souls into your stomach to be useful here."

Maveric sprinted into the burning city to do as ordered. *It won't be enough*, I glowered to myself. *Hecrûshou may actually be my end.*

I dug my heels in the wet sand. *But not before I remember who HE is. Be prepared, Hecrûshou. I will not die easily.*

52

FOUND

WILLOW

The ship crashed against the sandbank, water spraying as the bow crunched against jagged rocks. I coughed up seawater and let go of the rope I'd gripped so hard, it was a wonder my fingers didn't crack straight off my knuckles.

Jaq bent over to retch, moaning over the deck beside Herrin, who'd been tangled in a net and was suffering the same queasiness. Dalen's ghost hovered over the scholar in concern, and I found Aiden and Nathaniel checking on the Treble family. Vendy's ghost floated to the twins to check on them, hopping in worried circles and demanding they resurrect her for backup. The twins obliged and revived her corpse from the Storagecoffin at their belt, the rabbit quickly unsheathing her Crystal sword.

Zylveia had taken flight to avoid the tidal wave alongside El, and they were now flying down with Lilli. Oliver was clutched in my Aide's arms and crying.

Sir Janson hadn't been so quick to jump off.

The Sentient had been thrown against the cabin wall and pinned by heavy crates, his wings crushed behind him. He shoved off the crates and allowed his bones to pop back into place, slithering with tar-like blood and mending. It looked painful, but I knew something as trivial as boxes wouldn't kill him.

A shame. I glowered, fox ears curling as I glared at Janson. The betrayer. The demon. How foolish I'd been to trust him! He wasn't our Brother—not anymore. He'd only pretended to care so he could bring the twins to Cilia. *I... I should have heeded Xavier's warning.*

I thought to ready my scythe, to end him here and now, but I'd dropped my weapon when that wave thrust us to shore. I scanned the ship and found my scythe across the deck, running over to pick it up—

"*Aaahn!*" that little Bindragon purred as it curled around my staff, happily oblivious to his surroundings. "*Aaahn?*"

I growled, ignoring the dragon, and snatched my staff off the deck. I stalked toward Janson, fury bubbling. But I was pulled back when Xavier took my shoulder. "Are you all right?" He asked.

He was staring at my forehead. Confused, I touched two fingers there, and they came back sticky with warm blood. *Had I hit my head?* "I'll be fine." I said, turning to the ship's bow.

Splashing onto the boat from an isolated wave was that shark shifter—Hecrûshou—whose tail touched the rail and slowly shifted into bare, smooth legs when the wave withdrew over the deck. The Bindragon gave a happy cheer and slithered down my staff onto the floorboards, crawling to Hecrûshou and wrapping around his bicep. The Demon King didn't protest, standing casually on the rail, staring past the rocky shoals at the burning city in the distance.

That Bloody Sentient! I scowled at the glowing trident resting on his shoulder. *It must be made with Spiritcrystal.* No other material gave off such a light. *How dare that demon pretend to do our work?*

Smoke plumed from the charring buildings in the city, the haze thick and peppered, stretching even here at shore.

"The air has become a bit dry," Hecrûshou murmured to himself, annoyed. His gaze drifted to the billowing clouds above, the rumble of thunder muffled within them. He pivoted to the Sky Princess and her Aide. "You two—the storm-brewers! This may sound difficult, but do you think you can keep focused enough to force that nimbus here faster than its current schedule? And no, this will not be play-time, if you even know such a concept."

Zylveia's red eyes brightened with offense, her wings flapping. "Of course we know what means, dumb fish! We not *Galect!*"

"Not *Galect!*" El echoed at her side.

Hecrûshou gave an unimpressed hum. "Splendid. If you will please go off and bring us that storm, we can douse this fire quickly. I may be able to draw out the moisture in the air with Aquavoking, but I have little skill *producing* that moisture when it's gone. The smoke is too drying now, and I can't bring the whole Bloody ocean with me, now can I?"

Zyl's nose crinkled. "Why we do what fish demon say?"

"Because if you don't," he said, "you and your lot may well be slaughtered by Cilia's pack. We haven't much time before this place is a giant pile of ash. Do your damned jobs as Sky Knights and bring us a shower!"

Zyl and El hesitated, but after glancing at the burning city, Zyl took flight into the storm clouds and El followed swiftly.

When the Stormchasers were gone, Hecrûshou sighed and rubbed his temples. "This will not be an easy battle. Damn that girl and her psychotic episodes… Newborn." He gestured for Janson to follow. "Come with me and bring your little corpse-puppets. It's time your mistress was stopped."

Janson flapped beside him with an eager grin, Rosette and Nikolai following obediently. "Lead the way."

Hecrûshou smiled. "Determination. A good thing to see when faced with a task such as this… Pray it helps." He nodded to Xavier and me next. "You will find the entrance to that shelter within the shoals. Look for an opening past the rocks. We will deal with Everland's rotten queen."

"Wait!" I stepped toward him. "You don't expect us to let you…!"

He and Janson hopped overboard and darted for the burning city. I thought to follow after—wanting to kill Cilia, and both of them with her—but Xavier grabbed my wrist.

"We'll deal with them later," he said. "We have more important things to take care of."

"You're damn right we do!" Ringëd shoved past us, climbing down the ship by a dangling rope. "I'm getting my parents out of this death trap!"

His feral ferret, Kurn, scuttled after him, pausing when the Bindragon slithered up to him curiously. The two ferals circled each other, cautious, but Kurn sniffed indifferently and crawled down the rope after Ringëd. Aahn followed him happily.

My head shook. *He's right.* I let my anger go in a breath. *Saving lives is more important than taking them.*

Seeing everyone else had filed down the rope after Ringëd, I hurried too, and stepped into the mucky shoals. The black birds flew to our shoulders—Chai being carried by Bianca up ahead, since his feathers still hadn't fully grown. Neal's raven, Ace, was on his shoulder. Jewel fluttered to my finger with concerned chirps, her wings buzzing in a blur to show her anxiety.

I hushed her gently, cupping my companion with a hand to shield her from the splashing water.

"I'm sorry, Jewel," I whispered to the songcrow. "I should have listened. You knew Janson was a Fera… Can you ever forgive me?"

Jewel twittered in scolding tones, fluttered to my face to rub against my cheek endearingly, then perched on my shoulder. I smiled, taking that as a conditional *yes*.

The waves were shallow, rising to my knees as we trudged into the forest of rocks. I was thankful I'd decided to wear these loose trousers. A skirt would have floated into an awkward mushroom in the water... not to mention, expose certain areas I'd rather not expose.

Ringëd led the way, since he claimed to know the entrance of the underground tunnels. Kurn was now riding the back of Aahn, swimming jovially in the water beside Ringëd's legs.

I waded next to Xavier—no, it was Alexander now—and Matthiel shoved his way beside me not long after. Miss Ana was being carried protectively by Kurrick. His face was set in a tense scowl as he looked over his shoulder like a rat walking into a trap that promised cheese. He acted as if her feet would rot off her ankles if they so much as touched the water.

He was muttering with Ana, something about how he didn't like demons coming and going as they pleased, how disastrous their civil disputes were...

"Their pretend 'kingdoms' are ridiculous anyway," he said, lion tail swishing furiously in the water. "These beasts and their unholy royals... setting their own laws as if their kind actually *had* the brains to follow them! Preposterous."

Splashing behind them, Linus gave a ponderous hum. "Perhaps you ought to consider a five-hundred-year-old Sentient's perspective? It must be an awfully dull life, walking around, never dying, eating the occasional soul, never having anyone but disgusting, slimy, illiterate beasts to talk to."

"You make a curious point," Ana considered quietly. "I suppose all souls seek some means of distraction, clean or rotten."

"A distraction that costs the lives of others," Kurrick growled, irritated. "It is childish behavior for century-old beings. Has living for so long done nothing for their conscience?"

Ana shifted in the warrior's arms, murmuring softly, "But this Hecrûshou seems to deviate from the norm, does he not? His laws sound more on the side of the Reapers."

"Hardly!" I scoffed, causing the lioness's ear to flick toward me. My arms crossed. "I must agree with Kurrick. You can't claim to fight the Necrofera and be one yourself. It doesn't make sense."

"But he *has* claimed to do so," Ana protested. "And he even departed to kill the queen."

"Perhaps he was lying."

"Perhaps. And perhaps not." Ana held a hand to Kurrick's chest to tell him to slow, and the Healer whispered to me. "Must all demons be condemned for being what they hadn't a choice in becoming, Princess? You yourself have said many times that your duties help even the Fera themselves, freeing them of their burdened life. Is this not true?"

I hesitated. "It... it is."

"Then is it not also true that, since their lives are seen as a burden, they may hate what they are and wish not to be monsters? Could this not cause them to create a personal vendetta against their own kind and seek their destruction as a means of atonement for the crimes they've committed? And you must admit, your rotten Reaper seemed more than willing to kill the mistress who had ordered your deaths. I do not think he wanted to obey her."

"Then why did he?" I demanded. *Didn't she see the contradiction? Why was she defending these fiends?*

Her head cocked, looped earring swinging. "Perhaps he had no choice but to follow her? There may be things about the demon world outside our knowledge."

"I…" Hang on. *Had that Demon King mentioned something about a 'Mark'? That sludge he'd pulled out of Janson's head?* After that thing was tossed overboard, Janson's behavior had changed drastically… and he'd stopped trying to kill us.

"I suppose it's possible…" I mumbled. *Could I have misjudged?* Did Janson really want us dead, or was he forced by Cilia?

"Then," Ana continued meekly, careful not to upset me. "Would it not benefit the Reapers' cause to have Sentients such as Hecrûshou fight alongside you? To tell you their secrets, set laws within the Fera societies that allow your knights to execute swifter action to exterminate the lesser creatures?"

I halted in the water. "Nira below." I glanced at Jewel on my shoulder, who twittered at me in consideration. "It… *would* be a great benefit if we knew more."

Shame flooded, so staggering I nearly backed into Alexander. *How could I have been so foolish?* I'd nearly forgotten my own Creed: *I'll let not actions souls once took deter me from my duty…* The line says nothing about the *state* of those souls. Clean or rotten, didn't everyone deserve fair consideration as well as scrutiny?

"I'd never even thought…" My voice was soft. "How could I have forgotten my own Creed?"

Ana clasped my shoulder, smiling. "You are young. There is time yet until you rule. Perhaps some things will change when that happens?"

"Yes… But the council will never agree to such a thing—and neither will Grim's citizens. The Everlanders already suspect us of working with the demons, if we *did* publicly, the reactions would be astronomically horrible."

Ana sighed. "I suppose. But perhaps one day, the world will see things differently."

"One day," I agreed solemnly, a hollow pit weighing down my stomach. "But not anytime soon…"

MATTHIEL

Her Highness and I walked together through the wet cavern with caution, our hands blazing with fire to provide light for our entourage in the dim tunnels.

That black haired, commoner cat—I couldn't remember her name—had her fire Hallows exposed for the same purpose as she sidled beside her new husband—whose name I *also* couldn't remember. We had too many people in our pack, I couldn't be expected to remember every blasted name.

Her husband was a local here, as I understood it. This had once been his home, or something of that nature. Scuttling at his feet was that feral ferret of his, and now wrapped around his ankle—which he tried in vain to kick off every few steps—was that demon king's little Bindragon. The thing seemed rather... stupid. It clung to his leg happily, without a care in the world, as if explosions weren't blasting above us.

The rest of our company covered the rear, the two cat brothers last and keeping an eye out for any unwelcomed Necrofera.

Alexander walked behind me. I could hear him muttering to himself again. *Who was he always talking to?* His two vassals were here, one ghost floating silently beside Lord Lucas's two specters and the other resurrected and stalking beside her *Da'torr* with a Spiritcrystal sword held at the ready. Which meant Alexander wasn't speaking to them through their mental connection. *I wonder, could he be talking with Xavier somehow?*

I blinked, suddenly realizing something. "Your Highness," I said to the Death Princess, "we've lost Xavier."

Her Grace glanced at me with dazzling, frosted eyes, searching for the right words. "He's... well, you'll have to trust me when I say he's still with us. Never you mind."

I glanced at the many faces of our company, still not spotting Xavier. I turned back to Her Highness. "I'm telling you, he's not here. He may have gotten separated at that last fork. Some of us should go back for him."

She sighed, exhaustion gleaning from the dark bags under her lids. "We're not going back because he's right here. It would be a waste of time."

"But what if he—"

"Matthiel, please. I don't have the patience to explain."

"Don't tell me he's found a way to disappear like a phantom?"

She groaned. "Don't be ridiculous."

"Then if you won't search for him, *I* will—"

"Matthiel," Alexander grunted, making me turn. He waved a finger at his mismatched eyes, like a patronizing parent to a toddler. "Look at me. Carefully."

My brow furrowed. "Why?"

"Just shut up and don't blink."

"But why..." I choked. His eyes had switched positions. Changed. Moved. Shifted—right before me, forcing my feet to a stop.

"I'm right here," Xavier—who had just seconds before been Alexander!—muttered. It sounded like his patience had ebbed. "I'm not lost, you clot, you don't have to go back for me. Now will you please keep moving?"

I stayed where I was, petrified. "What in Death?!"

"Xavier!" Willow gasped. "You can't just show him!"

"It doesn't matter anymore." Xavier shoved past us, running into my shoulder along the way. "According to Linus, my body is at the end of this tunnel. Being exposed won't make a difference if Alex and I return to normal."

Return to normal? I thought, bewildered. *What was he saying?* I snatched his arm. "What is going on? You... your eyes—"

The blue eye switched back to the right, *Alexander's* face dropping to a scowl. "They change when we do. You can only see because you have soul-sight."

They switched again, Xavier rolling his eyes. "Now that that's out of the way, could we continue on?"

He tugged his arm free and kept moving, determined to reach our destination. I was blinking dumbly, forcing my feet to follow. "But I... I don't understand. You and Alexander...?"

"Share a body." Xavier's tone was terse and dismissive. "For six Bloody years, my soul's been trapped in here, and there was nothing I could do about it. Until now. So, if you'll excuse me, Matthiel, I have a reunion to attend."

He sped ahead, pacing nervously. *Or was he excited?* I followed skeptically. "But—I—*how?*"

Willow shook her head beside me. "We'll explain at a later time."

From the back, there were murmurs of agreement. *So, they all knew about this and thought nothing of it?* I was still trying to wrap my head around the insanity, rubbing my temples. "But how can... How is it even possible?"

"We don't know," said Xavier. "One minute I was falling off a cliff, and the next, my soul had separated and moved to my brother."

"But..." I ran a frustrated, beguiled hand through my hair. "Your NecroSeam is still intact?"

He muttered, "Obviously."

"And your soul didn't rot?"

"Clearly."

"There has to be some reason for—"

My shoulder was seized by the cat father—er, what was his name?—who shook his head at me. "Maybe you can interrogate him some other time, kid? People are trying to focus on what's happening here and now."

I tore away. "But it's outrageous! Xavier, taking out his own Bloody soul without cutting his NecroSeam? And then placing it in another vessel? It's unheard of!"

Xavier narrowed an eye at me. "I never said *I* did it."

"Well, who else could have? You have the soul half of your split Hallows, you're the only Necrovoker alive who could have that sort of power."

That seemed to surprise him, and he slowed to face me. "The only Necrovoker... What in Death gave you that idea?"

I paused, not actually certain. Our old combat instructor's words came to mind, something Sir Gail had said years ago in the palace training room...

"Those twins are prodigies in their own right," Sir Gail had said. *"And someday, they may very well become the strongest Necrovokers to ever live."*

That's right, I'd forgotten that day. I knew back then they were strong, infuriatingly so, but... could Xavier really do something as unthinkable as... whatever this was?

Xavier gave up waiting for my response and continued forward. "Regardless... I have yet to repeat the Evocation. Even if I can pull out my soul again, what if I can't place it back into my vessel? Even ghosts with temporary Seams can't just walk into their risen bodies. They need a Necrovoker to sew them to it... a Necrovoker who's already *in* a body, to serve as a medium for his Hallows."

"Well," I hesitated. "What if you practiced on someone *else* first?"

He gave me a crinkled glance. "Why would I do that?"

"Why?" I was almost laughing now. "Do you even understand the magnitude of your situation? Such a thing has never happened—never in Nirus's history! Whoever can cast such an Evocation... well, it would be talked about for ages."

"I just want to exist again," he sighed. "I don't need to be talked about."

One of the rebels from our company, Kurrick, growled. "I agree with this one." The brute grabbed Xavier's collar, shoving me aside. "If you once had the power to defy the laws of magic, then you can do it again now. Test if you can cast the Evocation at all, before we go any further."

Xavier tried to pry off his fingers, but the giant had too firm a grip. "What are you saying?"

He pulled Xavier closer. "Push out my soul. And then replace it."

Xavier went Deathly silent. Then he said, "Shove off, Kurrick."

Kurrick shook his catch. "Prove you can. Otherwise, there is no point to this journey—"

"Kurrick," the brute's gentle companion—Ana?—snapped behind him. "Leave him be."

Kurrick craned to her. "We were wrong, Ana. He is not our quarry. Neither of them are. The true Shadow is still out there, and we have been wasting our time with these imposters."

Miss Ana held her ground. "You must be patient."

"I have been patient for five centuries, Ana," he bellowed, keeping hold of the squirming Xavier.

Xavier managed to pull back hard enough to let his shirt collar rip free, and he stumbled back against the cavern wall—

Kurrick slammed his fingers over Xavier's throat to pin him in place. "We've wasted precious months on you. I am sick of the wolf hunt. Our End draws ever nearer, and the one we truly need may have already been killed during this useless game!"

"Kurrick!" Xavier sputtered under his grip. "I don't... know what you're talking about...!"

"I cannot fathom why Dream bothered with—"

"*Enough!*" Xavier shoved him back, black Hallows flaring from his hands. Kurrick collapsed.

A cloud of dirt puffed around the warrior. Everyone froze, a long silence following. Hesitant, I knelt, seeing the rebel's eyes were closed. He was unconscious.

"K... K-Kurrick?" Xavier asked, his certainty gone.

I looked up at Xavier in alarm. "What did you do to him?"

"I don't know." Xavier seemed just as worried. "Theoretically, that should have... er..."

I lifted the man's thick arm, released it, and watched it drop limply to the ground again. His chest was steadily rising and falling, so he wasn't dead... "Did you push his soul out?" I asked.

Xavier swallowed. "That was the intent... but I'm not sure if it worked or..."

Her Highness yelped, and my head snapped to her. A new ghost had appeared beside her, a white string bright and gleaming from its chest.

It was Kurrick.

I laughed. *He's done it!* Death's Hallowed Head, Xavier had pushed Kurrick's soul right out of his Bloody vessel.

XAVIER

"Kurrick...?" I was frozen on the wall, gawking at Kurrick's detached, pale soul in front of me. His sleeping body lay at my boots. "Mother of Death... I-I did it."

"Did what!" Ana piped in fright, her voice shriller than her usual whisper. She grabbed Bianca beside her and shook the rabbit by the shoulders. "Lend me your soul-seeing glasses! Please!"

Bianca fumbled to fetch the rose framed glasses from the satchel at her hip—

Ana snatched them and shoved them over her nose, her gaze flicking every which way to find the ghost of her warrior floating above his slumbering body.

"Kurrick?" Ana gasped. She held a shaking hand to her warrior's pale face—it phased through without touch. "Kurrick…! Oh, what have you done?"

Kurrick's ghost grinned wide, looking at me. "So, you *can* repeat it. Good. There is hope for us yet."

I backed away and tripped on a stone, landing on my rear, fixated on the translucent soul. I let out a laugh. "I did it. I Bloody *did it…*!"

Matthiel, who'd been kneeling beside Kurrick's slumbering body, pushed to his feet in a thrilled chuckle. "You see! The test worked. But now… er, hm. Can you put him back? Or is he stuck like that?"

I ducked when Kurrick's ghost shot me a pointed glare.

"I'll… try?" I offered.

Kurrick shut his eyes and exhaled—or, motioned to, since ghosts couldn't actually *breathe*. "That doesn't inspire confidence."

"R, right. Sorry." I reached a trembling hand to the NecroSeam within his chest.

The Seam tingled coolly under my grip, radiant beams shooting between my fingers. It was the oddest sensation, in my grasp. I was used to temporary Seams, ones that I fabricated for deceased souls. This was a living soul: a genuine, strong, *raw* NecroSeam still laced within its host specter. And I was holding it. Death, I may be the first Necrovoker to *ever* hold one.

That thought brought a rush of pride. I sucked in a breath, held it in place… then…

Slowly, steadily, I evoked my Hallows and pushed the soul back into its slumbering body, feeling the NecroSeam wrap around the beating heart. I then threaded the Seam to the muscle, weaving my glowing hand back and forth until I was sure it was secure.

When I dismissed my Hallows, I gasped for breath and leaned over the ground in a heavy pant. Whatever I'd just done had taken a lot of stamina. I was sweating from exertion.

Kurrick lay there for a long while, unmoved. Unchanged. I was beginning to worry. *Perhaps it didn't work?*

But soon, he grunted awake and heaved himself upright, his grin wild. "*There* is the power I searched for. Well done, Shadow-half."

I stared at the Crest on my left hand. Alex sounded incredulous from my thoughts. *"I guess we know it's not impossible now?"*

"Maybe not." I turned my hand over, awed—but the cave shuddered, bits of ceiling crumbling down. It sounded like explosions. I hurried to my feet. "W-we'll celebrate later. We have to find that shelter!"

We sprinted down the tunnels, tremors shaking the caverns from up top. The shelter wasn't much farther. We followed the soft glow of torchlight ahead. When we reached the end of the tunnel in hard puffs, we found ourselves in a wide, rocky enclosure, filled with cobwebs and a pool of water at the center. It was the size of a common gymnasium. There were only fifteen people I could see in the dim light of a firepit. Ringëd found his parents with this group, and he embraced them, babbling in Marincian while tremors shook the tunnel. Some of our group scattered to check on the survivors while I hurriedly searched the rest of the dark shelter for any signs of my body.

I had to be here somewhere—Linus Saw a vision of it. Somewhere in here, so close… so incredibly *close*…

I stopped. Three figures were crouched in the corner, their backs facing me. One was a teenaged, black-haired girl with long pigtails, wearing a lavender nurse's tunic. Another was… *Wait. I know this person.* It was that reptile woman, Rochelle, from Nulani… and the third woman next to her was cat-eared with orange hair. She was tending to a patient, evoking her remedy Hallows over a cut on the unconscious man's arm, oblivious to us.

She was Sirra-Lynn. And looking down, I saw her patient's skinny, chalk-grey, malnourished hand.

My hand.

53

FINAL HESITATION

~~~~~~

XAVIER

My limbs—my *borrowed* limbs—numbed.
Sirra-Lynn finished mending the cut on her patient's boney arm and turned to Rochelle, who blocked the man's face from view.

Move, I ordered silently to myself, *move, damn you. Speak—anything!* My lips were sealed shut, legs heavy and shaking. I licked my lips. "Sirr—"

"Sirra?" Claude interrupted in a whisper behind me. Her husband shoved in front, dazed and elated. "Sirra is… is that you?"

Sirra-Lynn flinched, spinning in shock. She found Claude's face and, for a moment, she lost her breath. "Claude?"

He swept her in his arms, tears hitting. "Damn it, Sirra!" he sobbed, holding her tighter. "What are you doing on the surface? You could have… you could have been eaten, and…"

"Claude…" Her eyes watered as well, returning the embrace as she laid her head on his shoulder. "It's all right. I'm safe. I have a Bloodpact with a Necrovoker… but what are you doing here?" She pulled him at arms' length, searching his face with a worried brow. "Is *he* here…? That snake?"

"No," he said, laughing between hiccups as he rubbed at his eyes. "Honey, I left them. Our kids—they got themselves out of the house, away from his people. I'm damn well making sure he doesn't come near them again."

"Oh, Claude!" Her smile split with uncontested joy, squeezing the breath out of him—

Another explosion ruptured overhead.

Sirra's cheer dripped away, turning to despair. She cupped her husband's face. "Claude, you shouldn't have come. You still have your life—oh, why are you throwing it away by coming here?"

"We have a way out." He gripped her fingers, determined. "We brought a ship. There's room for the other survivors."

"But why are you here at all? Where are the kids?"

Octavius sidled past me, interjecting. "We're here, too, Mom."

She blinked at him, dumbfounded. "Tavius?"

"And us!" Neal cut in from the crowd, bumping into my shoulder on his way past me. Neal trotted to his mother, crushing her lungs brightly and lifting her up in a laugh. When he set her down again, he gave a toothy grin. "Good to see you, Mom!"

Sirra chuckled. "Neal! Bloods, you two have grown. You're taller than me, now."

"Mom?" Mikani called next, running over with Ringëd at her heels. Mikani hugged her mother as well, her smile warm. "Bloods, it's been a while."

Sirra gaped at her daughter, staring at the glittering marriage-vines and centerpiece that dangled from her forehead. "Mika!" she cried, looking at Ringëd's marriage stud pierced in his left ear. She held a hand a hand to her lips. "Oh, you're married finally…! Damn me, I missed the wedding!"

Ringëd chuckled, taking Mikani's hand and kissing her knuckles. "It's all right, Sirra. It was a quick one anyway."

Sirra wiped desperately at her leaking eyes, sniffling. "Bloods, but… what about Connie?"

Octavius threw a thumb over his shoulder. "She's back in Everland, in Reaper territory. She's safe."

Sirra sounded stuffy now, her eyes rubbed red. "B-but… but what are you all doing here? This is the worst time to show up…!"

Octavius scratched his nose. "I'd say it's the best time, since you look like you could use a way out of here. But we actually came here looking for…" He blinked over her shoulder, glancing down. "Oh. Well… *him*, actually."

She stiffened, pushing him back. Her gaze moved to me standing here, and her face flushed with dread. "Octavius," she whispered, her cheerful tone snuffed in a heartbeat. "What have you done?"

I couldn't speak. Alex gave no comment from the psyche either. I stared at the skinny hand—*my* hand—lying at her feet.

"It's all right, Mom," Octavius assured, gesturing to me. "It's hard to explain, but let's just say they came a long way to get here."

"You have no idea what you…!" Sirra's hands clenched, and she slid between us and my sleeping body protectively, glaring at me; then at Willow. "Your Highness Death, I know why you're here. You're arresting me for my crimes. For saving a vessel with no soul… But you aren't laying a damn claw on this boy, not before I go to Nira. I spent too many years keeping him alive—hiding him—caring for him…" Her voice shook.

Neither Willow nor I offered a reply.

Sirra's cheeks reddened, anger rising. "You of all people should understand…! Princess, he was your betrothed, wasn't he? And Howllord, your own brother! No one else would care for him! When he washed on Everland's shores, they all wanted him to die on his own, to waste away because he was the Bloody Devouh's son…!" The last word fractured, and she cupped her mouth, choking on her sobs. "He was just a kid…! Probably sent off that cliff by the same man who killed me!"

She sniffed, composing herself, but barely. "Call me a criminal if you want, but I couldn't stand aside when a victim of that monster was right at my feet. I'm sorry, Claude. Princess… Howllord." She bit her knuckles, another sob choking. "Your brother's soul is gone. He's just a shell… If you take him back, you'll have to hand him over to your parents and have him killed because of that *ridiculous* law. And I… I can't let that happen—"

"Then step aside," I said, finally finding my voice, quiet though it was. "Let my soul return to its body."

She held her breath. In the dim light, I saw her squint at me. "What…?"

I walked toward her. "Thank you for watching over me. Truly. If I'd died, I don't know what I'd have done."

At long, long last, I gazed upon my slumbering body.

It wasn't what I'd expected. My grey hair had grown to my shoulders, hollow face lined in a thick beard that trailed down my throat, limbs skinny as bone, ribs visible from my bare chest. A scar ran down my right brow and skipped to my cheek at a jagged angle. Oddly, I noted, it looked much like Chai's scar.

I knelt, brushing my fingers over my—*my!*—face. "It's real," I breathed. My blood bubbled. "It's *real*…"

Willow lowered beside me, clutching the boney hand of the slumbering figure. "And alive."

"*How do you go back in?*" Alex asked anxiously from the psyche. "*If you pull out your soul, you can't use your Hallows afterward. Not without a body to serve as a medium.*"

I couldn't look away from my thin face. It was eerie, seeing myself without the aid of a mirror. The full effect of seeing through my brother's eyes—to stare at myself—truly sank in. I cupped my mouth broodingly. "How had I done it before…?"

"How indeed," a new voice hummed behind me.

I whirled, startled.

An azure haired boy with icy blue eyes had appeared. He looked my age, but his face held no obvious emotion. He was a blank slate; his stare as stale as month-old bread.

I wasn't sure what to make of him. His oddly colored hair baffled me, but I noticed the crowned Dream mark on his forehead, then took a breath and pointed weakly. "Are you—?"

"Grandfather!" Willow rose in a jolt. "Why are you here?"

Miss Ana must have overheard because she turned to us, seeming to recognize the newcomer. She gave a delighted gasp and left Kurrick's side to embrace the blue haired boy. "Dream!" Ana whispered gleefully. "At last, you've come to meet with us! Oh, it's a glorious sight to see you…!"

The boy, the King of Dreams, hugged her in return and chuckled. "And you as well, Anabelle. Always the sentimental one, aren't we?"

This is the illustrious King of Dreams? I wondered in silence. *This… kid?*

My mind simmered with memories of the strange king. They were faint and few, but there was no mistaking that placid gaze and flighty voice.

As I remembered, Dream looked nothing like his holy depictions in *The Choir*. Instead of an oracle's sage robes that were said to glitter with row upon row of silver chains and bejeweled buttons, he donned a boring, grimy sweater, its orange hood swallowing his curly blue hair. He had a white-gold crown etched in prancing foxes that he wore in a tacky fashion over his hood, but that hardly did anything to break his un-regal demeanor. His legendary shepherd's crook was nothing more than a blasted tree branch, frayed and splintered down the staff, and he bobbed it lazily over his shoulder.

Willow didn't seem fazed by his unimpressive visage. "Grandfather," she began, beguiled. "What are you doing here?"

"Assisting you all, my dear." Dream patted his granddaughter's cheek—the woman no younger than himself—and crouched to face me. "Hello, Xavier. It's been a while. Do you remember me, by chance?"

I stared, trying to recall more than the few scenes clinging to mind… A barefoot boy in the palace gardens by a trickling fountain… He'd said a few words, I think, though I couldn't remember what… Mostly, I remembered being confused.

"Er," I said, my face twisting with effort. "I faintly remember… something."

"Well, that's all right. I imagine something will click when I give you your gift later. Can Alexander hear me in there? Tell him King Dream says hello."

"Tell him I said to go fu—"

I ignored him.

Dream laced his fingers over a knee, humming. "I'm sure you're wondering how I intend to help. Well, it's taken me some time to think of the solution to this predicament… But I think I know what needs to be done now. Willow?" He turned to his granddaughter. "You must be the one to start it."

Willow didn't seem sure what he meant. "Start what?"

"His soul's sleep, where he will be brought into Aspirre," he said. "When he pulls out his soul, you'll have to use your dream Hallows to put him to sleep, where *I* will then guide him to his destination. I cannot touch a detached soul out here, and therefore can't put him to sleep to begin with. But you have the advantage of being a daughter of both the Death *and* Dream families. You are the only candidate capable of helping Xavier presently."

Willow frowned. "Couldn't his soul just… fall asleep on its own?"

Dream hummed. "It could. Though, I doubt he's feeling tired, given all that's happening above us. Best we sped up the process and escape quickly, don't you think?"

Willow glanced at me, her gaze uncertain, but determined. "All… All right. Then let's begin."

"Very well!" Dream clapped his hands as I rose to my feet. He waved a hand at me. "Xavier? If you'd do the honors of removing your displaced soul?"

"I… er…" A knot pinched my throat. "Right now?"

"Yes, now. We haven't much time."

"You're sure this will work?" I asked doubtfully.

He shrugged. "Fairly. It's more of a hunch, really."

"That doesn't spark much confidence—"

"Xavier." Dream gestured a hand out. "This is the only option left, I'm afraid. We're running out of time."

"But what if…" A tremor ruptured overhead, shaking the cave and sent a dust storm of debris over us. I shut my eyes, hoping to Gods I wasn't going to regret this, and pressed my left hand to my chest. "All right. Fine." I breathed out slowly. "Alex? Are you ready?"

I heard my brother inhale nervously. *"Ready."*

"It's been fun."

"Fun. Yes."

"I suppose we'll need to find a different way to speak in private—"

"Xavier," he interrupted gently. *"You're stalling."*

"Right… Sorry." I sucked in another breath. This was happening so fast, my brain raced to catch up. But this had to be done. Sooner rather than later. *Best jump in head first… right?* "Let's do this."

I evoked my Hallows, using the same method as before, and felt two cold vibrations in my heart: Alex and my NecroSeams.

I pulled on one, but didn't feel a connection. It must have been Alexander's. I tugged on the next one—felt it. *There*, I thought, breathing slowly. *Goodbye, Alex.*

I pulled.

A chilled breeze rushed over me, color draining from my surroundings, and every sense of touch was left behind as my soul was thrown out of its six-year prison. I had to take a moment to regain my wits, feeling winded, though I didn't have any lungs to breathe. I glanced up. Everything was white and grey. Turning, I—

Stopped cold.

My achromatic brother was staring at me. *At* me. Not through a mirror, nor through the psyche's window. His mismatched eyes were wide with shock. *It's done*, I realized numbly. *We're... separated.*

"Xavier," Willow called softly. She was as colorless as everything else. She held out a pale, glowing hand. "Are you ready?"

I set my jaw. Nothing for it now, was there? I was out of Alex. Forever. No turning back. Not ever again...

"Yes," I said. "I'm ready."

I took her hand, and the physical plane vanished around me.

The grey cavern vanished, replaced with an empty abyss of blackness as I fell downward in a yelp.

My feet landed awkwardly over some sort of paved road. It was suspended in the abyss along with other crisscrossing roads in the distance.

"Now then," a voice chimed in the darkness. "To your body?"

I spun on my heels, finding King Dream. Though there wasn't a light source, everything here seemed to emit its own light. Dream, me, the wavering roads and distant cities suspended in the abyss...

Dream floated in the air, his bare toes a foot off the paved road where I was grounded.

"Aspirre..." I gazed in all directions, not sure which way was which in this emptiness. Then a new thought struck me and I turned to Dream, staring at his azure locks. "You're in color again. What happened to the grey?"

He hummed. "Aspirre doesn't abide by the rules of the physical plane."

"That doesn't explain anything."

His head cocked. "Hm. I suppose it doesn't." He hovered forward, leaving the matter unanswered, and I scrambled to keep pace on foot.

"Wait," I called, "do you know where you're going?"

He stopped and pointed with his shepherd's crook. "To that light."

Squinting, I found a tiny, radiant ball of white light. It hovered in the blackness, moving with wispy tendrils like a living creature.

"What is this?" I asked, reaching a hand to the light. A shock spread through my hand when I neared it. I retracted my fingers, a pulse rippling painfully at my chest. Yet, there was something else to it. Something… fulfilling.

A bright gleam leaked from my chest, stretching toward the light. My feet slid forward as it drew me nearer.

My breath spilled. "Is this…"

Dream's lips split into a smile. "It's your heart, Xavier."

The lights spewing from my chest latched onto the wisp, and my lungs went numb, heaving a breath as the lights yanked me toward my heart's wavering glow.

Then it swallowed me.

54

A DANCE OF DEMONS

CILIA

The round buildings smoldered with flames, embers dusting off the collapsing frames as I stalked through the streets, gathering my scattered soldiers one cluster at a time.

These damned pests were so distractible. One whiff of a clean soul, and they forgot all other dangers. That is, until I came to press my Weight over them. They always bent under the pressure when I focused on them. That would be where this little game proved tricky.

If that Demon King was on his way, there was a chance he would try and control my army if I let any minions stray. Best I kept them close at hand for the coming battle. It would be difficult. Water Hallows could easily douse my fire, especially since I was surrounded by the Bloody ocean. I only hoped my current fires had dried some of the moisture in the air—

A sudden ball of water hit me, soaking both of us and extinguishing my flames. My teeth clenched, already feeling his Weight.

"Hello, Hecrûshou…" I chewed. "Fine weather we're having, don't you think?"

His Royal Pain-In-The-Arse Majesty waited on the other side of the street. His glowing trident rested on his shoulder.

The charred building behind him dripped with water, its fire having been doused. My gaze flicked to the trident. It was made with Spiritcrystal. The last few times I'd seen him, he had told me so. More as a warning for if I broke the treaty, as I've just done.

He'd brought an army of his own, straight from the waters surrounding us, no doubt. My previous commander, Janson, was with him, along with his two vassals. *Damn him.*

I glanced sidelong, seeing my second commander, Maveric, had come with the rest of our army. *Now Hecrûshou has a Necrovoker, Astravoker, AND a Glaciavoker.* My throat clicked, irritated. *All I have is a Bloody HEALER. Useless idiot...*

"Cilia," Hecrûshou greeted venomously. "I imagine you wish to enjoy your holiday to its fullest? Shall I give you the grand tour?"

I cracked my neck, summoning my fire. "I'd be delighted."

I ordered Maveric to take out Janson, then hurtled my fire at the Astravoker. The flames hit the small girl, distracting her from shocking me, and I rushed for Hecrûshou.

He swung his trident. I ducked and swirled round, throwing fire. He doused it with his Aquavoking, flame and water clashing in a beautiful display of wavering liquid and licking inferno.

Janson's Glaciavoker threw spikes of ice at me, and I melted them with a quick wave. I was nearly impaled with Hecrûshou's trident, but I dodged so the fork only speared my arm. With a yell, I ripped free, black blood pooling at my feet before it slithered back to me. My gaze scorched at the shark.

A challenge indeed. I barred my teeth, grown ears curling tight. *I'm at a disadvantage.*

I would just have to kill them all quickly, one at a time. Starting with the king.

I screamed and charged again.

55

FIRST BREATH

~~~~~~

WILLOW

Explosions burst above, rumbling the shelter as dirt crumbled from the ceiling. I crouched over Xavier's body to shield him from the showering bits and shook out the debris that dusted my hair, wiping my brow with a sleeve.

Xavier's eyes were still closed, his breath steady. I touched his sunken cheeks and the jagged scar running down his right eye, brushing away a strand of his long hair. *Please wake up soon...*

I didn't know what was taking him and Grandfather so long. We were running out of time. Everyone was panicking as the tremors grew stronger. Alexander seemed the most stressed. His face was set in a dreaded glower as he paced round Xavier and me, his wolf ears folded to his neck and gaze flicking to Xavier's slumbering figure obsessively.

Bianca crouched beside me and set down her satchel, medical tools and vials clinking inside. Her orange hair was pulled in a messy tail, probably done on the way here, as her rabbit ears draped to her neck, still dripping from all the splashing water on the ship.

Bianca plugged her ears with a stethoscope, holding the silver disc to Xavier's boney chest.

"Normal heartbeat," she murmured, wrapping the stethoscope round her neck. She then began massaging Xavier's reedy muscles. "Atrophied to Void, but still functional to a degree..." Her nose wiggled in thought, mouth twisting. "But *how* functional? Science says the muscles shouldn't be functional at all after a six-year coma... not without proper surveillance and tonic administration—"

"Both of which were given," a voice said behind. Sirra-Lynn stepped around us and knelt to Xavier's other side, her orange cat ears curled in thought. She combed her fingers through Xavier's shoulder-length hair. "I did what I could to retain his muscle strength... though, it isn't much. I wasn't exactly expecting his soul to walk in here and..." She sighed, measuring the scraggly hairs of Xavier's thick beard with two fingers. She chuckled. "I was going to give him a trim today. So much for that... I hope he isn't mad when he wakes up."

I shook my head. "Believe you me, Mrs. Treble, the only one he will *not* be angry with is you." I gave a laugh. "You've given him the life he's sought so desperately."

Sirra's cat ears rose, but only slightly, a blush blooming over her cheeks. She bowed her head. "I'm... sorry, your grace," she said. "I feel like an idiot. I was trying to hide him from you, from your father, from the man who killed me... but I just ended up hiding him from himself."

I snorted. "Better that you did, Mrs. Treble. My father and I were sure he was dead. *I* only learned of what'd happened not months ago." *How many months had it been?* Oh, when would I see home again...?

I squeezed Xavier's boney, limp fingers, my heart fluttering. *Regardless*, I reminded silently, *I'll return with Xavier.*

"What is taking so long?" Alex demanded, ceasing his pacing above us. "Did something happen?"

"Give them time," I said, clutching Xavier's thin hand. He looked weak, so lanky... Sirra-Lynn assured they'd given him tonics to retain some strength over the years, but how much would it help?

Alex didn't seem satisfied with my answer, growling, "Something's wrong. It shouldn't take this long."

Jaq, thank Nira, came to clasp his quivering arm. "Calm down. I'm sure he's fine."

"How do you know?" Alex shoved the viper off, trembling. By the Seamstress, he looked downright terrified. "I can't hear him. What if they couldn't find the way? What if it didn't work? I don't know what's going on in there and *I can't hear him...!*"

Jaq grabbed his lapel. "Will you get a hold of yourself? Stand still and calm down! Throwing a fit isn't going to help—"

Screeches blared within the tunnel up ahead, making us turn. It sounded like Necrofera, screaming from the way we'd come. *They've found the entrance by the shoals?*

Sirra-Lynn cursed. "Bloods, the only other entrance was already caved in from the tremors!"

Her reptile friend, Rochelle, lifted her glasses in concern. "Shel help us, and the last of the island's Reapers have already been slaughtered..."

Alexander stopped his pacing around us and plucked the scythe-spheres from his neck, summoning his weapons. "If they get in here, these people will be vulnerable," he said to me. "We have to do something. And Xavier…"

He glanced down at his slumbering brother, anger flaring. Then he exhaled and cast me a pleading look. "Stay with him. Watch him for me." He turned to Jaq, Lilli, the Treble brothers and Matthiel. "I'm going to try and clear the exit so we can leave without being killed. Who's coming?"

All agreed. With a nod, Alex trotted off with them. "Matt, I need you up front for light. Vendy, at my side with your sword. Octavius, keep an eye on your brother, since he's never been on a hunt before. Jaq, Lilli, I need you to…"

He ran off with them, leaving me with Xavier.

The tremors continued, and everyone gathered in huddled groups with terrified whispers.

Gods be with you all. I hated to sit here when there were Fera lurking, but Alexander was relying on me. I'd never seen him so frightened…

I nearly jumped when I felt a twitch under my hand. My head snapped to Xavier.

Nothing. All was still… His eyes remained shut, and my heart sank. I was sure I felt something…

Another twitch from his fingers.

My breath caught and I hovered over him, gaze sweeping his thin face for signs of consciousness. "Xavier…?"

XAVIER

"Xavier…?"

I almost couldn't hear the wispy voice. It was muffled and dim, hundreds of miles away and trying to find me in a fog.

"Ngn…" I tried to move, but couldn't. The only sign that my mind *wasn't* floating aimlessly in a black abyss of inexistence was how my lungs blistered with each heavy breath.

My eyes cracked open—*my* eyes—but sight was unfocused and bleary. There seemed to be someone leaning over me. My vision sharpened more, and the blurred figure's white hair shifted into focus.

"Xavier?" the quivering voice called again, hope and thrill brimming.

My throat scratched. "Willow…?"

"Oh, thank Nira!" Her lips fastened joyously to mine. "You're awake! You're awake…!" She began weeping, kissing me again.

As much as I wished to enjoy the reunion, I found I couldn't move. At all. My head wouldn't even turn, I felt utterly... drained. So *weak*.

I tried lifting an arm, but it rolled to the side like a limp creature reaching for life. My legs were a lost cause; I couldn't even feel them beneath me. Only the small grip from Willow's twittering messenger on my toe assured me they were still there.

Chai croaked by my face happily as he pushed his beak against my cheek, urging me to get up. The tattered raven's touch brought a reviving surge of relief. Chai screeched more determinedly, demanding me to keep going. Our connection was taut, the messenger feeling my distress as I felt his push, reminding me that I wanted this; I needed this; I couldn't simply lie back and surrender, could I?

Preparing myself, I focused on controlling my arms. They strained, Chai urged, and I silently commanded the limbs to *move*. They finally did as asked, and when I attempted to lift myself upright—my lungs cracked with a pained grunt and my arms collapsed.

Willow pulled me up to sit, leaning me against her cushioned chest.

"Willow," I panted, my cheek meeting hers for support. My long hair fell over my face, blocking half of my view. "I... I want to go back to Alex."

She kissed my brow, hiccupping a laugh. "You'll regain your strength over time. I promise." Chai screeched at me in agreement.

The others gathered round, each face looking more stunned than the next. The ghosts of Aiden, Nathaniel and Dalen had floated to my eyelevel in shock.

"I'll be damned," Dalen breathed while inspecting my face. "Ya look... well, ya look *different*, that's for sure, Da'torr."

"That's one way 'o puttin' it," Nathaniel grunted. "Ye look downright sallow there, Lad. Thin as bones."

"Indeed." Aiden made a wincing face. "Perhaps some food and a shave would do you some good, young sir?"

"A shave can wait." I coughed, throat sore and burning. "But food... Now that is a grand idea. And water. Is there water?"

"Yes, yes!" Willow called for someone.

But King Dream was already there. He knelt and offered me a bowl of water. "Welcome back, Xavier. I thought you'd need this."

I raised my quivering hands to the bowl, but couldn't lift it on my own. Bloody Void, even a bowl of *water* was too heavy for me. Dream assisted and tipped the edge to my lips, slowly letting the water pour down my throat.

Some of it dribbled from the corners of my mouth, tasting of minerals as specks of dirt peppered the water, but I didn't care. Never in my life had I thought water tasted so wonderful—so *reviving*. Like ice washing over coals. Swallowing was a challenge, but my thirst turned ravenous as the liquid drained. I choked after a moment, and Dream lowered the bowl while I hacked away.

"Are you adjusting well?" Dream asked.

I cleared the last of my coughing. "If by adjusting you mean *dying*, then yes… I don't think I can walk."

"I imagine not." Dream's frosted eyes examined me curiously. "I suppose that will take time to fix. But now, I think it's best if you all left. Is there any way off this island?"

Willow answered, "We have a ship out in the shoals. I'm not sure how we plan to get it back in the water, or if we can even *arrive* there without running into the Fera and endangering more lives."

"Don't worry there," Dream assured. "If we run into the Fera, I can bring everyone to the ship from Aspirre."

My brow furrowed and I shifted weight against Willow. "How will putting us to sleep solve anything?" I questioned. "Only your soul can go to the Dream realm. Unless you bring us *physically* there, we may as well let the Fera eat us. But such would be impossible."

Dream's lips rolled into a sly grin, winking. "Unless you're a Relicblood of Dreams with a particular set of Orbs."

Willow hissed under her breath, as though not wanting me to hear, but I caught it regardless. "You have the Orbs with you?"

"Of course, dear." Dream gestured to my left hand. "That should have been obvious, with his Crest gleaming so."

Startled, I looked at my Evocator's mark. The black diamonds over my knuckles were shining, pulsing in a dark light with a purplish outline. When I weakly waved it back and forth, the diamonds began changing direction. Each time, they pointed to King Dream, until I oriented it correctly and all three began pulsing again. *How long has it been doing that?*

I glanced back at Willow; at her music watch. *The Crest lit for that before…* I regarded Dream again. "Why is it glowing for you?"

"Not me." He gave a smile. It looked formulaic, as if displaying emotions escaped him and he was making a habitual effort to show that he felt any. "I'll save that explanation for a more opportune time. Right now, I think it's best to retrieve your brother."

Brother.

The word shoved everything else from my attention.

Brother!

"Alex?" I called, my cracked voice echoing back.

No reply came. Panic sank, made worse by the utter silence. I was too used to his voice answering me from the psyche. Now that it was gone…

Clasping my ears and taking deep, steady breaths, I strained to listen—to hear even the tiniest response.

My thoughts remained blotted with silence. Pure silence. He wasn't sleeping this time; wasn't ignoring me. He was gone. Gone…

Shaken, I looked at Willow. "Where is he?"

Even if we weren't sharing that forsaken psyche anymore, I shouldn't have been alone now. It didn't make sense. The one damned person I expected to be here wasn't? For Death's sake, this was *the* most crucial moment for both of us! He wouldn't miss this. Something must have been wrong.

Willow hushed me. "Alexander is keeping the Necrofera at bay with the others. He'll be back soon."

I limply clenched my hands. "It was too early." I shuddered, hating the newness of it all. "We separated too soon. We should have waited."

"Don't worry," she said encouragingly. "I'm sure he's fine. He'll be back in a moment."

"Right… You're right." I inhaled sharply, collecting myself. "I just… just need to acquaint myself with being… *normal* again. But I still want to be sure… wait—Dalen?" Our ghostly vassal swept to me right away when I called. "Can you contact Alex?"

This would have to be our new method of communication, I decided. Dalen and Vendy were bound to both of us. They could transmit messages.

Dalen nodded and relayed the message under his breath. "*Da'torr* Alex? Your brother's askin' for an update."

56

LATE REUNION

ALEXANDER

The darkened tunnels were damp and caked with mildew, smelling of sea water and mold as my shoes trampled over beds of soft moss. My wolf ears curled back, annoyance budding. *Or was it anger? Fright...? Did it even matter?*

The Fera's screeches could be heard ahead, the others rushing beside me with their glowing weapons poised.

It wasn't the demons I was afraid of—I was accustomed to the massive hordes by now—rather, it was the silence. Pure, *utter* silence from my thoughts. The moment Xavier's soul slipped out of me, I felt so... empty. He wasn't asleep anymore; he wasn't ignoring me. He was gone. Gone...

"... He's gone, Alex," *Lilli had murmured when I awoke in the palace infirmary. The bat's wings were draped low to the floor, tears and dirt streaking her narrow face.* "Willow told me what happened. She'd been found on the surface by other Reapers, but Xavier... I... I'm so sorry..."

I shut it out. *Never again.*

The gleaming white eyes of the Necrofera swerved within sight at the mouth of the cave. My fingers tightened on my dual blades.

"Don't let any of them through!" I barked to the others and stormed out to the shoals.

I swiped my blades at the nearest beast that charged for me. The scythes' crooks tore into the skeletal creature's neck, seared through the bone and ripped its head clean off. The skull rolled at my feet and I drove one blade into the thing's chest, cut its NecroSeam with a distinct *snap* and kicked the corpse to the ground.

Cut after cut, the beasts were taken down. But there were so many—as Bloody usual. My body moved methodically around them, piercing chests, cutting limbs, cracking bones... The only thing to worry about now was stamina. And that was draining quickly.

When there was a lapse of enemies in my area, I took a moment to catch my breath, checking on the others. To my left, I found Lilli and Jaq... and frowned.

They were maneuvering around each other with impressive ease. Whenever Jaq's chain-scythe swooped round, Lilli deftly leapt over it, soared around him and cut down the demons he would miss. And whatever *she* missed, he'd clean up without so much as a word. There was little communication, yet they instinctively moved as a team.

What in Death happened in that prison? My lids narrowed at them, wiping sweat that leaked into my eye, bearing the sting.

Hollering sounded to my right, and my attention snapped to the Treble brothers. They were also faring well, it seemed. Both were directing the other about which beasts to aim for. Neal was a better shot by far, but Octavius's infecting Hallows gave him the advantage. Neal was hitting their chests easily enough—hitting *through* them even, with his outrageous speed and deadly thrust—but his glowing blades wouldn't always slice close enough to the NecroSeams. Octavius's Hallows gave him more leniency, since he only needed to hit the general area and allow his Infeciovoking to seep into the creatures' chests.

Neal apparently noticed this, and he called out, "Lil' bro! Think you can load up some of my scythes with that stuff?"

He gently tossed one blade to Octavius, who coated it with black veins, tossed it back to Neal and warned, "Don't hold onto it too long, or it'll spread to you."

"Got it." When the newly infected scythe touched his fingers, Neal launched it at the nearest Fera bounding for him. When it died in a shriek, Neal smirked and brought out another blade. "Awesome."

Vendy was a girl on a wild rampage, heaving out guttural war cries and slashing beast after beast in a frenzy with her Crystal blade—

A small fizzle filtered over my brain, freezing my breath. It felt like a mental connection with a vassal. Since Vendy was here, it must have been Dalen.

Sure enough, Dalen's voice sounded in my thoughts. *Da'torr Alex?*

My brow knitted. I couldn't recall him ever specifying which '*Da'torr*' he was speaking to.

"What is it, Dalen?" I yelled over the noise.

Your brother's askin' for an update.

I stopped cold. "Say that again?"

It's Xavier. I could imagine the smirk with his tone. *He's akin' if you're still alive out there?*

"He's awake?"

He's awake.

I erupted with laughter and dashed for the last two Fera in sight, slamming my scythes into both their chests, killing them. Making sure the last of the beasts had fled, I put away my scythes and trotted to the others, grinning like a madman. "He's awake!"

"Thank Bloods," Jaq puffed, coiling his chain and wiped the sweat and sand from his chin. "I think that's the last of them, too. I don't know why they just left, but I sure as Void don't care."

"Whatever's going on in the city must be intense," Lilli speculated, looking at the bursts of fire and water that crashed against each other in the distance. "Those Sentients are probably gathering all the troops they can find, if Cilia and Hecrûshou are really at war. Should we see how that battle is faring—"

"Void no, let's go back and get the Death out of here!" I clasped Lilli's wrist and dragged her back the way we came, the others following. I'd been waiting six years for this day, I wasn't about to miss a second of it—

I screamed when something thick and sharp lodged into my shoulder blade and *ripped* through the other side, a bloodied horn sliding out of my collarbone.

Pain exploded, fizzling like scorching ice, nerves shocked and blood flooding when the bull-horned demon behind me tore the spiked horn out. I collapsed to the wet sand, wailing in agony as I held a hand to the large gash coming from my clavicle.

XAVIER

"*AAAAGH…!*" I screamed, my back and shoulder met with excruciating pain.

Everyone was startled. Willow crouched beside me, hesitant to touch my back as if worried she'd make it worse. "Xavier? What is it?"

A groan squeezed out my throat as I waited for the pain to settle. It dimmed, but didn't vanish completely. It was stuck in some layer that didn't quite reach me—didn't quite affect me.

"I don't know." My breath was ragged. "It felt like… like something just…"

The pain was familiar. Too familiar. Not so much the agony in my shoulder, but the strangeness of the static. It was there, yet it wasn't.

"Alex…!" I remembered screaming through the streets of a Grimish city—Low Drinelle?—at Dim Light hours.

I was six, I think, and Alex had gotten lost. I'd found him by some grace of the Goddess, some phantom pain that had been exploding from my stomach for the last few minutes.

I found him being beaten by a pack of commoner children. His nose looked broken, and I could see a splintered bone cracking out of his arm, one of the boys kicking his stomach over and over and over, synchronized with my phantom pain…

The present hurtled back as the pain in my shoulder pulsed, making me gasp.

"Alex…!" With as much pitiful strength as I could conjure, I tried to stand, but my legs refused me. I fumbled to the ground, straining and cursing, then began dragging myself over the dirt.

That's what the pain is! His, not mine! He was hurt somewhere outside, I was sure of it. I just… have to reach him in time…

"Xavier!" Willow came to hold me back. "Alex will be all—"

"He's hurt!" I shoved her away, though I knew she only drew back out of courtesy. The Gods knew I hadn't the strength to overpower her right now. "Something's happened!"

"How do you know?"

"I-I don't know! I can't explain it, just—*AAAGH*…!" Another wave of pain flared. "Just *bring me outside!*"

ALEXANDER

My left arm wouldn't move. Every attempt was an excruciating failure.

The bull-horned Fera screeched and charged for me again, forcing me to abandon one of my scythes to leap up and whirl behind a closely-fitted series of spiked rocks for shelter. *I* could slip in, but the creature was too large to fit. It clawed at the rock and shrieked at me, butting its horns, futilely trying to force its way in.

I took a moment to seethe, still clutching the gushing wound. I was getting dizzy. My left arm still wouldn't respond and it hung limp at my side, drenched in warm blood.

"Well!" a surprised, flighty voice huffed above me. "Isn't this just my luck?"

My head snapped up—and I cringed.

Staring down at me were the glowing-white pupils of Cilia. She was crouched on the spike I hid behind, peering down curiously. "It seems we both were seeking shelter for a time. How convenient. Is my descendant with you, by chan—*ah, ah, ah!* No you don't!"

She grabbed my collar before I could duck away. I was lifted over the rocks and plopped at her feet as she gave a long, satisfied sigh. "There we are. My, you look exhausted, don't you? Quite a lot of blood you've lost, by the looks of it."

I squirmed against the precarious surface, her hand pressing my face to the rock and scraping my cheek. I tried to shout for the others—Vendy, Jaq, *anyone*—but all that surfaced was a sputter of mangled groans.

"This changes plans drastically," Cilia hummed, examining me. After a while, she said to the sky. "Everyone! Bring the other Reapers here to me. Do not harm any of them, merely herd them."

The hole in my back and shoulder still burned. I realized I'd dropped my second scythe when she'd pulled me up, so I had nothing to defend myself with.

Everything was spinning as the other Reapers raced around the rock formations one by one. They were being pushed back by the horde of Necrofera, and when they were all corralled together, they were trapped in a circle.

Among them, Lilli gasped, spotting me. "Alex!" She spread her wings, flying up.

Damned girl, stay where you are! I wanted to scream, but didn't have the breath—nor the freedom. My jaw was crushed against the rock so closely, I thought it would crack.

Lilli hadn't flapped three feet when Cilia raised me upright by a tuft of hair, making the bat swerve back when Cilia held an enflamed hand to my chest.

"Keep your distance," Cilia clucked, a playful twang crawling from her lips. "I have little reason to keep him alive already. I know his twin is here somewhere, and I could simply kill him now and wait until the other arrives."

Lilli set her jaw, as if debating what to do. She kept her dual scythes ready and questioned, "Then why are you waiting?"

"I'm *so* glad you asked!" Cilia giggled like a schoolgirl, her smile wide as she looked down at our group—specifically at Octavius. "Hello, Descendant!"

Octavius grimaced. "Gods damn it."

"What sort of greeting is that for your cherished relative?" she cried, holding an ostentatious hand to her chest and carelessly ground my face into the rough rock. "Aren't you happy to see me?"

"Ecstatic," Octavius spat.

Her face dripped into a scowl. "It's the Reaper's influence… You'd change your tune if you only knew. Perhaps we need to separate you from their poisonous drivel."

"I've already told you I'm not going anywhere with you."

From my vantage, I barely saw Neal lean toward his brother and mutter, "When did Mika dye her hair?"

"That's not Mika." Octavius held a cautious stance. "This is our ancestral Demon Queen I told you about."

"Why does she look like our sis—?"

"Because we're related I guess, I don't know!"

Cilia looked at Neal, curious. "What's this? A brother?" They stiffened when she gave an overjoyed gasp. "How wonderful! Don't worry, I have room for both of you. Just come stand behind me and—"

"*Neither* of us are coming with you!" Octavius roared.

I yelped when she lifted my head higher, nearly yanking out the hairs. "You'll come if you want me to set him free!" she sneered. "I don't care about him if I have you. And your brother will come as well, of course, all family is welcome. Now! Stay with me and allow your friends to walk free, or let them die—"

An enormous wave shoved against our rock, knocking Cilia and me to the wet sand below. She tumbled to one side while I thudded ungracefully to the other.

Lilli soared down and crouched over me as Cilia rose to her feet. The Sentient's face was creased with fury.

Hecrûshou had been the source of the large wave. He stood between us and the Demon Queen. Beside him flapped Sir Janson and his vassals, all taking offensive positions to guard us. *When had they come?*

Cilia's anger leaked from her throat. "Why are you so determined to get in my way, sea dweller?"

Hecrûshou flipped his glowing trident over a shoulder. "You were the one who broke our treaty. Perhaps I should ask why you are so determined to ignore my laws?"

"Oh, for the love of Shel, it's always about laws with you! Just get out of my *way*!" She charged him.

The Sentients crashed into a frenzied brawl, the lesser demons screeching and clawing at each other. It was utter chaos. I could barely keep up with what was happening, the world swirling nauseatingly... vomit climbed from my stomach and flooded up, sloshing onto the beach.

It barely missed Lilli's lap, and as my head dropped onto her knees, I saw the bile was mixed with blood, which poured from that damned hole at my collarbone.

I felt Lilli's hands quivering when she pressed against the hole on my back. The pressure hurt like Death, but I was too dizzy to complain. *Was she in tears?* It was hard to hear, from the constant noise of spraying sea water.

It sounded like she was talking frantically with Jaq, both of their voices projecting over me and debating what to do. Their voices were fading, and my lids were dropping... but then I heard a new voice calling me, sounding neither like Jaq nor Lilli.

"Alex..."

My lids were so heavy, my mind thumping numbly.

"Alex...!"

I was so close to sleep. So close to relief from the pain, the dizziness... but something was nagging me, keeping me awake.

"Alex!"

Who was that? The voice was too deep to be Lilli's; too far away to be Jaq's. I could swear it almost sounded like—

"ALEX!"

My eyes shot open. "Xa... vier?" The fog vanished from mind, and I forgot the pain in my shoulder, stumbling to my feet. "Xavier?"

I looked around the chaos of battling Necrofera. There, three rocks down, being carried over Kurrick's back...

Was my brother.

57

CAVEATS

XAVIER

"Alex!" I yelled over Kurrick's bulky back, spotting my brother. He was bleeding from a large hole at his collarbone, looking paler than usual. His left arm lay limp at his side and I guessed from that monstrous wound he wasn't able to use it.

His bleary, mismatched eyes lit into focus after I called, and when he staggered to his feet I barely heard him holler back in the chaos of warring Necrofera.

Cilia and Hecrûshou were in the midst of combat. Their rival armies tore out each others' hearts in a confusing display of splattered tar and cracked limbs. I had no idea which beast was on whose side, but if they were focused on each other, then they weren't paying attention to *us*.

Alex staggered toward us, but stumbled and curled on his side, trembling.

Lilli and Jaq scrambled to help him while Kurrick rushed me over and set me down beside them. Kurrick kept me upright, and I watched Lilli push her hands over Alexander's gash, trying to stop the bleeding while Jaq squeezed my arm.

"Xavier." Jaq gave a wary grin. He was clearly thrilled to see me here, *physically* here, beside Alexander. But that delight didn't last long and the viper's grin soon faded to a dark, pertinent frown when he looked at Alex.

"What happened?" I asked, clutching my brother's hand as tightly as my boney fingers would allow.

"Fera with horns," Jaq explained. "Some kind of bull-shifter. Hit him from behind when we were heading back."

"Damn it, Alex…" I tightened my grip on his fingers. It was a weak effort, but he soon squeezed back.

"Xavier," my brother puffed, sounding disoriented. "You're... awake..."

I gave a thin smile. "I wasn't about to let you die before we had a chance to be face to face again."

He hacked a chuckle. "Does that mean you'll... let me die now that we are?"

"Ah, well. You're in luck. I *had* planned to leave you here, but I've decided to take you with me after all. If you think you can make the trek?"

His head shook. "I'll be fine. Let's just... leave. Now."

I glanced at Kurrick. "Can you carry both of us to the ship?"

Kurrick made a hard face. "If given time for travel and a clear path. Of which we have neither."

"Please, try anyway."

Something caught my eye past the warrior. There were four figures making their way through the chaos of Necrofera. It looked like... Willow. The Death Princess had taken out her scythe and was ripping at the demons, her arcs and spins precise with unrivaled grace. Ana, who was with her also, had fashioned an enormous, glowing sword out of stone with her Terravoking and was cutting a path through the demons to make way for Sirra-Lynn and...

"Oh, Gods," I cursed, seeing *Bianca* sprinting alongside them, scared out of her wits and following the three girls. *Alex is not going to like this.*

Bianca tripped on a low rock, cried out, and fell behind.

"Bianca!" I shouted. "Stay close to Wil—!"

A Fera leapt for the girls, making Bianca duck and scream in fright, but Willow was quick to slice the beast in two. The rabbit made a run for it, driven by panic as she collapsed beside us.

"A-A-Alex...!" she panted in a shiver, fumbling to take out her medical tools from her satchel. "W-w-what happened?!"

Alex scowled at her, wheezing, "What in Death's name are you... doing here...?"

Willow came beside me and touched my shoulder. A single look held an unspoken question and answer: 'Will he be all right?' she wanted to know. 'I hope' was my reply.

Sirra-Lynn and Ana knelt to Alexander, cleaning the front gash at his clavicle alongside Bianca. The rabbit was shuffling through a plethora of vials, the clink of glass rattling from her bag.

She gave a shuddered breath. "I-I heard Xavier saying you were hurt or something and-and I got worried and... Nira, does it go all the way through?! Roll him on his side again!"

Alex groaned when Sirra and Ana pulled him sideways, and Bianca hurried to sanitize the back wound that was caked in a layer of bloodied sand.

Lilli, meanwhile, had been brushed aside, her stained-red hands shaking. "Will he be all right?" the bat asked Bianca.

Bianca's eyes flicked at her, resentment buried inside, and her gaze fell back to her medical work. "We'll seal the holes. It won't return the motion in his arm right away, but it'll stop the bleeding. Alex, you were damn lucky it missed your heart. Bloody *idiot*."

He muttered something like a pained laugh as the three Healers used their Hallows to make his skin scab over the holes at both ends. They dressed the wounds, though it was a rushed job, and propped him upright against a rock.

"All right," Bianca huffed, wiping tears. "You'll be fine. Just fine. Okay—uhm—we need to get you out of—"

"Cilia," a new voice snapped from the top of a rocky spike. I glanced up, seeing a scaled man in a midnight blue cloak was watching us. He didn't look pleased as he barked louder over the noise. "Cilia! Why are you still wasting time with this nonsense?"

Bloods, I thought with a groan. I recognized the cobra, though not entirely by his face. We'd only met once, months ago in Nulani, but I'd heard enough about the man from Claude to know exactly who this was. *The puppeteer himself.*

The two Sentients didn't cease their battle after Macarius had called for Cilia.

"Cilia!" Macarius clipped again, piqued. "Are you listening?"

Cilia barely ducked away from Hecrûshou's thrusting trident. Her brow twitched with annoyance. "I'm a bit preoccupied!"

"Just kill him and be done with it," Macarius ordered.

She skidded around an electric bolt Janson's vassal, Rosette, had aimed at her. "I *said* I'm—"

Janson's *second* vassal showered her with a flurry of icicles, pinning her to a pillar in a *spliksh* of black blood. Her chest was nearly sliced open by Janson's crooked blade, but she ripped free and pushed him back with a burst of blue fire.

Then, before Janson could regain his footing, a *fourth* Sentient rushed forward and charged Janson, the newcomer's leopard ears curled back in a snarl and claws drawn long and sharp.

Beside me, Sirra-Lynn gasped at the new demon, her orange cat ears folding to her neck. "M... Master Maveric...?"

Alexander and I simultaneously growled. "Mother of Death."

58

THE ARCHCHANCELLOR

~~~~~~~

HERRIN

The tremors shook the underground tunnel we migrated through, dust and rocks showering from the ceiling.

Ringëd was shepherding the island's survivors through the tunnels, all of them talking to him in Marincian and acting like they knew him. Maybe they did… well, except for that teenaged Grim girl—the cute, Necrovoking nurse with the black pig-tails.

She had all kinds of hair clips pulling back her straight bangs and she wore a lavender nurse's tunic over teal stockings. Three rows of earrings sparkled from her ears in the firelight, which Mikani had provided with her Pyrovoking, and the girl's arms were covered with purple, fingerless gloves.

The girl was muttering something under her breath. *What was she saying? Would it be weird to start talking to her?* Prepping myself mentally, I inched my way over.

"… Your old *maiser*?" she whispered with a fluid accent, looking shocked. "Are you sure, Sirra?"

Oh. She was talking with her vassal. The twins did that with Dalen a lot.

I decided to leave her alone. What would I even say? The cavern tunnels were still rumbling like all Void was breaking loose up there, so flirting didn't really feel appropriate right now anyway.

And how were we even going to get past all those demons? I know the blue-haired guy up ahead kept saying not to worry about it, but how were we *not* supposed to worry about being ripped to shreds?

So, that's King Dream, huh? I squinted at the crowned boy's back as he led us through the tunnel. *Why does he look so… YOUNG?*

He looked the same age as his Bloody granddaughter. Wasn't he supposed to be two-thousand-years-old or something? And what the Void was with that ratty looking sweater? I thought royalty was supposed to have a sense of propriety or whatever.

King Dream suddenly turned around and looked at me. "Herrin? Could I have a word?"

I stiffened. *Oh Bloods.* Was this about the book his wife gave me? The one I lost? I swallowed and meekly shuffled next to him.

"So, you're the one Crysalette chose?" he asked, head cocking. I couldn't get a read on his expression. There wasn't a smile; wasn't a frown. Just curious, azure eyes. "Interesting… You're much younger than the other Enlighteners. I suppose my wife finds value in youth. She was the one to suggest bringing back the old texts, you see, so I left her to choose whomever she saw fit to read them."

I winced. "I… I lost the book, actually. Kurrick took it and threw it in the ocean, so…"

His expression still didn't change. "Did he? Oh, dear… I apologize for Kurrick, he's always been a bit overzealous. Especially when it comes to Ana."

"The text was ruined." I had to keep my voice in check. Remembering how the pages sopped out of the binding in my hands made me sick. "I-I *lost* the book she gave me."

"Ah, well, it's only a book. You can write another."

My brow furrowed. "*Write* one?"

"I don't see why not." He, for once, smiled. It seemed forced and formulaic, but the voice was sincere. "In fact, why don't you add something else? A scripture of your own?"

"What would I put in it?"

He waved a shrugging hand. "Perhaps about the twins? They have quite an intriguing story to tell of their own, don't they? And who better to scribe it than the Archchancellor himself?"

I stumbled to a halt. "The *what?*"

"Oh, didn't Crysalette tell you?" He chuckled. "Your full title is Chief of Knowledge, Archchancellor Herrin Tesler of the Enlightener's Guild. You were the first to be chosen, and will be the one to direct the other Enlighteners. They will follow whatever system you wish to establish. It's something of a school, an army of scholars, you could say. We'll certainly need one to combat the Lightcaster's propaganda—"

"Why in Bloods am *I* the Archchancellor?" I interrupted, throat tight with panic. "Wh… what did *I* do?"

"You're traveling with the Shadowblood, for one thing," he said, keeping that forced smile in place. "Who better to speak of their existence than one who is with them? Also, my wife believes you have the intellect to study the text, interpret it, and establish a sound structure of how to teach it to others."

"How would she know that?"

"She's watched your dreams for the last few months here and there, before she made her decision. She approved of what your subconscious showed her."

"Uh…" *What did I dream about that long ago?* I couldn't even remember anymore.

He chuckled again. "Yes, I think another scripture would be most interesting. Ah, here we are."

We stopped at the mouth of the tunnel where the rocky shoals started. I staggered, horrified. It was utter chaos. Demons were killing demons in an all-out war and I had no idea who was on whose side. *Did* they *even know?* Sure didn't Bloody look like it.

Dream gave a short hum. "We don't want to go out in that, do we? Very well. It seems the Orbs will be of use here after all. Let's get a look at the ship…"

He rose to his bare toes, craning past the misted rocks to see the ship we'd left behind in the sand. "Not too far, that's good. If I gauge the distance from here, I'd say it's nearly… eighty-two paces."

I frowned, disagreeing. I'd studied geographical measuring enough to estimate the number of paces a structure was. "It's one hundred and *seven* paces."

His smile remained stagnant. "Eighty-two."

"If it were a straight line, maybe," I protested. "But not if you have to move around the rocks."

"Oh, we won't be walking through this plane," he said and reached into the wide pouch of his greasy sweater, pulling out three glittering, azure orbs. "We're going to take a trip into Aspirre."

What? I was about to question him, but one of the orbs gleamed with a blinding flash—

The world was sucked away.

The ground disappeared and I yelped when I dropped a full foot down, my stomach lurching before I slammed onto a random, stone street that had popped into existence out of nowhere. Literally nowhere.

I groaned and pushed to my belly, scraping my hands bloody against the rough stone beneath me. I glanced around, confused as Land. Except for this one piece of street, it was black all over. Our whole group was isolated in an empty abyss of nothingness.

"What the Void...?" I whispered, staggering to my feet.

Dream showed up beside me and patted my shoulder, chuckling. "Sorry for the rough stone," he said, nodding at my scraped palms. "I nearly forgot to weave anything for you all. It was a last-minute correction."

"Where are we?" I asked. "What happened to the shoals? The ship? The Bloody Fera?"

"They're back on the island," he murmured, and I jerked back when the Dream mark on his forehead gleamed bright.

Azure lights streamed under his hands as he gripped his shaggy tree-branch-crook, its decorative bell jingling. "For now, the demons we have to worry about are far different."

Screeches echoed overhead, along with some kind of shifting noise, like sand in the wind. But there wasn't any sand, and there sure as Bloods wasn't any wind.

Dream lifted his shepherd's crook and slammed it down on the road, everyone gasping when an enormous bubble blossomed from the staff and engulfed our entire group.

Shadowy sand creatures started clawing at the bubble, sending ripples over the bubble's protective surface. Dream stared emptily at the creepy monsters, and I noticed his feet were hovering a few inches off the ground. How was he doing that? The rest of us had to adhere to gravity.

"Come along everyone," Dream called with a smile, floating forward as the bubble followed him. "Stay close, and pay no mind to the noctis golems. The barrier will keep them at bay so long as you stay within its walls."

No one was about to protest, and the herd followed close at their shepherd's heels through the black abyss.

59
CAUGHT IN THE FRAY

XAVIER

Maveric raked his claws down Janson's wings, causing the Sentient to scream and turn on the rotted Healer.

Janson had the advantage: wings and a weapon. Maveric's strategy dealt mostly with dodging and striking from behind, neither of them getting far. Maveric's approach was sloppy and unrefined, unlike Janson's purposeful strikes as his long-handled scythe arched and bowed with efficient vigor.

The tar-coated underlings were still bursting around us, their allegiances seeming as reliable as a single strand of horsehair keeping a boulder from falling.

I had Kurrick set me against the nearest rock so I could sit up on my own. Ana, Bianca and Sirra-Lynn propped Alexander beside me after he was properly bandaged. The dressings at his chest and back were seeping with blood, I noticed. He was breathing hard, looking as if he were straining to stay conscious.

"Some mess we've walked into," he grunted.

"*You* walked," I reminded, my head rolling back against the rock. There was only so much my weak neck could take without support; my skull may as well have been made of lead. "I had someone carry me."

He glanced absently at my boney legs. His eyes were red and glossy, maybe trying to focus on a thought. "Do your legs work?"

"No. Muscle degeneration."

"Grand." He shut his eyes and sighed hard.

"—Young sirs?"

Alex and I flinched when Aiden's ghostly head popped between us from the rock we rested on. Our mother's vassal looked rushed. "I think we ought to be going, don't you?"

Nathaniel's head came to the other side of Alexander's face. "Aye, best be gettin' off this rock, says I."

Dalen next, by my own face. "Yeah, *Da'torr*, we need to go. I mean, Vendy's resurrected and kicking ass out there, but I say call her back and skedaddle while those things are distracted with themselves."

"Fair point," Alex and I spoke in unison, clearing our throats. "Vendy, fall back."

In the distance, I saw Vendy slice through a Fera and freeze, her head snapping toward us. *Bloods, Da'torr*, she said through our mental connection, too far to be heard by our physical ears. *That was just downright spooky, hearing both of you guys talk.*

We shrugged—though Alex could only use one shoulder for it. "You'll get used to it."

Vendy hacked her way through the mass toward us, sliding beside Willow as both women stood guard with their glowing weapons drawn.

Ana and Kurrick assisted them in pushing the creatures back, all of them unwittingly inching farther and farther away from Alex and me. Even Sirra-Lynn ran after them, calling Maveric's name, and Bianca chased after the insane Healer in a panic.

After long, Alexander and I were left alone. We were the only ones who could do nothing but sit and watch, Alexander too faint from blood-loss and I too weak from my six-year coma. *Marvelous.*

The ghosts fled back into the rock behind us, only keeping their heads visible to see what was happening.

"How're we gonna leave with all these things crawling around?" Dalen asked skeptically.

Alex coughed, his throat sounding sore. "I don't know. But since Xavier and I are here, we can go ahead and resurrect you, Dalen. It will at least be better protection."

Dalen's spectral face sagged. "But my Crystal daggers are back on the ship."

"It's better than nothing," I considered.

Alex's head swayed when he began evoking his death Hallows, fingers gleaming with violet light as he reached for the three Storagecoffins strapped to his belt.

He'd only begun to single out Dalen's coffin when Nathaniel turned to Dalen and said, "ey, thief bird, think ye can give me 'n feather-brains here a lift when yer sown? Ye can fly us outta here pretty easy, right? Not like we weigh anythin' worth a lick."

Dalen shrugged his translucent shoulders. "Worth a try—"

Alex gave a startled gasp, gripping the three coffins at his belt.

"What's wrong?" I asked.

"I..." Alex didn't seem sure what to say. He stared at the sky in thought, brow furrowed as he fingered the Storagecoffins with small *clinks*. His hands were still pooling with violet light. "I felt something. With *all* of them. They just... moved."

There was silence. It took me a moment to respond. "What are you saying?"

"I think... I think I can..." He sucked in a breath, held it, then ripped his hand upward.

All three skeletons tumbled out with his dragging Hallows.

I gaped at the pile of bones. "What in Nirus?"

"How in the five Bloody realms did ye do that?" Nathaniel blurted, staring at his aged bones. "Not in two hundred years has a corpse raiser done *that* when I was under contract with someone else!"

Alex's eyes glazed dimly, as if drunk. "Huh. I think I just broke the Necrovoking laws of physics. How about that?"

He inhaled and strained his Hallows more, sweat beading his brow as he collected each skeleton and pieced them into whole puzzles. With a determined yell, he sent a surge of violet light onto the puppets, filling the bones with nerves, tendons, muscles, skin, hair, feathers—and jumpstarted their hearts until they were fully alive and breathing.

I sat in shock as my brother collapsed over my lap, coughing and wheezing.

"Alex?" My voice shook. "How did you...?"

"No idea." He hacked blood onto my patient's tunic, puffing. "That... that took a lot out of me, though... Your turn."

"What do you mean *my turn*? I can't sew all of—"

"*I* just did," he growled. "By default, that means you can."

"But—"

"Try. It's difficult, but... possible." He didn't get up from my lap. "Just push harder than usual."

I clicked my teeth, hesitant. *Oh, what the Void?* I may as well give it a shot.

I raised my hands to the three ghosts who phased out of the rock to stare at their resurrected bodies. With a slow inhale, I evoked my Hallows. The lights streamed from my fingers and stretched to the ghosts, engulfing them.

But only Dalen was affected. The other two didn't move. I sighed. "Well... I tried." Committing to our vassal, I created a temporary NecroSeam for Dalen and slid his soul into the awaiting body.

Dalen awoke and stretched his wings, kneeling down to us. "What about the other two?" Dalen asked. "Can ya do whatever *he* did with 'em?"

"I tried." I said.

"You—" Alex fell into a coughing fit. He let it subside before rolling onto his back to stare up at me with bloodshot eyes. "You have to push harder."

I scowled at him. "I did."

"You Bloody well didn't and you know it!" he accused. "You have to use the same stamina as when you took out your soul! And Kurrick's!"

My lips pursed. "You think that will work? It's an entirely different Evocation."

"It'll work." He pressed his right hand against my chest, letting me stare at his Crest. "Trust me."

I glanced at Nathaniel and Aiden: my parents' vassals; the souls I shouldn't be able to control. *Yet Alex could...*

I exhaled, uncertain, but lifted my hand to the two remaining ghosts. I held my breath. My crest of black diamonds morphed into the Death mark and shined white as I evoked my Hallows again. I strained, the stream of Hallows thickening from my palm. Still, nothing happened.

"Keep going!" Alex barked.

I pushed again, the breath draining from my lungs, stamina fading as if drawn from an already empty well. I felt a bead of sweat drip down my temple as I tried to shove the remaining ounce of power in my quickly leaking reserve, hands trembling.

Alex ducked under a flying demon's claws and yelled. "*Xavier!*"

My hands exploded with violet light.

The glow poured through the two ghosts, filling them. It collected in their chests, and I wove two shining NecroSeams at their centers.

"Hold it there!" Alex ordered, seeing that I'd nearly fallen over. "Now sew!"

I threw the ghosts into their resurrected vessels, stitching them to their beating hearts. At last, Nathaniel and Aiden blinked awake as I gasped and curled over Alex, puffing profusely.

Alex breathed a ragged praise as I leaned back against the rock. "Gods! That was worse than any of Mistress's training..."

"Unbelievably worse," he agreed, closing his eyes and lifting a finger to the newly risen vassals. "All right, everyone—get out of here and return to the ship. Make sure it's ready to go before we get there. Nathaniel, I trust you'll know how to handle everything?"

Nathaniel still seemed unfamiliar with... *whatever* just happened. "Uh, yeah... 'o course. But don't ye want to be comin' with us?"

"We'll be right behind you." Alex waved his hand in a 'shooing' motion. "Kurrick will take us. But we need the ship ready, and fast. Now that you're resurrected, you can fend off the Fera with your Hallows. Keep Dalen safe, please, he's not an Evocator."

They hesitated, but did as asked, the three vassals hurrying off and disappearing behind the misted rocks.

"Kurrick," I coughed, weakly lifting my head. "Follow them to the…" I trailed off, seeing Kurrick wasn't crouching next to me anymore. I'd forgotten the warrior went off to keep the Fera at bay with the others. I grimaced. "Death. Now what?"

Alex didn't open his eyes, and I thought for a moment he'd fallen asleep until he gave a tired grumble. "We leave, don't we?"

"That would be ideal. But you can't seem to stay upright, and my legs may as well be twigs."

His mouth opened, then shut. "Hm. Then we wait, I suppose."

"Brilliant."

60
FAMILIAR FACES

~~~~~

WILLOW

Sirra held a horrified hand to her throat beside me as I cut down the Fera pouncing for her and Bianca.

Why the Bloods are they here? I thought furiously, slicing beasts left and right. *Don't they see this disaster?!*

At least Bianca was aware of the danger, shivering and shrieking in fright with every lunge the demons made for us, but Sirra didn't seem to notice any of it! She was too preoccupied with watching Janson and Maveric's brawl.

"He… he's been Changed?" Sirra whispered, tears misting. "My old master is a demon…?"

I watched Maveric claw at Janson's side, but the crow kicked him back and brought down his scythe—

Maveric's head was torn off. Janson swung a second time, at the leopard's chest, and *snapped* his NecroSeam in two. Then Maveric fizzled with a mist of black tar before reverting to an aged corpse and splashing to the wet sand.

"*Maveric!*" Sirra cried, running to the headless corpse. She hovered over him, cupping her mouth and choking on sobs. "Maveric…! Why…?"

"He's gone back to Nira, now!" I yanked her up by the arm. "There is nothing we can do for him! Come, you must go where it's safe!"

This was no time for grieving! Didn't she see that? We were caught in a war that we needed to flee. I started to pull her back to the others, but stopped after locking eyes with Sir Janson.

His one white pupil shone in the darkness, face long with hesitation. "Princess," he began. "I… wanted to…" He trailed off, leaving it there.

He didn't need to finish. With a forgiving smile, I said, "Even in death, you wear your badge with honor, Brother… Perhaps the Goddess will spare your rotten soul for it."

His lips curled up, bowing with a fist to his chest.

—A black-stained hand pierced out of his ribs. Janson gave a gurgled choke, collapsing forward as Cilia plucked her arm out of him.

"Hmph," she flipped her hair over a shoulder. "Just scraped the NecroSeam, eh? Hadn't quite snapped…"

Janson's wound didn't heal. Black blood spurted from the hole in his back, the winged Sentient gasping for breath.

"No…!" I cried, my shock wrenching into absolute rage as I glared at Cilia. "You…! Bloody…! *Monster!*" I screamed and charged for Cilia.

I almost cut her throat when she bent back and twirled away, then she leapt when I swung for her legs. On and on I went, tears streaming, my only thought to kill the crazed girl that'd caused me so much grief, so much pain, so much insatiable *fury*…!

"Cilia, for Gods' sake," the cobra man hissed from his safe perch above us, his voice echoing off the rocks. Bloods, I'd nearly forgotten he was there. "You can play later. I need that one alive. And I can see the twins clearly from here, cease your games and kill—"

He was cut off when Hecrûshou sent a giant wave over his pillar and landed in front of the cobra. The shark's finned brow furrowed low.

"You're an annoying one." Hecrûshou's glowing trident was raised to the snake's throat. "Are you the reason Everland's queen has been acting so vicious?"

The man regarded him as a genius would a dimwit. "You say vicious. I prefer *efficient*."

"You have some gall, Clean One." Hecrûshou thrust his trident into the man's stomach—it phased right through, like a phantom. The shark blinked. "What in Nirus…?"

He's a Somniovoker, I realized. That must have been a copy of the original man. *But then… a dream walker has caused so much chaos?* Somniovokers were passive people, from my experience. Not fit for violence.

"Cilia!" the man barked again. "I will not be left waiting!"

"Oh, all *right!*" Cilia propelled off her perch to land with a puff of scattering sand—directly behind Xavier and Alexander.

The others were forced away from them when she evoked her fire Hallows to make a flaming wall around the twins.

Then Cilia came for them.

"Xavier!" I scrambled forward, passing through the wall of flames without heed—clothes and hair catching fire—and skidded in front of Xavier in time to slice off Cilia's groping hand.

The fabric of my tunic and breeches slowly burnt away, the heat of the flames radiating as it licked over the ever-growing bare spots of skin. The ends of my long, bundled hair had been singed, white strands flaking into ash, stopping at my back when a splash of ocean water doused it.

"Willow," Xavier breathed behind me, startled. "Your hair…"

"It will grow back." *Grow* wasn't the right word for it. *Did he not remember?*

Cilia's detached hand slithered back to her in a string of black slime, her wrist cracking back into place as she set the hand at her hip in a sigh. "Do you ever give up, Princess?"

My fox ears curled back. "You will pay for your crimes, Demon. For what you've done to our Brothers and Sisters… to Sir Janson." Tears came again, Janson's writhing body flashing to memory.

Cilia rolled back her head, her neck cracking. "I'm sure I will, one day. But not until I have what I want—"

"CILIAAA!"

We jumped at the booming voice, our heads snapping to the abandoned ship outside the shoals.

Standing at the bow was a black-haired man, a fist clenched around a thick rope that dangled from a mast. A flash of lightning illuminated his yellow eyes like a blaze of fire, and he bellowed once more. "CILIAAAA!"

Cilia fell dead still.

A light rain drizzled from the billowing storm, no doubt courtesy of the Sky Princess, which doused the surrounding fire.

"Cilia Treble," Claude called over the thunder. "I have a question for you."

Cilia's green eyes grew wide. I barely heard her whisper, "Treble…?"

"Do you remember Kael?" Claude asked, rain dripping from his chin. His yellow eyes glinted in the lantern-light of the ship, visible even from this distance. *"Do you remember Kael?"*

"Ka…el…?" Her lips quivered. "Kael…?" Her eyes welled, a bubble of joy sprouting with the name. "Kael…!" She clutched her head, screaming. *"Nnh…! Ka*el*…!"*

Ana tugged my arm, nodding toward the ship. It was time to leave.

Kurrick had already taken Xavier on his back and lifted Alexander in his arms, hustling both twins out of the rocky shoals and onto the ship with everyone. The island's survivors had—somehow—slipped onboard during the distraction. Nathaniel was at the helm, miraculously resurrected. *How?* Oh, never mind that now.

Grandfather Dream was waiting for me on the lower deck.

"Ah, Willow," he said, patting my cheek. "I should think that's everyone, then." He turned to Nathaniel at the helm and cupped his mouth, shouting, "All accounted for, captain!"

"Aye!" Nathaniel called back, waving at the surrounding crew. "Bring down the sails!"

Lilli, Jaq, and Octavius hurried to pull down the sails, the fabric rustling in the harsh winds.

"Yer Highness Sky!" Nathaniel called next, pointing to Zylveia from the clouds. "If ye wouldn't mind, we could use some winds!" He flapped a meaty hand at Aiden beside him. "And you, too, feather-brains! Give us a gale and get us off these bloomin' rocks!"

Aiden flapped to join Zylveia in a hurry, tugging on his goggles and hollering, "Aye, Captain!"

The two Aerovokers lifted their hands to the billowing clouds, their fingers glittering scarlet lights as they thrust them at our sails. The fabric was blown backward, pushing the ship off the shoals in gritty crunches as we finally drifted out to sea.

The shore fell away inch by inch, and I stood at the bow beside Claude, my now shoulder-length hair blowing in front of me and letting me see the flaky, ashen ends.

I watched Cilia sob alone, sprawled over the sand like a desperate, miserable creature.

We were still close enough for me to see tears streaming down her face when she looked up at us—at Claude. She rose like a machine, wet hair sticking to her face.

"Kaaaaaaeeeeel!" we barely heard her screech, voice fading under the storm. "KAAAAAEEEEeeeelll!"

She vanished in the fog.

Her faint voice was all that was left of Y'ahmelle Nayû, crying the name one last time before the ocean's currents took us.

61

A DAUNTING TASK

HERRIN

I sat in the galley alone. Everyone had already gone to sleep, I think. If they hadn't, they weren't hungry. Not that I was, either. I just wanted a place to think. This whole night was just so... so...

I sighed, folding my arms onto the table and practically dripped into it. I didn't even have a word for it. *What was with that Sentient girl? Who exactly is Kael and why is he important?* I didn't get it.

I flinched when footsteps creaked from the stairs up top. Ana was coming down.

"Hello, Herrin," she said softly, reaching the bottom and sat beside me on the bench. Her crimson eyes were sullen as she cupped her hands on her lap. Her tan face was covered by the petal-like curls of her chestnut hair.

"Hi..." I mumbled, fidgeting.

There was silence. The calm sway of the waves outside made the floorboards creak and groan, filling the empty space of our non-existent conversation.

"I think it's time," she finally murmured.

When she didn't expound, I prodded. "Time for what?"

"To tell the Shadowblood who they are. It is time they were told, by the Chief Enlightener. You have my permission to do so. Although..." She paused. "Perhaps tonight is not appropriate. All must be aware, including the Death and Sky Princesses. Willow has other concerns at the moment and may need time to... heal. The twins will also need rest."

My stomach sank, nerves shaking. "How long should I wait?"

"Until you determine they are in a reasonable state." She rose. "I give you full control of the decision, Archchancellor."

She began climbing the stairs. I stretched to my feet and called after her. "There's still one problem, though, isn't there?"

She paused halfway up the stairs, one lion ear flicking. Her looped earring wavered with the motion. "What problem is that?" she asked.

"We're missing a Relicblood." My fingers squirmed nervously. "The King of Land. The true heir… I know you think he's still out there, but what if he's not? What do we do then?"

Her lips curled into a smile. "That is not something to worry about, dear Herrin. Good night." She continued up the stairs… and disappeared.

62
A NEW BEGINNING

※※※

XAVIER

"Willow?" My crutches clipped over the deck outside, my useless, limp legs trembling under me. *Damned, weak muscles...* I sighed. *But at least they're mine.*

I found Willow sitting on the edge of the ship, staring at the vast sea. She fiddled with her music watch, the amulet open and playing the Requiem with mournful twinkles.

I noticed my Crest was gleaming black and purple over my knuckles, as it always did when that amulet played. The white stones inside the watch glowed and dusted like pale embers, swirling round the revolving discus in time with the slow, ringing music.

Y'ahmelle Nayû had disappeared hours ago. The storm had passed and now, only a light breeze swept by, wavering Willow's long, ashen hair behind her. She'd taken off her ribbon and bell to let the strands fall freely to the floor, her morose figure outlined in silver moonlight.

Dazzling, she is, I admired in silence, smiling. Chai gave a soft croak beside my foot as I hobbled to her. He used his beak and talons to climb onto the rail beside me.

Willow gave Chai a welcoming pat on the head, and Jewel twittered in greeting from her shoulder. Still, her expression was morose.

When I propped myself beside her, I lifted her chin and took her lips. The heat blazed from her flesh, so sweet and tender, the hush of the sea fell to silence. *Now wait a moment.* Had that been the first time we'd kissed in so many years? That *I* had kissed her? Not as my brother, but as myself?

No, now that I recalled, she had taken that initiative while I couldn't move. *Hrm...* How disappointing. *Well, there's plenty of time to correct that.* We had years, perhaps decades ahead of us... For the first time in a very long time, I... had a future.

I smiled, and she attempted likewise, but her eyes were still laden with gloom.

"What's wrong?" I asked. "I'm myself again. I'm alive. Is it not enough?"

Her head shook. "It's wonderful, darling. I can hardly believe we've made it this far, it's only... I'm only... tired."

An obvious lie. But if she wasn't willing to explain, then I supposed she didn't want me asking any more of it. I started with a different topic. "I see your hair's grown back already?"

She gave a low hum, letting the music ring out its final, sorrowed note, and clipped the amulet closed. "It always does."

"How?"

With a sigh, she let the amulet slink along its glistening chain and rest over her bosom. She then plucked her hair-stick scythe from her Storagesphere and twirled it idly between her fingers, having her scythe materialize in a golden glitter. She took the glowing blade to her long bundle of strands and sliced them off.

I drew back when the strands deteriorated into flakes of ash, swirled in the wind for a moment—glowing in the moonlight like brilliant specks of dust in the blue ray—before they reattached themselves to the rest of her hair where they belonged.

"It isn't just ashen in color." She leaned her scythe over her shoulder, still watching the waves. "It *is* ash... All the Relic Children and their incarnations have something similar. Ocean's hair is water, Sky's hair is lightning, Land's hair was said to be flower petals..." She chuckled hollowly. "Grandfather Dream's hair is sand. You and Alexander didn't believe him once, and he cut a lock of his hair to show you. The look on your faces was hysterical..." Her chuckles died, smile weakening. "I suppose you forgot, when you lost your memories..."

"I suppose so..." I murmured, awed. It was fascinating... But her depressed tone was still concerning. I leaned against the rail and stared at the lapping waves. "What are you looking for out here?"

"I don't know," she admitted. Jewel stretched up to rub against her chin. "Sir Janson, perhaps..."

Ah. So, that was it. "Did Cilia really kill him?"

"He was dying when we left. I imagine he's gone now. I only wish..."

"...you could have said goodbye?" I offered.

She thought on that. "Yes. There'd been no time. Neither for that nor..."

A splash sounded below us, and we craned to peer down. Hecrûshou was bobbing in the water in front of our ship, carrying someone on his back. Someone with black wings.

Willow gasped, making room when Hecrûshou climbed up a dangling rope to the deck and threw Sir Janson on the floorboards. The withered crow flopped onto his back, his two vassals crouching beside him, their faces wet with tears and seawater.

Hecrûshou's Bindragon slithered to Janson's face, its head cocking as it gave a curious, "*Aaahn?*"

"Brother," Willow said and bent to Janson, her eyes misting while she kept hold of her scythe. "I thought you were gone?"

"Al… most…" Janson wheezed, black blood sloshing from his chest. "She hit… part of my Seam. It's not fully snapped, but it's…"

She hushed him, then gripped his fingers. "Is there no way for you to heal?"

"Not from this. Bodily wounds are… no problem… but our Seams are irreplaceable…"

I hobbled with my crutches over to them and stood beside Hecrûshou to watch, saddened. "Is there nothing we can do for him?" I asked softly.

Hecrûshou folded his arms, Aahn curling around his bicep. "Nothing will save him. He will die. I would have left him there on the island, but he fought bravely with me and so I thought he deserved a proper reaping from his king's daughter."

Willow's gaze hardened at Janson's sickly face, her fox ears growing. "Yes. I will be the one to reap his soul."

Willow rose and clutched her scythe. "Brother Janson," she began in a dismal note. "You have proven yourself a true Reaper of Grim. Though your afterlife had been stolen from you, you still sought to protect the souls to whom you swore a life-bound oath. The fact that these vassals are standing here today is proof that you kept your vow to the Mother Goddess and watched after them… For this, She will bless your spirit in the Void. You will be forgiven for your sins… For this, you will be given a Reaper's farewell."

"Wait," Janson croaked. He lifted a weak hand toward Rosette and Nikolai. "Please… take my vassals. They've… agreed to serve you. To repent."

New vassals? That was unexpected. Willow hadn't seemed to expect this either.

After a long silence, she nodded, then raised her scythe and twirled it gracefully in one hand while hovering the glowing crook over his chest. "I am a guide of fallen souls, for those death's taken hold."

Hearing her speak the Reaper's Creed, I bowed my head and leaned on one of my crutches, holding a fist to my chest.

She continued, "Not a bringer of the end, all souls I will defend. Never will I turn away if there are Seams untied… beside my Brothers I will stand, living… or otherwise…" She took a breath after that line, then went on. "I'll let not actions souls once took deter me from my duty. I will forgive old histories and never show one cruelty.

"I am a destined guard who has been chosen from the masses, who only kneels and places faith within the wolf of ashes. Protect, defend, preserve and foster every life and afterlife. With this creed I will swear to conquer rotted strife." She raised the scythe over her head. "I am a knight of Death…"

Janson exhaled softly. "A Reaper… of Grim…"

"Whether this life or the next…"

"Both in life… and after death…"

She gave a final farewell, and brought the blade to his chest.

As black mist rose from his pores, his lips released a final breath that swelled in our ears before it was swallowed by the night.

"It's our time, Nile…"

After Janson's send-off, I left Willow with her new vassals to grieve in private. I clopped my way to my cabin, fumbling with the crutches while opening the door, and shut it behind me with some difficulty.

Alexander sat by the window, watching Mal and Bridge chatter in their croaking language on the curtain rail. We were sharing the room with Jaq, but he seemed to be absent for now.

Alex leapt up when I came in. "Xavier." He helped me into a chair, setting my crutches aside. He only had one arm to assist, since his other was in a sling. Still, he was in better shape than me. "Should you really be moving around so much?"

"Sirra said I have to be *in* motion to regain my strength," I grunted, straining to hold myself against the chair's back. When I was better settled, I rubbed the scruffy beard at my chin, the thicket of hairs warm and unfamiliar.

"But you only woke up hours ago," he protested. "Shouldn't you be resting?"

"I've spent the last six years resting, Alex. The last thing I want to do is lie in bed."

He began a reply, but thought on it and lowered into the chair beside me. "Where do we go from here, then?" he asked.

"Exactly where we planned to go." I shrugged. "To the Ocean King, to ask for military aid."

"Ah. I'd almost forgotten that bit…"

I lifted the window curtain, staring at the waves. "How long will it take to reach Marincia's capital?"

"One month," he speculated, then amended. "Perhaps two. Aiden and Nathaniel are taking wagers."

Months. It would take months to reach our first destination. *When will we see Grim again?* The concept of returning home seemed to be falling farther and farther out of reach.

I let out a long, tired sigh, a grin rolling over my lips. "Right, well… Despite all that, I never did say: Hello, Alex. It's good to see your face again." I held out my hand.

Alex grasped it firmly, smirking. "Yes… Welcome back to life, Xavier."

Epilogue I
OLD ACQUAINTANCES

~~~~~~

MACARIUS

"Kael..." Cilia sobbed in the rain, her hair a tangled mess as the tide swelled and receded over her arms. She didn't care to move, just simpered there, mewling, "*Kael...*"

"Get up," I sneered, fangs unfolding. *Damn that Claude. What was he doing here?* Ruining everything I've worked so hard for... "I said *get up.*" Venom leaked from my glands. "Worthless witch, look at yourself. You couldn't even fend off that shark long enough to *touch* the Shadowblood."

"Why?" she asked condemningly. "You knew Kael, you *knew* him...! I remember. And all this time, you said *nothing* of how he was... he was alive. My Kael...!"

"Kael is dead." I was growing so, so tired of this nonsense. "That man you saw was only your descendant."

She shivered. "But he looked..."

"Of course he looked like him, you blubbering idiot!" I threw my hand at her face—it phased through. I'd nearly forgotten I was only a copy. My hand clenched. "I told you he was your descendant. Your blood, along with Kael's. But he is *not* Kael."

"How did he know my name, then?"

"The Reapers must have told him. Now stop whimpering like a child and get off this pathetic excuse for an island. If you find those brothers again, I'll... return *all* your memories of Kael."

Her eyes brightened at this, breath frozen.

Good. At least I still have hold of her. "They were headed west," I continued. "We will meet at Garuule ne La'quine off the Flowering Trail in three weeks. Go ahead of me."

She wept lightly, staring out at the waves that rippled from the rain. "Kael…"

"*I SAID GO,*" I screamed, causing her to jerk back and dive into the waters.

She would find fish-tailed demons to ferry her, I knew. Time was of the essence, and I damn well wouldn't tolerate any more delays. It was terrible enough that she remembered even the slightest glimpse of Kael. And she lost the Shadowblood. *And* the Death Princess. *And* the Sky Princess.

I was in *no* mood to deal with a defective asset. I would have to report back to my original, to assess what must be done now—

"Macar."

I stiffened. *That voice…* that hollow, stale, lamenting voice… It was a phantom from a time long remembered; a time that had been ripped from me. *It couldn't be…*

"Macar, please."

It'd been five hundred years since I'd heard that voice, but oh, how *familiar* it sounded… A wicked grin tugged at my lips, and I slowly turned to my dear, ancient friend.

"Why, Dream," I purred, "what a delightful surprise."

Dream stood in the rain, staring at me with morose, azure eyes. His blue fox ears were grown, a rare sight to see. The rain didn't physically touch him. He was only a copy, like myself.

"And what brings you here on this fine, drizzling evening?" I asked.

His expression didn't soften. "Macar, please. Stop this. There does not have to be a Lightcaster."

"There is a Shadowblood, and such cannot exist without the other. Those were your own words."

He was barely audible under the rumble of thunder. "You cannot kill the Relicbloods, Macar. You cannot make your Sanctuary."

I hissed, "Sanctuary is the only way to survive, Dream. The only way to protect us from the destroyers—from your pampered *pets*."

"They won't bring our End," he said in an almost whisper. It sounded pleading.

Perhaps he struggles to believe his own sermon? I chuckled. It was amusing, to see such confliction in his sage eyes.

"I suppose we'll have to see," I said, "but I tell you now, Dream, if you don't kill them, they'll kill us all. You're fostering our demise."

He gazed away, pain contorting his features, and he whispered. "Why did you do it?"

He lapsed into silence, and when I saw he wasn't about to expound, I mused. "I've done a number of things over the years. Could you perhaps specify?"

"Why did you kill your brother?" His fists shook. "Accursius hadn't a part in this. Why kill him, of all people?"

I scoffed, flicking a dismissive hand. "Oh, I don't remember anymore. Perhaps I was sick of seeing my face on a lumbering mule." I glared at the waves behind me, an old anger simmering. "He was a pawn of that monstrous king, regardless… I am done being strung along by your brothers and sisters, Dream. You will all be the death of us, and I'm through being their Bloodlines' puppet. It makes me sick to see little has changed in the last five hundred years." My smile curled at the horizon, hope brimming. "The people of Nirus will rise, Dream. Kael took care of that tyrant Land King and his Bloodline, but four still stand in our way."

Including you, I thought with a bitter growl. Yes, Dream would have to die. It was inevitable, if he still couldn't see the good that would come of Sanctuary. *Though…* A pang of guilt crushed my chest. *His is perhaps the one death I will regret.*

"You're wrong," Dream said.

I paused, attention broken. "Wrong? About what?"

"Kael did not end Land's Bloodline."

My head craned to him, baffled. "You were there when it happened. I hope your memory hasn't deteriorated over the years?"

"It hasn't." Dream's voice grew rough. "Adam's heir lives."

"Adam's son died at childbirth, along with the queen. He had no heirs."

"Ah, but he did," Dream murmured. "The original heir survived."

My brow knitted. *What was he saying?* "His daughter was also stillborn, years before. Who else is left?"

Dream's lips rose into a flat, vindictive smile. "The daughter lived through the birth. I'd hidden her from the world. And I've brought her with me to this era… Land's heiress still stands to destroy you, Macar. Prepare yourself."

He vanished, leaving me alone and raving on the storming, desolate island.

Epilogue II
THE RIGHTFUL RULER

~~~~~~

ANABELLE

The cabin door creaked when I pulled it open, stepping in. Kurrick was waiting for me, a single candle wavering from the lantern on the desk. He sat bare chested on the floor by the window, his swords and daggers scattered as he sharpened them with a whetstone.

"I see you decided to return," he muttered, the scrape of metal on rock singing with each stroke against the blade. "And here I thought you would spend the night in the hawk's bed."

Fool. Annoyance bubbled. His tone had been envious; spiteful. Why must he insist on ignoring my passes, yet treat me like his precious little flower that no one must touch? Why so possessive, yet so cold?

He stopped his sharpening when I didn't reply. "Ana?"

I unfastened my looped earring, setting it on the desk. I watched in the window's reflection as my chestnut hair bled to a metallic, sun-gold sheen. My crimson eyes glinted to a brilliant gold, shining like coins in the firelight.

Kurrick scowled fiercely. "Anabelle, you know well Dream gave you instruction to keep that illusion while…"

My hands glimmered with golden Hallows, his sword ripped from his grip when I yanked it aside with my Terravoking. I pushed the other weapons under the bed in a noisy clatter.

I disrobed, my tattered gown falling at my feet.

Kurrick's head snapped away in a blush, his eyes fixed on the wall. "Ana, please…"

I crouched over his lap, kissing his thick neck.

"No!" He grabbed my shoulders and pushed me back. "That time is gone, now…! I… am no king, for you… There will be others. Others who are worthy of a queen…"

I met his gaze, whispering, "Tonight, your queen deems *you* worthy."

DEAR READERS,

Thank you so much for reading Orbs of Azure, Book Two of the NecroSeam Chronicles pentalogy. Now that you've completed this second part of the Reapers' adventure, I would be extremely grateful if you tell others what you think by writing an honest review. It doesn't have to be long…a few words, or even just a rating would be much appreciated. Reviews are vital to an author's career and helps us not only sell books, but provides valuable feedback. For your convenience, my website has links to various book review sites at www.necroseam.com/reviews.

Want to find out more about the NecroSeam Chronicles universe, including world notes, deleted scenes, character artwork, and even recorded songs from the books? Visit my website at www.necroseam.com!

And while you are there, feel free to sign up for my newsletter to receive announcements on new releases, upcoming conventions I'll be attending, and special promotions!

You can also follow me on my social media accounts below:

http://www.NecroSeam.com
www.Facebook.com/officialEllieRaine

Thank you again!
~Ellie Raine

Sneak Peak for Book III: Pearl Of Emerald
PROLOGUE: BLOOD AND FURY

KING DREAM

500 Years Prior

Screeeeee...

The scrape of metal on stone screamed, the soft points of my fox ears brushing my neck with each heave of breath.

I didn't wish to peer round the open doorframe; I didn't wish to see what was there, not in person. The vision of what lay inside was clear enough through my Third Eye; the stink of death profuse.

There were bodies strewn about the floor, nobles and servants alike. Not even royalty was exempt. The Queen of Ocean hung impaled against the wall; the King of Sky lay dead at her feet, his scarlet wings plucked from his back. His daughter's head had been removed and rolled beside her father's limp arm.

I only hoped to Gods my daughter Myra—my little Myra—hadn't seen. This slaughter was not for the eyes of such a small thing.

The vision burned in my Third Eye, though I was looking through someone else's point of view. I could hear the scraping blade both behind and in front of me, listening with two different sets of ears, but only Seeing through *his* eyes. His stinging, bleary eyes, wet and misty, glaring at the man with the golden crown.

The king's lion ears were grown and curled back, his glittering golden robes the only garb left unstained in the ballroom. He had no sword, but outstretched a hand and evoked his rock Hallows to the nearest blade that lay discarded on the ballroom floor, the weapon lifting in the air and flying to his grip.

The protagonist of my vision felt a tug at his own sword, and saw the king was attempting to rip it from his grasp. Black veins spewed from his hand onto the blade suddenly, the mirrored surface shrouded in stringy poison.

He gave the king a look that said, *take it now, if you dare.*

The king's expression fell, dismissing his Terravoking lest he grab the poisonous blade and bring his own death.

"Madman," King Adam growled, his timbre disgusted. "You're a damned madman."

The killer kept his dragging pace, his poisoned blade scratching the floor behind him. His gaze went placid, more machine than man, with but one mission.

King Adam's bronzed face paled at the look. "Why…?" he asked. "Why torment me further…? I've lost Genevieve—I've lost our *child*—what more do you want?!"

The blade whined over the marble quietly, the killer as silent as the dead men and women he stepped over.

Adam's voice shook. "All this, over a damned dismissal…? Good Gods, Doctor, if I'd known a lunatic was buried within, I…"

"Where?" the doctor croaked, his feet slowing to a halt at last.

The king kept his distance, blinking. "What?"

"Where is he?" His voice was a meager whisper, exhaustion and pain—*crushing pain*—weighing down his soul. "Where is my son?"

His memory flickered with bloodied walls—pooling floorboards—the red dripping, dripping, dripping from her open neck—

Agony writhed within him. He remembered her smile, her entrancing green stare, her laughter— her blood, painted on the wall of their home—*your failure's payment* glowing hot against the wood—her scattered pieces tossed about like morbid scraps—her head hung from the wall by her silken, Grimish hair—her heart carved out of her naked, appendage-less body and placed between her legs—

Fury *ripped* through his blood again, his vision flooded with tears and blocking my view of the king, but oh, the man's neck had never looked so tempting to *wring* the breath out of…!

Yet he knew now was not the time to grieve. He could mourn her when their son was safe.

He'd seen King Adam not hours ago, his golden locks and coin-like eyes glinting from under his cloak as His Majesty fled from the streets with the youngling in tow.

The doctor focused on the present at hand, his cheeks wet as he screamed, "*Where is my son?*"

His roars echoed through the ballroom, heard mostly by dead ears. Barely a moment lapsed before he came for the king in a wild rage—

The first *clang* of swords sang from inside, and my Third Eye suddenly slammed shut, my own perspective swimming back into focus.

I hurried to look through the doorway, watching the two men trade blows. The surgeon had the advantage: Kael's Infeciovoking was not something Adam had ever fought against. Now, seeing the surgeon for myself with my physical eyes was more sickening than having Seen through *his* view. The state of the ballroom was the same as the vision. Every speck of crimson that oozed from the floor, every stale stare still caught in a silent scream, hadn't changed. But Kael's face, full of fury and sorrow, each thrust with the sword deadlier than the next, the anguish ripping from his cries…

I cupped my mouth as my eyes misted. "Gods help us…"

Their swords collided and held for too long. Kael's poison-infested blade spread its black veins onto Adam's weapon. The veins seeped into the king's hands and rooted into his fingers, which went rigid as his weapon clattered to the floor.

Kael turned his blade downward and thrust its tip at Adam's chest, but the king rolled away. The surgeon's blade cracked the marble instead. Kael lifted his weapon for another strike, but he staggered when the floor beneath him began to quake.

Adam had evoked his rock Hallows onto the marble under Kael's feet and lifted the man off the ground.

It was only a distraction, I noticed, as the king's blackened hands shone with gold light, perhaps in an attempt to heal the infection with his remedy Hallows.

But Kael sprang off the floating piece of floor and *plunged* his sword downward. Adam hadn't had enough time to heal. He saw his attacker too late.

Kael's blade sank into the king's shoulder, the black veins rooting deep in his soul. Adam collapsed onto his back with a scream as veins crept over his skin.

Kael removed his soaked blade and towered over the fallen king, whose golden eyes peered up at the surgeon in a shiver.

"Why…" The veins spread to his throat, Adam shaking violently like a rabid, feral dog. Foam bubbled from the corners of his lips and dribbled onto his beard… then, suddenly, his glassy eyes looked past Kael. "Ana… belle…?"

Kael turned, searching for what the king had been staring at, yet didn't seem to notice anything. But from my place by the door, *I* could see a tiny, golden-haired lion girl hiding behind a pillar.

Ana!

What was that blasted girl doing in here?! And without her disguise?!

Keeping hidden from Kael's sight, I rigidly went inside and ducked under a table, making my way to the girl. I couldn't risk going into Aspirre to get to her.

There was no guarantee that I'd come back outside unseen. Even with as much practice as I've had, there was no perfecting that kind of coordination. Especially when they kept changing the layout of this damned castle every few years.

My sheltering table came to an end, and I peeked out from under the decorative cloth. Kael had his weapon raised above the king. He asked once more, "Where is my son?!"

The king's only reply was a gurgled sputter, drool slipping from his slacked jaw.

Kael snarled, "If you've so much as *touched* a hair on his head—!"

Kael leapt back when a scythe nearly tore through his neck. He staggered to regain his footing and saw his newest opponent.

I let out a relieved exhale. The Death King had been late to the ball this year. Too late perhaps, but I thanked Nira that Ysthavon was here to, at the very least, distract the crazed surgeon. Both men had infection Hallows. Ysthavon was now the only match for Kael. Iri knew *I* was useless against him. What was I going to do? Put him to sleep? The moment I'd come close to him, all he'd have to do was touch me and that would be that. A two-thousand-year-old king gone in a flash. But Ysthavon's own Infeciovoking would give him some immunity. Hopefully, he could keep Kael distracted long enough for me to grab Ana and flee.

As the two crossed blades, I crept from pillar to pillar toward Anabelle. She waited two pillars away. But there was an older boy with her, perhaps in his twelfth year. The boy wasn't what I would call handsome, especially not with his face contorted with sheer horror at what was happening.

My gaze narrowed at this newcomer. I didn't like strangers seeing Anabelle. And they *never* saw her without a guise. I went through much effort to make the world believe Adam's daughter had died at childbirth, I wasn't about to have it ruined by some stray lion cub.

When I hurried behind the next pillar, I hissed, "Ana!"

Ana gasped and found me. I held a finger to my lips, then waved for her to come to me. She took a step in my direction.

"Anabelle..." the dying king wheezed again from his place on the floor. "My Ana... You came. Dream said you'd come today. He said you'd come..."

He coughed up blood, remaining on his back. Ana hesitated, then glanced at me before turning round and going to the king.

"Ana...!" I hissed after her, but she ignored me. *Damn Land and his reckless, recycled soul!*

I went to the pillar she *had* been behind, exchanging a glare with the older boy she'd left behind.

Ana was whispering to the king. Her father. She'd only just learned who he was. This was not the reunion I had planned. You'd think I'd have Seen it coming. *Some wise oracle I made.*

Then there came a straggled grunt from the balcony outside. I turned, noticing the curtain was drawn halfway, snow blowing inside with the chilled wind. Slowly, I walked over.

The white flakes dusted my cheeks as I came to the curtain, the scent of ice eerily serene compared to the stink of death inside. Another sound came behind the curtain, a struggle of air.

I peeled the cloth open.

The noise came from King Adam's chief military general, Accursius Lysandre. The strange breaths on which he choked were caused by the thin sword lodged in his scaled throat, shoved in further by his own brother. The snow speckled red around them.

His brother gave a low chuckle. "For all your precious foresight, you never were the brighter half, brother… I suppose we each have our *talents*." He grunted and ripped the sword upward, slicing open his brother's neck and kicked him to the ground. The snow fell lightly over the body like a soft veil.

"Macar…?" I whispered.

He turned to me, and I shuddered. Something had changed in that stare. Behind his blood-splattered glasses, his eyes were no longer wide and curious, eager to learn the mysteries the world had to offer. His lust for knowledge had curdled into lust of a different sort.

He smiled like a lunatic. "Ah! Dream, my friend. I wondered when you'd arrive for the show." He kicked his twin's boot with a grin. "What do you think? I dare say I've finally gotten the best of this brute. Perhaps it wasn't the most graceful of executions, but I think with practice, grace will come more naturally."

I stood in silence, my bones numb to the freezing snow and gentle gale that batted against my robes.

Macar frowned. "Dream? Are you that amazed?"

"Macar…" My lungs quivered painfully, tears hitting as I realized I'd made a grave, *grave* mistake. "What have you done…?"

"What have I done?" He laughed, using his tunic to wipe blood from his spectacles. "Why, I'm doing precisely what I swore to do when you knighted me, Dream." He replaced the lenses on his nose and his lips split with a fang-filled grin. "I'm doing what's necessary."

NIRUSSIAN TRAVEL GUIDE

CHARACTER REFERENCE LIST

Aiden Rogeteller	Vassal of Alice Devouh, robin shifter, former Stormchaser, Aerovoker
Alexander Devouh	Half Shadowblood, wolf shifter, fiancé of Lilliana, half-Half Necrovoker with an emphasis on vessel manipulation (Vassals: Vendy, Dalen, and Hugh), Reaper (Messenger: Mal)
Alice Devouh	Twins' mother/ Death King's General, wolf shifter, wife of Lucas, Necrovoker (Vassals: Aiden and more unmentioned), Reaper (Messenger: Ethil)
Anabelle Goldthorn	Relicblood of Land, rightful Queen of EverLand and Neverland, Land's reincarnation, Lion shifter, Terravoker/Healer/Arborvoker
Apsonald Coult	Jaq's grandfather who was executed by Galden, now Lucas Devouh's vassal, viper shifter, Hallowless
Bianca Florenne	Childhood friend of the twins, Doctor and Alchemist, rabbit shifter, Healer
Cilia the Grim	Kael's wife and Everland's Ancient demon queen, ancestor of the Treble family, cat shifter, Pyrovoker
Claude Treble	Father of: Octavius, Cornelius, Connaline and Mikani. Descendant of Kael and Cilia. Cat shifter, Infeciovoker
Connaline Treble	Octavius's youngest sister, cat shifter, Healer
Cornelius (Neal) Treble	Octavius' brother, cat shifter, son of Claude and Sirra-Lynn, descendant of Cilia and Kael, Hallowless, Reaper (Messenger: Ace)
Crysalette Sandist	Queen of Aspirre and Dream's wife, Dreamcatcher, fox shifter, Somniovoker
Dalen Tesler	Vassal of the twins, hawk shifter, brother of Herrin, Hallowless
Daniel Tessinger	Lilli's father, Bat shifter, Necrovoker, Reaper (Messenger: Dawn)

Dream Sandist	Relicblood of Dreams, King of Aspirre, original Relic Child of Dreams, Dreamcatcher, fox shifter, Somniovoker/Decepiovoker/Seer
El Lochīst	Zyl's Aide, cat/blue-jay hybrid shifter, Dual-Evocator: Pyrovoker/Imbrivoker, Reaper (Messenger: Salfwy)
Hecrûshou the Hunter	Ancient Demon King of the Western Seas, shark shifter, Aquavoker
Henry Cauldwell	Vendy's uncle, blacksmith, rabbit shifter, Terravoker
Herrin Tesler	Archchancellor of Enlightener's Guild, Dalen's younger brother, hawk shifter, Hallowless
Hugh Lowery	Vassal of the twins, Xavier's apprentice Reaper, younger brother of Syreen, lion shifter, Arborvoker, Reaper (messenger: Lady Lilac)
James (Jimmy) Grieves	Dreamcatcher, elk shifter, Somniovoker
Janson Stane	Sentient Necrofera under Demon queen Cilia's control, crow shifter, Necrovoker, former Reaper (Messenger: Nile, deceased) (Vassals: Rossette and Nikolai)
Jaqelle (Jaq) Mallory	Xavier and Alex's friend, viper shifter, grandson of Apsonald, Hallowless, Reaper (Messenger: Bridge)
Kael Treble	Macarius's partner, Cilia's husband, Surgeon, ancestor of Treble family, cat shifter, Infeciovoker
King Galden Relekin	False King of Land, father of: Cayden and Rilla, Lion shifter, Terravoker
Kurn	Ringëd's pet ferret who thinks he's an exiled emperor from the planet *Hcah-Ah-Ah-Hcah*
Kurrick Everstien	Ana's bodyguard and lover, Lion shifter, Hallowless
Lannyse Lysandre	Headmistress of the Lysander Academy, snake shifter, Hallowless
Lëtta Russeaux	Sirra-Lynn's *Da'torr* & apprentice doctor, bear shifter, Necrovoker
Lillianna (Lilli) Tessinger	Willow's Aide, Bat shifter, fiancée of Alexander, Necrovoker, Reaper (Messenger: Dusk)
Linolius (Linus) Rennegaurd	Cayden's friend, Goat shifter, Seer: emphasis on visions of the present
Lucas Devouh	Twins' father / Death King's Eyes, wolf shifter, husband of Alice, Necrovoker (Vassals: Nathaniel, Thateus, and more unmentioned), Reaper (Messenger: Barrach)

Macarius Lysandre	Lightcaster half, cobra shifter, Dual-Evocator: Decepiovoker/Somniovoker
Matthiel Inion	Willow's former fiancé, wolf shifter, Dual-Evocator: Necrovoker/Pyrovoker, Reaper, (Messenger: Paschal)
Mikani Fleetfûrt	Octavius's eldest sister and Ringëd's wife, descendant of Cilia and Kael, cat shifter, Pyrovoker
Myra Ember	Relicblood of Dream, Queen of Grim, Dreamcatcher, wife of Serdin, mother of Willow, fox shifter, Somniovoker/Seer/Decepiovoker
Nathaniel Jorrechoh	Vassal of Lucas Devouh, bear shifter, former pirate captain, Pyrovoker
Nikolai Voux	Vassal of Janson, tigerfish shifter, Glaciavoker
Octavius Treble	Xavier and Alex's friend, cat shifter, son of Claude and Sirra-Lynn, descendant of Cilia and Kael, Infeciovoker, Reaper (Messenger: Shade)
Oliver Tessinger	Young Owl shifter, Seer of the Future, Reaper (Messenger: Clover)
Prince Cayden Relekin	Crowned Prince of EverLand, also known as Land's Servant, son of Galden, Lion shifter, Terravoker
Ringëd Fleetfûrt	Seeker detective & Mika's husband, feral human, Seer: emphasis on visions of the past
Rojired (Roji) Skrii'etey	Relicblood of Sky, heir to Culatia's throne, Sky's reincarnation, brother of Zylveia, son of King Rojired, Stormchaser, husband of Dalminia, swallow shifter, Astravoker/Aerovoker/Imbrivoker
Rojired Skrii'etey	Relicblood of Sky, King of Culatia, Stormchaser, swallow shifter, Astravoker/Aerovoker/Imbrivoker
Rossette Roroan	Vassal of Janson, macaw shifter, Astravoker
Serdin Ember	Relicblood of Death, King of Grim, Reaper, husband of Myra, father of Willow, wolf shifter, Necrovoker/Pyrovoker/Infeciovoker (Messenger: Locke)
Sirra-Lynn Treble	Claude's deceased wife, mother of: Octavius, Cornelius, Connaline, and Mikani. Vassal of Lëtta, cat shifter, Healer
Syreen Lowery	New Queen of Neverland, older sister of Hugh, lion shifter, Arborvoker
Vendy Cauldwell	Vassal of the twins, rabbit shifter, niece of Henry, Terravoker

Willow Ember	Relicblood of Death and Dream, Heiress to Grim's throne, Death's reincarnation, Reaper, fiancee of Xavier, daughter of Serdin and Myra (Granddaughter of Dream), fox-wolf hybrid shifter, 6 hallows: Dream and Death (Messenger: Jewel)
Xavier Ember	Half Shadowblood, wolf shifter, brother to Alexander, fiancé of Willow, half-Necrovoker with an emphasis of soul manipulation (Vassals: Vendy & Dalen), Reaper (Messenger: Chai)
Yulia Vivelle	Devouh's hired Dreamcatcher, fox shifter, Somniovoker
Zylveia Skrii'etey	Relicblood of Sky, Princess of Culatia, sister of Prince Roji, daughter of King Rojired, Stormchaser, swallow shifter, Astravoker/Aerovoker/Imbrivoker

NIRUSSIAN WORLD NOTES

Dragons of Nirus: For every element of magic Hallows (with the exception of Dream Hallows), there is a dragon that embodies that element. Land realm: Stonedragon/Barkdragon/Landragon, Sky realm: Skydragon/Shockdragon/Nimdragon, Ocean realm: Seadragon/Bindragon/ Frostdragon, Death realm: Bonedragon/Flamedragon/Poisondragon.

Evocators: A shifter born with magic Hallows is called an Evocator. Most Evocators only possess one element. In rare cases, some are born with two Hallows and are known as Dual-Evocators. Only the Relicbloods have ever possessed all three of their realm's Hallows.

Land:	Terravoker		Healer		Arborvoker
Sky:	Astravoker		Aerovoker		Imbrivoker
Ocean:	Aquavoker		Glaciavoker		Pregravoker
Dream:	Somniovoker		Decepiovoker		Seer
Death	Necrovoker		Pyrovoker		Infeciovoker

Hallows: These are the "Gods' Blessings", which are elemental magics to which certain shifters are born. A shifter's Hallows element is defined based on the realm they are from. There are fifteen Hallow elements in total. For each of the five realms in Nirus, there are three elements, as shown in the charts below.

LAND		SKY		OCEAN	
Rock	Terra	*Wind*	Aero	*Water*	Aqua
Plant	Arbor	*Rain*	Imbri	*Ice*	Glacia
Remedy	Healer	*Storm*	Astra	*Pressure*	Pregra

DREAM		DEATH	
Dream	Somnio	*Fire*	Pyro
Illusion	Decepio	*Death*	Necro
Prophecy	Seer	*Poison*	Infecio

NecroSeam: A ghostly thread which sews a soul to its vessel. When a shifter of Nirus dies, the soul is still bound to its body by their NecroSeam. If three days pass without a Reaper coming to cut the NecroSeam and free the soul from its deceased vessel, the trapped soul rots inside its corpse and merges into an undead creature called Necrofera that can only be killed by a weapon made of Spiritcrystal.

Nirussian Calendar: A month in Nirus is 60 days, or six weeks. One week is 10 days. There are 5 months in a year (300 days).

Realms of Nirus: There are 5 realms in this world. Land (surface realm split into two continents: Everland & Neverland), Sky (floating islands of Culatia in the sky inhabited primarily by flying shifters). Ocean (seaside isles of Marincia inhabited primarily by fish shifters), Dream (subconscious realm of Aspirre where shifters' souls visit in their dreams), Death (underground caverns of Grim where souls of the dead are protected in their afterlife).

Relicbloods: Shifters who are descendants of the Relic Children (those chosen by the Gods to be the ruler of a specific realm). The only Relic Child still alive today is Dream, who doesn't age at a regular pace due to his timeless residency in the subconscious plane of Aspirre.

The Relics: Magical artifacts of the Gods which are the sources of each realm's Hallows. (Land: Blossom of Gold, Sky: Phoenix of Scarlet, Ocean: Pearl of Emerald, Dream: Orbs of Azure, Death: Willow of Ashes)

Sentients: Necrofera who possess Hallows (Class 1), or a mongrel demon who has eaten ten thousand souls (Class 2). Sentients look like normal shifters, except their pupils are white.

Shifters: The world of Nirus is inhabited entirely by shifters, but they aren't quite the traditional shapeshifters who can transform from one human form to a full-on beast form. The shifters of Nirus are seen possessing traits of some kind (Ringëd Fleetfûrt is the only exception) but these traits usually only consist of wings, horns, claws, teeth, ears, tails, scales, fins, etc. Most shifters are born with a majority of their traits already showing (referred to as Primary Shifts), but some only appear when they are threatened or upset (teeth/talons/claws and even extra feathers/scales/fur). Mammals seem to be the main beings whose traits actually shift, with their ears, claws and teeth. Antlers and horns are always out and don't retract, nor do wings and scales. The fish shifters are the most unique due to their inherent ability to switch their Primary Shift to tails or legs when they are in or out of water, and this is the largest range of shifting that happens among the shifters.

The Void and Great unknown: A place that is considered purgatory for rotten and sinful souls in the Harmonist religion. It is believed that once the Goddess Nira has Cleansed these souls of their rot and sin, she takes them to the Great Unknown, which is thought to be the "waiting room" for souls to be reborn again.

NIRUSSIAN MINERALS/TECHNOLOGY

Olium: a lightweight, extremely durable mineral that is found in the deeper caves of Grim, where the veins are closest to the planet's magma-filled mantle and are in a constant liquefied state until extracted and left to cool. Once cooled, the metal can be crafted, but forging the material is incredibly difficult and only skilled smiths are able to handle the task.

Spiritcrystal: a mineral found in the caverns of Grim. It is a unique crystal which physical skin cannot touch. Adversely, it is one of the few things ghosts can make contact with. The Reapers use this crystal to forge their specialized scythes which allows them to cut a shifter's NecroSeam without damaging the body.

Vision-gems: minerals found in the Land realm's mines which, when broken apart, can show what the other piece is reflecting. Modern technologies led by Culatia's top inventors in 2102 A.B. have learned to harness Vision-gems to bring devices such as Vision-screens, communicators, and other numerous devices.

Levi-stones: magnetized rocks that are repelled only by the planet's core, causing them to be pushed into the air and kept suspended so long as the oppositely-charged side is facing the core. Culatia's islands are made of these stones, which is speculated by many geologists as to the reason Culatia's islands float.

Storage-gems: a gummy, gel-like mineral found in Everland's mines. When an object is pushed inside it, that object's size and weight shrinks to a small percentage of its original mass until that object is removed.

Yinklit Gel: a sap from a long-leafed plant that is native to Culatia. It is similar to the Aloe vera plant, but instead of possessing soothing properties when applied to burns, Yinklit Gel dampens all Hallows effects when an Evocator's hands are coated in the substance. If the gel is ingested, it can cause serious damage to an Evocator's Hallows for several days, and in some cases, it can wipe their magic connection permanently.

Shotri: The latest ranged weapons created by Culatia's top weapon-smiths. They require ammunition made of meta-glass pellets with entrapped elemental magics which, when fired, cause damage or temporary paralysis on a target, depending on the element the pellet housed.

Meta-glass: an alloyed material which combines Flexi-glass as the outer layer and Yinklît Gel as the inner layer. With this, Culatia's top weapon-smiths have used these to make Shockspheres, Flamespheres, Splashspheres and the like, which are then used as ammunition for Shotri.

Flexi-glass: A gummy, gel-like glass found in Culatia's mountain peaks that can be stretched and manipulated with ease while still wet. Once it has been through a kiln, it solidifies and become as fragile as normal glass.

ABOUT THE AUTHOR

Ellie Raine is a voracious BookWyrm when it comes to epic adventures, detailed world-building, and thrilling battles. Growing up in a family of book lovers, comic readers, and video gamers, she always dreamed of making the next explosive game that would catch fire with her darker themes that put the spotlight on her favorite fable: the Grim Reaper. Her ongoing Hard Epic Fantasy pentalogy, *NecroSeam Chronicles*, was originally intended to be that video game series, but she's found that the book adaptation is far more fulfilling and exciting. Her other works include a paranormal-noir novella entitled *Nightingale*, published with Pro Se Productions.

Fueled by coffee-bean concoctions brewed by the finest caffeine alchemists in Georgia, Ellie only emerges from the depths of her daring tales when she is summoned by her loving king and their darling daughter: the Dragon Princess Felicity. She is a lover of ravens and a dreamer of dragons, but above all else, she is a scribe to the stories that guide her.

You can find out more about Ellie Raine and her books at: https://www.NecroSeam.com

Made in the USA
Columbia, SC
10 October 2021